THE
DAWNING
OF
DELIVERANCE

Books by Judith Pella

Lone Star Legacy

> *Frontier Lady*
> *Stoner's Crossing*

The Russians (with Michael Phillips)

> *The Crown and the Crucible*
> *A House Divided*
> *Travail and Triumph*
> *Heirs of the Motherland* (Judith Pella only)
> *Dawning of Deliverance* (Judith Pella only)

The Stonewycke Trilogy (with Michael Phillips)

> *The Heather Hills of Stonewycke*
> *Flight from Stonewycke*
> *Lady of Stonewycke*

The Stonewycke Legacy (with Michael Phillips)

> *Stranger at Stonewycke*
> *Shadows over Stonewycke*
> *Treasure of Stonewycke*

The Highland Collection (with Michael Phillips)

> *Jamie MacLeod: Highland Lass*
> *Robbie Taggart: Highland Sailor*

The Journals of Corrie Belle Hollister (with Michael Phillips)

> *My Father's World*
> *Daughter of Grace*
> *On the Trail of the Truth**
> *A Place in the Sun**
> *Sea to Shining Sea**
> *Into the Long Dark Night**
> *Land of the Brave and the Free**
> *Grayfox**

*Michael Phillips only

JUDITH PELLA

THE DAWNING OF DELIVERANCE

BETHANY HOUSE PUBLISHERS
MINNEAPOLIS, MINNESOTA 55438

Cover by Dan Thornberg,
Bethany House Publishers staff artist.

Published by Bethany House Publishers
A Ministry of Bethany Fellowship, Inc.
11300 Hampshire Avenue South
Minneapolis, Minnesota 55438

Printed in the United States of America.

Library of Congress Cataloging-in-Publication Data

Pella, Judith.
    The dawning of deliverance / Judith Pella.
       p.   cm. — (Russians ; 5)

    1. Russia—History—Nicholas II,—1894–1917—Fiction.
2. Russia—History—1801–1917—Fiction. I. Title. II. Series:
Phillips, Michael R., 1946–   Russians ; 5.
PS3566.E415D39   1994
813'.54—dc20   94–25131
ISBN 1–55661–359–8   CIP

To my niece,

Sarah Storbakken,

for her love and support as this book grew.
"Peace I leave with you, my peace I give unto you: not as the world gives, give I unto you. Let not your heart be troubled, neither let it be afraid."
John 14:27, KJV

JUDITH PELLA is the author of five major fiction series for the Christian market, co-written with Michael Phillips. An avid reader and researcher in historical, adventure, and geographical venues, her skill as a writer is exceptional. She and her family make their home in California.

CONTENTS

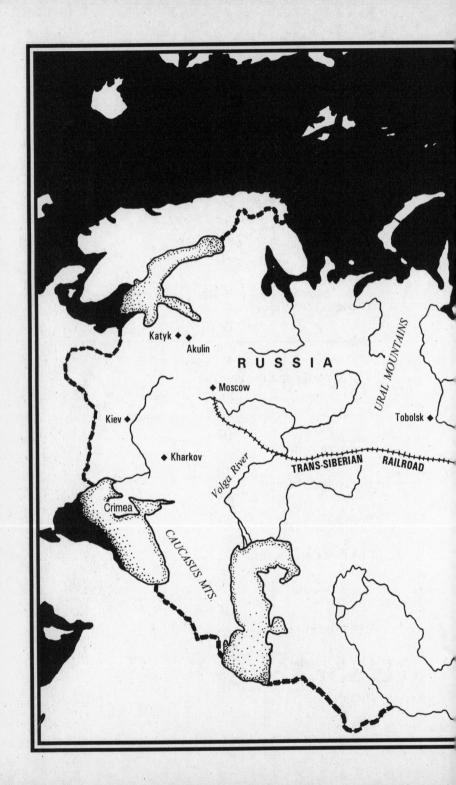

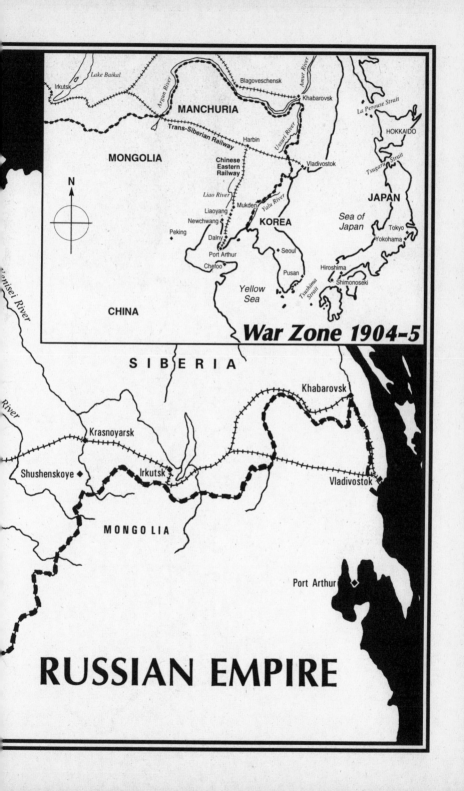

Irkutsk
Lake Baikal
Argun River
Amur River
Blagoveschensk
Khabarovsk
La Perouse Strait
HOKKAIDO
MANCHURIA
Trans-Siberian Railway
Harbin
Ussuri River
Vladivostok
Tsugaru Strait
MONGOLIA
Chinese
Eastern
Railway
Liao River
Mukden
Yalu River
JAPAN
N
Liaoyang
KOREA
Sea of
Japan
Tokyo
Newchwang
Peking
Dalny
Yokohama
Port Arthur
Seoul
Chefoo
Pusan
Hiroshima
Shimonoseki
CHINA
Yellow
Sea
Tsushima Strait

War Zone 1904–5

S I B E R I A

Khabarovsk

Yenisei River

Krasnoyarsk

Shushenskoye
Irkutsk

Vladivostok

MONGOLIA

Port Arthur

RUSSIAN EMPIRE

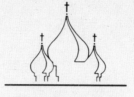

Prologue

WHAT HAS GONE BEFORE . . .

The years following the ascension of Nicholas the Second to the throne of Russia were, at least by Russia's volatile standards, relatively serene. Nicholas and his wife, Alexandra, lived their lives in a rather idyllic fashion, raising their four daughters to the Victorian standards by which Alexandra herself was raised. Each day brought a pleasant succession of afternoon teas, lavish receptions, and evenings at the opera or ballet. In summer the royal family retreated to the Crimea where they lost themselves in warm balmy days on the beautiful seaside.

Political unrest seemed to be under control. But strife was merely lurking just beneath the surface, simmering like a broth that needs only a bit more heat to bring it overflowing furiously from the pot.

Unlike the royal family, the lives of the Burenin and Fedorcenko clans seemed intent on upheaval. When Prince Sergei Fedorcenko angered the tsar with his writings, he was exiled to Siberia, far from his parents and his sister Katrina. He escaped and returned to Russia, taking on the guise of a peasant and marrying his sister's maid, Anna Burenin. For many years Sergei and Anna Christinin (Fedorcenko) lived contentedly as peasants in Katyk. They raised Katrina's daughter, Mariana, and had two sons of their own. Then the unexpected appearance of Dmitri, Mariana's real father, changed everything. Mariana left her beloved Katyk to live with him in St. Petersburg and there abandoned her peasant ways to take her rightful place as a countess. The transition was not always easy for the sixteen-year-old girl, especially since her father,

13

Dmitri, proved to be as irresponsible and unreliable in middle age as he had been as a youth.

A young American journalist named Daniel Trent was the one bright spot in Mariana's new life. Both were in strange, new circumstances, and those common bonds seemed to draw them together, cementing the friendship. Mariana openly confided her most private emotions to Daniel, and when he used his friendship with her to write an authorized story about Mariana and her family for his newspaper, she was deeply hurt by the betrayal. His heartfelt repentance seemed to come too late to help their wounded friendship. Daniel was suddenly called back to America to be with his father, who had taken ill. Mariana accepted this as proof that their friendship, not to mention their budding love, was not to be.

Anna and Sergei, concerned about Mariana's difficulties in St. Petersburg, decided to leave the safe haven of Katyk to be with her in the city. Unable to reveal his aristocratic background because he was still an escaped fugitive, Sergei found life in the city hard and unrelenting. Employment as a laborer in a factory nearly drove him to his death until he was rescued by their longtime friend Misha, a Cossack guard. Misha directed Anna and Sergei to the widow Raisa Sorokin, who was struggling to raise her daughter, put food on the table, and pay rent on her modest apartment. Sergei and his family moved in with Raisa, establishing a mutually sustaining relationship that would last years.

Sergei found employment as a tutor, and just as life appeared to be taking a turn for the better, Cyril Vlasenko made his greedy presence felt. Vlasenko, a cousin of Sergei's father, Viktor, had long envied the Fedorcenkos. Even when Viktor went insane and Sergei was sent to Siberia, Vlasenko could not be satisfied. He usurped control of the Fedorcenko estate, the last vestige of the once-mighty Fedorcenko holdings. When Viktor attempted to reclaim his property at gunpoint, Sergei came out of hiding and, in the guise of a family servant, convinced his father to surrender. Viktor lost his estate but regained his sanity and was reunited with his son after years of discord.

The Burenin family, too, experienced some bittersweet reconciliations during those years. Anna's revolutionary brother Paul finally returned to Katyk when he received news of his father Yevno's illness. And he found, like the biblical Prodigal, that his father's arms were open to him.

In Yevno's final talk with Anna, he passed on to her the mantle of spiritual caretaker of the family. "You, my little daughter!" Yevno gently informed Anna. "Don't you know yet that those slim, delicate shoulders of yours have the strength of an ox? In your weaknesses, Anna, you have been made strong because you have, more than all my children, allowed God to dwell in His fullness within you. I have no doubt that you can shoulder the burden of this family. But you must remember that you need bear no burden alone—otherwise I would not place such an expectation upon you."

Thus the Burenin and Fedorcenko families enter into a new century. They do not know what strife and upheaval the world will mete out to them. They know only one thing—that with God's help they will survive. After all, they are Russians, and that is what Russians do best.

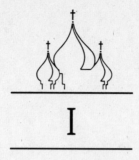

I

JOURNEY

1

Black smoke coughed from the engine's smokestack, streaking the clear summer sky with an ugly ribbon, like a battle scar. The train was passing through the heart of Siberia now. The Urals, with their lovely green foothills and meadows covered with violets and kingcups, had been left behind long ago. With Europe left far behind as well, a new world had opened up before the mighty iron engine of the Trans-Siberian Railway.

At least it seemed so to Mariana Remizov, who had never before traveled beyond St. Petersburg.

The flowery steppes and black earth of Tiumen had been followed by the dismal city of Omsk, on a sandy plain populated as much by huge mosquitos as by people. Then had come the flooded Barabinskaya Steppe. In spite of the swarms of insects, the steppe was like a wonderland to Mariana. Lakes and swamps bubbled up from the earth in an eerie fashion. Water surrounded farms, and sometimes even whole villages looked like floating islands. Amazed, Mariana had gazed for hours out the dusty train window at the scenes.

Abruptly the steppe had given way to woodlands, then the taiga. This vast primeval forest, which appeared as if it had never seen the blade of an axe, made Mariana realize just how small the Russia she had always known was, and how much more there was to her beloved Motherland. She had passed through the virgin forest as if in a dream, its swampy mists enveloping her with darkness and cold. She wondered if the sun ever penetrated the thick canopy of foliage.

Several breakdowns on the way, causing hours of delays,

had provided Mariana ample opportunity to view the countryside. The trip across Siberia should only take fifteen days, but she had already been en route for more than two weeks, and she was still less than two-thirds of the way to her destination.

The train was approaching Irkutsk—"the pearl of Siberia," as it was called. No doubt Mariana would only catch a quick glimpse of the "pearl" as the train made another quick stop at the station and then resumed its course. There was so much to see, and so little time. It would take a dozen lifetimes to experience everything Russia had to offer.

Even with all the changes of scenery and the interminable drone of the train beneath her, Mariana could still hardly believe she was more than three thousand miles from home. But she had made her decision, and there was no turning back. Not that she *wanted* to turn back. This was one of the greatest adventures of her life, almost as life-changing as the day she had left her adopted parents' peasant izba in Katyk for the big city of St. Petersburg.

Mariana could hardly believe the direction her life had taken. She had grown up in Katyk as the peasant daughter of Anna and Sergei Christinin. Life in the village was simple and satisfying, and Mariana could not have imagined anything else.

Mariana had always known that Anna and Sergei were not her real parents, but her aunt and uncle. They had told her she was the daughter of Princess Katrina Fedorcenko, Sergei's sister, who died in childbirth. When her father, Count Dmitri Remizov eventually returned, the time had come for her to take her rightful place in Russian society.

That first giant step had sent her catapulting through many new and exciting and frightening experiences. She had not only gone from country girl to city girl; she had leaped from peasant to countess in the blink of an eye. And once she had made that move, each successive step became easier. Now she hungered for adventure—she who had once been content with the prospect of spending all her days in sleepy old Katyk!

Her mama Anna told her it must be from the blood of her real mother, Katrina, that flowed in her veins. Katrina had had such a zest for life, Anna said. She was afraid of nothing, always confident to enter a new situation with gusto. Of course Mariana's real father, Dmitri, had no small part in this also. Stories of his wild exploits, especially in his youth, always left Mariana in awe.

Mariana wasn't quite so audacious. She had to admit to some fear of what lay ahead, but, as when she left Katyk, her fear was mingled with anticipation. Mama Anna had told her that her apprehension was a positive sign.

"The fear shows your maturity, Mariana; it says you have good sense. But you don't let your fear control you. It doesn't keep you from a new challenge."

Mama Anna had spoken those words with tears rising in her eyes. Certainly, a good part of Mariana's courage had come not by blood but by a lifetime spent in the loving care of a woman who had met and conquered her own share of fears and challenges. Mariana knew it must have been hard for Anna to let her adopted daughter travel halfway around the world, undoubtedly to encounter many dangers and hardships. Yet Anna had often said that the goal of parenting was to raise children so they could eventually step out on their own. Her own dear papa, Yevno, had taught her that much.

Yes, Mariana had matured in many ways in the years since she left Katyk. People seemed to think she was pretty and were always admiring her smooth skin, dark hair, and green eyes— *her mother's eyes*, people now said. But her hair was apt to be pulled back into a practical bun, and long hours of study indoors had left her skin pale and her eyes weak. She was forced to wear eyeglasses most of the time.

She was twenty-three years old and still unmarried—a fact that never failed to amaze others, especially those from her village where girls were usually married by age fifteen or sixteen. As Countess Mariana Remizov, she had numerous suitors from the best families in St. Petersburg. But she had too much to see and do before she could commit her life to another. Singleness didn't bother Mariana at all, for it was her choice.

Papa Sergei commended her self-awareness, although her real father, Dmitri, was beside himself with fear that his only daughter might become an old maid. Her grandmother, Eugenia, was outraged.

"How can you throw your life away, after all I have done for you!" the woman had ranted.

Dmitri was more tender: "Dear child, you are so beautiful, so lovely . . . it is such a waste."

"Just because I'm not married?" Mariana had replied with some affront—perhaps she *had* been spending too much time with the liberal women at the medical school. "That doesn't mean my life is wasted, Père. I'm doing something valuable and important with my life—helping others."

"But you could do that if you were married."

"Would I have the freedom to follow this call to the East, if I were married? I don't think so."

"Oh, don't even mention that, my dear!"

Mariana knew that her father wished she were married just so she couldn't go on what he called "this fool's journey of hers." He wanted her safe and secure on the estate of some count or prince, surrounded by babies, and booked up with parties and concerts and ladies' luncheons. A life like his mother's—a life that, once the initial glamor had dimmed, had become increasingly empty and meaningless to Mariana.

Thoughts of marriage had, in fact, been a little more frequent lately. She even told herself that as soon as the war was over, she would seriously pursue that path. She did want someone special in her life, and after this current adventure, she would be ready to give up her freedom for him, whoever he might be.

But a hunger after adventure wasn't the only reason for her hesitancy. She had to wonder if her spinsterhood was also because she had been unable to find a suitor who interested her. She had fallen into the annoying habit of comparing all men to one particular cocky American. She had neither seen nor heard from Daniel Trent in nearly four years, yet he still managed to intrude into her life, especially when she was introduced to an eligible male. She had met many handsome young men who were far better looking than that wiry little American with his perpetual smirk, probing eyes, unruly brown hair, and that silly cleft in his chin. But none who had been more exciting, more stimulating, more—

More self-centered, arrogant, and insensitive, Mariana reminded herself sharply. Hadn't he deceived her and won her
friendship in order to write a story about her for his newspaper?

Still, he seemed sincere in repenting of that error. When
they had spoken before he left Russia to return to America and
his sick father, he had seemed so contrite. By then, though, it
was too late. He would be thousands of miles away, and she
was embarking upon a new life at the St. Petersburg Medical
School for Women. It was hardly a good time to begin a romantic relationship.

She had written to him once in America but never received
a response. Perhaps she should have been more persistent, but
she had been hurt by his silence and it seemed best to surrender to fate. No doubt he was getting on with his life without
her, and she resigned herself to do the same. And, after four
years, it was apparent she would never see him again.

Why, then, couldn't she forget him? Was there something
to what she had once read about "soul-mates," two people who
just *fit* together, who had the right ingredients to perfectly
complement the other? She had felt that way with Daniel—
that is, before his newspaper article had ruined everything.

Well, if for no other reason, this journey of hers, this adventure, would be just the right thing to distract her mind
from a hopeless romance, once and for all.

Just then the train jerked to a sudden stop. Mariana was
thrown hard against the back of the seat ahead of her. Several
other passengers were pitched from their seats entirely, one
crashing into Mariana before landing in the aisle.

2

Although there had been innumerable stops and delays along the way, none had been like this. When Mariana recovered from her momentary surprise, she jumped up to aid other passengers. One woman had broken her arm, and an officer had a nasty bruise on his brow.

All the passengers were buzzing with curiosity. Many had crowded to the windows to peer out.

"What happened?"

"Can't see a thing!"

"Cursed railroad. It's a wonder we weren't all killed!"

It wasn't long before the conductor appeared. "Everyone calm down, please. We . . . ah . . . are going to have a . . . ah . . . little delay."

Two officers exited the train to make their own assessment of the problem. Within moments, several other passengers decided to do the same. They knew by experience it was almost impossible to get straightforward information from train officials.

As soon as Mariana had helped tend to the injuries, she joined the throng of curious passengers.

It was about an hour before dusk, and a chill wind was blowing. Mariana had left her cloak in the car, but she was too curious to return for it. Shivering, she joined a knot of passengers who stood gaping ahead.

Mariana gasped with shock.

Not twenty feet away, a huge canyon stretched before them. The railway bridge spanned a dozen yards out over the gorge, then ended in a tangled mass of support beams and pilings. Someone had blown up the bridge. Had the train stopped a few seconds later, the engine and all the cars would have tumbled into the raging river below.

One woman in the group of spectators fainted at the dreadful sight. Mariana herself was quaking a bit, although she forced herself to remain at least outwardly calm. They had been only seconds from a horrible death.

"Sabotage," one of the officers said.

No one wanted to hear that. They had expected danger at the end of their trip; many were even prepared to die when they arrived at their final destination. But it was unnerving to think that they could die this far away from Manchuria—suddenly, unexpectedly, by an unseen hand.

It was Mariana's first hint of the real implications of her decision to embark on this journey.

Was she traveling to her own death?

It seemed more possible now than ever.

Anna and Sergei had tried to support her in her decision to come, but even they had been confused by their adopted daughter's unexpected turnabout. Four years ago, Mariana had been so certain the Medical School was what she wanted. But she had been disillusioned by the mountains of study and work involved in becoming a doctor. She had always worked hard on her parents' farm in Katyk, but the intellectual work that faced her in school was worse than milking and threshing and baking all put together!

She had chosen to pursue medicine because she had wanted to help people. Although that might be the end result, in order to get there she had to wade through endless mounds of mathematics and science. Mathematics, especially, was as tough as an old Russian bear for her. Even with Sergei tutoring her, she barely passed. It was the same with science, though at least that was interesting—what she could understand of it! Chemistry was impossible. When she failed her third-year chemistry final, she knew she was in way over her head. The school allowed her to take chemistry again in her fourth year, but in addition to all her regular classes. By the time Christmas came, she was a wreck. Her eyes had completely failed her. She was losing weight and had a terrible chronic head cold. She could not face another minute of school, much less over a year and a half more.

The outbreak of war with Japan in February provided an unexpected outlet for Mariana. There was a desperate call for nurses to go to the front. The Russian Red Cross Organization was recruiting and training women by the dozens to answer that call. Mariana was welcomed eagerly into the fold. Her education might not have seemed much to her, but to the Red Cross it was more than their nurses were required to have. All she lacked was practical training, which they provided at the Red Cross Hospital in St. Petersburg. By summer she was ready to embark on her journey to Manchuria, the theater of war.

The protests of Dmitri and Eugenia went unheeded. They bemoaned her stubbornness, and Dmitri mentioned more than once how, indeed, she was just like her mother.

But Mariana had chosen the medical profession in the first place so she could serve. She loved her work in the hospital, directly serving the needy. She didn't need trigonometry, or biology, or chemistry for that. And now she could serve her country as well. Her uncle Ilya had been called back into the army and sent to the front. For him, and for all the men like him, she would do what she could. If she didn't get killed before she got there, that is.

Shaken, but feeling an undeniable sense of gratitude that their lives had been spared, the passengers returned to their cars. Once the sense of disaster had dissipated, however, the event quickly turned into just another of the many frustrating delays they had been forced to endure on the tedious trip.

Mariana joined the grumblers when they learned they'd be delayed several days while the bridge was being repaired. At least it wasn't the middle of winter, and a nearby village could provide makeshift accommodations for the women. The soldiers and officers would remain on the train.

She closed her eyes and tried to sleep while waiting for the wagons that would take the nurses to the village. But the seat was hard and uncomfortable, and she squirmed like a cranky child. She tried not to think of the delay, which if Russian efficiency were true to form, would probably be even longer than the original repair "estimate." It could be worse. The poor soldiers were packed into the freight cars, which were filled with three times more human cargo than they could comfortably hold. The nurses were allowed the privilege of traveling in the passenger cars with the officers.

The conductor must have realized his passengers needed a distraction, because it wasn't long before a porter arrived with hot tea. At least there was plenty of that. As Mariana sipped her tea and munched a barley cake she had bought at a previous stop, she started to feel a little better.

Mariana shared one of her cakes with Ludmilla, the nurse next to her, and they talked while they finished their tea. Then the girl laid her head back against the hard seat and was soon asleep.

The wagons arrived a couple of hours later and took them to a village as poor as Katyk, but large enough to have a small school, where the nurses were lodged. It wasn't comfortable, but at least they had safe shelter while they waited.

The days of the delay seemed to drag on forever. Mariana availed herself of the fine weather by taking walks in the countryside—sometimes alone, sometimes with Ludmilla or the other nurses. But the long hours of idleness gave her ample time, perhaps too much time, to race away with endless thoughts. She wondered what her family would think of the incident of the bridge. She knew there would be few neutral opinions. Everyone had attitudes about the war, from Dmitri's rampant nationalism to her little brother Andrei's budding radicalism. Andrei liked to quote the university students her father tutored, spouting things he probably understood little of.

But at the outbreak of the war, nearly everyone had been caught up in initial nationalism, herself included. Without a formal declaration of war, the Japanese had attacked the Russian fleet at Port Arthur. They called it a surprise attack.

The only real surprise was that it hadn't happened sooner. Trouble with Japan had been brewing for years.

———

In 1894, after war with China, Japan had received the Liaotung Peninsula, where the Russian Port Arthur was located, as one of its spoils.

Japan's budding military power was a far greater threat to Russia's interests in the Far East than China's crumbling empire. Russia was determined to keep its foothold in the East. Port Arthur provided a much needed warm-water port, and it satisfied Russian expansionist visions as well. Once the Trans-Siberian Railway was completed, it took only a few weeks to reach the Pacific Ocean instead of a year and a half.

On an international level, Russia was not the only one that was concerned over the growing strength of Japan. She was joined by others of the European powers that had political interest in the Far East. The tsar was especially egged on by his German cousin, Kaiser Wilhelm II. The cunning German was fond of referring to his cousin as the "Admiral of the Pacific," while he called himself the "Admiral of the Atlantic." Nicholas felt quite flattered that the tsar of all the Russias was known for such power in the Pacific. In actuality, his cousin "Willy" was only showering him with praise in regard to the Russian power in Asia so as to distract Nicholas from his political ploys in European affairs.

The European powers managed to pressure Japan to return control of Port Arthur to the weaker China. Then, as foreign nations scrambled to extend their colonial powers and seize pieces of China, Russia took advantage of the opportunity and moved in on the port, which was then leased to them by China. To ensure dominance in the region, Russia immediately began to fortify this vital position by building a spur of the Trans-Siberian Railway from Harbin to Port Arthur. This aggression, not only by Russia but also by other colonial foreign powers attempting to claim hold of parts of China, incited the Boxer Uprising in 1900.

After this, Russia's continued presence in Asia caused British anxiety. Consequently, the British saw the Nippon Empire as a perfect ally against their perennial foe, the Russians, and thus made an agreement with the Japanese that if a conflict should arise they would remain neutral. No doubt encouraged by this, the Japanese began to pressure Russia to loosen its hold on Korea. Russia ignored the Japanese while continuing to strenghten its position in Manchuria and Korea.

Finally, in early January of 1904, the Japanese declared that Manchuria was outside its sphere of influence, hoping to receive a similar assurance from Russia regarding Korea. But the Russians stonewalled the request until Japanese patience finally eroded. As a declaration of protest, the Japanese ambassador was recalled to his homeland.

After a few years of this political shadowboxing, the Japanese finally made their move. Russian diplomats assured the tsar that Japan would never fight over the Peninsula. Indeed, how could the tiny island nation, which only a few years ago had been totally isolated from the world, possibly have the nerve to cross swords with the Holy Russian Empire?

But the Nippon Empire rose to the challenge. One night in the first week of February, the Japanese fleet quietly entered the harbor at Port Arthur and opened fire on the anchored Russian fleet. Considering that tensions between the two nations had been mounting for weeks, the Russians were shamefully unprepared. Two Russian battleships were completely disabled, along with several smaller ships; Admiral Togo of the Japanese fleet steamed out of the harbor unscathed.

———

The unprovoked attack raised Russian nationalism to fever pitch. The only person Mariana knew who showed no enthusiasm for the war in those first weeks was her papa Sergei.

"I have been through one Russian war," he said shortly after the attack, "and nothing I have seen of late shows me that anything has changed in twenty-seven years. We have the stoutest, bravest soldiers on earth. Unfortunately, they are led by a bunch of incompetent nincompoops. Admiral Alekseev completely bungled the defense of Port Arthur."

"But wasn't it a surprise attack, Papa?"

"He's the viceroy of the Far East, for heaven's sake! There is no way he couldn't have known how badly relations with Japan had deteriorated. The fleet should have been placed on alert weeks before the attack."

"I must agree with you, son," said Viktor as they sat together around the dinner table. "But as an ex-army commander myself, I do take some offense at your comment about 'nincompoops.'" He spoke with a hint of amusement in his eyes, but Mariana saw that his words stung Sergei nevertheless.

"I'm sorry, Father. I suppose I was a bit rash. There are worthies in command, and you were definitely one of them, but they are far too rare."

"Too true," lamented Viktor. "I'll never understand why our emperors insist on surrounding themselves with inept fools."

"It's the only way the tsar can make himself look good."

Raisa Sorokin, the friend with whom Anna and Sergei lived, clucked her tongue. "Please, gentlemen, the walls have ears."

"Forgive me, Raisa," said Sergei. "I love Russia, but sometimes . . ." He shrugged his shoulders and smiled apologetically, but Mariana had seen the look of frustration in his eyes.

3

Many days later, the train conductor came to the schoolhouse and announced, "We'll be getting underway soon."

A great cheer rose from the bored and miserable women. Much to their surprise and delight, the time estimate on the repairs had been fairly accurate. Mariana welcomed the monotonous vibration of the moving train again, and she was soon lulled into the best sleep she'd had for days. She awoke several hours later to a beautiful sunrise.

The new day revealed a sight almost stunning in its beauty. As the train rounded a bend, Mariana glimpsed a huge body of water, the light behind it giving it an ethereal quality, golden and shimmering. Her guidebook told her this was Lake Baikal, but few Siberians ever referred to it as a lake—to them it was a sea, and indeed, Mariana could not deny the accuracy of the description. It was the largest freshwater lake in all of Europe and Asia, three hundred and ninety-five miles long and, at its widest point, fifty miles wide—approximately the size of Switzerland.

For all its glorious beauty, Lake Baikal was, at the present, something of a thorn in Russia's flesh. It was one of the weakest links in Russia's war effort. In order to save money, the builders of the Trans-Siberian Railway had decided that instead of building the costly rail around the lake's southern tip, they would ferry freight and passengers across. A tenable plan in normal times, it was becoming a nightmare during wartime. The lake was frozen at least six months out of the year, forcing soldiers to hike forty miles over the icy, windswept lake, which added days to the already ponderous trip to the front.

Mariana was lucky to arrive during the thaw because the women were to be ferried across with the supplies while the soldiers still had to march around the lake. On the ferry she was able to enjoy the scenery and see at close range the exceptionally clear water of the lake. But even late in June, it was chilly and windy.

As she pondered the wonders of the lake, she also began to consider the events that had brought her to this faraway place.

For all Papa Sergei's dissatisfaction with the war, he had been the only one not to discourage Mariana from answering Russia's call for service at the front. He didn't *like* the idea, but he seemed to understand and trust her motives.

Sometimes Mariana wondered if even she really understood what was driving her toward Manchuria and war. And as she drew closer to it, she became even more uncertain. Normally Mariana couldn't be bothered with the intricacies of unraveling her hidden motivations. Such pursuits were probably best left to the likes of Stephan Kaminsky, her onetime friend and suitor. He had always known just where he stood and why he stood there. So far all Mariana really knew was that at the end of this journey there existed a need she was trained to fulfill. At last her life would have real purpose. Did she need to fathom the deeper nuances of this war? Did she even have to agree with it? There was a war out there, no matter that it might have been caused by incompetence or greed or arrogance. Men would be hurt and in need, and she was prepared to minister to those needs. In the end, that's all that really mattered.

What she was doing had little to do with nationalism or politics or even altruism. From the beginning she had simply known this was the way she must go. Moments of fear and wavering—or even near-brushes with death—could not change that inner sense of "rightness." She belonged here, on this journey, and she already sensed that the journey's end would bring her to both a physical and a spiritual destination.

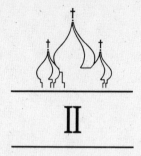

II

WAR ZONE

4

Mariana knew she had reached foreign lands. Since entering Manchuria, the train had been passing peculiar pagoda-shaped buildings. The laborers in the fields wore high-collared jackets that looked like pajamas and wide-brimmed hats an officer called "coolie" hats. Mariana thought the villages dotting the mountainous landscape were more squalid than those in Russia, but then, she might just be showing her prejudice. All available land, even the slopes of the mountains, was covered in beans, or in millet growing as tall as fifteen feet.

But not until the train passed Mukden did Mariana truly feel she had entered a world unlike any she had known. Here were the first real signs of war. All along the way since crossing the Urals, she had seen soldiers guarding the all-important railroad to try to prevent just the sort of sabotage her train had experienced. She had heard that at least fifty-five thousand men were thus employed along the length of the railroad. But here, in the Liaotung Peninsula, there could be no doubt that a war was being waged. The troops of soldiers marching in the fields were not crisp and clean like those guarding the railroad in Siberia. These men were worn and filthy, dragging their feet as if they had been marching for years without halt. No doubt the oppressive heat weighed them down as much as their rifles and knapsacks.

But even more disconcerting than the sight of these war-weary soldiers was the distant sound of artillery and explosions. Mariana and her companions were not so close as to be in immediate danger, but the sounds were frightening nevertheless.

At Liaoyang, however, Mariana received her first real initiation into her chosen career. Her supervisor informed her that she and five other nurses would debark in order to help load wounded onto the Russia-bound train on the adjacent track. Mariana's original assignment was to serve in the hospital at Port Arthur, and her supervisor assured her that she would get there eventually. But for the moment the greater need was here. Apparently a major battle was being fought south of Liaoyang, and casualties were pouring into the station faster than they could be evacuated away.

With trembling fingers, Mariana straightened out the white apron of her pale gray uniform. She had put it on fresh that morning, so it was still white and stiff with starch. Glancing at her reflection in the car window, she determined that her veil was on straight, then she donned her navy cape—not that she needed it in the heat, but it looked so professional. She smiled weakly at Ludmilla, who was also to debark, then rose and made her way off the train.

"Over here, girls!" yelled an orderly as he boosted a stretcher up into a train car.

"This isn't going to be like in the hospital at home," said Ludmilla.

Mariana swallowed and shook her head. "We didn't think it would be, did we?" Her question was directed as much to herself as to her companion. In reality, she had given very little thought to what nursing at the front of a war would be like. They had learned in theory about treating traumas, but had little firsthand experience.

In another moment they found themselves busy working among the stretchers, and there was no time to muse over their situation.

"Come in here," a woman called to them from the open door of one of the freight cars of the converted hospital train.

Using an overturned crate as a step, Mariana and Ludmilla climbed aboard. Inside, the walls were lined with eighteen suspension beds, nine on each side of the car. The beds were fitted with springs intended to help absorb the jostling of a moving train, but after spending weeks on a train herself,

Mariana could imagine how excruciating such a journey would be for a wounded man.

Besides the beds, there was little else in the car except a small cabinet for storage and a few buckets for waste. The car was filled with foul odors, and even with the huge sliding doors wide open, the heat was stifling. Mariana quickly tossed aside her cape.

The car contained little room for the nursing personnel to move about, and situating the patients on the beds was at best a difficult maneuver, resulting in frequent moans and cries from the wounded. Mariana tried not to think of any of this, but instead focused all her energy on the task at hand. Not thinking, however, proved to be her most difficult job. She could not keep from regarding these poor men as individuals—frightened, in pain, and dying. Many would never make it to their destination—the hospital at Irkutsk—and she felt completely helpless to do anything for them.

"What are you doing?" the nurse in charge asked. As the long lines of stretchers waiting by the track increased by the minute, the woman's patience was quickly ebbing away.

Mariana had paused by one of the wounded soldiers and had begun to read a letter to him that he had handed to her.

"He asked me to—"

"Not now, girl! We have three more cars to fill, and the wounded keep coming."

Mariana smiled apologetically at the soldier.

"It's all right," he answered weakly. "There'll be time later."

But Mariana wondered; the man's coloring was gray, and the fresh bandage she had applied to the stump of his amputated leg was already soaked with blood.

They worked past sundown. When the train was full, they had to transport the remaining wounded to the hospital at Liaoyang, which was already filled to overflowing. Mariana hardly remembered having a hurried dinner, and when she was finally relieved for the night, she was as exhausted as she ever recalled being. Since she and the other nurses had not been expected to stay in town, however, they had to wait while sleeping accommodations could be arranged.

She and Ludmilla and a couple of the other nurses found

a supply area where some stacks of crates offered the only seating available. Two of the orderlies Mariana had worked with that day had also availed themselves of the makeshift seating, and they welcomed the girls. It seemed safe enough to mix with the men unchaperoned—if for no other reason than that the men looked as exhausted as the women.

"I have never worked so hard in my life!" Ludmilla said as she plopped down on a low crate of tin goods.

"And this is only the beginning," said the orderly named Fedor. "Wait till the wounded really start coming. In the last two days we've handled hundreds of casualties—that's including the dead. It was the same last month and the month before that."

"You've been here a long time, Fedor?" asked Mariana.

"Since the beginning. So has Boris here. Boris, tell them about Yalu—" He turned back to the girls. "That was the first real land battle of the war."

"These young ladies don't want to hear about that," said Boris glumly. He was more serious and morose than his companion, and far less talkative.

"I was at Port Arthur, so I missed that one," Fedor said. He seemed almost disappointed.

Mariana decided to overlook his overzealousness and try to get as much information from him as possible, since he seemed so eager to talk. "I heard a rumor that the Japanese now control most of the railway stations south of here. Ludmilla and I were bound for Port Arthur. Will we be able to get there?"

"For one thing, missy, you got to know that rumors fly around a war zone thicker than artillery. But in this case that particular rumor is pretty close to true. We haven't won a battle since . . . well, we haven't won a battle *period*."

"How can that be?" asked Ludmilla in innocent shock. "We are Russia, the mightiest nation on earth. Japan is just a tiny island."

"If we've learned nothing else, we have learned not to underestimate them Japs. They're tough 'little monkeys,' as the tsar calls them, and they've got a loyalty to their country and emperor that—"

"You talk too much," growled Boris, glancing quickly over his shoulder.

"Can you give us an idea of the direction of the immediate fighting?" asked Mariana, hoping to steer the conversation back to the beginning.

"Well, in a nutshell, the Japs are pushing north, trying to push us Russians out of the Liaotung Peninsula. We're trying to stop them—" Fedor glanced toward his companion. "None too successfully. Telissu, where this most recent battle is being fought, is about a hundred miles south of here. But it won't be long before they get to Liaoyang." He lifted his eyebrows at the sudden pallor in the nurses' faces. "But it'll take the Japs weeks, maybe a couple of months, to get here."

"What about our assignment in Port Arthur?" asked Ludmilla.

"You can still get through," said Fedor cheerfully. "But you may not be able to take the train the entire distance—there'll be wagons and such, and the Red Cross trains can get through."

"So, do we still have the port?" asked Ludmilla, who had next to no understanding of warfare.

"Of course," said Mariana. "That's what this is all about. If the Japanese take Port Arthur, the war would be as good as over." With her father, grandfather, and uncle all ex-military men, Mariana had a little better grasp of these matters, especially because Dmitri and Viktor had both plied her with many war stories before her departure. Sergei had said very little.

"So, don't worry," said Fedor. "If that's where you want to go, you'll get there."

Boris shook his head grimly. "Don't think you'll be escaping anything by going there. The Japanese could take all of the Liaotung and Manchuria as well, but if they haven't got Port Arthur, they haven't got anything. And believe me, they'll soon be fighting like the devil to get it."

"I wouldn't be so anxious to get to Port Arthur, if I was you," added Fedor. "It's only a matter of time before the Japs seal it off good—you know, lay siege to it."

Mariana suddenly felt trapped. But she was no quitter—at

least she didn't want to be labeled as one. After the fiasco with the medical school, she had to prove to herself, if to no one else, that she could finish something she started. Her options however were frightening; she could stay where she was and face a fierce battle, or go south and still face heavy fighting and probably a siege. But she had never once believed she was going to a picnic; her papa Sergei *had* tried to enlighten her about that.

In the end, of course, the choice was not hers to make. She was under the authority of the Red Cross, which in turn was under the thumb of the army. Unless she decided to quit altogether, she would go where they told her to go.

And the very next day her orders were changed. She was assigned to the field hospital attached to the Fourth Siberian Army Corps, located about a day's journey south of Liaoyang. With fighting raging all around, she wondered if it would have been better to risk the possible dangers at Port Arthur. But the decision was made without consulting her. She would go—no matter what the outcome.

5

The bumpy wagon that seemed to find every crevice and pothole in the road gave Mariana a new appreciation for the train. The railroad was smooth as a glass highway by comparison.

The field hospital was about twenty miles to the south, but the treacherous steep roads, now clogged with mud because it was the rainy season in Manchuria, made it a lengthy journey. They were traveling at the rear of the battle, but that was not a total guarantee of safety. She hoped that the huge red cross, the internationally accepted emblem for neutrality painted on the side of their wagon, would afford them safe passage. It took them two days to make the trip, and never once did the sound of distant gunfire and artillery cease.

Mariana's traveling companions in the cramped wagon included Ludmilla, also assigned to the field hospital, the driver, and two soldiers along as escort. Around midmorning of their second day they were caught in a torrential rain. Because there was no place near to go for shelter, not even a shanty, the driver opted to continue. They were only a few miles from a village, he assured them. But he was finally forced to stop when the wagon wheels became mired in mud.

All the passengers climbed out of the wagon to ply their shoulders to the task of freeing the wagon. It was wet, miserable work, and when the wagon was finally mobile again, the party found little comfort within the leaky canvas shelter of the wagon. They were a little happier when the sun came out an hour later. They lifted the side flap of the wagon to allow the blazing sun to dry their soaked clothing. Once they were dry, however, the sun became almost unbearable.

Mariana had begun to lose track of time, but the rumbling in her stomach indicated it must be near lunchtime. The driver had said they ought to reach their destination about this time, but so far there was nothing in sight resembling a field hospital. She hoped they would get there soon because, by the look of the sky, they were in for another drenching. Suddenly they heard loud bursts of artillery fire—much too close for the "rear" of a battle. And the sound was getting closer, not farther away.

"How close is the hospital to the front?" Mariana asked one of the guards who was riding in the wagon. She made a concerted effort to quell the tremor in her voice.

"Half a day's ride, at least," he said in a patronizing tone. He and his comrade had spent most of the morning flirting with the two nurses, but Mariana's comment caused him to take closer note of their position. His complexion paled. He nudged his comrade. "What's going on?"

They shouted to the driver to stop.

"You're heading the wrong way," accused the soldier. "There's fighting a mile from here, if that."

The driver began to defend himself. "We had to alter our course a bit because of the rain—"

"Do you have any idea of where we are?"

"Well . . . we might have gone a little past the hospital." The driver drew up the reins and looked back at his passengers apologetically. "We'll get back on track, don't worry."

Fifteen minutes later it became quite apparent that the driver was thoroughly lost and had no idea where the correct road was. The gunfire had stopped, but it was still disconcerting not knowing if they had stumbled into "no-man's-land."

A few minutes later they came upon a squadron of Russian soldiers.

"By the saints!" shouted one. "This is close to being a true miracle."

"What do you mean?" asked Ludmilla.

"We were just hit pretty bad, and we have wounded. Never thought an ambulance would get here this fast."

"We aren't exactly an ambulance," said the driver. "I'm transporting personnel to the field hospital."

"You're going in the wrong direction for that. The hospital is about six or seven miles in the other direction. You're right in the middle of a battle zone now."

"Which way to the hospital?" asked the driver, ready to turn around and race away as quickly as possible.

"Just a minute!" The soldier grabbed the harness. "We have wounded to be evacuated, and there's no reason why you can't take them. Our dressing station was hit pretty badly. Our surgeon's dead, and two of our medics are wounded. They have more casualties than they can handle."

The driver was none too eager to comply. He was strictly a part of the rear echelon and hadn't been this close to the front the entire war. But Mariana and Ludmilla insisted they help out. The two guards supported the nurses.

Thus, the driver reluctantly proceeded to the camp headquarters of the squadron. The captain in command welcomed them, then took them to the battered dressing station—little more than a ragged tent to house the wounded. There they found about fifty stretcher cases, two dozen ambulatory wounded, and twenty men who only needed minor patching in order to be returned to their posts. On duty were four feldshers—highly trained male nurses able to assume many of a physician's lighter duties. Female nurses were only slightly less trained than feldshers, but there were none at this particular station. There were six attendants, untrained male personnel that performed mostly menial tasks as opposed to direct patient care. The ten workers had their hands quite full, especially with the loss of their only surgeon. They crowded four of the most critical patients on the wagon, but the frantic atmosphere in the tent continued unabated.

The head feldsher, whose name was Kask, greeted the women as they entered the tent. "Help at last! And Red Cross nurses, too. Very good!" He was a stocky, round-faced man, and in any other setting he might have appeared quite jolly. But at this moment there was such a grim aspect to his cherubic face that it had a most depressing effect.

He set the girls to work immediately. When he found out they hadn't been officially sent to him, he just shrugged and told the driver to unload their baggage and report to the field hospital that he was "borrowing" the nurses for a while.

"By the time they object," he said offhandedly, "it'll be too late."

Mariana wondered fleetingly if she should tell Kask they were novices. But he seemed too busy to notice their inexperience and too desperate to care.

Ludmilla drew the worst duty—a soldier whose right leg had been shattered. He was bleeding profusely, and the fragmented bone in his upper leg was perforating his skin in several places. His wound, combined with the summer heat and the surrounding horror, would have been enough to sicken many a veteran—much less a novice. Ludmilla tried gallantly to hang on, despite her trembling knees. Then the feldsher she was assisting pulled a bone fragment from the patient's hip.

"This isn't a femur," he said upon examining the bone. Then, after giving the patient a quick appraisal, he exclaimed, "Dear Lord! This isn't even *his* bone!"

43

Ludmilla crumpled to the floor.

In spite of her concern for her friend, Mariana was too busy to stop and help. She was assisting Kask in setting a dislocated shoulder. In the next stretcher a man with a terrible abdominal wound was screaming in pain.

"Can't we do something for him?" Mariana asked, appalled that no one was attending the man.

Kask shook his head. "He's a goner. We can't waste our time on him when there are others we *can* save."

When the shoulder popped into place, Kask grinned. "There you go, fellow! You'll be back on the line tomorrow." Kask turned to Mariana and, indicating the man in the next stretcher, said, "Give him an injection of morphine, a quarter grain." Then he moved to another patient.

Mariana stood immobile for a moment, shocked at the medic's brusque, matter-of-fact attitude. Then she saw two attendants carrying Ludmilla out of the tent.

"Ludmilla!" she cried and started after her.

Kask stopped her. "She'll be fine—just couldn't take it, that's all." He stopped and peered closely at Mariana. "You're not going to break on me, too, are you?"

Mariana had no answer to that. Her knees were weak, and the dying man's screams echoed horribly in her head. A huge knot in her throat made her speechless. She just shook her head rather unconvincingly. Where she found the inner stamina to go to the medicine chest, draw up an injection of morphine and administer it to the soldier, she never knew. Somehow, though, she kept going, her actions dreamlike and detached. The screams of the dying man continued to haunt her long after he had died and was carried away by an attendant.

Carts finally began arriving to take the patients to the field hospital, but evacuation was a slow process. Ambulance wagons were rarely used in Manchuria; instead, a two-wheeled cart called a *dvukolk*, drawn by one or two horses, was the primary means of transportation. There was room in the cart for four slightly wounded men who could sit up, but only two stretcher cases would fit—and the patients had to lie on their sides with their knees flexed so their feet didn't hang over the

end. There wasn't even a seat for the driver; he walked alongside the cart. Thus, the removal of patients could not keep up
with new arrivals, which seemed to come in by droves. The
war showed no mercy to an untried girl fresh from her papa's
home.

Shortly after nightfall, Kask nudged Mariana aside to eat
dinner and take a short break, but he returned for her long
before she was rested. There were no more breaks for the rest
of the night.

Around midnight a soldier came in with a hemorrhaging
chest wound. Even if a surgeon had been present, this man
needed the better equipped facilities of a field hospital. Kask,
who was not only the head nurse but also the most experienced of the staff, did what he could for the man, but Mariana
knew it might not be enough.

"He needs to go to the field hospital," he said, "but he'll
surely die if we move him."

"We could move him if we stopped the bleeding, couldn't
we?" asked Mariana.

"That could take hours, and I can't spare the personnel.
There are others who have a better chance of surviving. Didn't
they teach you anything about triage?"

"Please, Kask, give me an hour with him. If there is no
change, then . . . well, at least I'll know we tried."

"Maybe that's the only way you'll learn."

"Thank you. Just tell me what to do."

Kask snorted dryly. "Are new-trained nurses all they have
left to send us?"

"Remember, no one *sent* me," Mariana corrected with as
much audacity as she could muster. "I shouldn't even be here."

"Then I should be grateful," Kask said. Mariana couldn't
tell if this was a statement or a question. Either way, he was
far from enthusiastic. "Go attend to your patient. We haven't
time for this chatter."

Mariana put her hour to good use. By applying continuous
pressure to the wound, she managed to slow the bleeding,
though it by no means stopped. The young man, named Yakov,
was conscious and in great pain despite heavy doses of morphine. As Mariana worked on the wound, she talked to him

constantly, trying to distract him. She hated to leave him when her allotted hour was up, but Kask had other pressing duties for her. She put a pressure bandage on the wound and found it only needed changing two or three times an hour after that. Kask examined her efforts and grunted, a sound Mariana soon learned was his way of showing approval.

A surgeon arrived shortly before morning. No more feld-shers, nurses, or attendants could be spared from the field hospital. The doctor praised Mariana for Yakov's condition, saying he couldn't have done more for him under these conditions. The young soldier was pronounced fit to be moved.

"Nurse," Yakov called weakly to Mariana as the stretcher-bearers were about to take him to a cart. When Mariana leaned close to hear, he continued, "Thanks isn't enough for what you did for me. I don't even know your name so I can pray for you."

"I'm sorry I never got around to introducing myself, Yakov. My name is Mariana Dmitrievna."

"God bless you! I . . . won't forget."

6

Mariana hardly noticed when the gunfire stopped. It made little difference, for the wounded kept coming. She was beginning to feel completely helpless. All they could do was staunch bleeding and clean wounds. Many of these men needed much more than that, and quickly. There was no time even for the surgeon to do more. They could only patch the patients up and hope they reached the field hospital alive, where more extensive surgery and care could be given.

The staff had no time for rest, especially when the battle began again in earnest. Ludmilla had gone on to the field hospital, and Mariana hoped that this unfortunate first exposure to fresh battle wounds did not sour Ludmilla completely on nursing. Mariana herself couldn't understand why she hadn't fainted or lost her breakfast; but there wasn't time to think of her own discomfort at all. These poor boys were facing much greater horrors than she could even imagine.

With only twelve on their staff, the dressing station was woefully undermanned. Since Mariana's arrival nearly twenty-four hours before, hundreds of wounded had already passed through their doors.

Hundreds!

No longer did Mariana wonder about Kask's incredible detachment from the whole appalling scene. She, too, began to distance herself from the reality—it was the only way to survive.

Help from the field hospital arrived after lunch—another physician, a feldsher, and a female nurse. Those who had been working the longest took the first breaks. The men wanted to defer to Mariana, and she was tempted to comply. After working around the clock, she was bone tired. She desperately needed a bath and a change of clothes, too, for her uniform, besides being wrinkled and smelly, was also liberally stained with blood and grime. She didn't even want to look at her smudged face and her greasy hair which kept falling in her eyes. But she insisted she be given no special treatment, either, because of her gender or her inexperience. Kask was the only one who refused to take a break. Mariana decided she would not go before him.

Her physical limitations, however, overpowered her good intentions. As she was taking a patient's temperature, the thermometer fumbled from her hand. At least the soft canvas floor had kept the delicate glass instrument from breaking.

"No offense, miss," said her patient, "but you look worse than me. Why don't you take a rest? I don't got a fever, but I'll tell you if I get one."

The other nearby patients heartily agreed.

"What kind of hospital is this," she said with a good imitation of a smile, "that the patients have to care for the nurse?"

They laughed, but they still insisted that she get off her feet for a few minutes.

"No . . . no, I'll be fine." She reached for disinfectant to clean the thermometer. She had been inhaling the odor all day, but this time the pungent smell must have been too much for her—at least that was the way she explained it. A sudden light-headedness assailed her, she swayed on her feet, and the thermometer fell again—this time on the hard instrument table. The glass split in two, sending beads of mercury everywhere.

Kask reached her in a few steps.

"You are a stubborn young woman," he said gruffly, catching her just before she fell. "You will take a break—now!"

"You've been working longer," she protested weakly.

"Go, or I shall carry you away!"

"Well, perhaps for a few minutes . . . I'll just go out and get a bit of fresh air. That's all I need."

Mariana made her way outside, wondering at one point if she *would* need to be carried. She sank down on the grass and leaned against the trunk of an old tree. She didn't need to go to the tent that had been cleared to provide quarters for the women; she would only rest a moment or two. In a few seconds she was sound asleep.

An hour later, Mariana woke, feeling disoriented and sluggish as if she had slept the night through. Her slumber had finally been disturbed—not by gunfire, but by a single voice that seemed to have come straight out of her dreams.

"Mariana!"

"What?" Mariana said dully, removing her glasses and rubbing her eyes, hoping to clear her head.

"It is you! I couldn't believe it when I heard your name at the field hospital—" The newcomer stopped abruptly. "I woke you up, didn't I? I'm really sorry. I guess I'm still the same insensitive clod—"

Mariana's eyes opened wide and she sat bolt upright.

"Daniel!" She scrambled to her feet. "I . . . I—what a surprise!"

"No less for me. Just when I thought—" He stopped speak-

48

ing and went to her, taking her hands in his. "You look wonderful!"

Mariana smiled. She didn't care if she looked and smelled
like a street vagrant, and she knew he was just being polite and
didn't mean a word of his compliment. All of her fatigue simply fell away, replaced by an unexpected surge of emotions.
She couldn't quite identify the feelings, and perhaps she was
a little afraid to examine them too closely, anyway. The only
thing that seemed important was that Daniel Trent had suddenly stepped back into her life.

7

Mariana brushed a damp strand of hair from her eyes
while Daniel held tightly to her other hand. Around them orderlies were busy moving stretchers onto the dvukolks that
had just arrived. But in that moment Mariana thought only of
Daniel's impish grin and her own sweet memories of picnics
at the Summer Gardens, pleasant walks along St. Petersburg's
quays, and quiet evenings talking in Madame Durocq's slightly
threadbare parlor. It felt as if hours instead of years had
passed since she and Daniel had last been together.

The sharp cry of a patient jarred her back to the present.

"I . . . I better help them," said Mariana.

"Oh, yeah, of course," he replied with obvious reluctance.
But when she started to turn, he held on to her hand a moment
longer. "Gosh, I feel as if it were only yesterday." Then, slightly
flustered at his sentimentality, he dropped her hand.

Mariana returned to work, struck by the incredible realization that they had been feeling the same thing. It had been

four years since they had parted in her father's parlor. They were now in a foreign land in the middle of a war, yet she felt as if they could just as well be back in St. Petersburg, strolling along a wooded path.

Surely they were not unchanged in all that time. She knew she had changed immensely, and she could only assume—or perhaps hope—that Daniel had too. But standing there, looking into his eyes, she had felt the same friendship and affection she once had for him. For nearly two years they had enjoyed a special relationship in which they both—yes, even Daniel!—had opened up their hearts to each other. He had been a friend and confidant when she had needed someone to lean on—someone to help her make the adjustment from her peasant life in Katyk to the aristocracy of St. Petersburg. She had trusted him. Yes, he had taken advantage of her trust and published that article without her knowledge. He had made her life into a public spectacle.

But later, when she thought about their falling out over his article, she had to admit that she had been somewhat unfair in her accusations. His affection for her couldn't have been merely a sham, a role he played to get her to open up for his article. The laughter, the joy, the moments of tenderness simply could not all have been a ruse. He had been deceptive and insensitive, it was true—but there was more to Daniel Trent, more to their relationship, than that.

Mariana wondered why he had never written to her. Now that time had passed and the wounds were healed, she began to realize that perhaps she had hurt him, too.

Still, he didn't seem resentful toward her. He was genuinely pleased to see her. They were, after all, four years more mature. They had both made mistakes and let their pride get the better of them, but that didn't negate all the good in their friendship.

Stubborn. Kask hardly knew Mariana and he had called her *stubborn.* Her father had said so, too. They were probably right. She was so stubborn that she had let someone she cared about slip away from her. Daniel meant more to her than her actions had indicated, for he had nagged at her thoughts frequently in the past four years.

Was this sudden, unexpected meeting her second chance? Was this the reason God had kept her from relationships with other men? Was Daniel the man she was ultimately going to marry? Startled at the question, she glanced toward where she had left Daniel.

He was gone.

She stopped her work briefly and looked around the compound. Finally she spotted Daniel, notebook in hand, talking to the captain. Mariana smiled to herself. Well, he was a reporter, and he had come to Manchuria to report on a war, not to court an old flame. She couldn't expect him to wait around like an adoring puppy until she found time for him. They *both* had work to do, and if they were to have a second chance, their relationship was going to have to fit in around very demanding schedules.

Mariana returned to the dressing station tent. As the fighting had diminished, things had quieted somewhat. The carts removing the wounded were finally able to keep up with the influx, and soon the crowd in the tent began to thin out. Mariana was pleased to note that Kask had gone to rest, and he remained away for two hours. When he returned he looked much better, but there was still no merriment on that cherubic face.

"Well, Mariana Remizov," he said, "it appears I must let you go."

"What do you mean?"

"I had to inform headquarters, of course, about our stray nurses. They gave me permission to keep you until the battle ended. Since our troops are in retreat, it is safe to assume the Battle of Telissu is as good as over."

"I'm sorry to hear that—I mean about the retreat."

"We're getting used to it."

"I suppose I should find my things and be on my way while it is still light."

"Of course." Kask turned to go and Mariana was about to be on her way when the feldsher paused and swung back around. "Thank you, Miss Remizov. You are a fine little nurse."

Then he hurried away before Mariana had a chance to respond.

The only hindrance to her leaving now was transportation. The wagons were filled with wounded, and the prospect of walking five miles to the field hospital was not at all inviting. It was, however, her only choice.

When she stepped outside the dressing station tent, Daniel ambled over to her, carefully putting his notebook and pencil into his coat pocket.

"The battle is over and lost," he said. "That must be the cause of the woebegone expression on your face."

"It didn't go well for us."

"Would you like to see why?"

Daniel took her hand, and she followed him to where a company of soldiers was parading before their officers. One of the officers was mounted and—if it could be judged by the ornate, medal-bedecked uniform he wore—was a man of importance.

"That's General Stoessel," Daniel whispered to Mariana. "Governor of the Kwantung Peninsula. Heaven only knows what he's doing here, but he should have—"

Before Daniel could finish, General Stoessel began to speak to the assembled troops. "I have never seen a more pathetic assemblage of brigands in my life!" His voice shook with rage, his eyes bulged.

"What did they do?" Mariana quietly asked Daniel.

"They retreated—after fighting their hearts out."

The general continued to rail at the troops. "Traitors, all of you—do you hear! Why, I'll have each and every one of you up for a court martial. Thank God the defense of Port Arthur doesn't rest on such worthless excuses for soldiers!"

Mariana nudged Daniel. "Let's go. I don't want to hear any more."

As they walked away Daniel took out his notebook and jotted down some notes.

"Are you going to write about that?" asked Mariana. When he nodded, she added, "You won't make them look bad, will you? The troops, I mean. So many suffered and died, Daniel. They weren't traitors."

"Anyone with an ounce of sense knows that," said Daniel. "It's men like Stoessel I'd like to expose. Arrogant, inept fools.

But I doubt anything I'd write would get past the censors."

"I feel so bad for the men," said Mariana.

"No wonder they're always talking about revolution."

"Here?"

"Sure, they *talk* about it a lot. But the conditions of war make it a pretty risky business. In Russia they can only get exiled for such talk; here they could easily get shot for treason."

"How will we ever win the war?"

"That's a very good question. If I were a betting man, I'd put my money on the Japanese."

<hr>

8

<hr>

"I'm afraid I put a cloud over our reunion," Daniel said after a gloomy pause.

"This is not the best setting in which to meet an old friend."

"Nevertheless, I'd like to do something to cheer you."

"Well, if you could produce a carriage so I wouldn't have to walk to my next assignment, it might help."

"You would ask the impossible! I'd offer you a ride on my own shoulders if I thought they were strong enough."

She chuckled at the image that presented, then taunted playfully, "Since when have you become so chivalrous?"

"How quickly you forget! But I do recall defending your honor once, in the face of a grizzly bear of an opponent."

"Yes, I had quite forgotten that." Mariana smiled at the memory. Stephan Alexandrovich, her first love and unofficial fiance, had found her and Daniel together. Daniel was trying to make it up to her after she found out about his unauthorized article. Stephan had jumped to the wrong conclusion and heaped accusations upon Mariana, and Daniel had defended her reputation. Had Stephan chosen to take up Daniel's challenge . . . well, Mariana didn't like to think what might have happened to Daniel; Stephan was indeed a formidable opponent.

"Unfortunately," Daniel went on, "my shoulders aren't nearly as broad as that other fellow's, and I fear even your slim, lithe figure would break them. However, I will gladly offer you my arm and whatever company I can give as I walk at your side."

"I suppose that will have to do—the walking part, I mean." Then, flustered, Mariana added, "I'd like nothing more than your company; I just wish it didn't have to be on foot. I've had only an hour of sleep since yesterday morning."

He gave her a look of sympathy, seeming to contemplate once more the feasibility of carrying her, then shrugged apologetically. "At least we can catch up on our lives as we go. Perhaps that will take your mind off your fatigue."

"That would be nice." She smiled and took his arm.

But he hesitated before going on. "Mariana, I'm glad you still consider us friends, and a little relieved, too. But I have to admit I had given up on us when you never answered my letters."

"Letters?"

"I wrote you several times—you mean you never received anything?"

"Honestly, Daniel, I never did."

"No wonder you stopped writing after that first letter." He frowned. "Do you mean that we drifted apart because of the *postal service*? It makes a person think, doesn't it?"

"What might have been. . . ?" Mariana sighed, then shook the musing away with a smile. "Perhaps we can forget all about the past."

"I'd like to try."

Mariana retrieved her few pieces of luggage and managed to convince one of the dvukolk drivers to tuck it away in a corner of his cart. By the time she and Daniel finally set out, it was late afternoon—the hottest, most stifling part of the day.

They hurried to catch up to the ambulance wagons. Walking alone in the countryside was unwise, even if the battle was officially over. At least the Red Cross flags on the wagons offered minimal protection.

The rush left Daniel and Mariana breathless and sweaty. But once in the company of the wagons, they slowed their pace and proceeded to resume the much-anticipated discussion. Mariana was dying to hear from Daniel, but he insisted that she go first.

She thought she didn't have much to tell. But once she got going, helped along by Daniel's probing questions, she found herself discussing feelings she had only thought about before. He listened so attentively that for a moment she wondered if he was merely trying to find some—as he would say—"angle" he might use for his benefit. She chided herself immediately for the unkind thought. He had thus far shown himself to be completely sincere. But hadn't he seemed that way before?

She sighed, frustrated both with herself and with the position their mistakes had put them in.

"Something wrong?" asked Daniel.

"Oh, no, just the heat—" Mariana stopped abruptly.

Deception and misunderstanding had caused their problems in the first place. Wasn't it best to have everything out in the open? Part of her wanted to sweep the past neatly under the mat and move on, but she wasn't sure that was possible if the past kept getting in the way. Her papa Sergei was fond of saying, "He who dwells on the past is bound to lose an eye. But the man who ignores the past will lose both eyes." She had to be honest with him, no matter what the cost.

"I never knew the heat to trouble a person so," Daniel prompted when her hesitation lasted a moment too long.

"I guess it's not just that," Mariana replied with resolve. "I know we agreed to forget the past. More than anything else, Daniel, I want to start over with you—to be the way we were when we first met. You were one of my best friends."

"But you can't keep from wondering if I'm not just sizing you up for another sly article. I don't blame you. Let me assure you that you are completely safe with me now; I do very little human interest these days—"

"Otherwise I'd still be fair game?" Mariana couldn't keep the hard edge from her words.

"That's not what I meant. How could you think—?" He stopped and gave an indignant shake of his head, causing his glasses to slide down his nose and a lock of hair to fall into his eyes. He adjusted his glasses and tried to fix his hair, but that unruly brown strand fell forward again. The action, however, seemed to calm him and clear his thoughts. "I guess there isn't any reason for you to think differently," he said finally.

"I want to believe in you, Daniel. I'm sure you really felt bad about what happened before."

"I'm so incredibly dense when it comes to saying what I feel."

"But I would like to hear nothing more, Daniel."

"And I believe you." He started walking again, and Mariana kept at his side. "Mariana, since I left Russia, you have never been far from my thoughts. I came to realize just how important you were to me, and I never stopped regretting how my selfish actions spoiled everything." He turned toward her. "Do you want me to be completely honest with you?"

She nodded, unwilling to speak lest it deter him from finishing.

"I've thought and thought about this, always hoping that one day I'd see you again. First, I have to tell you that I would still do almost anything for a story—and, to tell the truth, in the last four years I have done some pretty outrageous things, even worse than I did with you, to get the news." He stopped walking again, then placed his hands on her shoulders and gazed intently into her eyes. "But, Mariana, I would never, *never* again willfully do anything to hurt you or deceive you. To me, you are sacred ground. I know you only have my word on that, but now that I have this second chance with you, I plan to do everything in my power to prove my faithfulness to you, to our friendship."

"I don't know what to say, Daniel—"

"Just say you'll give me another chance. I can't say what might come of it, but I don't think it was mere coincidence that we ran into each other here."

"I agree. And I never had any other intention but to give

our . . . friendship another chance." Her slight hesitation over the word *friendship* went unnoticed by Daniel, but Mariana could not prevent herself from wondering if they would ever be more than friends.

Daniel gave her a relieved grin and they walked a little farther in relaxed silence before Mariana spoke.

"So, Daniel, what have you been up to since I last saw you?"

"Working. You know what a slave I am to my typewriter." He paused, obviously not comfortable talking about himself. "My father died."

"Oh, Daniel, I'm so sorry. Recently?"

"Four years ago. Actually, he died while I was en route to the States from Russia."

"So, you didn't get to see him?"

He shook his head. "I'll always regret that. I suppose I am a very wealthy man now—although I really don't care about any of that."

"No, you never did. All you wanted was to be a reporter."

"My priorities are a bit more balanced since you last saw me, but I must admit my job is still very important to me. I almost quit, though, when I found out about my father. He never approved of my aspirations to be a reporter and wanted me to work with him—or at least do something more respectable than being a newspaper hack. For a while I felt I owed it to him to become an executive in the steel company that is now half mine. You know, sort of a penance for my rebellious life."

"You must have been miserable."

"It was pure agony. I'll never understand why my brother loves it all so much. After a year I was going crazy."

"Then you quit?"

"Not exactly. I was ready to, even if I had to go through the rest of my life feeling guilty. But I was spared that when I found a letter from my father. He had written it with the intention of giving it to his lawyer to pass on to me in the event of his death, but it never got that far and was lost for a time. I found it while sorting through his papers after his death. In it he told me how proud he was of my accomplishments at the newspaper, and that he could never be so cruel as to expect me to give up something I obviously loved and had a talent for in order to please him. I carry that letter with me everywhere I go. I know it sounds silly, especially for someone like me who never needed to rely on the praise of others for my confidence. But there is something immensely gratifying about a father's praise, probably because we so seldom hear it."

He paused and made a visible effort to lighten the serious mood of the conversation. "So, the world of journalism need suffer no longer from my absence. I've been in Manchuria several months now. When hostilities broke out it was only natural for the *Register* to send me, with my experience in Russia and in China during the Boxer Uprising."

The rest of their trek passed quickly, in spite of Mariana's weariness. They talked about their lives; they laughed over old memories. They even walked in comfortable silence, neither one needing to say a word. Mariana thought it was the most pleasant walk she had ever taken.

They reached the field hospital shortly after sunset. Mariana hated to leave Daniel, but she was too tired to visit any longer. After dinner they said good-night, and Daniel promised to join her for breakfast in the mess tent the next morning.

Mariana settled into her bunk in the nurses' quarters for the night. But the tent was stifling, and in spite of her fatigue, she couldn't sleep. She tossed and turned for a while, then finally gave up and began writing a letter home.

The full moon shone through the open tent flap, giving enough light for her to see by. She had just mailed a letter from Mukden a few days ago, but so much had happened since then. She wrote a whole page, but as she began a second, her eyelids drooped. Her pen fell from her hand onto the canvas floor, and she slept soundly the rest of the night, dreaming of Mama and Papa and the izba in Katyk. Only once did Daniel enter her dreams. He was harvesting a field of grain, sickle swinging high over his head; but he was dressed in his American suit with waistcoat and bowler hat.

9

Daniel felt good when he left Mariana that first night. Being with her had been almost like those wonderful days in Russia. How easy it had been to share his heart with her. He had never told anyone else the things he told her about his father.

Perhaps that made it all right that he hadn't told her everything.

He had really wanted complete honesty between them, especially since he had botched it so badly last time. But he was afraid that telling her everything about that terrible time surrounding his father's death would reveal some weaknesses—things even he hadn't fully come to accept.

He had shared enough so that she would know what an impact it had on him. But he said nothing about the true depth of emotions he had felt, or how he'd tried to cope with them.

What occurred on that blustery November day when he stepped clear of his ship's gangway in New York was simply too personal to reveal.

Daniel could still visualize his brother's grim face greeting him from the dock. One look at William, and he had known he was too late.

"I'm sorry, Daniel," William said. "He tried to hang on until you got home."

"When was it?"

"Two days ago."

Daniel couldn't speak. He had never lost anyone before—in fact, his life had always been somewhat of a carefree lark. His mother had died so soon after his birth that he had been spared the kind of grief he now experienced. The greatest loss he had known had been Mariana. Odd, that one loss should come so quickly on the heels of the other.

At that moment, he couldn't think of anything but the terrible emptiness he felt. During the journey home, he had given considerable thought to what he would say to his father when he saw him. Daniel wanted to tell him how he admired him and wanted to be like him, and how his love for writing was not so much out of rebellion as it was his way of forging his own path through life, make his own personal mark—just as his father had. He had rehearsed many speeches, imagined his father's encouraging responses.

Now all his words were useless. What do you say to a corpse? He would get no acceptance, no forgiveness, from a dead man.

"Listen," Daniel said to his brother, "do you mind if I find my own way home? I'd like to walk for a bit."

"Are you sure you'll be okay?"

"Yeah. It's just a shock, you know."

Daniel walked up and down the streets of New York that day, but all the walking in the world could not fill that empty hole in him. His steps took him to the Brooklyn Bridge—ironically appropriate, he thought, for he had come here before his trip to Russia to sort out the events of his life. His father had arranged for the assignment to Russia, in hopes of making a responsible man of his rowdy son. Had the plan been successful?

Archibald Trent certainly wouldn't have been pleased about the fiasco with Mariana. He would have liked Mariana and thought Daniel an immature lout for using her so.

But maybe, Pop, you would have been a little proud of how I owned up to my mistake. I probably wouldn't have done that before.

Now, Daniel would never know. That was the worst thing of all about death—it was so final. He desperately wanted to reach out and grab his father back.

I'm not finished with you, yet, Pop!

Tears filled Daniel's eyes. He felt silly standing in the middle of that busy bridge, crying like a kid. He wished there had been some fog like on that other day to hide his desolation, his emptiness.

Then he thought of Mariana. He needed a friend now, as he had never needed one before. He needed to hear her voice. She would know just what to say, and somehow her gentle, understanding words would ease his pain. And that's when he realized just what he had lost in Mariana—not a girlfriend or a potential wife, but a *friend*. She was the only real friend he'd ever had. He probably wouldn't have had to say a word to her—she would have known what he was going through.

Mariana would, no doubt, have offered him her faith. But even Daniel knew that someone else's faith didn't do a fellow a whole lot of good. If only he could have the kind of peace she had—*serenity*, he had called it in his ill-fated article. If only he could dredge up something from that empty hole in his heart. If only he had listened closer to Mariana back in Russia. But it's hard to care about such things when your life is rosy—and it's too late when the thorns start to prick you.

Is it really too late? he asked himself that day. Maybe not. But what good would faith do now, anyway? Would it bring back his father?

Daniel couldn't answer those questions, but he determined to try. If there was something out there that he was missing, something that would spread a balm over his wounds and fill the chasm in his heart—well, it was certainly as critical to track down as a news story. His editor at the *Register* had often compared Daniel to a scrappy little dog, gripping a news story with his sharp teeth and not letting go until it was his.

On that bridge, as he had before, Daniel reached a significant milestone in his life. He became a seeker.

Since he was not the most introspective of men, his path sometimes became obscured by the more mundane aspects of life. When his father's death necessitated some crucial decisions, he sometimes forgot about his resolve and fell into old habits. But he did ask questions about religion, and he attended church and talked to the minister. He even read a Bible. He wrote to Mariana, too, and almost gave the whole thing up when she didn't respond.

As time passed he seemed to need *something* more than

ever. His life was steadily deteriorating. Thinking that God would probably want him to give up the newspaper and do what his father had wanted him to do all along, Daniel quit the *Register*. His brother found him an office in the Trent Building, and he tried to settle into the life of an industrialist—whatever that was. Paperwork, board meetings, analyzing charts and graphs of markets and trends—how could anyone find this satisfying, or even interesting? Most days, the greatest enjoyment Daniel had was pitching wads of paper into his trash can.

The only positive aspect of this period was that the more miserable he became, the more he attended church. Then one day he asked himself if God really intended for him to be this miserable. The God Mariana always talked about didn't seem to be the kind who meted out misery. The words she used to describe her life of faith were joy, peace, contentment.

If he was trying to seek what God wanted, why didn't he have any of those things?

One morning Daniel was greeted by his brother as he entered the office.

"Daniel, do you have those reports ready for the board meeting today?"

Daniel slapped his forehead. "I forgot. I'll get right on them. When's the meeting?"

"You'll never get them done in time." William shook his head. "Daniel, I was really proud of you when you came into the firm. But sometimes I think your heart isn't in it. This is what Father wanted most in life, to see us working together in the company he built. Don't you care if his company remains successful? What would he think about your attitude? You were too late to please him while he lived—the least you can do is to try now."

Daniel isolated himself in his office, locking the door against intruders. He dropped his head into his hands, and though no tears actually came, he was filled with agony. His father wanted him in the business; his brother wanted it; God seemed to want it. No one cared about what *he* wanted.

"Well, I've had it with you all!" he shouted to the empty room. "Tomorrow, I'm tendering my resignation. I don't care if I go to hell for it; I don't care if my brother hounds me about respecting the dead. I'm through trying to please others.

"And, God, if you don't like it, then show me some other way! But it better be something I can live with."

That very night their accountant requested some of Archibald Trent's personal papers—apparently some items in the will were being disputed by Archibald's sister. Daniel spent the evening searching through his father's house, and he stumbled upon the letter. With so many business matters to be dealt with, it was not surprising that this letter, in a plain white envelope, had been overlooked. But Daniel couldn't refrain from wondering if its timely appearance had something to do with his rather belligerent prayer that morning.

The letter was from his father, addressed to Daniel.

Dear Daniel,

I have never thought myself to favor one son over the other. But I have to confess that my heart always had a slightly softer place in it for you. Perhaps it was because your mother died in bringing you into the world, making you the closest part of her I had to cling to. Perhaps, too, it is because I've had to agonize over you so much more than your brother. He always did what was expected of him, but you fought every step of the way. You clutched at your independence and your identity as if it were gold. In short, you are so much like I was in my younger years that it is frightening—and pleasing.

Unfortunately, I didn't realize the pleasing aspect of this until lately. But now, as I lie here on my bed, I feel my mortality tugging away at me. A man has to be pleased to know he is leaving behind an image of himself. I regret all the years I tried to force you into a different mold. If someone had done that to me I would have done just what you did. I would have pursued what I wanted, anyway.

Well, son, they say I am a very sick man. I may not live long enough to see you again. This meager scrap of paper will have to suffice to communicate my heart to you. Please forgive me my mistakes. Know that I only wanted your good. I can tell from your letters that going to Russia was a good thing for you, so perhaps I did one thing right. I have read your work and realize that you are, unquestionably, where you belong—at least in the right profession. I am proud of you. I'm afraid I haven't told you that enough, but now, more than ever, I want you to know this. And you have my blessing—not that you ever really needed it!—to do the work that is obviously dearest to your heart. I would be the last to rob the world of such a talent. The most important thing to me is that you are happy, content. I can die in peace as long as I know that.

Daniel resigned from his father's company and got his old job back at the *Register*. And his fledgling faith was greatly bolstered. He rode high on a kind of spiritual euphoria—for a while. But as his life began to get back on track, with accompanying contentment, he began to slip back into old routines and patterns. One thing led to another, and now he just didn't remember to think much about God. His work once more became his joy and contentment. Occasionally he would think about how the Lord had brought him through that tough time in his life, and he told himself he'd get out that Bible or go to church. But something always seemed to get in the way of his admirable intentions. Before long he was too ashamed to think about the Lord—and thus have to admit to God that he was not much of a Christian.

Now Daniel was afraid to admit that to Mariana. It was best to ignore it altogether. What Mariana didn't know wouldn't hurt . . . them. He didn't purposely set out to deceive her; it was just natural for him to leave the spiritual matters out of his account. He had been doing it quite well these last two years, after all.

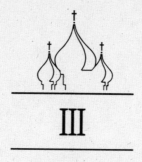

III

HOME

10

Summer in St. Petersburg was sultry and warm. Anna and Sergei had seriously considered an invitation from Sergei's father, Viktor, to spend the season with him in the Crimea, but in the end decided that they had to keep their distance from the Fedorcenkos. An occasional visit by Viktor when he was in the city was no problem, but anything more extensive could cause unwanted questioning. Sergei could never let his guard down, never forget that he was still a fugitive. It was harder, of course, now that his relationship with his father had been restored, and Viktor had been healed of the burden of guilt and shame he had borne for so many years. But if anyone discovered that Sergei Christinin was actually Sergei Fedorcenko, he would be sent back to Siberia—or worse.

Sergei even had a new pride in his family name and heritage. He did not often speak of it, but Anna had sensed in him lately a regret that he could not pass on to his sons the name and prestige of his family. Yuri and Andrei by rights were both princes of Russia, yet they lived in a poor flat that did not even belong to them, dressed in patched hand-me-downs and often dined on nothing more than black bread and kasha. Sergei had once extolled such a simple life, but much had changed since those idyllic days in old Katyk.

Anna knew Sergei did not envy the rich or wish to trade places with them. But as his sons grew, he saw their great potential, and the sad possibility that, like so many of the poor in Russia, they would be crushed, mind and spirit, beneath the weight of their poverty.

Anna understood Sergei's fear. Yet their sons were different from the peasant boys in Katyk and the children of the work-ers here in the city. They might not be able to claim their princely titles, yet they had been raised with all the fierce pride and independence of every Fedorcenko prince before them. Granted, she and Sergei had liberally balanced this with Christian humility, but their boys were unlikely to become downtrodden, drunken Russia peasants simply because their aristocratic blood was denied.

Maybe she was just a proud matushka, but her sons were special. At fourteen and twelve, Yuri and Andrei had already mastered Anna's knowledge of math, science, and grammar, and were nearly as proficient as she in history and geography. For years, Anna had been teaching them herself. Now they were ready to move on. Sergei worked with them when he could, but financial necessity forced him to concentrate on the students he tutored for pay.

Nevertheless, the children were not suffering in their pov-erty. Misha, the Cossack guard who had befriended Anna years ago when she was a maid to Princess Katrina, had re-mained their faithful friend through nearly three decades. Thanks to him, they had been rescued from the wretched life of factory work. He had helped them find a home with Raisa Sorokin and her daughter, Talia. Three years ago they all had to move to a less expensive flat, but they were still in the same fairly decent neighborhood. And they were more fortunate than many in the city—only their two small families occupied the three-bedroom flat. Raisa and Anna had become like sis-ters, and the children were inseparable friends. To part com-pany now would be like ripping a family apart. But there was no reason for that to happen; they were content and happy.

The evening meal was nearly done. Talia was setting plates around the table in the small kitchen. Raisa was mashing po-tatoes while Anna sliced bread. Cabbage soup, with a few bits of beef added for flavor, steamed on the stove, filling the kitchen with a pleasant fragrance. Anna marveled at how sim-ple fare could be made so inviting, but Raisa was something of an artist. She had a special talent for the creative use of seasonings—a bit of garlic, basil, or fennel was enough to make even simple cabbage a gourmet delight.

Andrei came in with an armload of wood for the stove.

"No more wood, Andrei," said Raisa. "The soup is done, and we don't want it any warmer in here than it needs to be."

Andrei dumped the wood in the box near the stove, then washed his hands. "Guess what I saw down the street?" When no one responded immediately, he went on, "Come on, Talia, guess."

"I don't know; it could be anything."

"Use your imagination."

She shrugged apologetically. "I don't know—wait a minute! I just thought of something."

"Well, what?"

"One of those fancy automobiles—a silver one, with a chauffeur and a grand duke and duchess in the backseat." She smiled, obviously pleased with herself for her inventiveness.

"I didn't say to make up a fairy tale. Whoever heard of an automobile in our neighborhood?"

"You said to be imaginative," said Yuri, who had followed Andrei into the kitchen.

"Oh, never mind. If there are no better guesses than that, I'll just have to tell you."

A knock on the door interrupted him.

"Who can that be?" Raisa frowned. "And at this hour?" She dried her hands on her apron and headed for the front room. Curious, everyone followed.

Raisa opened the door to reveal a postal clerk, a satchel slung over his back, and mail in his hand. From the kitchen doorway, Andrei grunted.

Anna realized that her son's announcement had been spoiled by its very object. But letters came so seldom—who would have guessed that the postman he had seen in the street was coming here?

"I've mail here for S.I. Christinin," said the man.

Anna stepped forward. "That is my husband."

Anna took the letters and glanced at the return addresses. She smiled. "They're from my niece," she said to the man, as if an explanation for this unusual event was necessary. "She's a nurse at the front—in the war."

"Well, you must be proud."

"Very."

"Good day to you, then."

The moment the postman left, everyone crowded around Anna, clamoring to see the letters and hear news from Mariana. But Anna had to disappoint them.

"We must wait for Papa to get home."

Sergei arrived fifteen minutes later. The children had a hard time restraining their eagerness while he paused at the "beautiful corner" to cross himself and offer a brief prayer. Andrei, ever impetuous, pounced on him as he was rising from his knees.

"We had letters today, Papa. Two, from Mariana!"

"Excellent!" Sergei braced his hand on his son's shoulder as he rose. "I was beginning to wonder when we'd hear from her." He straightened up slowly, groaning a bit.

"Andrei," said Anna, "let's let Papa wash up and have his dinner first. He's had a long day."

"I'm too anxious to wait," said Sergei. "We'll read the letters around the table."

Mariana's account of distant places—the wonders of Siberia and the exotic Far East—left everyone in awe. Of the group, only Sergei had traveled more than two hundred miles in any direction from their present home. It suddenly occurred to Anna that Mariana might grow beyond her family and home in Russia. She would never disdain them, but could she be content here after the war? Still, Anna knew a fledgling bird must be given its wings. Her own papa had taught her that when he let her "fly" from little Katyk many years ago. It was the natural way of things.

11

Later that night, Sergei and Anna discussed Mariana's letters. One of the great luxuries they had since moving in with Raisa was having a little room of their own. Since their marriage, they had almost never been alone. Mariana had been with them right from the beginning, and the extended family continually surrounded them in one way or another. Poor peasants knew nothing of "honeymoons," and so Anna and Sergei had never had one. But this little cubbyhole in their flat was like a honeymoon haven for them where they could interact and talk as intimately as they wished. Anna often said it made her feel like a newlywed all over again. Sergei countered that he had never stopped feeling like a newlywed.

"Sergei," Anna began after they climbed into the bed that nearly filled the little closet of a room. "I need to have my worries about Mariana eased a bit. I know they are futile and we have been over this ground before, but every now and then those motherly anxieties try to overtake me."

"Anything specific? It sounds like she is quite close to the fighting."

"I'll worry about that until she is safe by my side again." Anna sighed as she shook her head. "What I really fear is that by allowing her to go so far away, we will have lost her. By comparison, her life here will seem humdrum and unappealing. And she says her American friend is in Manchuria. What if he should want to marry her and take her with him all the way to America?"

"It's not something I like to think about either, Anna. But we want her to be happy."

71

"Yes."

"The old proverb says, *Let your child follow her own path and it will always lead back to you.*"

"Sergei," Anna said tenderly, "you are sounding more like my papa every day with your wonderful and wise proverbs and sayings."

"Ah, dear Papa Yevno! Thank you for such high praise." Sergei propped himself on an elbow and gazed with open love at his wife. She never seemed to age, somehow always retaining that fragile loveliness that had captured his heart twenty-eight years ago on an ice pond. She had been sixteen, timid as a baby fawn exploring a new world, delicate as a spring bloom. In the ensuing years he had come to realize Anna was about the strongest woman he knew, though she had never lost those qualities he had first fallen in love with.

Anna blushed under his frank admiration, then quickly changed the subject. "Now, I've sensed since you came home this evening that there is something on your mind. I can't promise you Yevno's wisdom, but I can give you a listening ear."

"This has been a very eventful day for me, Anna. First, I spoke with Mr. Cranston. When Daniel Trent mentioned his editor here in Russia, I never thought that it would affect me. But suddenly the man has become a very important part of my life—at least he has control over an important part of my life."

Over the years Sergei had never stopped writing, though he had done so mostly for his own benefit. He never dreamed—except in the wildest parts of his imagination—that he'd be published again. But since coming to St. Petersburg, he had begun mingling with more literary types at the university, and friends had encouraged him to attempt to publish his work again. His first—and last—book had landed him in Siberia, but he had become much less political in his tendencies since then. He was able to get two short stories and several poems published in mainstream magazines—under a pseudonym, of course. It didn't pay much, but the sense of accomplishment was enormously satisfying.

About two years ago Sergei had begun compiling an anthology of many of the poems he had written over the years.

Viktor had suggested Sergei try foreign publication for this book. Though the poetry was not as politically incisive as Sergei's first book, *A Soldier's Glory*, many of the poems were still a bit too sensitive to pass Russian censors. Sergei remembered Daniel Trent's editor, George Cranston, and, on a whim, visited the man. Cranston, himself an admittedly poor judge of poetry, agreed to pass the volume along to an American publisher he knew. That had been nearly six months ago. Since then, every time Sergei was in the neighborhood of the newspaper office—sometimes even when he wasn't—he would drop in to inquire if there had been any response yet. Sergei feared he was beginning to make a nuisance of himself, but under the circumstances they felt it was best for all communications with the publisher to be made through Cranston.

"Mr. Cranston had mail from America," Sergei said, and Anna knew by the gleam in his eyes that he had good news.

"And?"

"The American publisher liked my poems."

"Just 'liked'?"

"Well, the word *loved* might have been used, and he did draw some comparisons between my poems and those of Pushkin and Lermontov—which only shows that such praise must be taken with a grain of salt."

"Your poems are wonderful, Sergei!"

"As Pushkin's? Never! As Lermontov's? Not a chance. However the man, a James Duke, of Duke and Sons Publishing, did show in his letter more than a passing understanding of poetry—more, I have to admit, than I might have expected of an American."

"Why, Sergei! If you recall, you were the one who opened up the world of foreign poets to me."

"English poets, mostly. But I suppose I do sound rather like a snob. The world of American poetry isn't exactly a desert. I've liked some of Whitman's and Whittier's."

"You gave me that lovely volume of Emily Dickenson's a few years ago. I've read it over and over."

"I am grateful to be published at all," said Sergei.

"Does that mean this Mr. Duke is going to publish your book?"

Sergei nodded, then grinned. Anna threw her arms around him and kissed him.

"That's not all," Sergei said, still holding his wife. "They will send me two hundred American dollars as an advance as soon as they have received a signed contract."

"That is a lot of money, isn't it?"

"Four hundred rubles, Anna! As much as I could earn in two years of tutoring."

"Oh my," breathed Anna in awe. "Sergei, would it be possible to use some of the money for sending Yuri and Andrei to the gymnasium? They are ready for a higher education."

"That was at the very top of my list also, Anna."

Anna could hardly believe their good fortune. She wanted to get new dishes for Raisa to replace the set that had gotten broken and chipped over the years. Sergei said he wanted to take Anna on a trip—a real honeymoon, perhaps to Paris. They laughed like children.

Then Sergei became a practical adult once more. "Of course, the wise thing would be to save what we can against a rainy day."

"I never thought we'd do anything else," said Anna. "But it was fun to dream for a while."

"Well, Raisa will have her new dishes," Sergei declared, "and you shall have a fine new dress and a winter coat with a fur hat and muff to match. And the children shall have new winter coats also."

"People will wonder about our newfound wealth."

"Let them wonder! We cannot always live in fear of my past, Anna." He paused thoughtfully, then continued. "Not that this has anything to do with my past, Anna, but it is as good a time as any to mention the other thing that happened today. I saw Oleg Chavkin."

Chavkin, a friend from Katyk, now lived in St. Petersburg. When they had first come to the city, he had taken in Anna and Sergei, and found Sergei a factory job.

"How is he? We see the Chavkin family so seldom now that we live on Vassily Island."

Anna still shuddered when she thought of the kind of existence she and her family had lived when Sergei worked at

74

the textile factory. Chavkin still dwelt in that rat-infested tenement with no heat, no running water, and twenty-five people jammed into two small rooms. Like the majority of workers in the city, there seemed no way for Chavkin to escape perpetual poverty. The factory owners saw to it that their workers remained virtual slaves.

"If Oleg has his way," said Sergei, "I will be seeing much more of him. He has asked me to take on the task of teaching the men at the factory to read and cipher. There are about a dozen men who are interested in learning. But it is not as simple as it sounds. The owners strongly discourage their workers from bettering themselves. Not only would I have to volunteer my services for no pay, but I must do it secretly."

"Sergei, do you dare?"

"Anna, I have thought about this all afternoon. God has blessed us richly all our lives, but especially in these last few years. I cannot forget where we would be if He had not sent Misha along to deliver me from that awful factory. God has interceded continually in our lives, and now I have a chance to repay to others the blessings He has given me."

"But you serve God every day as you witness to the boys you tutor."

"It's not enough, Anna." Sergei's countenance bore a look of such taut determination that Anna knew it was useless to argue with him. "I can't turn my back on the need Oleg has presented to me."

Anna should have been proud of him, she knew . . . and in many ways she was. Still, it was hard for her to agree to something that could bring danger to him. But he hadn't asked for her approval. He was going to accept Oleg's offer—in fact, he had probably already given his consent.

"You're upset with me, aren't you, Anna?"

Anna shrugged silently.

"I thought you would understand," he said.

"I'm just afraid of what could happen."

Sergei put his arm around Anna and drew her close to him. This tangible sense of his strength helped to buoy her. She sighed and attempted a smile. It was no use to fight against both God and her husband. If this was God's will, then somehow she would find the resources to accept whatever came.

12

Changes did not come quickly to the home of Anna and Sergei. The summer passed in its usual manner—warm and rather lazy, almost oblivious to the fact that war raged in a far-off land. The children, especially, were unaffected by the broader national events. A Saturday in August meant a day off from the lessons that their mother made them do during the summer.

This particular Saturday, each of the children had a few kopecks, earnings they had saved all month long from doing odd jobs for their neighbors. Anna and Raisa gave them permission to go on an outing by themselves if they promised to stay together and be home by five in the afternoon. The only problem the children had that day was agreeing on their destination and mode of transportation.

Yuri wanted to walk to Nevsky Prospekt and spend his money at Wolff's huge bookstore, or one of the secondhand stores. There were no free libraries in St. Petersburg, and purchasing books was rather hard on the family's small budget. Yuri never seemed to have enough books; he read them as quickly as his parents could buy or borrow them. In fact, he usually read each book many times before a new one found its way into his eager hands.

But it was a long walk from Vassily Island across Nicholas Bridge to the downtown area of the city. The reward of a book at the end was not much motivation to Andrei and Talia, who were of a less studious bent than Yuri. Andrei had seen a hand-bill posted advertising a circus in town, and that's where he wanted to go.

When they found the handbill on a wall around the corner from their apartment building, they realized that the admis-sion price would have drained all their money. Only Andrei was that eager to see the circus. In the end, Talia's quiet sug-gestion won out. She proposed taking the steamer down the Neva to the Summer Gardens and having a picnic there. An-drei liked the excitement of being on the water, and Yuri liked the idea that he would still have money left over—money he could spend at the cheaper used-book vendors at St. Andrew's Market on Vassily Island.

Raisa packed the adventurers a lunch, and they set out about ten in the morning. The day promised to be a scorcher, with temperatures already approaching eighty. The breeze off the water and the river spray was a welcome relief, and the children stood at the bow of the boat to get the full effect.

"Let's pretend we're sailing on the ocean," said Talia, "go-ing to some romantic, faraway place."

"The South Seas," put in Yuri, "where coconut trees wave in the warm sea breeze and the water is so warm you can swim all day and bask in the sun on a sandy beach."

"And brown-skinned natives pick armfuls of beautiful flowers for us—orchids and hibiscus of every imaginable color." Talia closed her eyes dreamily.

"Don't forget the buried treasure we're seeking," said An-drei.

"Of course," said Yuri. "And pirates."

Talia opened her eyes. "Do there have to be pirates? Our island was so nice and peaceful."

"Too many flowers and dancing natives could get boring after a while," Andrei said.

Yuri had a solution to the problem. "Talia, you'd be the damsel in distress, and we'd rescue you."

"But I didn't need to be rescued before you brought the pi-rates."

Andrei grunted impatiently. "Girls! Do you have to make everything so difficult?"

"It was my idea in the first place," Talia replied quietly, almost as if she was sorry to have to make that point.

"Who wants to go to some boring island, anyway?" said Andrei. "If I could really be on an ocean liner, I'd go West, to America—a place that's exciting and real. I'd visit all the tall buildings that are said to reach up to the sky, and I'd look at the Statue of Liberty. Papa says it's so big a grown person could stand inside one of its fingers! That I'd like to see!"

Talia smiled. How could she be upset with her friend when his eyes were dancing with so much excitement? The South Seas hadn't been her idea, anyway, though it had been in her mind when she had mentioned going to a far-off place. She glanced at Yuri, then at Andrei, her two best friends in the world, and wondered if there could be a trio of more different characters. Were they friends only because they had been thrown together in the same home? She liked to think, instead, that God himself had thrown them together on purpose because He already knew what good friends they would be. And she didn't care what imaginary adventures they went on as long as they did it together.

"Well," said Yuri, "we just spent five kopecks for the real adventure of riding the steamer, so why don't we just enjoy that."

No one could deny that the little blue steamer was a fascinating world in itself, with its stewards in white waistcoats and an elegant restaurant where the more affluent dined. The children boldly sat at a table and bought raspberry ice, but they ate quickly and left because they felt like intruders. They preferred to be out in the open anyway, watching the dazzling river swirl under them, waving to the many other ships and boats that passed by. Only too soon the trip came to an end.

"Look!" exclaimed Yuri, pointing to his right. "Our stop is next. We better make our way forward."

The boat docked near the Summer Gardens and it was only a short walk to their destination. Once at the gardens, however, the walking did not end. They explored the grounds from one end to the other. They loved the statues of mythological characters and the swans in the little pond.

They had been to the Summer Gardens many times, but it never grew old or humdrum. The garden wore a different face at every season of the year, always promising new discoveries each time.

On this hot summer day, the water in the pond was especially inviting. In this trim and aristocratic setting, of course, swimming wasn't allowed, but the children found a deserted spot by the big pond, took off their shoes, and dared to dangle their toes in the cool water for a few minutes. It was Andrei who started the splashing, and though Yuri and Talia tried to stop him at first with verbal protests, he kept it up until they could do nothing else but retaliate in kind. It wasn't long before their squeals and laughter were noticed.

"All right, you kids!" came a stern, deep voice. "That'll be enough of that, now." It was a policeman, tall and rather imposing in his uniform, but a twinkle in his eyes indicated that he understood childish ways and wasn't about to exile them for splashing in the pond.

The children jumped up and back from the water nevertheless. Yuri, assuming the responsibility of being the eldest, said, "I'm sorry, sir. It was just so hot."

"That's a fact, but rules are rules."

"We'll be on our way."

"No need for that, just remember to behave like I'm sure your mama taught you."

"Yes, sir."

After the policeman walked away, the children put on their shoes and socks and vacated the place anyway. Besides, they were hungry and wanted to find a nice shade tree under which to eat the good lunch Raisa had given them—apples, thick hunks of black bread, and slabs of cheese.

"I don't know why you backed down so easily," said Andrei to Yuri as they ate. "This is a public place, you know. We have as much right to it as the nannies and their pampered children."

"And no one bothers us as long as we follow the rules."

"I'll bet he wouldn't have said anything if we had been of the gentry or bourgeois."

As with Mariana, Sergei and Anna had only told their children the barest minimum about their background. Only that the family had once had a little money but had lost it over the years. That was enough to explain Viktor and his obvious nobility as well as Mariana's sudden change in position. Why encumber the children with more? It was a life they'd never be able to have anyway. Besides, Sergei had, at least until recently, completely disdained that life.

Yuri gave his brother a derisive laugh. "Have you been hanging around the university again?"

"What of it?" challenged Andrei belligerently.

The potential confrontation between the brothers was mercifully interrupted by the sudden sounds of distant explosions.

"The war!" cried Talia, almost in tears.

"No, no," soothed Yuri, "the war is too far from St. Petersburg. It must be something else."

"Revolution!" offered Andrei.

There was always talk of revolution, and there were occasionally demonstrations at the university and strikes at the factory, but never were such events accompanied by gunfire. In a few moments, after the children's initial surprise had calmed, they noted that the explosions were even and deliberate.

"It's cannon fire announcing something," said Andrei at length. "Maybe the end of the war."

But Yuri had been trying to count the blasts, and he held up his hand so the others wouldn't interrupt him. After a few minutes he announced, "At least ninety shots."

A passerby corrected him, "A hundred, lad."

"A hundred and one!" they all said in unison as another shot blasted. The children still were uncertain why the cannon was being fired.

Then, "One hundred and two!"

"Saints be praised!" said the stranger. " 'Tis a glorious day for Russia."

"What is it? What is it?"

"An heir has been born!"

80

13

It had not been a nice summer for His Royal Highness, Nicholas II of Russia. The disastrous reversals in the war in the Far East weighed heavily on him. He hated war and felt he had done everything in his power to prevent this war with Japan. But when the Japanese had forced his hand with their surprise attack on Port Arthur, Nicholas had been confident that his army could whip the "little yellow monkeys" in no time. Six months of fighting, however, had delivered no major victories to the Russian army. It was not only sickening and disheartening; it was downright humiliating for the tsar of all the Russias.

At home, the summer had been vilely marked by the assassination of two highly placed officials—the governor-general of Finland and the Minister of the Interior. Such acts made it appear as if the nationalism at the beginning of the war would not be enough to sustain the tentative internal peace of the last months. Nicholas knew only too well what a war, much less a lost war, could do to the political stability of his country.

Lately, the emperor of Russia felt keenly his fate of being born on the Day of Job the Sufferer.

As he climbed the stairs to the family dining room at Peterhof, the summer palace overlooking the Gulf of Finland, about twenty miles from St. Petersburg, his mind was far from the anticipation of a pleasant lunch with his wife. He had just come from an interview with Count Kokovtsov and an artillery officer who had been wounded in Manchuria. How he hated to be reminded of the war!

Thus was his joy, his absolute ecstasy, that much deeper when he was informed that his wife had gone upstairs and retired to her bed in labor with their fifth child. Less than an hour later, she had given birth to a son!

That evening Nicholas wrote in his diary: "An unforgettable day in which God has clearly shown us His blessing."

Mother and child were doing well. The baby was fat and fair with blue eyes and a wisp of yellow hair on his well-formed head.

Nicholas named his son Alexis after his favorite tsar, Alexis I. Chuckling, Nicholas said, "I must break the chain of Alexanders and Nicholases that have ruled Russia for nearly a hundred years."

Alexis the First had been the son of the first tsar of Russia, Michael I. In Nicholas's mind, he was a great ruler because he had quietly and meekly brought reform to the emerging nation. Nicholas disdained Peter the Great, not only because of his strong-arm tactics but also because he had forced Western ways upon Russia. And Peter had caused the name Alexis to fall out of favor among the Romanovs when he ordered his son and heir, also named Alexis, murdered.

Thus, the tsar's choice of a name for his heir was greeted with disapproval by some. Still, his will prevailed, and the child was christened a week later as Alexis Nicholaevich Romanov. The emperor and empress could not refrain from entertaining dreams of Russia one day seeing their son, Alexis II, sitting upon the throne. Perhaps he would be Alexis the Wise. Anything seemed possible in those joyous days immediately following his birth.

———

Alexandra, Empress of Russia, gazed at the icon of Saint Seraphim, thankful she had managed to get the Church to canonize the early nineteenth-century holy man. She was sure her devotion to Seraphim had led to the long-awaited birth of a son and heir.

Alexandra had been searching for something upon which to attach her hope since Phillipe, the healer and mystic of France, had been forced to leave the Imperial Court. He had fallen out of favor after his faulty prediction of a son prior to the birth of Anastasia, the fourth daughter of Nicholas and Alexandra. The empress's friends, the two Montenegrin princesses, had spearheaded the tsaritsa's mystical journey, first with the introduction of Phillipe. Seances and sorcery became an important part of the empress's court. The Montenegrins said that what she needed was a person more mysterious than the Frenchman. They believed the more bizarre the character, the more indicative of his disdain for the world, thus demonstrating his closeness to God. There followed a progression of such strange "birds" at court that even Alexandra began to weary of them.

Seraphim was more to her liking. A holy man who died in 1833, his life was marked by healings and prophecies and spiritual visions. The rumors of his cavorting with the nuns were completely unsubstantiated. He was deeply misunderstood, and that fact strengthened his appeal to Alexandra.

The birth of an heir further deepened the man's saintly worth.

A year earlier, for the consecration of Seraphim's relics, she had gone to the saint's last earthly home, Sarov, for the ceremonies. There she had bathed in a healing spring, and now she held her son in her arms. Even Nicholas's faith in Seraphim was now unshakable.

As her boudoir door opened, Alexandra looked up and smiled a welcome greeting to her husband. He knelt down by her side so as to better view the child she held in her arms.

"I don't think I have ever seen such a quiet, beautiful baby," he said, sounding as if he were a new father who had not already welcomed four babies into the world.

"And why not?" smiled Alexandra. "He has the blessing of Seraphim on his dear head."

"Oh, Sunny, I can't thank you enough for bringing this joy into our lives. I don't know how I would have made it though this terrible year otherwise."

"We don't have to think of that, Nicky. It will be different from now on."

"Yes, it must be so. It couldn't get much worse. The coming of our Alexis is a turning point."

Perhaps it wasn't right to place so much hope upon one tiny child. But an heir was lifeblood to a monarchy, and Alexandra knew how important it was to Nicholas that the Romanov heir be his own son, not a nephew. He was as committed to the continuance of the Romanov line as he was to his own life. Many of the tsar's opponents had reveled in the fact that he had only produced daughters, and they were eagerly looking forward to the end of the direct line of heirs that had begun with Nicholas I. Should Nicholas II have passed without a direct heir, his brother Michael would have ascended the throne. Since many believed the tsar's younger brother was the weakest of the lot, it would have been an easy matter then to wrest the monarchy from the Romanovs.

Alexandra was thrilled. The arrival of Alexis would foil those vile rebels and anarchists. No one would steal the crown from either her husband or her son. She had suffered and prayed and fought too hard to bring this assurance to the Romanov line. The forces of hell itself would not prevail against them.

14

Count Cyril Vlasenko dabbed his thick lips with a linen napkin. No matter what the state of the union he served, he saw no reason not to fully enjoy the gourmet repast set before him that evening. His chef, a talented Parisian, managed to produce a new delicacy each day—tonight's *Chateaubriand*, *poulet roti* smothered in garlic, and *potatoes au gratin* were exquisite, not to mention the vintage Cabernet Sauvignon and cream-filled pastries so light and sweet they made Vlasenko's mouth water just remembering them.

"Ah, a fine meal," he said to his wife, Poznia. He leaned back in his chair, eyeing the last pastry remaining on the silver serving tray.

"I could tell you liked it, dear," she replied. "But you know the doctor told you only last week you should watch that rich food."

"Bah! He also told me I was the picture of health."

"What about your gout? Our son was concerned when he last visited—"

"And I'm going to take his word over that of a real doctor?"

"Karl is a real doctor."

"I practically bought his degree for him!" These were perhaps the two most unsettling subjects to Cyril—his diet and his good-for-nothing son. "I only hope serving as a medical officer in the army will teach him a thing or two before he has to practice on real people. As long as they keep him away from officers, we're all right."

"Oh, Cyril! I worry every day about him there at the front, facing God only knows what kind of dangers."

"Let's hope it makes a man of him."

After a moment of silence, his wife said, "We have been invited to pay a visit to Their Royal Highnesses following the christening of the new tsarevich."

"Excellent! That is good news." Watching his wife out of the corner of his eye, he reached a hand toward the pastry tray. No sense letting it go to waste—or worse, be consumed by some unappreciative servant. Being invited to the palace, especially at such an auspicious time, was quite an honor, and he deserved a small reward—his gout be hanged! He hadn't yet had a chance to celebrate the birth of the heir, and he had every reason to do so. The continuance of the Romanov line meant the continuance of his own power and glory in Russia.

Ignoring his wife's raised eyebrows, he popped the whole pastry into his mouth and chewed with utter delight, then washed it down with a cup of tea.

She rose and looked at him. "If you will excuse me, I need to dress for the evening."

"Do we have plans?"

"Have you forgotten our invitation to Princess Gudosnikov's birthday party?"

"Indeed I have."

"We must be there in an hour."

"I'll have the coach brought around."

It was turning into a decidedly fine evening. A satisfying
meal, good news about the invitation to the christening, and
a life fit for a prince of Russia. He was now lord and master
of the Fedorcenko St. Petersburg estate, once occupied by the
haughty Viktor Fedorcenko. Even most of the furnishings had
come with the house, and it was a good thing; after purchasing
the estate, Vlasenko hardly had enough money left to buy a
doormat. Only some wise—and lucky—foreign investments
provided Vlasenko with enough income to afford a few luxuries—his French chef not the least of these.

The last three or four years had not been entirely smooth,
but he had managed to hold his own in the extremely volatile
world of Russian politics. That alone was a feat of amazing
proportions. But he was becoming quite a master of charm
and wisely placed flattery, of greasing the right palms, juggling
alliances and, most importantly, being in the right place at the
right time. Case in point was his presence at that silly ceremony last summer consecrating the relics of that charlatan
saint, Seraphim. He had done his career no harm in presenting to the tsar ornately matted and framed photographs taken
of the ceremony.

And now, because of his manipulations, he was being considered for the illustrious post of Minister of the Interior. Such
an appointment would be the crowning achievement of his career. Even Viktor Fedorcenko had never been that close to political power. Every day Vlasenko waited for a messenger to
appear with the announcement. Why the tsar was taking so
long to make his decision, Cyril could not even guess. It had
been a month since the post was vacated by the tragic death
of Count Plehve.

Plehve's death did make Cyril wonder why he was so eager
to assume the job himself. It was, without a doubt, the most
hazardous position in Russia. The last two Interior Ministers,
Sipiagin and Plehve, had been assassinated, while countless

unsuccessful attempts had been made on others. It simply was not popular to be an Interior Minister, especially if it was your policy not to cave into the clamoring of the radicals. Vlasenko had every intention of continuing the policies of Plehve; that's why he was the tsar's first choice for the position.

There were rumors afoot, however, that the zemstvo leaders opposed his appointment. Everyone knew how powerless the zemstvos were, but rumors indicated that these bloated so-called leaders had enlisted the aid of the Dowager Empress Maria Fedorovna to appeal to her son, the emperor, about an alternate candidate. That's all Vlasenko needed was for that old woman to meddle in government affairs. She was dangerously moderate—perhaps even liberal—in her political views, and she had little respect for Vlasenko, whom she apparently considered a pompous bore. Unfortunately, the mama's boy Nicholas still listened to his mother. Her recommendation was Prince Svyatopolk-Mirsky, the governor-general of Vilna who had opposed the policies of both Sipiagin and Plehve. The prince sounded like Loris-Melikov, another bleeding heart liberal who would advocate lifting censorship, giving freedom to religious minorities, and instituting a constitutional monarchy. His kind wouldn't be satisfied until Russia was reduced to resembling England—or, worse still, America!

Vlasenko was determined to fight back by making the best use of his invitation to the palace. He would ingratiate himself shamelessly to the tsar. He would shovel flattery upon the tsaritsa; everyone knew the tsar listened to her even more than to his mother. Yes, that would be the best way to play it. Win over the empress, and he'd be as good as assured of the job. He would attend Mass a couple of times beforehand just to be in the proper frame of mind. The empress had a weakness for spiritual things.

Poznia ought to be able to help in that area. Lately she had been hobnobbing with the two Montenegrin sisters, who were quite devoted to spiritualism and such foolishness. Poznia had attended a seance with them recently. According to his wife, the two princesses were always entertaining holy men, *starets*. The tsaritsa also was friendly with the Montenegrins and quite interested in all that mystical business. Cyril thought it was a lot of rot, but it would be quite a coup if he could be instrumental in leading the empress to the acquaintance of a monk with miraculous powers. It was said there was a *starets* from Siberia at the Montenegrins' last year who had healed the grand duke Nikolasha's dog of the colic.

Ha! Even pathetic young Karl could probably do that.

Nevertheless, if such things appealed to the impressionable rulers of Russia, then Cyril was certainly not above using such methods to further his own career.

So, he was in an optimistic frame of mind for the upcoming festivities honoring Princess Gudosnikov. He could hardly bear that woman and her liberal views, but she and Poznia were old friends. Cyril often moaned at the company his wife sometimes kept, but he couldn't deny that her peculiar liaisons often had come in handy for his political and personal schemes. The party tonight was important, if only to give him a chance to evaluate liberal viewpoints.

Everyone would be there; they were all in the city anyway to pay homage to the new heir. How convenient for Marya Gudosnikov that her birthday fell so close to that of the new tsarevich, Cyril mused. If only *he* had that kind of luck.

"Well, I'll just have to make my own luck." He had done it before, and he could certainly do it again.

15

About fifty people gathered at the home of Princess Marya Gudosnikov. Represented among the guests was a wide variety of the St. Petersburg nobility, from important government officials to creative forces like Tchaikovsky and Anton Chekhov.

But there was also a sprinkling of insignificant nobles, and those whose stars had once shone brightly but had long since dimmed.

Viktor Fedorcenko well knew he was in the latter category. And it really did not bother him except that he still loved his country and grieved at the injustices so prevalent in Russian society. Once he had been in a key position to do some good, to change Russia for the better; once he'd had the ear of a tsar; once he had economic leverage, if nothing else. Now . . .

He was barely noticed in society. His presence at this function was only by virtue of his long-standing friendship with the princess. Those who remembered him from the old days tended to shy away; they only remembered that Prince Viktor Fedorcenko had lost his mind, had a nervous breakdown, and fallen out of favor with the royal family. It simply wasn't politically healthy to associate too closely with someone in that position. Viktor probably would have done the same himself in the old days.

Now he was fairly content to stand with his wife, engaging her in conversation. After all, Sarah Remington, now Princess Sarah Fedorcenko, was an intelligent woman whose company had sufficed and sustained him for many years as his housekeeper and protector during those years when he could not be trusted to care for himself. She was far more interesting than most of the blowhards now present in Marya's parlor.

As if on cue, Cyril Vlasenko and his wife arrived at that very moment. Now, there was the prince of blowhards! Viktor would never forgive the man for his crass opportunism in stealing the Fedorcenko St. Petersburg estate away from Viktor. He still harbored suspicions about Cyril's *convenient* takeover of the property. But there was no way for a penniless, powerless noble to investigate the onetime chief of the Third Section. Cyril's ties to the secret police had given him power that continued to linger years after he had left that position. And now it was rumored that Cyril was being considered by the tsar to become the new Minister of the Interior. Viktor found it inconceivable that a man like Cyril Vlasenko could rise to such a position. Perhaps he ought to be more thankful that he was no longer involved in government—it might only drive him insane again.

"Viktor," Sarah said, drawing her husband's attention back to their conversation, "I'm surprised so many have turned out in St. Petersburg in the summer."

"Marya is well liked, and her parties are renowned," he replied. He dragged his gaze away from Cyril, but not before Sarah saw where he had been looking.

"I suppose she can't be too selective in her guest list."

Viktor smiled. "I am here, am I not? The outcast of St. Petersburg society."

As if to refute Viktor's statement, the hostess herself swept up to them. "Oh, Viktor, I am so glad you were able to come. It is not every day a woman turns sixty-five, and she wants her dearest friends near her when she does." She turned toward Sarah. "And her new friends, also, Princess Fedorcenko."

"Please, if we are to be friends, do call me Sarah. The 'princess' part is still a bit hard to take," said Sarah.

"Of course," said Marya, "but I just wanted to emphasize that I do accept you fully as the new princess. Viktor's first wife Natalia and I were dear friends, as you know, and I'm certain she would be pleased with how things have turned out." Marya took Sarah's hands in hers and gazed intently into her eyes. "As I am," she said earnestly. Then more lightly, "Now, you must have some champagne. And do mingle—not all my guests are as stuffy as Count Vlasenko." She added this last in a mischievous whisper, then said more conversationally, "Tchaikovsky will be here soon, and I will introduce you."

Marya bustled away to greet more guests. In a moment a waiter appeared with a tray of glasses filled with French champagne. Viktor sipped his thoughtfully, pondering Marya's words. Would Natalia truly be pleased at how his life had evolved? She would, if nothing else, be shocked that he had married their former housekeeper. Even more surprising than that to Viktor was the depth with which he loved Sarah. He hadn't even loved Natalia in that way—he simply hadn't been capable of such intense feelings back then.

His thoughts were interrupted by the approach of a rather large, broad-chested man. He was tall and well dressed, but a certain coarseness about the man made him stand out among so many polished Russian noblemen. Viktor had never met Sergei Witte, but there were not many who wouldn't recognize the man who had been an important minister to two tsars.

"I don't think we have met," said Witte in a strong, confident voice.

"No we haven't, sir," Viktor said. "But I know you by reputation, and I am honored to meet you."

"You know me by reputation and are *still* honored to meet me?" He laughed.

"Indeed," said Viktor. "You have made a most positive impact on this country. I am Viktor Fedorcenko, and this is my wife, Sarah."

"Prince Fedorcenko, is it not?" When Viktor nodded, Witte continued. "When a couple of busybodies this evening informed me of *your* reputation, I said to myself, 'I must meet this fellow; he sounds like a man after my own heart.' However, your reputation was known to me even before this evening. And I must say, if we had more men in government of your ilk, Prince Fedorcenko, we'd all be better off. Ah, but for the whims of our rulers."

Witte, easily the most brilliant man in Russian government, was no doubt referring to his own unstable tenure in the Imperial Court. He had begun his career in railroading, demonstrating his genius even then. He came to the attention of Alexander III, who saw in Witte a man of vision and administrative talent. By 1893, he had been raised to the highly influential position of Minister of Finance, and his political power continued to grow.

When Nicholas II came to the throne, Witte remained in power even though the new tsar did not especially like Witte and his coarse, arrogant ways. He became the most powerful man next to the tsar. With his power, however, came a full tally of enemies, especially among those ultraconservatives with whom he was constantly butting heads in order to wrench Russia out of its backward slough. He also found himself in frequent opposition to the tsar himself, and eventually that precipitated his downfall. Fearing that the Minister of Finance was becoming too powerful, Nicholas transferred Witte to the figurehead post of Chairman of the Council of Ministers. Witte continued to make matters worse for himself by his outspoken opposition to the war with Japan.

Viktor admired the man, and could empathize with him because of his own similar experiences. It surprised him that Witte appeared to have some knowledge of Viktor's background, and, he had to admit, he was flattered that a man like Witte bothered with him at all.

"It would be a naive man who believed service to his country would be simple," Viktor said.

"I have been called cynical among other things, but I must say, I had hoped to have some effect on Russia's future."

"And you have, Sergei Witte. Most have already forgotten me, but I doubt the same will happen to you."

"We'll have to see in twenty-five years, won't we? In the meantime I would not mind having a man like you working with me—if I had a job these days! But if I ever do—"

Viktor held up a hand to stop Witte. "I have been in retirement too many years. I would be an anachronism in government today."

"So, you have no desire to return?"

Viktor hesitated too long to belie any protests he might try to make. He smiled sheepishly. "I suppose I'm occasionally assailed by such crazy ambitions, but, realistically, I am sixty-seven years old and doubt I have the kind of stamina required for such work."

"Still, the honor would be mine," Witte offered as he turned and walked away.

Later that evening, Viktor found himself in a clique of men who were discussing the pending selection of a Minister of the Interior. Unfortunately, Cyril was among them. But Viktor noted that Cyril had become a lot more subtle these days; he almost sounded believable when he responded to a remark about his own candidacy.

"I shall be honored to serve wherever the tsar deems me worthy," Cyril said. "The good of Russia is always the first consideration."

Viktor still cringed at the thought of Cyril in such a key government position. Surely Nicholas was not that addlebrained!

Viktor could not help but imagine what he himself would do with such an opportunity. He shook those thoughts from his mind, for they were as insane as when he truly had lived in a fantasy world.

Sarah came up to Viktor from where she had been conversing with a group of women. She slipped her arm around his.

"I could use some air, Viktor."

He gave her a relieved smile, excused himself from the group, and led her out onto the veranda. "Ah, my dear Sarah, you are indeed a lifesaver."

"Do you wish to return to our hotel?"

"No, for Marya's sake we must stay at least until cake is served and a toast is offered to our hostess. I believe I am doing well, all things considered, for my first large social gathering since my . . . ah, illness."

"You are."

"Actually, even at my best, I never enjoyed this sort of thing."

"Viktor," Sarah gently chided, "in my opinion you are at your best at this very moment!"

"Only because I have the support and encouragement of such a remarkable woman as you."

Viktor inhaled the sweet fragrances wafting over them from the garden. Was that a hint of roses in the air? Viktor recalled that Marya had magnificent rose gardens which she managed to keep in bloom all through the summer. He wondered if she would mind him coming out tomorrow to make a watercolor of them.

He would ask her when they returned to the party. And oddly, that prospect excited him as much—and perhaps more—than the thought of resuming his once-lofty Imperial position.

IV

GENEVA

16

Tolstoy once told the story of how he was walking along a country road when, in the distance, he noticed a man squatting in the middle of the road, waving and flailing his arms about frantically. Tolstoy decided the fellow was a madman. When he drew near, however, he saw that the man was actually sharpening a knife on a stone.

The activities of Paul Yevnovich Burenin often bore a great similarity to Tolstoy's story—even on this warm, hazy summer day when Mathilde had insisted they take a break from their work and have a picnic in the country. As he lay on a blanket upon the grass, he watched his wife picking a bouquet of daisies, looking so carefree and relaxed. The idle time seemed only to make Paul's mind work harder, thinking about things that perhaps were best ignored.

No wonder Tolstoy's little anecdote came to mind. It not only seemed to mirror his personal life, but that of the revolutionary movement as well. Sometimes it all seemed crazy, disjointed, purposeless. For a hundred different revolutionists there were a hundred different agendas. They debated and argued constantly, falling out over insignificant trifles. And Paul all too often felt caught in the middle, being pulled back and forth, and flailing his own arms desperately about.

Only Vladimir Ilyich Lenin demonstrated uncanny focus. He was sharpening his knife with unfailing precision. And for that reason, Paul had been drawn to Lenin and had remained with him even though, ideologically, they were often worlds apart. Lenin was so single-minded, almost to the point of being obsessed, that it was inconceivable he would fail at anything he set his mind to. Paul recalled Lenin's wife, Krupskaya, relating how as a young student Lenin had loved to ice-skate; but when he saw it made him too tired to study, he gave up skating. It had been the same with chess—and even Latin, which Lenin loved. He gave them up because they interfered with his all-important studies.

Paul had followed Lenin into European exile. He worked with him on *Iskra*, the radical newspaper he published and smuggled into Russia. Paul and Mathilde had been with him in London for several months. Their attempts at learning English together made Paul laugh. None of them had ever heard English spoken before, though all except Mathilde had taught themselves to read the language. How comical they had sounded trying to form the awkward foreign words! They had spent hours visiting Hyde Park and listening to the soapbox speakers, until they could finally render the language with some ability. But Lenin, in his way, was obsessed with learning everything he could about the English.

Paul wondered what his papa Yevno would have thought of the socialist church they had attended in London. The preacher sermonized about how the Exodus of the Jews from Egypt was symbolic of the deliverance of the proletariat from the kingdom of capitalism to the kingdom of socialism. They sang a hymn that intoned: "Almighty God, put an end to all kings and all rich men."

In London they met Lev Bronstein, also known as Trotsky. Fresh from Siberian exile, the twenty-three-year-old Jewish revolutionary with his vivid blue eyes and thick shock of black hair had made an immediate impression. He had been called a young eagle, and Paul, one of the elders of the group, saw that the appellation fit Trotsky well. His writing talents were put to work on *Iskra*, which had become the prominent voice of the Social Democratic Party.

Last spring they had returned to Geneva from London in preparation for the Second Congress of the Social Democratic Party. Lenin had opposed the move, probably in part because he wished to operate *Iskra* away from the interference of the venerable Plekhanov, who was considered by many to be the leader of the party. Lenin had had many disagreements with

Plekhanov over the years. Even in London there had been conflict, of course—clashes with others over such fundamental issues as whether change and reform could happen in Russia without a revolution. Lenin's all-or-nothing attitude was bound to ignite controversy anywhere.

The stress of all the controversy, however, took its toll on Lenin. He ended up with a horrible case of shingles and spent the first two weeks in Geneva in bed. Yet as he recovered he became optimistic and enthusiastic about the upcoming congress that would be held in Brussels.

The congress got off to a fine start in the summer of 1903. Plekhanov was elected chairman and Lenin was one of the vice-chairmen. There were about sixty in attendance, quite a large number compared to the First Congress with only eight. But when some delegates to the Second Congress were expelled from Belgium by the police, it was feared there might be danger to others, so the congress was moved to London. When the meetings resumed a week later, they were plagued by tensions and conflict.

If only Lenin had been able to bend a little, to compromise on something. But that simply was not his nature. Martov, Lenin's chief adversary, wanted a party of a broad scope with more appeal to the masses, one that entailed more participation with the Russian people themselves. Lenin insisted on a party controlled by a "Central Committee," a very small, elite group of leaders.

Trotsky had commented to Lenin during one of the breaks, "What you are promoting sounds a lot like a dictatorship."

"That is the only way," Lenin had replied.

After much maneuvering and some of the opposition withdrawing, Martov's faction, the *Mensheviks*, or minority, found itself with slightly less support than Lenin's opposing group, the *Bolsheviks*, or majority. It helped that Plekhanov, in spite of their many conflicts, stood with Lenin.

"I am reminded of Napoleon," Plekhanov said, "who had a penchant for insisting that his marshalls divorce their wives. Some of them actually did, regardless of the fact that they loved their wives. Well, I will not divorce Lenin, and I hope he has no intention of divorcing me."

Laughing, Lenin had assured Plekhanov of his fidelity with a shake of the head.

Paul recalled that little interchange vividly, because he had at the time been deeply struck by his own sense of infidelity. He had voted for Lenin, but his heart was divided. He knew Lenin planned on being a dictator in the government of the new Russia—of course there was little question in his mind that Lenin would be the leader of Russia after the revolution. But Paul had probably read too much Jefferson and Paine to be completely comfortable with the dictatorial style of government. He did have to admit to himself, however, that Russia—with its millions of illiterate, grossly poor peasants—might not be capable of the kind of democracy found in America. At least not by the time the revolution occurred. In that case, wasn't a man like Lenin best equipped for leadership? Only a man of such vision, drive, and charisma could direct the sweeping—yes, radical—changes that must occur in Russia.

Ironically, Lenin himself was a democrat. He once wrote, "Whoever tries to approach socialism by any other path than that of political democracy will inevitably arrive at the most absurd and reactionary conclusion." At best, he saw a dictatorship as temporary, until the proletariat attained economic and social prominence. At the worst, there would be in Russia a kind of democratic dictatorship, in that it represented the overwhelming majority of the population.

Paul was willing to bend to achieve a worthy goal. But he wasn't sure how much bending he could do without breaking. He simply was not the kind of diehard Marxist Social Democrat that Lenin usually surrounded himself with.

But Paul was not *surrounding* Lenin much at all these days. Claiming poor health as an excuse, Paul had, since the congress, curbed his activities in the organization. His health, in fact, could be better, but it wouldn't have proved a burden if he had been in a mental state to work in the way he knew was expected of him.

If only—

"Paul, you have that faraway look in your eyes again."

Paul's head jerked up sharply. Mathilde's approach had

startled him, and he grinned sheepishly.

"I made no promises," he said.

"Yes, but I had hoped this little excursion would help you lay aside your worries and inner debates for a while."

"Believe me, that's what I want also. My endless thinking only seems to lead me around in a circle."

"Come with me—we'll walk those thoughts out of your head."

"Or, *talk* them out?"

"We shall see."

They walked for half an hour by the little stream, its gentle gurgling, mixed with the occasional rustling of leaves, providing an idyllic and relaxing setting for the couple's afternoon stroll. Paul truly wanted nature to work its calming magic upon him. But he sensed the tension within him had a purpose that he must respect.

A time of decision was coming—he must finally make the choice he had been putting off for years. Either he would stand wholeheartedly with Lenin, or . . .

Well, if he knew what else, his decision would not be nearly as difficult.

17

Paul quietly sat with a glass of hot tea in his hand while Lenin read the article he had just finished for *Iskra*. They were in the kitchen of Lenin's tiny flat in a working-class neighborhood of Geneva. The kitchen was the largest room of the house and served as the main meeting place for guests. It was usually a crowded and busy spot, furnished mostly with packing crates serving as chairs. A large enamel kettle filled with water sat on the stove, steaming and ready for the steady stream of visitors who often came unannounced.

Paul had been glad when he arrived that only Lenin and his wife, Krupskaya, were present.

Lenin glanced up from his reading and tapped the page with his pencil. "This statement here sounds rather conciliatory."

Paul leaned across the low "table" of crates and read the indicated statement. Lenin's incisive observation was especially keen today.

"It's intended to be that way," said Paul. "I still believe it is in the best interest of the party to find some common ground."

"I doubt that's possible after the vicious depths to which Martov and his Mensheviks have sunk. I have tried—ask anyone! No one knows better than I what this rift is doing to our strength. Many of our supporters are reluctant to give us money. Several people no longer wish to offer their houses as secret meeting places. Even after my victory at the congress, I let the Mensheviks have a place on the board of *Iskra*. I even offered to resign. Krupskaya, isn't it true? Haven't I been in agony over this whole thing? Haven't I tried everything?"

Lenin went on for ten more minutes about the split and all its ramifications and repercussions. He took every opportunity to expound on this issue, usually with great passion, to anyone who would listen. Paul wondered if the most difficult part of the whole matter was the fact that Martov had been one of Lenin's closest friends.

Lenin was so obsessed by these affairs that he hardly took note of the momentous events in Russia. He had only mentioned the war briefly two or three times since it began, and that was only to say that the way things were going for Russia in Asia, the war would be a good boost to the revolution, for it would show the masses the ineptness of the Imperial government. It was the same with the entire exile population; any mention of the war was merely in passing.

But the split in the party was another matter. All those in the emigreé community—at least the Social Democrats—were depressed over the squabble. It seemed to dominate everything and even was being felt among party members in Russia. By comparison, the war was a mere speck of dust on the horizon.

All at once Lenin leveled his narrow, piercing eyes at Paul. "Are you one of those conciliators, Pavlikov? I have no use for you, then. I'd rather have a small fish completely devoted to the cause than a big beetle I can't depend upon."

Paul didn't know how to answer the question, or even if Lenin wanted an answer. It sounded as if Lenin already knew. But Paul was spared immediate comment by a knock at the door.

Three young men entered. Paul recognized one as Stephan Kaminsky from Katyk, the other two were named Chicherin and Lunacharsky. The room immediately filled with energetic chatter as Krupskaya placed glasses of tea in the visitors' hands and they found crates on which to perch. Conversation quickly turned to party affairs. These men were unreserved Bolsheviks and devoted to Lenin.

Paul himself could not help being caught up in the zestful spirit. Yes, he had his differences, but wasn't that the nature of freedom, their very goal?

They talked for over an hour. Lenin was making plans to start another newspaper as an alternative to *Iskra,* which had become pro-Menshevik. It was to be called *Vperyod,* or Forward. Money needed to be raised, and plans were being made for Lenin to begin a speaking tour to help the cause.

"We must have a mouthpiece for the party, an organ to spread our message!" Lenin exclaimed.

Paul thought of the name of the paper—*Forward!* That's really what it was all about, moving forward. That's what Lenin was doing. And what Paul wanted to do. He had been working toward this goal for nearly thirty years, had sacrificed and suffered much in order to see the dream of freedom for Russia realized. True, he often felt as if he were acting out the title to Lenin's recent pamphlet, "One Step Forward, Two Steps Back," but the path he had chosen had never been easy. Why should he expect it to be any different now?

He and this small band of revolutionaries were attempting to radically change an entire nation, the largest nation in the world. More than that, they were trying to topple a system that had reigned for nearly three hundred years! It was pure delusion to think they could do so without some compromise of ideals. Even Lenin was known to compromise occasionally, especially when he knew it would benefit the greater goals. In fact, Lenin had probably compromised some of his "ideals" by working with Paul all these years. After all, Paul had criticized Marxism and expressed doubts about the idea of a "popular dictatorship." But Lenin knew Paul was a level-headed, dedicated man, and no matter what he said about "fish" and "beetles," such men were hard to find, especially one who could write as well as Paul.

When a lull came in the lively conversation, Paul rose to leave. Mathilde had expected him home an hour ago.

Lenin held out Paul's article. "Are you willing to work on this, Paul?"

"Yes, Ilyich, I am."

"I'd like to use it in the first issue of *Vperyod*."

"I want to be part of it."

"No conciliation?"

"You know, Ilyich, I am dedicated completely—my whole heart!—to the revolution. If that's not enough for you, then you are asking the impossible."

Lenin chuckled. "I always knew you were a good man, my friend. I'll try not to wear you out with the impossible."

"Then good day to you all," Paul said as he gathered up his hat and coat.

"Give our regards to Mathilde," Lenin called as Paul left.

Paul felt good as he walked away, even lighthearted. He had finished his article and taken it to Lenin that day with the express purpose of trying to resolve some of his inner conflicts. He had feared the resolution would take the form of a break with Lenin and the Bolsheviks. Now he could go on, do the work he wanted to do—*needed* to do—and not fuss with minor inconsistencies. Leave that to the Martovs and others. Paul had better things to do.

He kissed his wife passionately when he arrived home. After she caught her breath, she examined him closely.

"Ilyich and Krupskaya send their regards," Paul said casually.

"Is that all? I thought perhaps the revolution had already taken place."

Paul laughed. "Not without me, it won't!"

"You're the only one who ever doubted that, my dear."

"Do you mind if I desert you for a while this afternoon? I have work to do—a lot of work."

———

Mathilde watched with pleasure as her husband sat at his desk. How glad she was that the people who had the flat before them had left it behind! It made up for the sparsity of other furnishings, and even added warmth to the room that doubled as both parlor and study. Paul shoved aside a couple of large volumes he had been studying—Locke's *Two Treatises on Civil Government* and a compilation of Thoreau's writings open to the essay, "Civil Disobedience." He laid several sheets of paper on the cleared area, then took up his pen and began writing with an inspired speed.

Mathilde smiled. She was pleased with the intense set of his mouth and the glint in his eyes. Could it be her husband had finally found his calling?

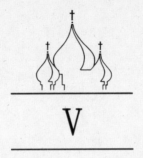

V

THE REPORTER
AND THE WAR HERO

18

Mukden, a teeming collection of a million inhabitants jammed into an area of about four square miles, was a little too far from the action to suit Daniel. The drab town had only one claim to fame—a graveyard. Well, in reality, the graveyard was the Imperial Tombs of the Manchu Dynasty, but they were literally nothing to write home about. Still, all correspondents had been evacuated to Mukden, and here he was resigned to await a new assignment.

Daniel and several other correspondents were residing in a Buddhist temple. Considering some of the second-rate inns he had been forced to rent in Manchuria, he should have appreciated the peace and cleanliness of the place. But he was coming up with fewer and fewer dispatches to send home, and he was anxious for a story with some meat in it. During the day he roamed about town cornering officers, especially those that appeared to have newly arrived, attempting to extract from them any news of action at the front. The correspondents were starting to behave like hungry vultures.

One day near the beginning of August, Daniel had been about his usual business. A morning downpour had kept him indoors, but the minute the rains stopped, he had taken to the streets and had spoken to several Russian soldiers. Then he made his way to the Green Dragon Inn, near the East Gate, where the newspaper correspondents often congregated to refresh themselves, exchange gossip, and hopefully hear the latest war news.

Entering the inn, Daniel went to a table where several reporters were seated. He knew them all well, and they greeted him enthusiastically. He ordered an ale and reclined in a vacant chair.

"That rain did nothing for the heat," Daniel said, mopping his perspiring brow.

"At least it dampened the dust a bit," said William Greener, a British correspondent for the *Times*.

"Give it an hour!" complained Dick Little of the Chicago *Tribune*.

The men continued to chat as Daniel's ale arrived. No major campaigns were afoot, only a few skirmishes. The Japanese advance up the railway had halted after Telissu because of supply shortage. The biggest news had come a few days ago, when the Japanese took the important Motienling Pass. Until then the mountains had proved a formidable barrier to the Japanese invasion of the Liaotung Peninsula. The Russians had tenaciously held all the passes, but the Japanese army, deployed in three strategic positions, was numerous and strong. And Kuropatkin, the Russian commander in chief, had weakened his forces considerably by sending a fifth of his troops to bolster the defense of Port Arthur, a gesture that garnered him some criticism.

Daniel had heard it all before and let his mind wander to more pleasant topics. *Mariana Remizov*. He still could not believe his good fortune in running into her here. How many times over the years had he imagined seeing her again? He hated to admit what a romantic dope he was at heart. But she had done something that no other woman had ever done; she had touched his heart in a way that he still could only begin to fathom.

For one thing, as he had realized when his father died, she had been a friend. All the other girls he had known before and since Mariana had been merely romantic liaisons—girls to date, take to parties, kiss when he could get them alone, and generally to woo and charm. He had done, or tried to do, all those things with Mariana, of course, but something happened between wooing and dating that had quite surprised him. Mariana had *talked* to him—really talked, not the banal chatter he had experienced with other girls. She had shared her heart and even her soul with him, and in a way he would never understand, she had gotten him to do the same. Not a man to wear his heart on his sleeve, he had told Mariana more about himself than he had to any other person. He had tried to kiss her a couple times, but she had been engaged to that oaf Kaminsky and had discouraged his romantic intentions. In the long run, the friendship that ensued had been better than a romance. He had never had a real friend before Mariana.

Too late, he realized that friendship was fragile. Only after he arrived back in America did he begin to understand just what his relationship with Mariana had meant. His father's death had made him acutely aware of lost opportunities. There had been so much more he had wanted to say to his father, but it was all forever left unsaid.

With Mariana, at least, there had been a possibility of recapturing what they had shared. But his unanswered letters had put an end to that hope. He might be persistent in reporting, but her rejection was too hard even for him to take. And later, after he had slipped away from his pursuit of God, he would have been too embarrassed to see her.

Then, suddenly, there she was.

Finding her, way out here, was almost like another miracle. But why would God perform miracles for the likes of him? It did make him think twice—he was certainly no heathen, even if he hadn't given much time to spiritual matters recently. Daniel had even found himself whispering a brief prayer of thanksgiving after first encountering Mariana. He might not be a fanatic, but he did like to give credit where credit was due.

And that same night after he had parted from Mariana, Daniel had promised—whether to God or just to himself, he didn't know—that he would take better care of their relationship this time. Whether their friendship blossomed into romance or not, he was determined not to mess it up again.

No need to rush things, though. She had to learn to trust him again. But Daniel had learned his lesson and wasn't about to make any more mistakes with Mariana.

What they needed was more days like those few they had spent together in the field hospital. Mariana had worked a lot, but they had found time to be together. Perhaps not like in St.

111

Petersburg—you could hardly go picnicking in a war zone. But they made the best of it. He smiled when he thought of one evening in particular. Mariana had gotten off duty late, about ten at night. Daniel ran into her on the way to the mess tent for a late supper. She had looked so beautiful—her uniform was stained and wrinkled, her hair was pulled back haphazardly, and damp strands tumbled into her eyes. But to Daniel she looked exquisite. This was no pampered society girl. She was very much a participant in *life*, and Daniel found that enormously attractive.

In the mess tent there was nothing left to eat but cold meat pies, bread, and hot tea. But at least they were almost alone; only three other people were hungry enough to eat at that hour.

Mariana put a greasy pie on a plate and wrinkled her nose distastefully. "Maybe if I close my eyes I can imagine we are sitting under a tree in a garden, enjoying my father's cook's delicious food."

"Okay, my lady," Daniel said, "close your eyes, and let's see what happens."

While Mariana's eyes were shut, Daniel hastily set to work. He grabbed a cook's apron hanging from a hook, spread it on a table, then took the tallest glass he could find, filled it with a couple of wooden spoons and a spatula, and placed it in the center of the apron.

"*Voila*, madame! Come join me on the banks of the Neva." Mariana opened her eyes and giggled. "See the lovely flowers—" He gestured toward the glass. "And listen to the river rushing by!"

"This is absolutely wonderful, Daniel! Just what I needed." Mariana set her plate down and slipped onto the bench. Daniel got them both glasses of tea.

The conversation turned to more serious matters as Mariana talked about her hospital work, her patients, things she was learning. Daniel listened.

"It can get pretty intense here," she said. "There are moments when I wonder if I'll make it."

"If anyone can do it, you will, Mariana."

"I have to keep reminding myself of how certain I was that

this is where God wanted me to go."

She talked about God so naturally, as she would about her mama or her papa. He almost asked her about it, but stopped himself when he remembered where such a question might lead. He wasn't ready to reveal his inadequacies in this area. Still, his silence left him frustrated.

Back in the States, when he had been seeking faith, he'd had so many questions he wanted to ask Mariana. Now here she was, and he was afraid. Would he always have things to keep from her? He didn't want it that way, but there were so many things about himself that he was ashamed of. Yet how could they have a deeper relationship if he held part of himself back? Maybe it was this, not his thirst for adventure, that had always kept him at arm's length from marriage.

Thus Daniel was rather ambivalent, perhaps even a little relieved, when he was ordered to Mukden. He was also disgusted with himself.

———

When Daniel finished his ale at the Green Dragon, he bid his associates a good afternoon and left the inn. There was no news to be had there, anyway. He went to the commandant's office to check on his application to join a military unit in the field, only to be assured that the commandant had his papers and was reviewing them carefully. As usual, nothing happened quickly where Russia was concerned. He should have stayed at the field hospital with Mariana. Interviewing some of the wounded there had inspired an excellent dispatch, called "Heroes in White," about the medical personnel. But after culling all he could from that venue, he felt he needed a change and decided to look for a battle. It was as good a reason as any— and it kept him from examining his real motivations too closely.

But then the correspondents had been recalled to Mukden. He saw Mariana briefly before leaving and hadn't seen her since.

Daniel returned to the temple. The hot Manchurian sun was dipping low in the sky. He hoped he was in time for dinner—the priests were a very disciplined lot, and everything

113

was done on a precise schedule.

The brick temple courtyard was an inviting place, with tall shade trees and potted flowering shrubs. The priests walked about, dressed in long robes of crimson and yellow, their pace methodical, deliberate, as if hurry were an unpardonable sin. They nodded welcome to Daniel as he passed. They spoke Mongolian and could not communicate even with the smattering of Chinese Daniel knew. Oddly, they were as foreign in this land as was he.

He entered the spacious but sparsely furnished main hall and headed directly to the dining room. The fragrance of dinner began to waft toward him. Simple, vegetarian fare was served at the temple—always including some variation of rice, with fruit and cheese and the best bread Daniel had ever tasted. He could smell the bread and realized he was hungrier than he thought.

Several priests were also heading in the direction of the dining room. He slowed his steps so as not to rush rudely past them, but it was no small matter to move at their measured pace.

"Honorable master Trent," called a voice from behind him.

Daniel stopped and turned. It was the Dalai Lama, the head of the monastery, whose name was Hui K'o. He was an ancient man, his bald head and arms covered with scars from some special rites of his sect. He was the only resident of the monastery who spoke English, and had, in fact, welcomed the correspondents in hopes of improving his usage of the language.

"Good evening, Father," Daniel said respectfully. This man might be of a heathen faith, but his age alone, not to mention the kindness with which he treated the correspondents, demanded respect.

"You will dine with us tonight?"

"If I am not too late."

"Even the most humble table always has room for a guest." The Dalai Lama smiled benevolently, then continued to walk with Daniel to the dining room. "I had hoped to see you today, and when I saw you enter our gates, I came as quickly as I could."

"There's nothing wrong, is there?"

"I hope not, but any message that arrives at our gates is treated with grave importance."

"A message?"

"Yes, I have it here. It arrived a few hours ago. I sent a boy into town to look for you, but he was not successful." The Dalai Lama reached into the folds of his robe and drew out an envelope.

Daniel did not immediately recognize the handwriting, but he knew it was not from his office. A decidedly feminine hand had produced the fine script. He tore open the envelope with a rising sense of apprehension. There were only a few lines to read, and he finished it quickly.

"It is not, as you say, bad news?" asked the Dalai Lama.

"I don't know," Daniel said. "A friend of mine who was serving with the Red Cross near Liaoyang has been transferred to Port Arthur. I had hoped to see more of her while I was here. Now . . ." He let his words trail away; he really didn't know what Mariana's transfer would mean to their relationship.

"Port Arthur is not a good place for a reunion with old friends," offered the priest. "Most civilians have evacuated the city with the threat of siege drawing nearer; few are going there except as duty calls them."

"I know. And her note is over a week old. It must have taken the long way to get here. And with each passing day, the Japanese noose around Port Arthur gets tighter and tighter."

"I will pray to Buddha for your friend's safety."

They arrived at the dining hall and entered. Inside, half a dozen long tables with wooden benches for seats were lined up neatly. They were filling up with priests, but the room was as quiet as a church service. His first meal with the priests had been quite a shock after eating in raucous mess tents with soldiers. Here, order and serenity prevailed.

One table at the front of the room was reserved for the correspondents. A handful of men sat there, and though they were talking among themselves, they were much quieter than they would have been at the Green Dragon—or any other place where that many newspapermen congregated. Daniel joined his associates, but he was distracted and quiet throughout the meal. He couldn't even enjoy the bread. All he could think of was Mariana's note and the fact that she was getting away from him again.

Daniel realized, of course, that their duties would command the majority of their time, but he had hoped that they could find some time to spend together. He expected to be out of Mukden soon—with or without the permission of the commandant. He was not a prisoner here, but for the time being it was in his best interests to placate the authorities. He had run afoul of them several times on matters of censorship and wanted to get on better terms in hopes of an assignment with a unit in General Kuropatkin's army.

Mariana's note changed everything. Aside from the danger her new assignment placed her in, her presence in Port Arthur—especially once it was under siege—would make her terribly inaccessible. He wondered if he could use some contacts he had in the high command to get her assignment changed. Then he recalled that the particular colonel he knew had been killed at Nanshan.

"I say, old boy, you seem rather out of sorts, today." The voice came as if from a distance, and Daniel looked across the table to see Carmichael, a British correspondent from the Manchester *Gazette*.

Daniel glanced around to find the dining room nearly empty. The meal was over, and he had hardly touched his own food.

"Bad news from home?" Carmichael continued.

"Not exactly." Daniel knew Carmichael better than most of the reporters, and he had mentioned Mariana to him. "It's that Russian girl I was telling you about."

"The nurse?"

"Yeah. Looks like she's on her way to Port Arthur. I don't know if I'll see her again soon."

"Nasty break. Why don't you just go there?"

"Just as easy as that, huh?"

"Since when do you take the easy way, Daniel? But, heavens! I wouldn't even suggest taking the risk only for love. If you could get into the port, imagine the exclusive stories the siege of the great Port Arthur might provide."

"If I could get them out."

"Where there's a will, there's a way, old boy."

"Bill, your sentimentality touches my heart. Is news all you can think of?"

"What else is there?" Carmichael grinned smugly. "Were you planning to go to your Russian girl anyway?"

"I hadn't gotten that far in my thinking." Daniel suddenly felt defensive. Why had Carmichael mentioned the news aspect of going to Port Arthur? He didn't need the possibility of a scoop to cloud his motives; Mariana would see right through him. But he probably would have gone after her anyway. And, once he was there, she couldn't blame him if he used the opportunity for other purposes as well.

Schmidt, the only other correspondent still at the table, shook his head. "You're crazy to even think of such an undertaking," he said. "Etzel was killed in the attempt a couple of months ago."

"We know about poor Etzel," said Carmichael, referring to the British correspondent from the *Daily Telegraph*. "But good reporting requires a few risks."

"It's not you, but Trent who will be taking the risks. And I for one wouldn't want to risk my life for any newspaper."

"But for love?" Daniel said, the suggestion vindicating him in his motives. "That's quite a different matter."

"I never knew you to be such a romantic fool," Schmidt replied.

Daniel shrugged and rose. "I'm just full of surprises, boys."

19

Evidently, the Russian government also had a few surprises, for the same day Daniel received permission from the commandant to travel to Newchwang on the northwest coast of the Liaotung Peninsula. During the early days of the war, Newchwang had been the war correspondents' headquarters, so Daniel knew many of the locals there and had quite a few contacts. It was the best—and perhaps only—available place from which he could obtain passage to Port Arthur.

In March, the last time Daniel had been in Newchwang, the town had been icebound and on a very nervous war alert. Now, with the Japanese encroaching closer and closer, they had even more reason for taut nerves. The town was under martial law, of course, and the port especially was closely watched. A Russian duty destroyer made regular runs between Newchwang and Port Arthur. All civilian traffic was strictly regulated.

Daniel knew from the beginning that he was unlikely to obtain transportation through legitimate means. Locals, mostly fishermen, went out at their own risk, for the coast was heavily patrolled. Both the Russians and the Japanese were likely to shoot first—and forego the formality of asking questions altogether.

Daniel arrived in the evening just before curfew. He reported to the Russian administrator as he was required to do, then sought out the Lotus Inn, where the correspondents had lodged during his previous stay. The place was quiet, and he learned that much of the civilian population had evacuated to Mukden—at least those who could afford it. Many of the poorer residents, and those who were too obstinate to abandon their homes and businesses, had remained.

The bartender at the Lotus, a Siberian Russian named Abegjan, was one of the obstinate ones who also saw a profit to be made from the soldiers. Because his Siberian heritage gave him an Oriental appearance, he could move about easily among the Chinese locals—and even the Japanese, if he chose. Thus he had become a valuable source of information for the correspondents.

"I'm surprised you're sticking around," Daniel said as Abegjan set a glass of ale down in front of him.

"As long as Russian soldiers with a thirst and money in their pockets are here in Newchwang," he replied, "I would be crazy to leave. It's quiet now, but in a while this place will be filled with off-duty soldiers, and my cash register bell will be singing like a happy bird." He leaned across the bar. "I think I could even stay after the Japanese take over the town. Yen spends just as good as rubles, eh?"

"I don't see why you couldn't pass yourself off as a local. You've done it before."

Abegjan laughed. "So, what brings you back to this foul old town?"

"I'm looking to take a little sail down to Port Arthur," Daniel replied casually.

"I thought you valued your life better than that."

"I do. That's why I'm coming to you. I have no doubt you know the best sailor to do the job."

"Of course I know the best—but you will have to settle for any old boatman who is willing to take the risk."

"I'll make it worth his while."

"That goes without saying."

Abegjan scribbled something on a slip of paper and shoved it across the bar at Daniel. "I ask only ten percent of his fee," said Abegjan. "He is likely to charge as much as a hundred rubles."

Daniel took the paper and passed back ten rubles. Abegjan took the money with a raised eyebrow, obviously surprised that Daniel sealed the deal without the customary bargaining.

"You must be very anxious to get to Port Arthur," said the bartender.

"Very."

"I hope you make it."

———

The boatman, Yin Chu, had waited an hour after high tide to take advantage of the outward tidal movements. Daniel would have preferred waiting until after the moon set, but by then the incoming tides would make passage out of the small bay nearly impossible. He glanced over his shoulder nervously as Yin Chu maneuvered the junk into the moonlit bay.

They rowed for about half a mile before hoisting the sail, keeping to the shadows cast by the coastal rocks and cliffs. Then the light winds pushed them along at about three knots. At that rate it would take three days or more to reach the port at the southern tip of the Liaotung Peninsula. Yin Chu claimed he had been cruising this coast all his life, and he knew several out-of-the-way coves where they could put in for rest. And with the full moon, they could sail at night and have a better chance of avoiding discovery by patrols.

But it was a perilous journey under any conditions. The British correspondent, Etzel, had been fired upon and killed even before leaving Chinese waters. The Japanese had a reputation for being far more efficient than either the Chinese or the Russians, so Daniel kept an especially sharp lookout the next day as they passed into Japanese-held waters. Losing their lives was perhaps the worst that could happen, but almost as serious was the chance of being arrested as spies.

Twice they observed patrols but were able to dodge them under cover of darkness. Their luck ran out on their third day. It had rained all night, with strong winds, and they had been forced to seek shelter ashore by negotiating a rocky inlet. By the time the rains stopped just before dawn, Daniel's patience was at a breaking point. He argued that the overcast skies would provide enough cover for travel and urged Yin Chu to set out immediately. Adding another twenty-five dollars to the boatman's already exorbitant fee encouraged the Chinese sailor to comply against his better judgment.

Having finally dried out from the rain, they had to plunge waist-deep into the water to tow the boat back out to the open sea. Noticing the rocks that surrounded them, neither man could believe they had traversed the same path safely in the dark the night before. When they climbed back into the boat an hour later, wet and miserable, their spirits were low and their tempers short. They had slept little the previous night because of the rain, and the winds now made sailing hard work. Yin Chu said there was a little cove not far down the coast; they should make for it in order to get some rest. Daniel put his impatience aside and agreed.

Two hours later they still had not come to the cove. It had rained again, a drenching downpour, but that was not nearly as disturbing as what Daniel saw when the storm abated: the coastal hills were dotted with gun emplacements. It seemed only a matter of time before the Japanese spotted the tiny boat in the water.

"Shouldn't we have reached your cove by now, Yin Chu?" Daniel asked, skittishly scanning the hills.

"I think so," said the boatman.

"You *think* so?"

"Yes, I was sure I saw a cove on my trip to Port Arthur."

Daniel's hand tightened into a fist. "Please tell me you mean *trips* to Port Arthur—as in more than one."

Yin Chu refused to meet Daniel's eyes as he answered. "Only one time have I been more than a hundred miles from Newchwang."

"You mean for the last twenty-four hours you've been *guessing*?"

"I got a good memory, and hear many things from others, too," Yin Chu defended himself.

"You said you knew this coast like your own backyard," fumed Daniel.

Yin Chu grinned sheepishly. "I got no backyard, most honorable sir."

"Why you no account—" Daniel lunged toward the skipper with mutiny in his eyes, but the boat rocked dangerously. Daniel crashed back into his seat, arms and legs flying askew.

All at once artillery fire rent the air.

Yin Chu screamed and hit the deck. The tiller, now unmanned, jerked toward the port, causing the wind to snap at the sail, making it jibe. Both men, still flailing around on the deck, barely missed being knocked overboard by the swinging boom. But the sudden movement of the boom and the strong winds forced the boat to heel over dangerously.

"We're gonna capsize!" yelled Daniel. He jerked around; the port gunnels of the boat were nearly in the water.

Yin Chu, only his pride injured, grabbed the tiller and brought it around, ordering Daniel to man the mainsheet. In a few moments the junk was out of danger, at least from capsizing. More gunfire, however, indicated their worries were not yet over.

Artillery shells chewed up the water all around them. But Yin Chu tacked, catching a gust of wind that pushed them forward, momentarily out of harm's way. Hearts pounding, hands shaking, Daniel and Yin Chu sighed with relief. The wind continued to favor them and for once that grueling day they were thankful for it. The treacherous hills receded to a safe distance.

"We did it!" laughed Daniel. "I thought we were goners—"

He stopped as Yin Chu began pointing excitedly toward the stern.

"Oh, no!" groaned Daniel.

A gunboat was steaming after them, and, from the look of the flag it was flying, with its yellow sun bright against a red background, it was not on a routine cruise. The flag was standing out straight as the boat approached on a full head of steam.

Yin Chu pulled in the mainsheet, giving them a little more speed. They must have been doing six knots, but it would never be enough to outrun a gunboat. A deafening roar crashed overhead and, thinking their pursuer had opened fire on them, both men ducked. The winds doubled in force, and the junk shot forward, flying through the water.

The gunboat was in range, and Daniel wondered briefly why their gunfire was not coming close to the junk. When the skies opened up, letting loose a deluge of rain, he realized that the crashing had not been gunfire at all, but thunder. And this new storm was worse than any they had yet encountered.

Yin Chu let off the mainsheet—for the junk was already being pushed to its limit. The gunboat was the least of their worries now. Visibility was too bad, the gunboat would have to call off pursuit.

"This is no usual storm," yelled Yin Chu over the howling wind and driving rain. "This is a monsoon."

"What'll we do?"

"Reef sail. You must do it—I have to steer."

"I don't suppose we can just stop?"

"Not yet. I can still handle winds. We'll stop when winds get worse."

"Worse?" Daniel couldn't imagine anything worse than the fierce gusts propelling them along at a breakneck pace.

Half an hour later, and a good distance from where they had encountered the gunboat, Yin Chu had heaved-to and they were waiting out the storm, bobbing in the water with the monsoon raging over them. For the first time Daniel began to seriously question his sanity in instituting this undertaking. What had he been thinking? Did his feelings for Mariana cancel all good sense? Surely she would only think him a worse fool than ever for attempting such a harebrained journey.

That is, if he survived.

Survival seemed a slim possibility, however, with the winds buffeting the little boat horrendously, tossing it about like a piece of driftwood. And even if the winds and rains stopped, the Japanese gunboat might still be waiting for them.

Was love really worth all this?

Love.

Did he truly *love* Mariana, then? Was that what this was all about? The thought was almost as frightening as the storm and the Japanese navy put together.

With such thoughts roaring through his mind like the unabated winds, Daniel fell into a miserable sleep. He awoke to darkness and a chilling silence. He had no idea how much time had passed, and for a moment he wondered if he was dreaming, or perhaps even dead. But when he saw Yin Chu crumpled over in sleep, his hand still gripping the tiller, Daniel knew that somehow, by some miracle, they had survived the storm.

20

As Mariana walked through the Old Town of Port Arthur in the early morning on her way to the hospital, she wondered why the foreign residents so extolled this mean and dirty city. The dirt paths meant to function as streets were clogged with mud when it rained, as it did frequently now during the rainy season. When the hot sun came out, they dried out quickly, sending up choking dust clouds. The squalid buildings were almost as primitive as a peasant izba in Russia. Foreign residents, of course, managed to have better accommodations, but still Mariana would hardly classify this as one of the great cities of the world, as she heard many of the locals boast.

Situated at the very tip of the narrow Kwantung Peninsula, Port Arthur was a landlocked harbor, surrounded by rugged hills rising to almost six hundred feet. It was considered—by its Russian inhabitants, at least—a glowing symbol of the Muscovite spirit and of Russian domination of the Pacific. Before the war, construction had begun on New Town, situated on a plateau to the west of the railroad. A grand city had been planned, fully illuminating the most stunning Russian vision. Hundreds of buildings were under construction, but less than a fifth of the new city had been completed so far. Old Town was still the center of activity in the thriving port.

The population had dwindled appreciably since the war, many having evacuated to Chefu, Vladivostok, or to European Russia, if possible. Only a few thousand civilians remained, a thousand of whom were Russians and other foreigners—mostly businessmen wishing to protect their interests and make money off the war, and about five hundred wives and children of the officers. A garrison of some forty-two thousand soldiers defended the town; the military presence was unavoidable.

The militant atmosphere of Port Arthur was made worse by the fact that the commander of the garrison was none other than General Stoessel, the same man Mariana had heard rail so unfairly at his troops. No one liked the man. He was pompous, arrogant, and, from some of the rumors Mariana had heard, completely incompetent. According to one story, while supply ships were still coming to the port, Stoessel had turned several away. One, containing a precious cargo of tinned milk, he had allowed to unload only after other officers applied great pressure on him, but Stoessel told the skipper not to return. His reasoning was that Port Arthur had enough stores—even with a siege looming in its near future! Other officers had protested that the city was in desperate need of supplies, having only enough to withstand three months of siege.

Mariana had also heard that Kuropatkin, the commander of all military forces in Manchuria, had recalled Stoessel, requesting that General Smirnoff, the fortress commander, be given full charge. Stoessel had ignored the order until it was too late for him to get out safely. So, in addition to all the other problems, there was great contention within the high command.

Fortunately, Mariana had little opportunity to cross paths with Stoessel. Her time, consumed with hospital work, left few spare moments, and even when she was off duty, Port Arthur offered little in the way of social activities. She usually spent her time off sleeping, writing letters, or reading. She worked twelve- or fifteen-hour shifts, often more. Although the city itself had not yet been attacked since that first bombardment in the early part of the war, there was frequent fighting around the outer perimeter as the Russians held back the encroaching Japanese. Wounded were brought into the city daily. There were several hospitals in the city—two real hospitals and several other buildings that had been commandeered for that use, including a new luxury hotel in New Town that had not even had a chance to open for business.

Mariana worked at St. Stephan's, a hospital in Old Town

that had about five hundred beds, all full. It was a dreary old building with peeling paint on the outside and a strong odor of disinfectant on the inside—a scent that did little to camouflage the other more unpleasant smells in the place. Not surprising, St. Stephan's was overpopulated and understaffed. But Mariana liked her work. She felt useful, and she didn't mind spending most of her time there. She was in charge of a medical-surgical ward with fifty beds—almost all occupied by soldiers, with an occasional civilian patient.

Mariana checked in with her head nurse and prepared to make rounds with the nurse assistant, who happened to be Ludmilla Tolsikov. She was glad that Ludmilla had decided to stick it out after that first awful experience, for she was proving a capable nurse.

They visited each patient and exchanged a brief, cheerful greeting to those who were awake. The men were always glad to see the young nurses, especially since the nurse on the night shift was a hard-edged, sour-faced woman who acted as if she hated her job and resented the patients for taking up her precious time.

Mariana paused at the bedside of a new patient who had arrived during the night. She took his chart from the foot of the bed and scanned it. His name was Captain Philip Barsukov, and he had come in with a badly shattered right leg. As soon as the surgeons had time, they would probably amputate it. For the time being, he was under heavy doses of morphine, but he was awake when Mariana and Ludmilla paused at his bed. He opened his eyes and gave them a weak smile.

"I must have died and gone to heaven," he said. "I'm surrounded by angels!"

"I hope heaven will be better than this old place," said Mariana. "And you'll think differently of us when we start to poke and probe you."

"Probe all you want—I'm not feeling much of anything for the moment."

"That's good. Is there anything I can do for you before I go?"

Captain Barsukov smiled, and a mischievous glint invaded his eyes. Then he shook his head. "Nothing, I suppose, right

126

now. But when I am well, I would love to walk through a rose garden with you." He paused, turning serious. "That is, if I shall be walking anywhere. Do you think it's possible?"

"We'll do everything we can to make it possible."

He raised a doubtful eyebrow. "I've heard how eager our Russian doctors are to chop off legs and arms."

Unfortunately the captain was only too right. Mariana hesitated a moment too long before replying.

"That's all right," Barsukov said, "you don't have to say anything. I'll just have to take what comes like a man."

"When I finish with rounds, I have to change your dressing—I'll have a better idea then just what your prognosis might be."

Half an hour later Mariana returned with a dressing tray and gave the captain a shot of morphine. While the medicine was taking effect, she asked him about himself. He was from Moscow, a prince from a prominent banking family. When Mariana asked how he received his wound, he seemed rather reluctant to answer, saying only that he was wounded on a scouting expedition with a detachment of a dozen men.

Mariana knew more than the captain was telling—everyone in the hospital, in fact, had heard the story of his heroism.

His detachment had been cut off and surrounded by a squadron of Japanese. When the Russian scouts tried to retreat through the ranks of the enemy, the Japanese major hurled taunts at the Russians. The major's insults had so inflamed Captain Barsukov that he grabbed his sabre, turned, and attacked the major. With the major killed and his men routed, the Russian troops were able to break through the enemy line. Barsukov would have made it unscathed had he not gone back to rescue his sergeant, who had been shot in the chest. He caught the dead Japanese major's horse and loaded the wounded sergeant on the animal's back. But just as Barsukov was swinging up behind the sergeant, an artillery shell struck his leg. Barsukov would receive the prized Order of St. Andrew for his valor.

Mariana lifted the blanket and began working on the blood-soaked bandage. The leg was a torn and bloody mess, but her medical training told her that the leg was not in as bad shape as it appeared on the surface. The tibia was broken, but not shattered beyond repair; the fibula was sound. More importantly, there was still good circulation to the captain's toes. He had lost a great deal of blood, and the possibility of infection or gangrene was still a threat, but Mariana believed the leg could be saved.

She hated to admit it, but his chances depended more upon other factors than on the leg itself. If the doctors were swamped, they simply could not spend the necessary time to repair arteries and mend torn muscles and ligaments. Often they had to be satisfied with just saving lives, foregoing the luxury of delicate procedures.

Unfortunately, time was not Captain Barsukov's only enemy. He simply might have the ill-luck of drawing a poor surgeon. Mariana didn't like to be critical; the doctors were, after all, working under a tremendous amount of pressure, in poorly equipped and sparsely supplied hospitals. But there were a few doctors who didn't deserve medical certificates, and one of the worst happened to be here at St. Stephan's. Since there were seven others on staff, there was a chance the captain might get one of the other surgeons. But she didn't want to raise false hopes in the patient, and as a nurse she wasn't permitted to offer diagnosis. She tried to be noncommittal, yet at the same time soothe the man's worries. "Well, Captain, it could be worse, really. I'm only a nurse and can't say for sure, but—"

A new arrival cut her off mid-sentence. "I'm certain the patient doesn't wish to hear an unqualified opinion, Miss Remizov."

Mariana glanced up and saw her worst fears realized. The very doctor she had dreaded was standing before her. She knew it was too much to hope that his presence was just a coincidence. Dr. Karl Vlasenko must be the unfortunate captain's surgeon.

"Dr. Vlasenko," said Mariana, ignoring his droll remark, "I'm glad you've come by. Perhaps you can ease Captain Barsukov's mind over the status of his leg."

Karl took a quick glance at the leg and said, "We'll get rid of that thing and you'll be happy to be alive afterward, Captain."

"You . . . you mean amputation?" asked Barsukov in a shaky voice.

"Of course. There's no other way."

"But, doctor—?" Mariana began, only to be sharply cut off.

"Nurse Remizov, do you have a problem? I will remind you I am the doctor; you are nothing but a nurse."

Unfortunately, this was not Mariana's first encounter with the ill-mannered doctor.

For good or ill, Karl Vlasenko had become a much more self-assertive man than he had been five years ago when, egged on by his domineering father, he had attempted to seduce Mariana. In fact, it seemed as if his inflated ego was in direct proportion to his blatant incompetence.

This was not the first time Mariana had been in conflict with him since they found themselves in the same hospital. She had been taught never to question a doctor's orders, but it was impossible to keep silent in the face of some of Vlasenko's misguided medical decisions. And there had been times Mariana could have sworn he had been intoxicated while on duty. In a couple of incidents, Vlasenko's orders—had they been followed—would have actually killed the patient. She had corrected him once about a wrong dosage of medication, and when he realized his error, he had merely grunted and said, "Of course, that's what I meant. How stupid do you think I am?" He even implied that if she had not caught the error, she would have been to blame for the results.

"Nurse Remizov," said Vlasenko, "I shall be able to take this man into the operating room immediately. Please prep him for surgery." He then spun around and strode away.

Mariana watched, somewhat dazed at the sudden rush of events. Captain Barsukov looked markedly pale.

"I suppose it's no more than I expected," he said. "At least I won't be like some of those peasant lads I command, reduced to pauperhood by such a crippling injury. My family can afford to take care of me, and . . ." All at once he choked on a stifled sob. There was only so much a man, even a hero, could take, and the thought of never being whole again, always the

129

object of pity, was Barsukov's limit.

Mariana took his hand and squeezed it, knowing that was a small comfort. Her eyes strayed toward the retreating figure of Dr. Vlasenko. How could he have so heartlessly dropped his awful pronouncement on the captain, then march away without a word of sympathy? Vlasenko, of all men, should have had *some* sympathy. He suffered with a club foot that made him slightly lame.

The thought of the man's insensitivity distracted Mariana from her patient's needs and made a hot anger rise within her. If only she had finished medical school and become a doctor . . . But even that wouldn't have helped; the Russian medical community would no more have accepted a female doctor than they would a female tsar. Had she finished her training, she probably would have ended up a feldsher or gone to some foreign country to practice.

But this was no time to spout a woman's right to practice medicine. A man's life was at stake. There was no reason for this man to live his life as a cripple, not if he had proper medical care. Mariana had no idea what she could do about it, but she knew she had to do something.

"Captain Barsukov, will you excuse me a moment?" Before waiting for a response, she grabbed Barsukov's chart and hurried away.

She reached Vlasenko at the door to the ward. "Dr. Vlasenko," she said. He turned but the look on his face clearly indicated he didn't appreciate being waylaid in his important work by a mere nurse.

"What is it, Nurse Remizov?"

"Doctor, I thought you'd want to see Captain Barsukov's chart before surgery."

"If I had wanted to see his chart, I would have looked at it," he snapped.

"It is usually routine."

"Are you trying to tell me how to practice medicine?"

"Of course not, it's just that you might not have realized there are X-rays—"

"That's enough, Nurse Remizov! I am about to report you for insubordination. You always were an uppity number with

130

little regard for authority. But those attitudes will be your undoing here."

She had tried to be calm, reasonable, biting down her fury; but seeing that tact would get her nowhere, she let her anger have vent.

"You simply can't doom a man to amputation by a quick, cursory glance!" she retorted.

"And how do you know I didn't examine him when he came in during the night?"

Mariana knew what doctors had been on duty last night, and Vlasenko had not been one of them, but she wasn't going to waste time on such a petty point.

"Had you examined his leg and looked at his X-ray, you would have seen that there is every possibility of saving it. The bones are sound, the circulation is sound. The muscles and ligaments will need suturing and repair, but—"

"That's enough, nurse! Consider yourself on report!"

Mariana shrugged at his toothless threat. What could they do to her, anyway? Send her home? Give her a couple weeks off from her backbreaking, grueling hospital duty?

"Do what you feel you must do, doctor," she said, "and I will do what I must."

"What does that mean?"

"I am going over your head."

"You wouldn't dare!"

In response, she turned and exited, leaving Vlasenko with his mouth gaping open.

The chief of staff was Dr. Vassily Itkinson, a highly competent physician who had been practicing medicine for thirty years. Just prior to the war he had been a professor at St. Petersburg School of Medicine. Mariana knew him on a more personal basis because he was one of the few in the old school of the medical profession who supported the Women's Medical School, and he had taught one of Mariana's classes while she was there. He had encouraged her to stick it out when things got really tough.

Itkinson was in his office, attempting to deal with the mounds of paperwork that passed over his desk each day.

When she knocked on his door, he looked relieved at the interruption.

"I was never happier, Miss Remizov, than when I could roll up my sleeves and work with the sick. Even working with eager students had its many moments of compensation. But this—" He waved a hand over the stacks of paper in front of him. "This is worse than being put out to pasture completely."

"You need another clerk, Doctor," she said, making an attempt at conversation in spite of her haste. "It's a shame for you to be kept from where you could do the most good."

"I've requested one half a dozen times in the last month. I am told another clerk for me would take a man away from the defense of the city. I can't argue with that, now, can I?" He smiled, and his pale blue eyes crinkled to slits. He was a pleasant-looking man, with a thick crop of white hair, a matching moustache, and a thin, lined face.

"But, I am sure," he continued, "you wish to discuss other matters."

"I do, Dr. Itkinson, and it's not an easy subject to broach. However, time may be of the essence, as they say."

"Then forget all the niceties and get right to it. I'll forgive any indelicacy."

"I have a patient who came in during the night with a wounded lower leg. Surgery was postponed until he stabilized, and just a few minutes ago Dr. Vlasenko said he was ready to take Captain Barsukov into surgery for an amputation."

"That's good, isn't it?"

"Dr. Vlasenko didn't look at the man's chart and only glanced briefly at his leg. But it seems very obvious to me that an amputation may not be called for in this case. X-rays verify that the bones are sound, and the circulation is still quite good. I tried to point this out to Dr. Vlasenko—"

Dr. Itkinson's laugh cut her off. "My dear girl, don't you know it's the height of blasphemy to question a doctor's diagnosis?" His tone was laced with sarcasm.

"Even Dr. Vlasenko's?" she ventured boldly.

This brought on a roar of laughter from the doctor. Dabbing tears of amusement from his eyes with a handkerchief,

Itkinson tried to compose himself. "Someday, I believe nurses will receive the respect due them from physicians. They will be able to hold their own in that realm—if not as equals, then at least as vital and indispensable assistants. Unfortunately it is not so now, my dear. Many doctors consider you little better than maids."

"Doctor, I don't ask you to take my opinion in this, because I realize I haven't near the training to make such judgments. All I ask is that you look at the evidence and, as senior physician, lend your input to Dr. Vlasenko. He is fresh out of medical school, himself, and surely would value the expertise of an experienced man."

"You must understand, Mariana, that I simply cannot intercede every time one of my doctor's judgments is in question."

"I'm not asking you to do it *every* time. But this one time, couldn't you speak to him? Think of the poor patient who will have to go through the rest of his life maimed. He is a hero of Russia, a recipient of the Order of Stanislaus."

"You understand, don't you, how desperate we are for physicians over here? Vlasenko isn't completely incompetent. He has saved a few lives, you know."

"Of course," Mariana replied respectfully, although she didn't altogether agree.

"I wanted to make sure you knew—" He stopped and shook his head. "What am I saying? I needed to remind *myself*! If only it were different."

"What about Captain Barsukov?" Mariana asked quietly.

"Let me see his chart."

Within five minutes Mariana and Dr. Itkinson were walking together back to the ward. They were only halfway to Barsukov's bed when Mariana saw that it was empty.

21

Philip Barsukov thought he must surely live a charmed life. A few hours ago he had believed that his life as he knew it was over, that he'd be a cripple forever, an object of pity to all who saw him.

When that boorish young doctor had him whisked away from the room so suddenly, he had almost lost all hope. Nurse Remizov had made him think that perhaps something could be done to save his leg, but then she had disappeared. Philip's protests when the attendants began to wheel him away were ignored. His complete helplessness only deepened his depression.

As he regained consciousness after his surgery, it took him quite a while to get the nerve to look at the foot of his bed. Someone had told him about "phantom pains" after an amputation. He could not trust the pain coursing through his wounded leg, and he was too weak at first to lift his head to look. He tried to ask an attendant, but they were all too busy. A large influx of wounded had just been brought in from a skirmish outside the city. He dozed off still not knowing the truth.

When he awoke an hour later, he was back in his ward. The first person he saw was Mariana Remizov, her smiling face a heavenly vision. She was gazing down at the foot of his bed, and the radiance in her eyes was his first indication that he was blessed above all men. By some miracle, his leg had been spared.

"The last thing I'd wish a pretty woman to notice about me," he murmured, "are my ugly feet."

"They are *both* beautiful to me! I am so happy for you, Captain."

Mariana said nothing about her part in the events surrounding Philip's surgery, and if it had been up to her, she would have had the whole thing kept quiet. But once the hospital rumor-mill learned of it, all chance of that ceased. Barsukov heard the story from Ludmilla.

Vlasenko, furious at Mariana's gall, had immediately ordered Ludmilla to ready the patient for surgery. Since Mariana left without apprising Ludmilla of the situation, she obeyed his orders—not that she was one to argue with a doctor, anyway. The patient was wheeled away while Mariana was still speaking with Itkinson.

Fortunately for Barsukov, an emergency case came into the operating room at the same time he arrived. Vlasenko tried to insist on his claim to the only available room, but even he had to admit that a bleeding chest wound had priority over a leg. Vlasenko was pacing and fuming when Itkinson arrived on the scene. Mariana had stayed behind in the ward. She told Ludmilla she had done all she could, and she was satisfied to leave matters in the chief of staff's capable hands.

Thus, when Barsukov's turn for surgery finally came, Dr. Itkinson held the scalpel. He had convinced Vlasenko that there were some new techniques he wanted to show his novice physicians. Karl was relieved from the case while saving face, but he was still not happy about the situation. No matter how gracious Itkinson had been, it was still galling that a mere nurse—and the Remizov girl as well—had so usurped his authority. He wasn't likely to forget the insult.

After hearing the story, Philip tried to thank Mariana.

"I won't have any of that," she said lightly, chuckling to hide her embarrassment. "Any nurse here would have done the same for you, and for any patient."

"But they didn't. *You* did."

"Nevertheless, I'd prefer not to be singled out."

"I'll say no more, then," Philip replied, "but know that you will always have my undying devotion."

She blushed outright because his words were so earnest, but she tried to lighten the moment with a little laugh. "If I

135

had a ruble for every time I've heard that in this war, I'd be a rich woman by its end."

He smiled, trying to understand her discomfiture. But he couldn't help his gratitude. Because of her he was a whole man. Now he had the right to court a woman, to love her, to take care of her. Hours ago he had nearly given up all hope of marriage and having a family—he was simply not the type of man who could burden a woman with his care. All that had changed because of Mariana.

Perhaps his growing devotion was confused with gratitude—such feelings were certainly not uncommon between nurse and patient. Yet it was not at all difficult to believe his stirring feelings were for other reasons also. She was a lovely woman, with a gentle and lively spirit to match. She was everything he could have wished for in a girl. And when he learned she was also of the nobility—well, it seemed they were fated to be together.

———

While Philip Barsukov's attentions were focusing on his nurse, she was holding him up to scrutiny alongside a brash, impertinent American.

Philip was everything a young woman could want in a man, with his thick, wavy brown hair and matching vivid brown eyes—eyes that had a striking way of mirroring his feelings in an open and honest manner. He had strong, broad shoulders, a gentle voice, and a pleasant sense of humor tempered by sincerity. Mariana's grandmother, Eugenia, would be delighted to make such a match for her granddaughter. And the fact that he was Moscow born and bred would have endeared him even further to the woman. But his social station did not impress Mariana as much as the fact that he seemed to be, above all, a very *nice* man who had somehow escaped the arrogance and self-absorption so common among members of the aristocracy. Mariana enjoyed his company, and over the next few days, she found herself frequently stopping by his bed just to chat.

Daniel and Philip were as different as two men could possibly be. The comparison wasn't fair, yet she couldn't help herself. The initial thrill upon seeing Daniel in Manchuria hadn't diminished. She thought about him a lot, even dreamed about him. But there were problems with Daniel. She feared he could never be as committed to another person as he was to his work. And, if they married, where would they live? Would he give up his home in America so she could be near the home she loved? She had once experienced this same worry with Stephan Kaminsky, to whom she had been engaged back in Katyk. It had worked out in the end, though far differently than she had anticipated. But moving a couple hundred miles from her village was hardly to be compared with moving halfway around the world to an entirely different culture, language . . . everything! Could she do it? Could she ask Daniel to do it?

But other more vital concerns nagged at her. There was, first of all, the matter of faith. Daniel was Protestant and she was Russian Orthodox, but that was not the real issue. She had learned from her mama and papa that there was far more to faith than the name on your church's doorpost. But Mariana wasn't even sure if Daniel truly believed in God. He always skirted the issue and made superficial statements, even as he listened so attentively to her own words of faith and belief. Sometimes he said he believed in God, sometimes he said he didn't know. She wondered if he was merely placating her, avoiding making any firm commitment.

Philip Barsukov, on the other hand, took his faith seriously. After his miraculous salvation from amputation, he had asked to be taken to the hospital chapel, and there had offered his thanks to God with utmost sincerity.

"I know I could have done this just as easily in my bed," he had told Mariana, "but I felt my thanks would be a sweeter offering if some sacrifice were involved." And it had been a sacrifice; the simple action of moving from his bed to a wheelchair had brought on immense pain.

Although Mariana liked Philip a great deal, she realized that something was missing. But, she had only known the man a few days, after all. Perhaps, given time, the intensity she sought, the passion, would grow. She was no child who believed "falling in love" with a man was everything. She knew that there was more to a relationship between a man and a woman than physical attraction. Yet she could not abandon the feeling that passion should be at least *part* of such a relationship.

The majority of marriages, however, were arranged without the slightest consideration of passion, and they turned out adequately. But Mariana wasn't sure she was willing to settle for only *adequate*. She longed for the kind of marriage Anna and Sergei had. Theirs was special. They seemed to know what the other was thinking and feeling; they talked like friends; and once or twice Mariana had chanced to see them kiss like young lovers. But perhaps their love was just *too* special to be repeated. Maybe adequate was the best a woman could hope for.

And Daniel Trent's reappearance in her life only added to her confusion. She had decided to give Daniel another chance—he had seemed different after all. But a relationship with someone like Philip would be much safer, more secure. Or would it just be boring?

Mariana sighed. Maybe spinsterhood wasn't such a bad thing after all. She wouldn't have to be plagued with all this inner turmoil. How simple her life would be then. How . . . lonely.

A week after Philip's surgery, he called her to his bedside. "They will be moving me today to a less critical ward."

She nodded. It was both good news and bad.

"I probably won't be seeing as much of you, Mariana, but I hope you will not forget me."

"I won't, Philip."

"Will you take this? It is a token of my gratitude—and also a sign of my hope that the friendship we have found here will not end with this war, but will go on for . . . a very long time."

He removed a chain from around his neck and held it out to her. On it was a silver cross, edged in a delicate filigree with a beautiful oval-shaped opal in the center.

"My sister gave this to me when I left for the war. It's all I have with me of any value except for my sword. It isn't much, as I said, only a mere token—"

"Philip, I couldn't take something so special. How would your sister feel?"

His wide, expressive mouth parted in a smile. "She gave it to me precisely so that I would have something to give a beautiful nurse who might chance to save my life."

"Oh, Philip, I'm not that gullible."

"Well, perhaps she never *said* as much, but I know my sister. She is a romantic; knowing the final destination of her cross would make her ecstatic."

"I don't know, Philip . . ."

"Please!" His smile was replaced with deep entreaty. He took her hand and laid the cross in it, continuing to hold her hand for a moment. "I have not known you long, Mariana, but you have become very special to me. I would not want you to forget me."

"I truly won't," she promised.

"Take this anyway. Who knows—someday it may find its way back into my family." He winked and grinned again.

She decided light banter was the best way to counter such a statement. "Watch what you say, Prince Barsukov. You may find yourself in deeper than you wish."

He clutched his hands theatrically to his heart and looked heavenward. "Oh, by the saints, if only it could be true!"

Mariana laughed, he joined in, and that was all that was said of the matter. She took the cross and slipped it around her neck. The tenderness of the moment was marred only by a fleeting thought of Daniel.

22

Daniel and Yin Chu made it to Louisa Bay to the north of Port Arthur. They hooked up with a blockade runner named Shen Kuo-hwa who reluctantly—and expensively—agreed to take them with him on the perilous five-mile overland trek to the port. Every mile they flirted with discovery by Japanese patrols, but Shen knew his business well and managed to get them to the port safely, along with his precious cargo of black market merchandise.

They were helped by the fact that the Japanese were some-what distracted by a major skirmish being waged twelve miles north of Port Arthur, and miles to the east of where Daniel and his party would pass. What they did not know was that even as they neared the town, the Japanese General Nogi had finally broken through Port Arthur's first line of defense and had pushed the Russian troops to within six miles of the town. The Russians had been fighting frantically to maintain that position.

As they neared Port Arthur, Daniel thought the sounds of artillery and gunfire were awfully close. He didn't realize as he slipped into the city with Yin Chu and Shen, who paid a large bribe to a guard to allow them entry, that Fock's troops had been ordered to withdraw to the city. He had no idea that the siege of Port Arthur had begun in earnest.

But Daniel's biggest worry at the moment was finding lodging and eluding the many Russian guards posted around the city. Shen had a prearranged setup with the guard he had bribed—after all, it was to everyone's advantage for goods to continue to get into the city. But there was no reason for the

Russians to welcome an unauthorized newspaper correspondent illegally entering the city. Among other things, he was just another mouth to feed, and that was the last thing Port Arthur needed.

About an hour of daylight remained. Daniel sent Yin Chu in search of lodgings among the Chinese locals, and he set out to investigate a source of his own. He wandered into the nearly deserted Japanese section of town. He remembered this street from his stay in Port Arthur at the beginning of the war. Several Japanese barbers had shops here, and he had often enjoyed their expert services. Daniel rubbed the four-day stubble on his face and wished they hadn't been forced to abandon their businesses and leave the city.

It was rather eerie here now and he hastened his pace, all at once feeling far too obvious. He rounded a corner and almost collided with a big burly Cossack sentry.

"What's your business here?" barked the sentry.

Daniel swallowed his trepidation, relying on his fine ability to think on his feet. "I was just hoping to get a shave." For added emphasis he scraped his hand over the sandpaper on his face.

"Where have you been to get a growth like that?"

"The last shave I got was from a Chinese barber over on Broad Street, and he nearly slit my throat. Thought I'd try growing a beard after that, but it's starting to drive me crazy."

"What's your business in Port Arthur?"

"I'm a clerk at the Colfax Bank and Trust Company."

"They are still operating?"

"We closed down a month ago and most of the staff evacuated to Mukden, but I was asked to remain as caretaker. We couldn't get all of our important papers out, you know. They've doubled my salary, so how could I refuse, eh?"

"Well, this area is off limits."

Daniel sighed as if greatly disappointed. "Those Japanese had some wonderful barbers."

The Cossack fingered his own excellent growth of thick, black beard, then started walking, indicating that Daniel should follow. Daniel obeyed; it would not have been healthy to do otherwise. He had no idea if he was under arrest or not.

The Cossack ducked inside one of the shops and Daniel entered behind him. He gaped in utter confusion as the large man set his rifle against the wall and stripped off his uniform jacket. Then, nudging Daniel into one of the barber chairs, he actually prepared to shave him.

After his shave, Daniel paid the Cossack a ruble for his services. It was the best shave he'd ever had, and Daniel had been able to extract valuable information from the erstwhile barber. Much to his chagrin, he learned not only that Stoessel was still in command of the port, but also of the reversals of the last couple of days. The Russians had finally been forced to retreat within the main defensive perimeter of the fortress. Daniel was unable to learn other vital details, such as the disposition of the Russian fleet, without giving away the fact that he had just arrived illegally in the town. But the Cossack revealed enough for Daniel to know he had come to Port Arthur at its most perilous hour.

When he met Yin Chu at a prearranged rendezvous spot, Daniel was told he had a place to stay in a Chinese inn—located in a part of town he knew to be a squalid slum. Not ready to turn in for the night, especially with such meager prospects before him, Daniel headed once more for the destination that his encounter with the Cossack "barber" had delayed.

A single light burned from the window of the office of the Port Arthur newspaper, *Novy Krai*. He knew many of the staff and was on especially good terms with one of the reporters, Eduard Nojine. He didn't want to place his friend in jeopardy with the authorities by asking Nojine to harbor him, but Daniel saw no reason not to contact him for information. Nojine might have some idea about where Daniel might locate Mariana. Finding her was his main objective, but it was quite possible Nojine would welcome Daniel's services on the paper, if his work could be done discreetly. For one thing, Daniel was fresh from the "outside world" and had much news he was certain even the authorities didn't have. He was even considering the possibility of using this information to entice the military leaders to allow him to stay legally in the port. First, however, he wanted to confer with Nojine to assure his bargaining position.

Nojine was working late, as Daniel had hoped. His initial shock at the unexpected sight of his American friend was quickly followed by an exuberant Russian embrace.

"My word! You are flesh and blood. For a moment I wondered." The reporter ushered Daniel into the office and quickly closed the door. "What on earth are you doing here?"

"An *affaire d'amour*," Daniel said coyly.

"What? Not you, Trent, the hardheaded, hardhearted American correspondent?"

"I think I deserve to be taken more seriously than that," said Daniel with mock affront. "I risked my neck to get here." For the next twenty minutes Daniel gave a brief account of his trip.

"I won't deny your dedication, my friend," Nojine said when Daniel finished. "It was pure insanity—that proves it must be love, eh? So, why are you here and not in the arms of your beautiful lover—at least, I must assume she is beautiful, to make you perform such a crazy stunt."

"I was hoping you could help me find her. It shouldn't be too difficult since she is a Red Cross nurse."

"Well, there are a dozen hospitals in operation—but let me see if I can find the names of the Red Cross hospitals." He turned to a file cabinet, talking as he searched in one of the drawers. "Do you need a place to stay?"

"I've got a place north of the quarry, in Chinese town—"

"Ugh! Trent, surely we can find you something better than that."

"Is your standing with the authorities so secure you could take such a risk?"

Nojine laughed, a low rumble that seemed out of place from the rather frail-looking man. "Stoessel just found out about a message I smuggled out of here to a friend in Chefu telling him to notify the tsar of the absolute necessity of relieving Stoessel of command. You should have heard Stoessel rant and rave at me, calling me—and all reporters—everything from liars to agents of the enemy. I don't doubt he'd be thrilled to find a reason for tossing me into jail."

"All the more reason for us to avoid each other."

"Trent, you aren't going to waste this opportunity of a lifetime just on love, are you? We've got to get the truth out. We can't—" He stopped suddenly, yanking a file from the drawer. "Ah, here it is!" Shuffling through the file, he withdrew a single page. "There you are, a list of all the hospitals. There are only four Red Cross hospitals, so that should help your search. First thing in the morning—"

"Are you kidding! The night is still young. I haven't traveled hundreds of miles through enemy lines and monsoons to wait another minute if I can help it."

"All right, let's go. I'm always for romance."

"Are you sure you want to accompany me? I mean, with Stoessel out to get you and all?"

"Wouldn't miss it for anything."

Daniel, full of confidence, tried not to think too much about things like love and romance. He gave little thought to the implication of his impulsive visit and the risks involved. It never occurred to him that Mariana might read too much into it. He figured she'd be thrilled to see him, they'd have a good time together, and . . . well, what more did there have to be to it?

His plans simply did not take into account the feelings of a young woman, nor the explosive milieu of war and siege.

23

Daniel found Mariana's boardinghouse that night, but the place was already locked and shuttered. A nurse on the night shift at the hospital had given him the address and informed him that Mariana was scheduled to be at work at seven in the morning.

He returned to his room at the inn, slept uneasily in a bed he was sure was lice-infested, and seriously considered No-jine's offer of a place to stay, risk or not. He rose while dawn was making its first mark on the Manchurian skyline. Maybe he could intercept Mariana before she started work.

———

As the sun rose over Port Arthur, General Nogi was giving a final inspection to his half dozen land-based guns. These six and 4.7 inch guns, the heaviest of the four hundred guns in his arsenal, could spit fatal shells toward their target from a long distance.

The ground gained by his army in the last few days had placed him within striking distance. He might not be able to capture Russian Port Arthur in one day, as they had defeated Chinese Port Arthur a few years earlier, but he was confident in his present army. His troops had already proven themselves successful against the great Russian bear.

The port's three lines of defense, however, were nothing to make light of. The Old Town was protected by an ancient Chinese wall a thousand yards from the town center, and the wall was reinforced by a series of formidable forts. In the hills to the northeast and northwest, the Russians had liberally fortified their positions with heavy guns. Especially fortified was the peak known as 203 Metre Hill which overlooked all of Port Arthur, including the harbor.

The Russians could not afford to lose this important hill—its loss would not only spell peril for the town, but it would also jeopardize the vitally important Russian fleet still anchored in the harbor.

Nogi was a venerated veteran and hero of Japan. Nevertheless, he was under great pressure to dispatch this obstacle quickly. Japanese success thus far had come only at the expense of enormous losses in manpower, and for the invasion of Liaoyang in the north to commence, the army required reinforcements from Nogi's troops. He didn't have time for a long, drawn-out siege. But more than that, Nogi's masters in Tokyo demanded victory simply to save face. The Russians had usurped the Liaotung Peninsula, and all of Manchuria for that matter, as if the Japanese were nothing. Now the Nippon Empire must prove otherwise.

Thus, as the rising sun crested the tall hills, Nogi gave the order he had been anxious to deliver for many days. The bombardment of Port Arthur was to begin.

———

Daniel realized it was Sunday only when he heard a church bell peal in the distance. A streak of light in the west outlined the 203 Metre Hill. It looked rather picturesque, with the ringing bells adding to the serenity of the morning.

Several nurses were leaving the boardinghouse as he approached.

"Has Mariana Remizov left yet?" he asked one.

"I don't know—"

"Oh, yes," answered another. "I saw her leave a few minutes ago. She can't be too far away."

Daniel listened no more but took off immediately toward the hospital. Because it would be too awkward to talk to Mariana at work, he jogged down the street, hoping to catch her before she reached the hospital.

Just then the first of the enemy's guns blasted in the still morning air. Daniel had been close enough to war zones to realize this was not distant battle. The city itself was being shelled.

The ground under his feet shook with the explosion. Behind him, he heard the frightened screams of the nurses at the boardinghouse, and he glanced back. They were unharmed; the blast had been several streets away.

"You'd better take cover inside," he called to the nurses. "Is there a cellar in there?"

"Yes, but we're expected at the hospital."

Another blast rent the air, then another and another. Daniel could see scattered puffs of black smoke rising in the sky.

"I think they'll understand. No one's going to expect you to be out in this—"

Suddenly it struck him—Mariana might be out in the open right now! Would there be some decent shelter for her to retreat to, or just the flimsy buildings that lined the street?

Daniel began to run. It was a good fifteen-minute walk to the hospital from the boardinghouse. Mariana might make it, but would even the hospital be safe? Those big Japanese guns would hardly be able to discern the Red Cross flag waving from its rooftop.

The artillery blasts came in rapid succession. All around Daniel, soldiers scurried to their posts and civilians raced this way and that—some in sheer panic, some in search of cover. Unfortunately, the inept Stoessel had forbidden the building of bomb shelters, probably in a vain attempt to seduce the citizenry into believing they were not in any danger. In an ironic way, he had been successful. The city had been braced for months for just such an attack, yet as time went by, people began to think it was all just idle talk. They were convinced the Japanese would be ousted from the Liaotung Peninsula long before such an attack could ever happen.

The shocked screams of people in the street mingled with curses at the government in general and General Stoessel in particular. But Daniel didn't care about any of that for the moment. Later, he'd do his best to expose the bungling of the siege; for now his only concern was Mariana.

Then he saw her—at least he saw a nurse dive into a narrow alley as a shell exploded a hundred feet ahead of her. Ignoring the rumbling of the earth under him and the dizzying rattling in his ears, Daniel made for the alley nearly tripping over his own feet as he came to a screeching halt next to the nurse.

She turned wide eyes toward him, and he realized his quest had been rewarded.

He gave Mariana a lopsided grin. "We meet again, Miss Remizov. What a pleasure!"

"Daniel?" Then she laughed. "I wasn't sure until I heard your voice. You're rather a blur—I've lost my glasses. What in the world are you doing here?"

"I came to see you."

"Me?"

Another shell exploded, closer this time. Mariana barely stifled a scream as she clamped her hands over her ears. Even Daniel had to suppress his own cry of fear.

147

"Daniel, you should never have come here." Mariana's voice trembled over the words. "But . . . but I am glad to see you. That is, I would be if I could see."

"When did you lose your glasses?"

"Just a few moments ago when I ran in here."

"Stay put. I'll look for them."

Daniel searched in the alley to no avail, then he cautiously moved out into the street. Sunlight glinting off the lenses led him to the eyeglasses, lying a few feet from the opening of the alley. He had just closed his hand around them when another shell burst a mere sixty feet away. The impact sent him sprawling, and he nearly lost his own spectacles.

"Daniel!"

Amid the dust and flying rubble, he scrambled back into the alley, then triumphantly held out her glasses.

"Oh, Daniel! I'm so frightened." Tears seeped from the corners of her eyes.

Her hands were trembling, and Daniel slipped the glasses on her face. Then he placed a calming arm around her.

"It's okay, Mariana." He was scared himself but he would never admit it freely.

Mariana sniffed and dabbed at the tears beneath her lenses.

A shell ripped a hole in the ground in the middle of the street, and the wall of the building they were leaning against shook. Rubble and shrapnel sliced at them; only by pressing their bodies against the brick wall of the building did they escape serious injury. Nevertheless a piece of wood ripped through Daniel's shirt-sleeve, gashing his arm. Across the street, the building that had been hit a few moments ago burst into flames.

"We really ought to get out of here," Daniel said with forced calm. "How far is it to the hospital?"

"Two blocks."

"Maybe there's a cellar nearby—"

"They're going to need me at the hospital."

"You'll get to the hospital soon enough. Better you get there in one piece, rather than on a stretcher."

"But—"

"And I thought I was crazy." He rolled his eyes, but the dust and grime on his glasses hid the motion. "Come on. The building next to us seems to be holding up all right. Maybe there's a cellar inside."

Without waiting for an argument, he grabbed her hand and started toward the street. Mariana followed without resistance.

They were about to make the sharp right at the front of the building when a shell burst dead center in the roof. The entire front of the building shattered, sending bits of glass, wood, mortar, and broken bricks everywhere. Mariana and Daniel were knocked off their feet and thrown about two yards back into the alley. It was their closest call yet. Pieces of roofing sailed down on them, one nicking Daniel in the head, another bruising Mariana's shoulder. But the wall adjacent to the alley held and provided some protection—otherwise both he and Mariana might have been killed, crushed by the weight of the wall or impaled by shrapnel.

Crouching on the ground, pressed for dear life against the wall, they did not move for several minutes. Mariana clung to Daniel, shaking and weeping. Daniel was shaking too, completely unable to maintain his courageous facade, and he inwardly cursed the tears that mingled freely with his sweat.

The bombing kept up relentlessly. Daniel had been in dangerous situations before, but this was completely unhinging. Bombs were falling all around them. It wouldn't have been so bad if he had been alone, but the weight of the responsibility he felt for Mariana made the fear suffocating. He felt so inadequate, so puny. What could he do? He was great at talking big, but *talk* wasn't going to stop one of those Japanese bombs from snuffing out their lives.

The ground rumbled with another blast. Though the actual blast was many feet away, the wall at their backs shook, and loose bricks toppled down on them.

"We gotta get out of here!" Daniel grabbed Mariana's hand and they tried to make a run for it.

A shell ripped up the street directly ahead of them, then another at their rear. They were trapped, and the brick wall

149

was crumbling more with every blast. There was no place safe to hide.

Covering her ears, Mariana buried her head against Daniel. "Why won't it stop?"

The weight of fear and responsibility nearly crushed Daniel as he looked wildly around for a way of escape. "Oh, God, help us!" he cried, hardly knowing what he was saying.

When a short lull came in the shelling, Daniel propelled Mariana toward the street but another explosion stopped him. He turned in the opposite direction. Maybe the alley went through. He tried not to think that if it didn't, they could easily be trapped.

Then he saw the door in the side of the building.

He headed toward it, Mariana following as if in a trance. Daniel tried the doorknob. It was locked, but it was an old lock, and the wood encasing the door appeared rotten. A couple of hard kicks and a ram with his shoulder splintered the wood so the door could be opened. A flight of stairs leading down greeted them.

"A cellar!" Daniel exclaimed.

The cellar was dark, and a thick shroud of cobwebs indicated that it hadn't been used for a long time, but it represented salvation to Daniel and Mariana. They huddled together in its black recesses and tried to regain their composure—not an easy matter with explosions still echoing outside and unseen things inside the building rattling and crashing.

After a few more minutes they noticed the silence. Utter quiet, like the silence of a tomb.

24

Mariana's voice, though frail and shaky, was like a light in the nearly complete blackness that surrounded them.

"Is . . . is it over?"

"For now."

"There'll be more?"

Daniel couldn't see Mariana's face, but he heard the fear in her voice.

"You better brace yourself." Daniel tried to be gentle in his prediction. "It could go on for the duration of the siege."

"I was never more frightened in my life." She paused. Daniel didn't like the darkness filling up the void and was relieved when Mariana continued. "Daniel, I really appreciate your praying for us."

"Praying? Me?"

"Yes, back there in the alley."

"Oh . . . I forgot about that."

"I'm glad someone had the presence of mind to do it. I hate to admit it, but I was so frightened I completely forgot to pray."

"I don't know what's worse, to forget when you're in trouble; or to only remember when you're in trouble." The irony so disgusted him that he spoke the words before he realized what he was saying.

"What do you mean?"

Suddenly Daniel realized he'd said too much. But so what? Wasn't it better that she know it all, know just what kind of sorry excuse for a man he was? Why lead her on anymore? She had seen him shake and cry during the bombing, too. If he lost her . . . well, maybe he didn't deserve someone like Mariana, anyway.

"Mariana, don't go thinking the wrong thing just because you heard me pray. I haven't told you everything about when my father died. I've been too ashamed of myself to do that. But what's the use? You'll find out what I'm really like sooner or later—all I have to do is get stuck in another shelling, and the real me will be revealed."

"Would you like to tell me about it now? I promise I'll try not to judge you."

"No, you wouldn't—and that would be worse yet. I don't deserve anyone like you."

"Daniel, what happened back in America?"

"I really went down into the dumps when my father died. I was heartsick and confused, and so empty because I hadn't had a chance to finish things with him, to say goodbye. Then I thought of you and the things you used to say about your faith. Believe it or not, I was listening back then, even if I seemed to ignore it."

"I knew you were." He could hear the smile in her voice. "I hoped it would come back to you when the time was right."

"I started going to church and reading a Bible. It all began to make sense." A part of Daniel's heart stirred as he recalled those first days as he set out to discover the truth. "The emptiness inside me began to fill up. Then I made the mistake of—I don't know, second-guessing God. I decided He'd want me to quit the newspaper and work in the family business as my father wanted. I told you how miserable I was. I started questioning God again. I truly wanted to know what this 'faith' business was all about. I came to the point where I couldn't take Trent Corporation another minute. I told God to do something—I guess that was pretty cocky of me, huh? Trying to tell God what to do."

Mariana chuckled, then said without rancor, "It sounds just like you, come to think of it."

"Mariana, He did do something!" His eyes danced as he remembered that day in his dreary office. "That's when I found the letter from my father. I think it was a real miracle. Maybe not like Moses and the burning bush, but the timing was too incredible not to have been from God."

"It does sound that way. But, Daniel, I still don't see what the problem is—it's so exciting what happened to you. Why didn't you want to tell me?"

He was glad at that moment for the darkness. It made his terrible confession easier.

"I stopped being miserable."

"I still don't understand."

"I finally had my father's approval, and I got my job back at the *Register*. It was great to be back to work—strikes, scandal, crooked elections—I couldn't have been happier. So happy, I forgot everything I'd been through to get there." He turned away, as if even the black cellar wasn't enough to hide his shame. "Don't you see, Mariana? I'm the classic 'fair-weather' friend. God helped me through a hard time and when it was over, I just went back to business as usual. Didn't hardly think of Him at all until a few minutes ago and I needed help again. So, there you go; you know it all now. And I wouldn't blame you if you told me to take a hike."

"Poor, dear, Daniel!" Mariana found his hand in the dark. She clasped it reassuringly in hers. "Why should I think any less of you? Because you are human? All I can see is that in your heart you are seeking God—"

"At least when the going gets tough."

"What better time to seek Him?"

"Shouldn't I be religious all the time? You are—that is, you talk about God naturally, and I'll bet you think about Him all the time, even when you feel great."

"Not *all* the time. I can't believe anyone does. But, Daniel, God isn't looking at how often we think about Him, or go to church, or read our Bibles. He's not up there with a big board keeping tally of the *things* we do for Him. I believe all God looks at is our *hearts*."

"But I don't know what my heart is like. Maybe it's rotten."

"Why do you think that? Because you haven't been going to church or praying?"

Daniel didn't answer.

"I know that I couldn't care for you the way I do if your heart were rotten," she said quietly. "Daniel, you didn't want

153

to tell me this secret about yourself because you were ashamed, you saw it as horrible. But I think it's wonderful. You're seeking God—that's what He wants of us more than anything. So, you stumbled a bit, or got sidetracked. The horrible thing would be for you to let that keep you from continuing on. Following Christ isn't a smooth, easy road. He knows that and isn't going to bar your way if you mess up occasionally, as long as you truly want to keep going."

"That's good news, because I'm apt to mess up a lot."

"I make mistakes, too, but we can help each other."

They fell quiet. Daniel couldn't believe that he had bared his heart, with all its gaping holes, and Mariana still accepted him. It gave him courage to reveal what else was troubling him.

"Mariana, what you say is fine. And from what I've learned about God, I do believe He's that way. But I'm still afraid of making a commitment then fumbling it. I'd lose respect for myself if that happened again."

"I understand, Daniel—at least I think I do."

"Well, I'm glad it's all out. I don't want any more deception between us. Where do we go from here?"

"I think we ought to see what's happening outside."

He laughed. He hadn't meant something so literal, but he was relieved to take a break from such deep realms. He could tell by her responding chuckle that she understood.

Still gripping each other's hands, they climbed out of the cellar into the brightness of the morning sun. Outside, the streets were busy with the activity of clean-up. A fire wagon raced down the street toward the burning building. Soldiers were already at the scene of the fire, attempting to beat it down with old blankets or whatever they had at hand. Other soldiers and civilians were sorting through rubble to insure no one was trapped.

Smoke and dust clogged the air, but Daniel felt as if he could breathe better than he had in years. Talking about his inadequacy had somehow made it more bearable. And at last he thought something actually could be done about it. He still wasn't sure what. Whatever he did would be a big step, and he wanted to be certain, no matter what Mariana said about how forgiving God was, that he didn't compound his previous mistake by repeating it.

25

The shelling of Port Arthur continued for the rest of the month. Not a day passed without the persistent, shattering blasts. They made Mariana's head throb, and even in her sleep—when she could sleep—the steady, jarring cadence of artillery continued in her dreams.

Even if the bombing did let up at night, there were the nightmares to contend with. Often, in them she'd be running down a street just as she had done on that first day of shelling. Bombs would dog her every step, and if she stopped, the inevitable happened. Even worse, a bomb would strike Daniel. Once in one of her horrible dreams, she was sleeping in her bed when a huge explosion woke her and she jerked upright. At that very moment a pair of wire-rimmed glasses—Daniel's glasses—flew through the air and landed in her lap. The lenses were shattered. She awoke trembling, even more weary than before.

The entire city was on edge. She could see it in the eyes of people she met on the street or at work. They were haunted by nightmares, too. If General Nogi would have asked any one of them to surrender, they probably would have in a heartbeat. And as if to further demoralize them, on August tenth, by order of the viceroy, the fleet departed the harbor for the safer haven of Vladivostok. En route, they were attacked, losing or sustaining severe damage to five battleships, a cruiser, and three destroyers. The port could no longer look toward the Russian fleet for salvation.

According to the soldiers who came into the hospital, Nogi sent Stoessel a request for surrender. Stoessel was insulted and refused to send a reply. Smirnoff insisted that some response must be made, if only for the sake of military etiquette. Again, internal strife reigned in the high command. With Russian refusal to respond, the Japanese redoubled their attack on the city.

As August wore into September, the numbers of wounded pouring into the hospital continued without letup. The staff worked on sheer nerve and grit. Food shortage was not yet a severe problem, but the quality of food had diminished significantly. Horseflesh had been fastidiously refused at the beginning of the siege, but now it was common practice to butcher any horse killed by gunfire. Fresh foods—milk, butter, eggs—were most missed, and cases of scurvy and dysentery began to mount almost as high as battle wounds. When the Japanese got control of the main water supply, reducing the residents to using wells out of fear the supply would be poisoned, bathing and doing laundry became luxuries. None of this made hospital work any easier. Water usage was limited, even in the hospitals. Officers' wives living at the port were put to work making bandages out of petticoats and other expendable items because medical supplies were not being replenished.

Mariana had heard what a siege would be like, and none of the talk was pleasant. As many people were expected to die of starvation and disease as from the battle itself. Sometimes besieged people went insane; there had already been a couple of suicides. She wondered every day if she could take it, if she had the courage to withstand deprivation, fear, and perhaps even hopelessness. When she visited Philip in his new ward, he tried to encourage her.

"You must depend on your faith, Mariana."

"I'm at the point that I wonder if I can do even that." She let out a troubled breath. "Sometimes it's hard to remember, or even to find God in all this mayhem and death. Surely you have felt that at times out on the battlefield."

He shook his head, truly bemused by what she was expressing.

"Don't you ever have questions about God, Philip? Aren't you ever confused?"

"Question God, Mariana? I wouldn't dream of doing that."

"I wish I could be so stalwart. But . . ." She shrugged to complete her unspoken thought. In truth, she didn't know what to say. Philip's firm assurance was somehow unsettling, perhaps because it made her feel weaker than ever. But even her papa Sergei questioned God and was confused at times.

"Mariana, I welcome you to lean on me," he told her. "At least you have work to do—that will keep you going. I only hope I can get back into the field before long. Lying here is already driving me mad; I shudder to think what a month more of siege will do."

"I hate to think of you going back." This would always be one of the hardest parts of being a war nurse—mending your patients only to watch them face danger again. And it was even worse when she had come to have a special concern for a particular patient. "But your leg is healing wonderfully." Her tone lacked essential enthusiasm.

"I want to go back, Mariana, you must understand. I have to do my duty."

She nodded, but she didn't understand at all. If possible, she'd have a doctor write an order sending Philip home. But that was a hopeless idea, especially since Karl Vlasenko was his doctor. Karl would never do *her* a favor. He seemed to take delight in returning his patients to their units—probably because so few of them lived to do so.

During Mariana's conversation with Philip, Daniel appeared in the ward. She had taken a break to visit Philip, and she was not at her usual station. Obviously Daniel had gone to some lengths to locate her. Since the day of that first shelling, they had seen each other half a dozen times, but usually they met at her boardinghouse where they would be close to the cellar in case of bombing. Those meetings had been easygoing, and usually short, because Mariana had so little time for a social life. She hadn't seen Daniel at all for three days.

"Is something wrong?" she asked, fearing the worst.

"No, I just thought that the only way I would get to see you was to come here. Do you ever quit working?"

"I'm taking a short break now, visiting—" She stopped, flustered, hoping neither man noticed. She tried to be gracious as she remembered to make introductions.

"Ah, an American," said Philip as he and Daniel shook hands. "You are the first American I have ever met."

"Really? I would have thought a man of your social standing, Prince Barsukov, would have had more exposure."

"I am from Moscow. We do not look out upon the rest of the world as much as they do in St. Petersburg. Being in the army also keeps me fairly insulated."

"Well, Moscow is a grand city," said Daniel. "I spent several days there when I lived in Russia a few years ago. I don't think I have ever seen anything quite as awesome as the Kremlin or Red Square."

They exchanged a bit of polite chitchat, and Mariana was somewhat taken aback at how casually and easily the two conversed, at first about Russia, then about the war. Mariana felt silly that she had been so nervous when Daniel had appeared unexpectedly. Maybe she was making too much of this after all. Philip and Daniel were both her friends, and certainly that shouldn't bother them. She had made no commitments to either. This was hardly like the volatile confrontation between Stephan and Daniel. Stephan could hardly be blamed for his reaction. They had talked of marriage and were unofficially engaged. She had not talked or even hinted with Daniel or with Philip about anything as serious as matrimony.

They were just friends.

She supposed her awkwardness came from the fact that she had *thought* about the subject of marriage in relation to both Daniel and Philip. But why was she thrust in the middle of two such choices again? Four years ago it hadn't turned out so well. Couldn't she just have Daniel and Philip for friends? Did she have to make a choice?

Mariana cast a covert glance at the two men and realized suddenly that friendship was not what she wanted. An odd thought flitted into her mind, seemingly of its own accord: *She was going to marry one of these men*. She blushed as if they could read her mind.

"See what I mean?" Philip was saying. "She gets embarrassed every time I bring up the subject."

"What?" Mariana exclaimed, turning even redder in her confusion. She wished she hadn't let her mind wander so.

"Mariana," said Daniel, "I didn't know you were such a hero. You said nothing to me about saving his leg."

"I'm not surprised," Philip said.

"Oh that." Mariana shrugged. "It was merely in the line of duty. I keep trying to tell him."

"Do you mind if I write a story on the incident?"

"Oh, Daniel," Mariana groaned.

"At least I asked first." Daniel flashed a disarming grin.

"I'll give my consent if Philip gives his, only you can't mention my name—it just isn't right to single out medical personnel in that way."

"Agreed. How about it, Philip?"

"I suppose I am just as reluctant as Mariana. All the men out there on the front lines are heroes."

"I can't tell *all* their stories. But, believe me, I am trying. Just one or two stories, however, will go a long way to garner Western support for your nation. You owe it to your country, Philip, you truly do."

"Put that way, how can I refuse? But you must make it clear that such acts are not isolated incidents. The Russian soldier is as courageous as a lion."

"Have no fear, I'll put just the right spin on it—"

"Spin?"

"You know, angle, slant. Anyway, it'll be perfect."

"Don't mind his modesty, Philip," Mariana said coyly. "Whatever he says, he is a good writer."

"Thank you, miss, it's a pleasure to finally hear that from you," responded Daniel with a chivalrous bow. Daniel and Mariana exchanged a brief glance, full of the kind of private things that go with a friendship that has spanned years. "And now, I should let you get back to your work," Daniel said to Mariana.

"As I said, I'm on a break. Let me walk you out, at least."

The two men bid each other a good day, Daniel promising to return tomorrow to hear more of Philip's story. Then Daniel and Mariana left the ward together.

"Mariana, will I ever get to see much of you?" Daniel asked.

"I'm so sorry you went to all the trouble to come here," Mariana replied as they walked through the crowded hospital corridors. "Many nights I don't even bother to go home to sleep. They've set up some cots in a little room for us. Since the shelling began, we've been swamped. They've opened up several more hospitals—well, hotels, large houses and such. My own boardinghouse may even be turned into a hospital; most of the residents are nurses and half the time our beds are empty because we're working."

"Is it good to work so much?"

Mariana shrugged. "What choice is there?"

"How are you holding up?"

Mariana was caught a bit off guard by the utter sincerity and concern in Daniel's question.

"It's sweet of you to care, Daniel."

"I do care about you, Mariana. That's why I risked my neck to come here."

"And I am ignoring you."

"I almost wish I could get wounded and receive all the attention Captain Barsukov seems to be getting."

"Don't even think it, Daniel! That's no way to get attention." Mariana hated to admit it, but she was a little pleased at the hint of jealousy in Daniel's tone.

"Barsukov seems like a nice fellow, though. Too bad about his leg."

"He is a nice man. And his leg is nearly healed. I think he will be released soon."

"Good."

"What?"

"I mean, good that he's better." Daniel countered. "I suppose they'll put him back on the line."

"I hate to even think about it." Mariana quickly changed the subject. "What have you been doing since I last saw you, Daniel? I know you can't have been idle, even if you must be in hiding."

"It doesn't bother you that I'd use my time here to work, besides seeing you?"

"Of course not. I couldn't be absorbed in my own work and yet expect you to wait around for me. At any rate, I know that would be asking too much of you—to pass up what I am sure is a prime opportunity for reporting."

"There are some dandy stories itching to be told here," Daniel replied with enthusiasm. "The problem is getting them out. Stoessel has declared war on all correspondents, so there's little hope of aid from that quarter. I've heard rumors he's threatening to close down *Novy Krai*, saying the enemy gets copies too easily, that they know better than he does what's going on inside Port Arthur. That may be true to an extent, but it's not the newspaper's fault that Stoessel's security is so poor around here. The citizens of Port Arthur have a right to know what's going on."

"But if it jeopardizes people, and our men—"

"It's hardly a significant effect."

"If even *one* person is hurt because of leaked information. . . ?"

"Hey, whose side are you on, anyway?"

"I'm on the side of the wounded and suffering men, Daniel," Mariana replied curtly. "There are so many, and sometimes I don't know how I'll be able to stand the arrival of another single one."

"I guess there is another perspective besides mine," Daniel conceded.

They paused in their walking as Mariana tried to compose herself. For a moment she thought he was about to embrace her, but then he drew back. Mariana found herself disappointed—she desperately needed the comfort of a tender hug. They continued walking and soon reached the front door of the hospital.

Daniel paused at the doorway. "Mariana, take the evening off tonight and spend some time with me. You need to get away from here for a while."

For a brief moment Mariana was tempted. The misery she encountered every day, the blood, the stench, the hopeless death—it was beginning to get to her, wearing her down, sapping the strength that had so astonished her when she had first arrived in Manchuria. Even her faith was hard-pressed to help her face each new day. But Mariana managed a halfhearted smile—it wouldn't help to worry Daniel. "So does everyone else around here," she answered, her voice sounding a lot tougher than she felt inside. "But I'm sure we'll be given time off soon. When that happens, you'll be the first person I call."

"Mariana—" But he stopped, and she never would know what he was about to say. He just took her hand, squeezed it, and offered her the encouragement of an especially endearing smile.

26

Daniel had plenty to keep him occupied when he couldn't be with Mariana, which seemed to be most of the time. His presence in Port Arthur might have given the city another mouth to feed, but it also provided another strong back. Many of the male civilians were conscripted into service by performing duties that would free up soldiers for the battle lines. Daniel found himself carrying wounded, digging trenches, delivering supplies, and doing any other non-battle task that was needed. No one asked any questions about his presence in the port, and no one cared as long as he worked hard. And always—despite Stoessel's ban on cameras in the city—Daniel carried his new Kodak snapshot camera with him, hidden in his knapsack. He was, first and foremost, a reporter, and he was determined to be prepared.

One day Daniel was on the front lines, running supplies out to the men in the trenches, when he paused to view the fighting and talk with some soldiers. After several failures, the Japanese were again trying to capture the strategic 203 Metre Hill. The fighting had been intense for several days. Twice the Japanese had captured different sectors, but they had been desperately driven back by the Russians.

Japanese loss of life was phenomenal. Corpses lay piled in heaps at the foot of the hill, impairing their maneuverability. Finally, a Red Cross flag, paired with a white flag of truce, rose above the Japanese trenches.

When the shooting died down in response to the flags, two Japanese officers carefully stepped out into the open. A moment later, two Russian officers did the same. Daniel hastened to join the Russians. Other soldiers, encouraged by the safe reception of the officers, began to emerge from their trenches. Like cautious but curious rabbits, Japanese and Russians began appearing out in the open.

Through an interpreter, the Japanese officer requested a temporary cease-fire so they could clear away their dead, of which there were more than fifteen hundred. He was very polite—in fact, Daniel was impressed by the cordiality shown by both sides.

This was his big chance—if he dared to take the risk. He retrieved the camera from his bag and held it up in a gesture that requested permission from the Japanese officer. The man bowed graciously to him, and as the Russian soldiers stood by, Daniel snapped pictures of the historic face-to-face meeting.

After a cease-fire of two hours had been granted, one of the Japanese brought out an earthenware bottle of *sake*, as if to seal the bargain.

"Please drink with us," said the Japanese officer through his interpreter.

When the Russians hesitated, the enemy officer bowed decorously, then drank a glass of the *sake* himself. "See, not poisoned."

The Russians accepted the wine, and before long they produced bottles of vodka—one commodity there seemed to be plenty of in the besieged city.

Then the gruesome task of clearing the bodies began. Because of the staggering number of dead, the Russians helped the Japanese with the removal. Daniel caught on film a shot he knew would make the front page of the *Register*—a Russian holding the torso and a Japanese grasping the legs of a dead Japanese lieutenant. What the photo did not show was the men trying to make friendly conversation in two different languages!

After exactly two hours, the soldiers of both sides crawled back into their trenches, and the shooting resumed.

With bullets flying overhead and artillery exploding all around, Daniel hunkered down in his trench and recorded on paper the entire bizarre scene. This was the kind of action that made newspaper work so glorious. It was also the stuff that sold newspapers. His editor at the *Register* would kill for such a report. And Daniel had not only the story, but photographs as well. Now he only needed a means to get it and several other dispatches out of Port Arthur.

Under cover of darkness, he returned to the city and went to Saratov's, one of the few restaurants still open in Port Arthur. Saratov's was also a good place to make contacts, and Daniel went there frequently in hopes of running into a smuggler willing to carry out his dispatches.

While waiting for his food, he thought about Mariana. He was worried about her. Every time he saw her, she looked more and more on edge. Her nerves were frayed; she jumped at the merest sounds and cried at the least provocation. She looked terrible, too, as if she'd been refusing meals so her patients could have more food. She wouldn't talk much about what the siege was doing to her. Once she let slip how worried she was about Captain Barsukov. He had been returned to duty, and though he was assigned to the adjutant's office, she feared he would request a frontline assignment long before he was ready.

No wonder she was so worn out, if she worried so about all her patients. Or was Barsukov special?

Daniel had a sickening feeling it was the latter. He had interviewed Barsukov as he had promised, and although he had to all but pry personal information out of the man, the captain was quite free with his praise of Mariana. He spoke of her with open admiration—no, rather with open *affection*.

164

How could Mariana not be drawn to this man, a handsome aristocrat, a war hero? Even Daniel's buoyant self-confidence wavered in the face of Prince Barsukov's obvious merits. Well, at least Daniel and Philip were now on equal footing. Had Barsukov remained in the hospital and in such close reach of Mariana, Daniel would have really worried. He did wonder if he'd always be in competition with someone for Mariana's affections.

That shouldn't surprise him. She was a beautiful woman, charming, kind, and gentle. It was a pure miracle she had remained available all these years. Daniel knew it couldn't last much longer, especially with a catch like Philip Barsukov plying Mariana with his winning charms.

Again Daniel asked himself, as he had on many occasions, just what he wanted from a relationship with Mariana. Marriage? Certainly a woman like Mariana would want nothing less.

But even the pleasures and the joy of being with a dear woman like Mariana brought certain sacrifices. Daniel liked his globe-trotting life, from one war to the next, one international crisis to the next. And how could his job mesh with a normal family life? The news didn't run on an eight to five schedule. Even when he had worked on the city desk, he had kept outrageous hours, sometimes working eighteen or twenty hours at a stretch.

No woman was going to want that kind of life. He couldn't count how many dates he had broken, how many women he had been forced to stand up because of work. He had never been able to sustain a relationship longer than a couple of weeks.

Daniel cared about Mariana too much to risk hurting her the way he had other girls. And what if they had children? What kind of father would he make?

Wasn't it better just to leave Mariana to someone like Barsukov? He was a steady fellow whose home and family were extremely important to him.

But he couldn't let go of her that easily.

"You are just a selfish, spoiled brat," Daniel mumbled to himself. He stared at the dinner before him—a thin slice of roast horsemeat and rice with a spoonful of rancid butter on the side. The only thing there was enough of was tea.

"Talking to yourself, old boy?"

Daniel looked up to see his friend Nojine standing before him.

"I can't believe I'm the only one in this pathetic town reduced to that malady," Daniel said morosely.

Nojine laughed, then swung his lanky frame into a chair opposite Daniel's. "I thought you'd want to know, Stoessel's gone and done it."

"Shot himself?"

"We should be so lucky. No, he's closed down the *Novy Krai*. I'm officially unemployed."

"That's rotten, Nojine. But don't fear being idle—there are plenty of trenches to be dug."

"For the time being, I'm quite busy trying to find ways to smuggle news out. And you might be interested in learning that I've found a blockade runner who is leaving tonight."

Daniel sat upright, suddenly alert and very interested. "He'll take our dispatches? You're a magician!"

"It'll cost."

"Doesn't everything? Let's go. It'll just take me a few minutes to get things in order."

Within half an hour they met with a Chinese smuggler in a small inn on the other side of town. The man took all their precious dispatches for two hundred dollars. In spite of his shrinking supply of cash, Daniel thought it was a bargain.

"This is my last run," the man informed them. "A German blockade runner and a Chinese junk were sunk in the last three days, and another German boat was detained by the Japs. This business is no longer healthy."

Daniel thanked the man so effusively that the fellow probably wished he had charged more. It helped lift Daniel's spirits enormously and almost made him forget about his confusion over Mariana. Almost, but not quite.

As the Chinese smuggler disappeared into the darkness, Daniel remembered that among his dispatches was one that paid homage to a Russian war hero. That story would make Barsukov appear more appealing than ever to Mariana.

"Good work, Trent," he mumbled sourly to himself. "Oops, there I go, talking to myself again."

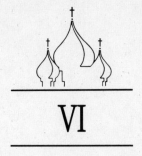

VI

FAMILY SECRET

27

Nicholas paced outside the nursery door. He could not stand the terrible uncertainty of not knowing what was going on inside, but neither could he bear the pain of watching Dr. Fedorov's examination of his beautiful infant son.

The child was almost two months old. He was such a chubby, pink-cheeked, happy little baby. And why not, with four big sisters to dote over him almost constantly and two parents who practically idolized him? They were such a happy family, loving and close. Nicholas had tried to comfort his daughters because they felt so bad about what had happened. But no one could say if it had been their fault from handling Alexis too roughly. Perhaps even he or Alix had somehow jostled the boy—

"Oh, God, all that matters now is Alexis. Please, God, don't let anything be wrong."

Two days ago the child had begun to bleed from his navel. It had been almost continuous the entire time. What a pitiful sight it had been, especially when Alexis had smiled and cooed through the ordeal. They had to change the little bandage several times. How much blood loss could a baby take? Nicholas had been afraid to ask the doctor that ominous question.

The nursery door opened and Alix joined her husband. She had been awake and by the baby's bedside the entire time. She looked terrible—worse, in fact, than the ailing child.

"How is he?"

"If it doesn't stop, the doctor may try to cauterize the area tomorrow."

"Alix, how ghastly!"

"We can only pray it will stop on its own."

"What could have caused this?"

Alix shook her head. The doctors were cautious in saying.

But the next day the bleeding did stop and Alexis seemed hardly worse for the ordeal. The family was relieved, of course, but the two concerned parents could not forget that the cause had not been determined. It could happen again without warning.

The only thing they could do was place the child in God's hands.

———

Alexandra prayed nightly to Saint Seraphim. Surely this holy man, known for his healings and prophecies, would protect her son. Hadn't she conceived the child after bathing in Seraphim's healing spring? Alexis was born with the saint's blessing upon him.

But Alexandra still thought about her uncle Leopold, Queen Victoria's youngest son, who had died of a brain hemorrhage when Alexandra was twelve years old. She also remembered her own brother who, at the age of three, fell, bumped his head, and died within hours of a brain hemorrhage. Her sister Irene's children also seemed to be plagued with this terrible bleeding infirmity. The baby, Henry, had bled to death at age four, not long before Alexis was born.

But why did such tragedy strike in Alexandra's family? It was not possible that her own child would fall victim to this bleeding malady. Alexis was so healthy. This thing was likely just a fluke, probably because at birth the doctor had failed to cut the umbilical cord properly.

In the months that followed, as bumps and bruises began to appear on the increasingly active boy, it became harder and harder for the tsar and tsaritsa to brush aside their fears. But except for the immediate family, no one knew. No one must ever know that something was wrong with the heir to all Russia.

28

A new demigod was on the rise in St. Petersburg. And Cyril Vlasenko felt utterly helpless to do anything about it.

Father George Gapon had appeared on the scene quietly a few years ago. As a religious zealot, an idealist doing missionary work in St. Petersburg's poorest working-class districts, he would have doubtless remained obscure. Then Zubatov, a former police officer who rose to head the political section of the Okhrana, had come up with his stupid idea of government-sanctioned trade unions. The intent of the plan was to mollify the workers into thinking they were getting a great concession—when, in fact, the government was in complete control, permitting no reforms without official approval. Gapon, a favorite of the workers and an ardent supporter of the tsar, had seemed to Zubatov a perfect choice—or, more correctly, puppet—to lead the experimental St. Petersburg union.

Cyril had opposed the idea from its inception, but Interior Minister Plehve viewed trade unions as a means to counter revolutionary activity among workers, and thus not only gave Zubatov his approval, but promoted the man.

In the two years since then, Gapon had worked tirelessly to build the unions and make them work. Gapon had recently decided it was time to establish similar unions in other parts of Russia and began to travel the country toward that end. In Moscow, however, his activities ran afoul of its governor-general, the grand duke Sergei, a favorite uncle of the tsar. The grand duke dashed off a strong letter of complaint to Plehve. The last thing Plehve wished to do was argue with the tsar's uncle, so he began to back off from his support of the unions.

173

Cyril had taken the opportunity to alert certain friends in the Okhrana, asking them to scrutinize Gapon's activities and take necessary action if he should get out of line. Vlasenko was certain it wouldn't be long before the sanctimonious union leader's career came to an end.

But when an assassin's bomb ended Plehve's life, it also spared Gapon's. In the rising political unrest that accompanied—and no doubt caused—the Minister of Interior's demise, Cyril was forced to stay his own hand against Gapon. The man's death could all too easily become a catalyst for demonstrations and even riots.

Making matters worse was the appointment by the tsar of Prince Svyatopolk-Mirsky as Minister of the Interior. That defeat stung Cyril tremendously, and he had been despondent for days afterward. He had been close enough to *taste* the sweet flavor of power! For a fleeting moment he even considered retiring from government service altogether. He had worked his entire life to achieve prominence in government, only to have his work suffer at the whim of a nincompoop who couldn't lead a pack of schoolboys, much less a mighty nation. The crushing blow had come close to making a revolutionary even out of a diehard reactionary like Cyril.

But there was more to be considered than his bruised image. Financial struggles made it imperative that he maintain his government position and contacts. There was money to be made in government, and he needed to keep his options open. Moreover, Cyril simply was not a quitter at heart. Greed might have been his primary motivator, but his political agenda was nevertheless important to him, and he wasn't ready to allow the moderates and revolutionaries a free hand in Russia, if he could possibly help it.

Someone had to balance out the likes of Svyatopolk-Mirsky, and to insure that demigods like Gapon were given only enough rope to hang themselves.

For that reason, Cyril was now on his way to a secret meeting with one of his most trusted henchmen. This fellow had been keeping a vigilant eye on the labor movement in the capital, and had Gapon under close surveillance. In a few days there was to be a general meeting of the Workers' Assembly, as the union was called. Under Svyatopolk-Mirsky's patronage, the general meeting, among other things, would provide the forum by which expansion of the union to other cities would be sanctioned. Cyril needed to insure that there were no surprises for him at the meeting. If he couldn't do anything about their activities, at least he'd be fully apprised of their seditious goings-on.

Cyril met his lackey, Cerkover, on the quay of Isaac's bridge, not far from the statue of Peter the Great. He chose the busiest time of day, early afternoon, when the meeting would blend easily into the general hubbub of the streets. The sky overhead was gray and the air was just chilly enough to remind him that autumn was not far away. Cyril had left his carriage a couple of blocks away, instructing his driver to wait. He walked the rest of the way, and he was huffing and puffing like a steam locomotive when he arrived at the base of the bridge.

Someday he'd make the powers that be pay for all this inconvenience!

"Good afternoon, Count Vlasenko," Cerkover said as Cyril sidled up next to him at the rail enclosing the quay.

"I'm glad you're on time," said Vlasenko, taking a handkerchief from his pocket and mopping his sweaty brow.

"I know your time is valuable," the lackey fawned. Cerkover was a husky man in his own right, but far from matching the girth and height of his master. In his early forties, his hair was lightly dusted with gray, but his round face, showing an obvious Mongolian heritage, was smooth, beardless, and amazingly free of wrinkles. His gray eyes were sharp and alert—indeed, after years of training under Vlasenko in the Third Section and more currently his work in the Okhrana, he missed very little. Vlasenko valued him as a storehouse of information, and as a man who forgot nothing. He was intensely loyal to his friends, but never forgot a wrong that was done him . . . *never.*

"In that case, let's get to it," said Cyril. "Anything new to report?"

"The meeting of the Assembly is taking on a very high profile. They've rented a hall in a nice neighborhood, and I've

175

heard that the governor of St. Petersburg will make an appearance."

"How many attendees do they expect?"

"Two thousand or more."

"Svyatopolk-Mirsky must be crazy to allow such a gathering."

"They will be ripe for influence by radicals, perhaps even demonstrations—maybe riots, eh?" Cerkover raised an eyebrow with a coy wink.

"It would be too risky for us to incite a riot," said Cyril, fully understanding Cerkover's meaning. "It would never do for such a thing to be traced back to me. Besides, a riot at this point could only serve to raise the workers' sympathy toward Gapon—and perhaps even that of such moderates as that Minister of the Interior. I want Gapon to cause his own downfall, and that's only a matter of time. The man is no saint, no matter what the workers may think at the moment. He was never exonerated completely in that affair of the mismanagement of the funds in the orphanage he headed. And then running off with one of the female orphans . . . well, we could ruin him if we wanted to."

"Then why don't we?"

"Timing, Cerkover. Timing is everything."

"And you are indeed the master of that, my good Count!"

"Thank you, my friend. I haven't done too badly." Vlasenko silently wished he'd had better timing with some of his investments, but there was no need to trouble his associate with that bit of enlightenment.

"I am ready to install my spies—" Cerkover began.

"*Spies*—what an indelicate word," said Cyril fastidiously. "I much prefer to think of them as agents."

"Of course, forgive my carelessness. So, as I was saying, my *agents* are ready; they wait only for your confirmation."

"You are certain no connection can be made to me?"

"Not a chance. One of my men is an American."

"That could prove tricky. He might stand out too much."

"This man, Jack Caine is his name, comes with a certain reputation I believe these union people will find irresistible.

He was involved extensively with the labor union movement in the United States."

"Are you sure we can trust him?"

"Let me tell you about his partner, then you be the judge. Caine has recently arrived in Russia in the company of a Russian emigré—well, *emigré* is rather a loose description. *Fugitive* would be more precise. This man is an ex-revolutionary whose activities are probably well known to you. He was the son of a now-deceased doctor, and he fled the country over twenty years ago. He was supposedly involved in the assault on the daughter of a once prominent St. Petersburg resident with whom you are well acquainted—the Fedorcenko family. Nothing was ever proved conclusively against the man in this matter, though it is pretty certain he killed a prostitute on Grafsky Lane."

"You can't mean you have found Basil Anickin! This is absolutely incredible—and dangerous! The man was always a bit unstable. How did you catch the fellow?"

"He was picked up during a routine raid of one of the brothels, again in Grafsky Lane. One of the police officers who had dealt with Anickin a few times in the old days recognized him—not easily, mind you, because there have been many changes in twenty years, but the officer followed his nagging intuition until it led to the truth. Being an old friend of mine, he informed me of Anickin's arrest."

"Did he inform anyone else?"

"No, and I don't believe anyone else made the connection."

"That's good. And you are blackmailing Anickin?"

"Not really necessary at the moment. Anickin needs money and is quite willing to work for us for a small stipend. The same with his friend, Caine. My impression of both men is that they will gladly work for the highest bidder. Political motivations come second to their greed."

"Men after my own heart!" chuckled Vlasenko.

"Anickin's police record is our insurance policy for keeping him in tow. The same with Caine, whose affiliation with the American socialist movement would make him an easy mark for deportation."

"From what I know of Anickin, using him will be rather

like holding a tiger by the tail." Vlasenko paused and rubbed his ample chin. "Ah, but this could promise to be quite a coup, if handled properly. Cerkover, you must keep on top of this at all times. If there is even a hint of it going sour, you must haul in Anickin and the American."

"I understand."

"And whatever you do, don't let the opposition outbid us for Anickin."

Walking back to his carriage, Cyril thought of those turbulent days twenty-some-odd years ago. It had been a tragic time for the nation, with the assassination of Tsar Alexander II. And much tragedy had also fallen upon the Fedorcenko clan. Cyril's grief in both matters had been superficial at best. He had rather enjoyed the toppling over of the mighty Prince Viktor Fedorcenko, though the death of his wife, daughter, and grandchild had been sad. Later—four or five years ago, in fact—it had come to light that the grandchild had lived after all. Because Cyril could find no way to use this information, he had let it drop, though he'd had a fleeting notion of forcing the girl to marry his son, Karl, in order to get his hands on the Fedorcenko holdings.

Well, Cyril got what he wanted without all that trouble, and thus forgot about the irregularities surrounding the Fedorcenko grandchild—her name was Remizov, daughter of that philandering Count Dmitri Remizov. Again he tucked this tidbit into the back of his mind, where he kept many seemingly trivial but potentially useful gems of information. Who knew when it might come in handy?

In the meantime another ghost from the past had resurfaced. Anickin would definitely merit watching, but there simply was no telling what a wealth of uses a man like that could present.

29

Sergei and Anna usually avoided such large crowds. But this first general meeting of the Workers' Assembly was an event of such importance that they made an exception this night. That is, it was important to Sergei. He knew Anna had come just to please him.

At least Anna only had to sit through the evening's entertainment—some fine musicians, a couple of jugglers, and a troupe of excellent traditional dancers. She had been spared the business part of the meeting that had occurred earlier in the day. The meeting had entailed four hours of speeches, reports, financial presentations, and much discussion. Sergei had been in attendance the entire day.

When he had agreed to tutor a group of workers, he had known that he would find himself drawn into the growing labor movement. He liked what they were trying to achieve, but more importantly he liked Father Gapon.

The thirty-two-year-old priest, the son of a Cossack father and peasant mother, had grown up in a strictly religious home in the Ukraine. But he had early been frustrated by his mother's emphasis on the external religious form. Always sensitive, and a bit of a romantic idealist, he was more drawn to the deeper spiritual depths of faith. Above everything, Sergei appreciated this in the man. If at times Gapon might tend a bit toward wild-eyed asceticism, he was a most sincere man, and his devotion toward helping the poor workers was very real.

In appearance, Gapon was rather average, with thick ebony hair and beard, and dark eyes that were both soft and intense. He sang in an excellent baritone with a passion that brought tears to many a hardened worker's eyes. He was physically strong for his size and, though usually gentle and soft-spoken, was known for his quick temper and iron will. Everything Gapon did was done with passion and zeal.

Gapon had recently won over the leaders of the Assembly, including Sergei, by showing them his "secret" agenda for the Assembly. In essence, he believed in reforms for the poor and for workers that would have pleased any revolutionary. He confided to this elite group that, as the government thought they were using him, he was also using the government until the worker's movement grew into a force of its own. Those who had previously reserved their full trust in Gapon because of his connections to officialdom became believers and swore never to reveal Gapon's agenda.

And that day at the general assembly, Gapon had fired the workers with his own zeal and vision.

"None of us present here," the priest had exhorted, "can even begin to envision what the future holds for our Workers' Union. Within three years, all two hundred thousand workers in St. Petersburg will be members. And our organization will spread far into the provinces of Russia. It will become a colossal organization such as the world has never before seen! And with this, the fine men and women who earn their living by the sweat of their brow will be given such power that all others will have to obey them."

Even Sergei had been caught up in the spirit of the day. Father Gapon made such a miracle seem possible. Sergei believed this movement might be the answer to his nation's desperate need for reform. Unlike the revolutionary movement, with which Sergei had serious problems, the Workers' Union stressed reform in a very practical sense, without all the political and theoretical jargon so often espoused by revolutionaries. Gapon himself was not a revolutionary. He loved the tsar and was committed to encouraging change within the existing system. He also lent the movement a strong Christian emphasis which Sergei appreciated.

As the day wore into evening and the crowd swelled to about two thousand, the air of unity and good-will prevailed. The owner of the hall in which the assembly was held said that he had never seen such a well-mannered group.

Sergei was enjoying the musicians and was happy to see a smile on Anna's face. They were gaily clapping their hands to the beat of the music when Oleg Chavkin came up next to Sergei.

"Sergei, I'd like you to meet some friends of mine," he said.

Sergei excused himself and followed Oleg to the back of the hall where he encountered two very alarming characters. How on earth could the stolid, kindly Oleg have hooked up with these sinister men? The younger of the pair, by at least a dozen years, was a little shorter than Sergei, solidly built with long muscular arms that gave him an almost comical resemblance to a gorilla. This impression was furthered by his thick curly black hair and two days' growth of dark beard. But there was nothing comical in his taut facial expression and deadly serious, probing eyes.

The taller of the two men was even more alarming. He had a gaunt and sinewy aspect, vulture-like, with his head jutting slightly forward on his long neck. His blond hair, dulled by gray, was close cropped and he wore a thin, pale moustache. Sergei felt an involuntary shiver go up his spine when he looked into the man's eyes. Those cavernous dark eyes were framed in pale, almost nonexistent brows and lashes, and looked as if they had gazed often and hungrily upon death. There was something else in those eyes—something hauntingly familiar, like the flash of a nightmare that you can't quite remember. But Sergei dismissed the thought. If he had met this sinister-looking man before he surely would have remembered.

Sergei glanced again at Oleg to insure that the simple peasant was indeed presenting these two as his "friends." Oleg introduced the younger man as Jack Caine, an American; the older was called Rolf Nagurski.

"They have been active in the labor movement in America," said Oleg with an innocent enthusiasm.

"Really?" Sergei tried to hide his wariness. "Have you met Father Gapon yet?" Sergei knew Gapon was against having foreigners in his Assembly.

"We haven't had that pleasure," said Nagurski curtly.

"How long have you been in Russia?"

"A few weeks."

Oleg added, "They have been working with me at the mill. I think they have a lot to offer us from their experiences."

"I would be interested in talking with you sometime about what is happening in America," Sergei said to the strangers. "Rolf, you speak Russian quite well. Are you from Russia?"

"Yes, but I have been away many years."

"What brings you back?"

"You ask a lot of questions, Sergei Ivanovich."

"I am so sorry; curiosity has always been a fault of mine. Please forgive me."

Nagurski gave a light, if incongruous, chuckle. "I am afraid that over the years, what with working so often at odds with the authorities, I have developed a natural aversion to probing questions."

"You can trust us," said Oleg.

But can we trust them? The question jumped unbidden into Sergei's mind.

"I am sure we can," Rolf said. "I have been especially impressed with the sense of brotherhood and solidarity I have sensed here today. Both are essential ingredients to the success of reform organizations."

"I am glad to have met you," said Sergei, "but I must return to my wife."

"Oh, Sergei," Oleg halted him. "I almost forgot why I called you over here. As you have probably noticed, Rolf's friend, Mr. Caine, doesn't speak Russian but would like to learn."

Nagurski added, "I have tried to teach him, but I seem to lack the skills of a teacher. Oleg tells me you are quite accomplished in that area."

"I suppose I make a living at it."

"Would you be willing to help my friend?"

"Of course. Bring him by the Assembly clubhouse. It's near the mill; Oleg can show you where. Come on Sunday afternoon when I work with a group of other factory workers."

"That is very kind of you."

When he returned to Anna's side and she turned and smiled at him, Sergei felt an odd sense of relief. She lent him a kind of warmth and safety that had been missing while with the strangers. Perhaps he was overreacting. Those men could not help the way they looked. And Nagurski seemed congenial enough. Nevertheless, Sergei wasn't looking forward to seeing them again.

30

Basil Anickin had no way of recognizing Sergei Ivanovich as the aristocratic son of the Fedorcenko clan; they had been adolescents when they last saw each other and both had since undergone dramatic changes. But when Sergei joined his wife, a bell from the past rang in Basil's head.

When Anna turned, smiling at her husband, Basil immediately saw something familiar in that lovely, fine-featured face. At first Basil could not identify the source of that familiarity. But there was something about her face that continued to nag at him the remainder of the evening. Who was she? An acquaintance from the past? If merely that, why was it disturbing him so?

It nagged at him all evening until, in a flash of deadly recall, a glimpse of the past shot through his brain. A dark night in the bedroom of a princess . . .

"Do you know what they did to me, Princess? Can you imagine waking every day to the screams and pathetic groans of human beasts? Breathing fetid air, eating what was not even fit for the rats. Then having my mind insidiously robbed by numbing drugs. They took from me my very humanity! All so that the fair little princess could play the fickle socialite. . . ."

"Basil . . . I'm sorry. I never meant—"

"On your knees, Princess! You are a dead woman. Your filthy husband is a dead man. Your unborn brat will never live to draw a single breath of this world's air!"

Oh, how close he had been that night twenty-three years ago while confronting Katrina Fedorcenko to the fulfillment of all his dreams of vengeance. His knife had been poised, ready to draw blood. Oh, sweet blood!

Then she had come, that interfering maid. That veritable spitfire of wild passion. She got hold of a sword that weighed nearly as much as she and wielded it with such mad—insane!—accuracy, Basil had been forced to flee for his life.

Yes, the interceding years were now etched upon her face, but there could be no mistaking her. The woman was the same person who had deterred him from his satisfaction—the maid of Katrina Viktorovna Remizov.

Basil was nearly beside himself with excitement over this discovery. He had never forgotten Katrina's rejection. He had returned to Russia less than a month ago with the express purpose of finding all the descendants of Princess Katrina . . . and killing them. It had been three years since he had seen the newspaper article that had first revealed that Katrina's husband and child were alive. He would have returned to Russia immediately had his finances been adequate. Toward that end, he had taken on the job of agitating among American coal miners and was arrested for assault. He had no way of knowing the kid he picked a fight with in a bar was the mine operator's son; that mistake had cost him a two-year prison sentence. Upon release, he hooked up with his old American friend, Jack Caine, who had wanted to go to Russia for his own reasons. They raised travel money and made the journey on a freighter, a grueling trip that took three months.

But Basil Anickin had proved long ago that he was a patient man. And he further demonstrated that fact after arriving in Russia. It had been an easy matter to locate Dmitri Remizov. But Basil restrained his blood lust for the promise of a more dramatic scenario. A straightforward kill simply would not be satisfactory. Had that been the case, Katrina's death would have finished the matter of his desire for vengeance. But that hadn't been enough. Her death should have come by his own hand, as he had planned that night in her bedroom. And he had dreamed of watching Dmitri's grief at the loss, just as Basil had grieved over the loss of Katrina's love.

Now Basil had a second chance. This Mariana was only the daughter, but her loss would still evoke pain and grief in the father—especially since she reportedly resembled her mother. That fact would surely make murdering her all the more pleasant.

Basil had learned from one of the Remizov servants that Mariana was in Manchuria working as a war nurse. She could be gone for months, or even years. And it would be impossible for Basil to go to the Far East. He'd have to wait and hope she wasn't killed in the war. His patience was being stretched mightily, but not yet to its limit.

Finding the meddling servant girl was a bonus. He would kill her, too, just for getting in his way before. But he must wait for Mariana. He didn't dare show his hand until all his pawns were together in one place. In the meantime, he would learn all he could about their lives and habits, and this time he would put together a plan that could not fail. If he was very lucky, perhaps Mariana would come home on leave and everything could happen much sooner. If not . . . well, he could wait.

Getting hired by the police would serve him well. As long as he was useful to them, he could roam about freely and with relative impunity. They would hold his past crimes over his head, but while they needed him, the threat of arrest was reduced. How long he could maintain this precarious cat and mouse game was uncertain—at least until he had Mariana in his clutches, he hoped. If not, he would go underground again. It was not an existence he relished, but he had done it before and could do it again.

So, that night, when the meeting ended, Basil began his odyssey of hatred, revenge, and death . . . especially death.

Keeping to the shadows, he followed Sergei and Anna home, to a flat in a quiet neighborhood on Vassily Island. A couple of days later he paid a street urchin to watch the house again. Basil could not risk being caught in the vicinity too often. Not only had he recently met Sergei, but he had to assume

185

Anna would also recognize him. His informant apprised him of the movements of the entire family—including the three children, two of whom were Anna's sons. The presence of the children was significant. Basil didn't yet know how they might be of use to him, but they represented many possibilities.

31

Sergei had spent so little time with his sons lately. Over the summer he had retained five or six of his most difficult students to tutor, and to make up for the loss of income when the regular school session ended, he had taken on odd jobs as well. He devoted Sundays, after Mass, to teaching his group of factory workers—that was the only day they had off from work. If these men were committed enough to give up their only free time in order to learn, he could make a few sacrifices to help them.

Saturday was usually his family day, but for the last three weeks he had been working on the galleys for his new book of poetry. The proofs had finally been turned over to Mr. Cranston to send to Duke Publishing, and Sergei was determined to make up for lost time.

Today he was taking Yuri and Andrei to the St. Vladimir Gymnasium for their admission interview. Anna had packed them a lunch; afterward, they would go to the Summer Gardens, or to the river where they could watch the boats.

Sergei had to admit he was a little nervous about the interview. Years ago his father had made generous donations to this particular school when it had been threatened with closure due to bankruptcy. Perhaps that was why Sergei had selected it, because his father had felt it was worthy of his support. Despite his financial support, however, Viktor would never have dreamed of sending his own son to St. Vladimir. Such a middle and working-class school was well below their station.

Now Sergei feared his present station might not be good enough for the gymnasium. Both boys had done well on their entrance examinations, but Yuri had done exceptionally, scoring in the top ten. The interview should have been a mere formality, but Sergei had worried all night. Dressed in his best clothes, Sergei surprised the whole family, including Anna, by appearing at breakfast with his beard neatly trimmed close to his face. Anna declared he looked just like a university professor. No one seemed to think any less of him for succumbing to this moment of vanity. He simply did not want to risk spoiling his sons' chances of attending this fine school because of his appearance.

He paid for a carriage to take them to the school so they wouldn't arrive all sweaty. And the entire way, Sergei coached the boys on proper etiquette for such occasions.

In the end, the interview turned out quite well. The headmaster was a soft-spoken, sincere man who had a way of making Yuri and Andrei feel important even if their clothes were a bit too snug and worn around the cuffs. Yuri was accepted into the second year of the four-year program, and Andrei into the first.

"I think we need to celebrate," Sergei declared as they left the school. He unbuttoned his stiff collar and slipped off his wool suit coat.

"What'll we do?" asked Andrei.

"I had in mind a pastry and tea from a shop we passed on the way here. Then we can go watch boats."

He received no argument from his enthusiastic sons. Purchasing something from a tea shop was indeed a momentous event; attending the gymnasium must be very important, if acceptance was celebrated with tea and pastries.

Each of them ordered a different sweet pastry, and Sergei cut them in thirds so they could have a taste of each. Sergei and Yuri ordered tea to drink, and Andrei ordered lemonade.

Sergei could barely remember the last time he'd been out alone with his sons, and he felt a deep urging within to make the most of it. With the boys going off to boarding school, who could tell when such a time would come again—and even if it did, none of them would be quite the same next time. The school experience would no doubt mature Yuri and Andrei. They were already losing their boyish qualities. Yuri had ordered tea like his papa; no children's drink for him. Andrei didn't seem to be squirming as much as usual.

Sergei thought he should feel some melancholy over this, but oddly, what he felt most was anticipation. The future was wide open for them, and Sergei was eager to see just what they would do with it. He firmly believed they would do well, make him proud.

His only regret was that they would never be able to embrace their full inheritance. There was precious little left to the Fedorcenko wealth, but he wished they could share in the history and pride that went with a name they could not claim. Their ancestors, their own grandfather, had walked with tsars. They had been heroes in war and counselors in peace. The Fedorcenkos had been involved in making Russia what it was, for good or ill.

Sergei was surprised when Yuri broached this very subject.

"Papa, when we were at the school, did you see the picture of our grandfather?"

"No, I didn't. Where was it?"

"Hanging in the corridor with about half a dozen others."

"Why would our grandfather's picture be hanging in the school?" asked Andrei, obviously skeptical.

"I'm sure I saw it," defended Yuri. "I'll prove it next time we go there."

Sergei hesitated. He had never considered such a situation arising with the school, and he wasn't sure what to tell his sons. He had always kept information about his side of the family vague. When Viktor had appeared on the scene, Sergei felt compelled to reveal his relationship with his father to the children. Viktor needed his grandchildren, and Sergei thought the risk was worth the benefits—both to Viktor and to the boys. Explanations, however, remained vague, and neither boy saw fit to question deeply. Perhaps they had an innate sense that this was an area to be treated delicately. The fact that their social circle was small and they were seldom off on their own simplified matters.

Things would surely change now as their world expanded. The Fedorcenko heritage was still present in this city, and Yuri bore a strong resemblance to his grandfather. No matter how careful they were, someday the two might be together, and a perceptive observer might draw an obvious conclusion. He and Anna had once thought they could guard the truth of Mariana's heritage from her. Maybe it was time to learn from that experience. Maybe it was not only impossible, but also irresponsible to hide the truth from his sons.

But were they old enough to handle the truth—and to deal with the reality of a double identity? Would Andrei ever be able to keep the family secret? He, far more than Yuri, was apt to act first and think later. But it wouldn't be fair to tell one and not the other; they were too close for that.

Sergei sighed and studied his sons for a moment. They appeared uncomfortable with this scrutiny and the silence accompanying it, but neither spoke. They were fine young men—yes, they were no longer children. He wondered what they would have become had they grown up in the Fedorcenko palace with a hundred servants to command, the finest education in the country, a place with the elite Guards, invitations to the best parties . . .

Sergei reminded himself that he had despised the aristocratic life and had rebelled at every chance against the things his father had extolled. Why, then, would he fantasize about his sons stepping into such a life? Did age tend to paint the past in rosy colors? He must not forget how he had suffered, how his father had suffered as a result.

He should be thankful his sons had grown up in a simple home, free of the constricting prison of the nobility. It was pure craziness to even think about placing such a burden upon them. They were free—let them remain so.

Then a completely new notion struck Sergei. Was the problem really one of wealth versus poverty, nobility versus peasant? How many unhappy peasants had he known over the

189

years, drowning their misery in a bottle of vodka?

He wanted to laugh at himself for his narrow vision. A smile did manage to bend lips, and Andrei noticed.

"You looked so serious a minute ago," Andrei said. "Now you're smiling. What's the joke?"

"No joke," said Sergei. "I was thinking of Grandpapa Yevno. I don't know how many times he told me that a man's contentment in life had nothing to do with how many kopecks were clanging around in his pockets."

"I remember, too," said Yuri. "He said something like: 'Faith is a man's roof, and God is his bread.' "

"Excellent, Yuri!" said Sergei. "But, let me see, I think you have it turned around. 'Faith is a man's bread, and God is the roof over his head.' When I heard that, I always liked to imagine looking up and seeing a huge, cloaked figure with a beaming, loving face floating over me. Yevno may not have meant it exactly that way, but it always gave me a sense of security to see it like that. It didn't matter whether the real roof I was under was that of a leaky izba, or of a grand St. Petersburg palace. When God was what I saw first, it just did not matter."

"Did the fine buildings of the school make you think of that, Papa?" asked Yuri.

"No, not really. It was what you said about the picture of your grandfather. It made me think of the past and . . . well, of many things I'd like to talk to you both about. Are we ready to go? I'd like to take you to a special place on the river."

They took the steamer upriver a couple of miles, then Sergei rented a little rowboat and they continued their trek up a small tributary to a place Sergei had not been to in many years. This stream was too shallow for large boats; only a few fishermen traveled these waters. The shores were lined with marshy reeds and a few trees, and this time of year many species of birds passed overhead on their way south for the winter. There was a peaceful quiet to the place, yet a huge city buzzed and throbbed a mere two miles away.

When he was a boy, he used to row out here and try his hand at fishing. He once caught a sixteen-inch trout, and because he knew the cook would scoff at him for bringing it home, he built a fire on the shore, cooked the fish and ate it all. He thought it tasted better than any of the fancy food served at home.

After rowing for a while Sergei was exhausted, and before a coughing spell completely disabled him, he handed the oars over to Yuri. The boys took turns rowing, both thoroughly enjoying the task.

"Why haven't we done this before?" Andrei demanded. His face was red and sweat trickled down his brow, but his eyes danced merrily.

"I never thought of it until now," answered Sergei. "I wish we had a fishing rod. Maybe next time."

"Papa," said Yuri, "I've been thinking about something."

Sergei smiled affectionately at his son. Yuri, the thinker, hardly ever said a word without first giving it great thought. "Go on, son."

"I have decided that when I grow up, I want to be a doctor."

"Really? I haven't heard this before."

"I've been thinking about it for a long time, but I didn't want to say anything because I didn't think the schooling would be possible."

"Ah, I see. Did something specific bring on this desire? Mariana's experiences, perhaps?"

"I first thought about it several years ago. Do you remember when Andrei and I found an injured bird back in Katyk?"

"That long ago?" A brief pang of guilt assailed Sergei at the thought that their financial position had caused Yuri to repress this dream.

"It felt so good making that bird fly again. I thought that doing the same for people would be even better. Hearing about what Mariana is doing at the front line only makes me more excited about it. I felt a little bad when she had so much trouble with the schooling. Some of the things I read in her books . . . well, I kind of understood them." He blushed at the immodesty of this admission.

"You have no need to be ashamed of that, Yuri."

"You don't think Mariana will be angry with me if I go on to achieve something she couldn't?"

Sergei chuckled. "Not our Mariana! She'll be thrilled. From her letters, I gather that she is quite happy as a nurse, and glad she discovered she could work in that profession without all the schoolwork."

Yuri shook his head. Sergei knew without asking that the boy would revel in the challenges of academics, especially the sciences.

"How about you, Andrei?" inquired Sergei. "Have you thought about what you want to be when you grow up? And I want you both to remember that we will do whatever we can to see that you get the education you need."

"I don't want to do anything that requires an education," huffed Andrei as he rowed with all his strength.

"The beauty of an education, Andrei, is that it allows you to have more choices."

"You didn't have an education, did you?"

"Yes, I did, a very good one, in fact—the best Russia has to offer."

Andrei stopped rowing, and both boys stared at their father with puzzled expressions.

"I want to tell you all about it, but I want us to get to a certain place on the stream first."

Yuri took over the rowing, and they continued to travel at an easy pace. The boys were curious and Sergei was growing anxious with what lay ahead, but he didn't want to spoil the afternoon with haste. He pointed out some unusual species of birds, and they fed some crusts of bread saved from their lunch to a family of ducks that waddled past their boat.

After fifteen minutes, the stream made a bend and there Sergei motioned for Yuri to lay down the oars.

Pointing with outstretched arm, Sergei directed their attention toward the right shore and some distance inland. "Do you see that hill?"

"The one with the mansion on it?" asked Andrei.

"Yes, take a good look at it." He paused. He had always wondered just how these words would come out, or if they ever would. For the most part they flowed naturally; Sergei had no doubt the time was right. "That's where I grew up."

"You, Papa?" both young voices said in unison.

"It's even hard for me to believe now," said Sergei, amused. He continued with more solemnity. "What I have to tell you is a very delicate matter. I have said nothing until now because I was never sure when you'd be ready to hear it. I think now you are. It will require some discretion on your part—that is, keeping a very important secret."

"Will we have to keep it from Talia?" asked Yuri.

"I know she is your best friend, and keeping a secret from an important friend is hard. My best friend, Misha, knows about it, and he has been faithful with my trust. Why don't we wait and see? But certainly you could tell no one else. Can you do that?"

"Yes," said Andrei eagerly.

"I don't know," breathed Yuri at the same time.

"I believe you can."

"I will try."

"I can expect no more from you. We will trust God to take care of the rest." Sergei laid a hand on Yuri's shoulder and squeezed gently. "I have no doubt about either of you."

"Then do tell us!" urged Andrei.

For the next fifteen minutes, Sergei told his sons all about the Fedorcenko family. He told them about their grandparents and great-grandparents. He told them how his father had earned the prestigious Order of St. Andrew in the Crimean War. Then, in a more somber tone, he told of his own place in that great Russian family and why he now lived as a fugitive.

"I'm not proud of the things I did, and that you, my family, must also suffer because of it. Your mother chose to follow me into this life, but you . . . I'm sorry you never had that kind of choice."

"Do you mean, Papa, that we are princes?" asked Yuri, confusion more than awe dominating his tone. "I've seen members of the nobility ride around the streets in their fancy carriages, looking down on the rest of us. Are you saying that could have been us?"

"I would hope that you would not have been arrogant and prideful," answered Sergei. "But if my book had not been censored and I hadn't been exiled to Siberia, I might not have met my God in a personal way, and I might not have been able to pass my faith on to you. Not that you might not have found humility through faith in some other way."

"Well, I'm glad all that happened," declared Andrei. "I'm glad we aren't of the nobility and hated by the peasants. You were right not to want anything to do with all that. I don't either. We've always been happy as we are."

"I'm glad to hear that." Sergei glanced at Yuri as he spoke. His oldest son had been too quiet since his first statement. "We have been content as we are." Sergei looked at Yuri as he spoke. "We can't do anything to change it. If I publicly claimed my rightful place as my father's son, I could be arrested again."

"Then why did you tell us, Papa?" asked Yuri.

"I don't know. I just felt it was time. I never liked keeping secrets from you, especially one that so deeply involved you. You have a right to know who you are. Also, you will be going away to school, meeting many new people. Questions might be raised, and it seemed best that you hear it from me and not some stranger."

"I wish . . ."

"What, Yuri?"

"Nothing."

"Boys, nothing has really changed. We will continue to live our lives as always. I suppose the only difference is that there will be times when you will have to guard what you say to others. Someone who thinks they are better than you might belittle you, and you might be tempted to tell them of your family. That would be unwise. But I believe you are strong enough to avoid this dilemma."

"They aren't better than us, anyway," said Andrei. "And not because of those Fedorcenko people, but because we are Russians, and men—well, almost men. That's why we can hold our heads high, Papa."

"Am I growing a little revolutionary?" chuckled Sergei.

"These are only things you taught me, Papa."

Sergei laughed heartily but then noticed that Yuri hadn't laughed, hadn't even smiled. Something was definitely eating at the boy, but perhaps it would be best to talk to him alone.

32

Fedorcenko.

Yuri silently intoned the name over and over in his mind. He even tried to say it out loud, but only in a whisper. It sounded awkward on his tongue.

But it was *his* name. Yuri Sergeiovich Fedorcenko. *Prince* Yuri Sergeiovich Fedorcenko.

The whole thing troubled him, though he couldn't exactly say why. His father thought that telling Yuri and Andrei was the right thing. Later his father tried to talk with him alone, attempting to find out what was bothering Yuri. But the four-teen-year-old boy didn't say; he couldn't say; he didn't know. At least, he only had a vague idea, but he couldn't tell his father.

They had been living a *lie* all these years. It was different when Yuri didn't know about the lie, but now he would have to lie, too. It wasn't that he was such a saint that he couldn't lie, although his parents had taught him lying was wrong. He had told a few fibs before, but this was a huge lie, a lie about *who he was*.

At his age, Yuri was already struggling with that very question. He also could not brush something so monumental aside with a glib acceptance. Sometimes he hated that in himself. Sometimes he wished he could be more like Andrei.

Yuri told himself it wasn't that he wanted to be a prince and live in that huge palace on the hill overlooking the Neva. He was happy and fairly content as the poor peasant son of Sergei and Anna. Well, there were times when he was frustrated, when he wished he could travel all over the world and see the places his mama taught him about—and have a better education than the one his mama gave him in the front room of their house. His papa said he could fulfill his dreams, but Yuri knew there were limits to what he could do. Yes, he could go to medical school, but an inexpensive one, not the best in Russia.

He remembered when Mariana's life had changed and she suddenly found herself a countess with all the fine aristocratic trappings. Yuri had been a little jealous. Not because he cared about wealth and money—he really didn't! But he did care about some of the things that went with it. Papa said an education gave a person choices; Yuri thought money and position gave far more choices. Papa said, "Faith is my bread, and God is the roof over my head." But God loved the wealthy as much as the poor, and you could love God just as much, too, no matter how much money you had.

Yet, weren't all these mental debates senseless? In the end, Yuri really didn't have a choice. The old-time power and prestige of the Fedorcenko name had dwindled to almost nothing. But more than that, if he claimed his place in society, it would endanger his papa—and he never, *ever*, would risk doing that. He'd have to live the lie, then. But it wouldn't be easy. There would always be a small part of him that would ask, "What might have been?"

———

Half an hour later, as Yuri was writing in his secret journal that he kept hidden under a loose floorboard by the bed, the door of the room burst open, and Andrei and Talia tumbled in.

"Don't you know how to knock?" Yuri said testily. His thoughts had left him in a sour mood.

"Oh, I'm sorry, Yuri," said Talia. "We were just so excited."

Who could stay angry for long at Talia's sweet sincerity? "Never mind. What's going on?"

"I told her, Yuri. Now Talia can share our secret, too," said Andrei.

Yuri knew without further explanation exactly what his brother meant, and he didn't much like it. "How could you do that without telling me first, without my even being there? You have a nerve, Andrei."

"Well, I thought—"

"You didn't think, just like always. Well, I'm sick of always having to be the patient big brother. You had no right saying anything—no right at all!" He snapped his journal shut as if he feared even that could be vulnerable.

Talia replied, "I'm so sorry, Yuri. I would never have—"

"You couldn't help it." Yuri tried to be gentle.

"I wouldn't have listened if I knew you'd be upset."

Talia the diplomat. Talia, for all her soft shyness, the rock. Like a calm, peaceful island between the turbulent waters of her two best friends. She absorbed the pounding of the waves, managing to diffuse the strife between the boys—strife that was growing more evident as they grew older and their vastly different personalities became more pronounced.

"Aw, just forget it." Yuri was beginning to feel a bit guilty for his overreaction. "So, what do you think, I mean about what Andrei told you?"

Talia and Andrei plopped down on the bed, all the previous strife forgotten for the moment.

"You do have the most unusual family," she replied thoughtfully. "I thought my family was interesting because I have a cousin on my father's side who is wardrobe coordinator to the tsar's sister, the grand duchess Zenia. But that's nothing compared to you. Your family is part of Russian history. Your name comes up in history books—I looked it up, too. I never dreamed that your grandfather had once been such an important man. And to think, he's dined in our simple dining room and complimented my mama's kasha!"

"Oh, come on!" interjected Andrei. "Men are men. It doesn't matter who they know or if their names are in history books. You were always a little awed by my grandfather."

"I guess so," said Talia. "I always sensed he was an important man."

"Because he *is* important!" Andrei replied with emphasis. "He hardly has two kopecks to rub together, but you just know he is the sort of man you ought to listen to."

"I can't argue with that. But that wasn't what I was getting at, anyway."

"What were you getting at?"

"Now I can't remember. Let me see . . ."

"You were saying how important our family seems now," prompted Yuri. Although he had been somewhat relieved that the conversation had wandered off track, a small part of him wanted—needed—to know what Talia thought.

"Oh, yes. But—" Talia looked at the two brothers, her eyes shifting back and forth a moment. "Nothing's really changed, though, has it? You're both the same; you're both my friends. That won't ever change . . . will it?"

"Maybe you'll change," said Yuri, hardly aware that he had ignored her plaintive question.

"I won't." Talia's eyes met Yuri's and held his for a long span, as if she were trying to burn the fact of her loyalty into his very soul.

Yuri looked away, suddenly uncomfortable. Couldn't he believe her declaration? Or, was it because he could not make the same promise in return? If he were ever given the choice, he couldn't say what he would do. Maybe he would change. He didn't know . . . he just didn't know.

Then Andrei, in his almost irritatingly confident way, said, "No one's going to change, and *nothing's* going to change. As long as Papa's a fugitive, we're going to have to keep on living just as we have. And I'm glad of it. Maybe there are some aristocrats out there that are good, like Grandfather, but I'd rather be associated with simple folk any day. They are the heart and soul of Russia, as Papa always says."

All at once a new idea struck Yuri. "What if . . ." He hesitated, almost afraid to voice the unpleasant idea.

"What, Yuri?" Talia urged.

He should have known better than to speak on impulse, for usually it caused him nothing but trouble. He simply should never have spoken his fear out loud—he should have let it go, forgotten it. But once a tiny crack was permitted, he seemed unable to stop himself. And the moment the words were out, it was almost as bad as if the thing had actually happened.

"What if Papa is reprieved, declared a free man—you know,

sometimes the tsar does that on his birthday, or something."

Andrei laughed at his brother. "Oh, Yuri, for a minute I thought you really had something earth-shattering to tell us. 'Reprieved'? It'll never happen. You're dreaming again."

"I didn't say it *would* happen," snapped Yuri defensively. "I just said what if, like a hypothetical question—something to consider, that's all."

"Oh, I'm bored with all your hypo—which-o-ma-call-its." Andrei jumped to his feet. "Come on, there's got to be something more interesting than this to do." Andrei strode to the door, then paused, glancing back at his friends who hadn't moved. "Well?"

"Not right now, I have to finish something." Yuri tried not to sound sulky.

"Talia?" said Andrei.

Once more Talia looked from brother to brother. It was an easy thing for the island to absorb the crash of the waves, but not to divide herself between them. Her eyes rested on Yuri.

"Well, I'll see you two later." Andrei exited impatiently.

"Go on," Yuri said to Talia. "I'm busy, anyway."

Talia began to rise, then stopped. "Yuri . . . I hope nothing ever changes."

"But don't you see, Talia, it's bound to change eventually. Papa could be pardoned; Papa could . . . die." He hadn't wanted to say that last part, he hadn't even wanted to think it, but it tumbled out anyway. "Talia, Papa *will* die someday. Then what? Then . . . what?"

"Can't you just not worry about it, Yuri? Let things happen as they will. But even if something happened like you say, it doesn't have to affect you . . . does it?"

He stared at her incredulously. She just didn't understand. Sometimes they didn't even have to speak in order to know what the other was thinking. Why now, with something so monumental, was she so dense?

"Look at Mariana," Talia went on. "She had that very thing happen, and she's still the same person at heart."

"She didn't have any choice, not really. She didn't want it; she just was being obedient to her real father."

"What difference does it make?"

"Talia, I think . . . I think I *want* it." Yuri took a sharp breath. There, the horrible thought was out. And he hadn't known until he blurted out the words that this was the core of what had been troubling him all along.

"Oh, Yuri . . ."

"Don't, Talia. Is that such a sin? Will I perish in hell for wanting my birthright? Is it so wrong to want to be important, even powerful? You can use those things for good, too, you know."

"I think you know what your papa would say."

"Talia, I want you to swear to me right now—" Yuri shuffled through a nearby bookshelf, pulling out a plain black volume. "Swear on this Bible that you will never—never, do you hear!—tell anyone, not my papa, not anyone, what I've just said."

"I . . . I . . ."

"Swear!"

Trembling, she lay her hand on the black leather binding. Her voice was soft, tentative. "I swear, Yuri."

He laid down the Bible, and suddenly feeling foolish, he tried to laugh off the tension. "I guess you think I'm an idiot."

Her lips twitched upward as she made a brave attempt at a light chuckle. "I'd never think that."

There was such expectation in her eyes, and he felt terrible for ignoring it. He knew she was hoping he'd take back the swearing.

But he didn't.

VII

BREAKING POINT

33

Lethargy seemed to prevail these days in siege-worn Port Arthur, or at least it seemed so on this particular cold November day as Mariana walked through the hospital corridors.

Every morning Mariana awoke a little surprised that she was still alive. By November, the siege had left hardly a corner of the town untouched by either bombardment or privation. The hospital had been hit several times by artillery; Mariana's boardinghouse had been destroyed completely, so she had no choice now but to board at the hospital. With death and destruction all around, it was no wonder she felt as she did.

Ludmilla had put it best: "I hardly care anymore; we're all going to die eventually."

Mariana wasn't as afraid of death itself as she was afraid of the *process*. The waiting. Any time she stepped out on the street it could happen. She avoided going out whenever possible, as everyone else did. The streets of Port Arthur were deserted these days. But the gaping craters in the hospital were proof that she didn't have to go outside to encounter death. It was lurking for her even in the halls where she worked. There was no escaping it. But often Mariana longed for nothing else but escape.

Oh, for her mama Anna's peaceful home! Père Dmitri's home, even with her contentious grandmother Eugenia, looked good.

How could anyone expect her to take this day in, day out? Her patients, her only motivation for continuing, appeared to have given up themselves. The injured did not even have the heart to cry out in pain. They just lay there as if in a trance.

The scant news from the outside did not help matters. Stoessel tried to keep any news at all from coming in, but word of the fall of Liaoyang at the end of September had steeped the town in a deep depression. The Russians were being disgracefully pushed out of Manchuria by tiny Japan. Kuropatkin was an able commander, but he had lost heart. Daniel had heard that Kuropatkin failed to commit reserves that might have turned the tide at Liaoyang. The army that had retreated to Mukden had been a substantial fighting force, with enough vigor left to provide a more aggressive defense.

Then, a month later, the rumor came that Kuropatkin was sending a huge force south to rescue Port Arthur. Stoessel set up a heliograph to communicate with the advancing army, only to discover it was all a mistake. No one was going to help Port Arthur.

The news that the tsar had ordered the Baltic fleet to the port was received with skepticism at best. They had eighteen thousand miles to traverse, and Russia, having no overseas colonies, would have to beg for fuel from an unsupportive world to power the fleet.

It often seemed that Port Arthur was merely going through senseless motions. Why bother if they were doomed to fail eventually? So many worthy men were suffering and dying . . . for what? Mariana could no longer remember what it had all been about in the first place. A deadening numbness had descended over her. She no longer cared.

Perhaps it was best, after all, not to think of such things. To try to find reason or purpose in all of this madness could drive a person insane. The only way to survive was to keep focused on the job at hand. Yet even that must be done carefully—only look at wounds, bandages, sutures, splints; try not to look at faces, individuals. It hurt too much to become attached to these poor boys, to hear about their loved ones, their hopes for the future. Many would have no future at all.

Absently Mariana gave the men the sacrifice of her smile, soothed their grimy, bloody bodies with her gentle touch. Sometimes when they would thank her for her kindness, it surprised her, for she hadn't even realized what she was doing. She tried to separate her motions from her mind, but caring for the wounded sapped her strength nevertheless.

One morning, when her stamina was at its lowest, Mariana circulated among the patients on her ward, and those that overflowed into the hall, as was her routine. She methodically glanced at each chart and assessed needs, even though the hospital no longer had the capability of meeting many needs. Supplies were alarmingly low. She had to ignore all but the filthiest bandages because they had so few clean ones. Men who might otherwise survive their wounds were likely to die from infection. Philip had been fortunate to have incurred his wound when he did; if he had been wounded now, his leg would never have been spared. Amputations were the order of the day, and even Mariana had stopped fighting them.

She paused between beds and commented to Ludmilla, who was accompanying her on rounds, "Nurses are useless around here anymore." She ran a hand through her stringy, unwashed hair.

"But we're stuck here, anyway," said Ludmilla.

"If only I felt I was doing some good . . ." Mariana ended her statement with a sigh that was interrupted by a cry and sounds of disorder from the corridor.

Leaving Ludmilla to finish rounds, Mariana hurried out to see what was wrong. Orderlies, bringing in a new patient, had stumbled and nearly dropped the stretcher.

"I'm very sorry!" exclaimed an orderly. "It's so crowded here."

"I understand," the wounded man on the stretcher said in a wracked tone.

When Mariana arrived, the orderly tried to apologize to her also.

"I know you're doing the best you can," said Mariana. "Let's just find a place for him quickly so there's no more jostling."

The cot was wedged into a corner, and Mariana turned to the patient to insure there had been no further damage done him. "Let's have a look—"

"He just came up from surgery," offered the orderly.

Mariana thumbed through his chart. Above-the-knee amputation of right leg, shrapnel removed from abdomen, and slight concussion. It looked as if this poor fellow must have walked right into a Japanese land mine.

She lifted up his blanket to check his dressings. They were already soaked with blood, and he was trembling with cold and shock and pain. There was no notation in his chart that he had been given any morphine recently. She knew they must conserve the precious pain-killer by extending time between doses, but such conservation could go *too* far.

"I'll get you something for the pain—"

Only then did she look at the man's face. She almost didn't recognize him, with his stubbly growth of beard, face smeared with grime, and a bandage nearly covering his right eye. But there was something familiar. . . .

"Uncle Ilya?"

His eyes snapped open.

Mariana leaned closer. "Uncle Ilya, it's me, Mariana." She took his hand in hers. "Do you recognize me, Uncle?"

His lips twitched in a weak smile. "Praise the saints, little Mariana . . . it's almost as good as being home."

"Don't wear yourself out with talk, Uncle Ilya. Let me get you something to ease the pain."

"That would be good. My leg hurts so, but at least it's still there . . . I'll be able to harvest the crops when I get home."

She didn't have the heart to tell him about his loss; he'd find out soon enough. Poor Uncle Ilya—strong, burly Uncle Ilya, so like Grandpapa Yevno, so full of vitality and gentleness. Now what would happen to him? How would he and his family survive if he could not work the land? He'd be too proud to take charity. Would he even make it that long? His wounds were serious, and Mariana had seen far less severe injuries end in death.

What would Aunt Marfa do? And Grandmama . . . to lose her baby son? Mariana shook the dismal thought from her mind and said a quick prayer for her uncle. He was alive now, and she would do what she could to keep it that way.

Mariana prepared a morphine injection, and after administering it, she sat by his bed until it took effect. When he was asleep she rose and kissed his dirty cheek, then turned to find Dr. Vlasenko approaching.

"Nurse, there isn't time for such malingering," Vlasenko

said. "I was told you've been sitting here for twenty minutes."

"I haven't the patience to put up with you, today, Doctor." She brushed past him, but he grabbed her arm before she was at a safe distance.

"I will not condone such disrespect!"

"I'm sorry." The apology was halfhearted at best, offered only because she did somewhat regret her rudeness. "That's my uncle."

"You know he's had an amputation." Vlasenko's tone held no emotion except perhaps a slight hint of gloating.

"Of course I know," Mariana snapped. "I, at least, read my patients' charts."

"Now, look here—"

"What do you want, Dr. Vlasenko? I have work to do."

"That's what I wanted to remind *you* of."

"All right, that's done. May I go now?" Mariana glanced down at his hand, still gripping her arm.

He dropped his hand, and Mariana strode away. She met Ludmilla at the door to the ward.

"I wish I could stand up to him like that," said Ludmilla.

"My mama would not be so pleased at my rudeness. She taught me better than that. But that man can make anyone forget her manners."

"Is that patient really your uncle?"

"Yes."

"I admire your strength, Mariana."

"My . . . strength?" Mariana didn't feel strong at all. She wanted to run away; she wanted to scream; she wanted to cry. . . .

Suddenly she realized she hadn't cried in weeks. When she saw Uncle Ilya, her heart had quaked, but that wrenching of her heart hadn't been accompanied by tears. Was that strength? She had tried to tell herself it was her duty as head nurse to be strong. But it was all just a whitewash, and she knew it. She didn't want to be hard. She *wanted* to cry. But she couldn't.

A few times she had seen Ludmilla go off by herself to have a good cry, and she had envied her. How odd that Ludmilla should admire Mariana for this weakness—for that's what it was. Mariana was just too weak to allow herself the luxury of tears. She feared that once she allowed herself to *feel*, she'd never survive this cruel war.

Mariana looked at her friend and shook her head. "Oh, Ludmilla, if only I could . . . cry. But if I start, I don't see how I would ever stop. I'll break, Millie, I know I will."

"Mariana!" Ludmilla put her arms around her friend.

Mariana felt her friend's tears soak the cloth of her uniform. But still her own eyes remained dry.

Finally she took a breath, managed a thin smile, and stepped away from Ludmilla. "We'd better get back to work before Dr. Vlasenko returns."

Mariana's uncle remained in very grave condition. When Dr. Itkinson learned what had happened, he gave Mariana permission to spend as much time as she needed by Ilya's bedside. A nurse in another ward offered to fill in, since Mariana and Ludmilla were the only nurses in their ward. These were kind gestures, but Mariana couldn't allow herself to ignore her duties because of one patient, even if he was her own uncle.

And when more wounded began pouring in from another major battle being fought at the gates of the city, Mariana became all the more determined to do her duty. It just wasn't fair to place one man above the needs of many. Simple rules of triage taught her that there were many wounded who, with her treatment, had a far better chance of survival than her uncle. Ilya would understand; Grandmama would understand; Mama would understand.

She had her duty.

She did stop by Uncle Ilya's bed as often as possible. He was slipping into a coma; he probably wouldn't know if she were there or not.

The day wore on, and Mariana moved through it as if in a dream. When she happened to glance up at the big clock in the ward, she realized with a sickening lurch that she had nearly forgotten about her uncle. Four hours had passed since she last saw him.

34

Mariana rushed into the corridor and to where Uncle Ilya was—where he *should* have been.

But a new cot was in his place, a new patient!

In a sudden panic, Mariana accosted the first orderly she saw. "Where's the patient who was there before?"

"What patient? Where?"

She pointed. "Where is he?"

"Took him away an hour ago, miss. Dead, you know."

"That can't be! I'm in charge here. Why wasn't I notified? You can't just go removing anyone you think is—"

"But the doctor was here. He—"

"Vlasenko?"

As soon as the orderly nodded, Mariana spun around and dashed through the corridor. She looked in several wards, then someone told her he was on his way to surgery. Running now, Mariana went to the stairway the doctors used to reach the operating rooms on the first floor. She ran down one flight before she heard the clicking of shoes against the hard steps.

She bore down on Vlasenko like a charging army.

"You heartless animal!" she yelled. "You were probably waiting over him like a vulture—who knows if he was really even dead. I wouldn't put it past you to send a living man to the morgue just to spite me. How could you—?" She was nose to nose with Vlasenko, screaming in his face, pounding on his chest with her fists. "I'll see you banned from the medical profession for this! I'll see you shot—"

"What . . . on earth!" Vlasenko could hardly speak in the face of Mariana's bombardment.

"You're finished here, Vlasenko! I swear you'll never practice medicine again."

"You're talking gibberish, woman. Have you gone insane?"

"*You're* insane!" she retorted. "Just because he was a poor peasant. You had no right! None, do you hear—"

"Mariana." The voice interrupted her tirade, a calming tone that tried to soothe her like an embrace.

Her head jerked around. It was Dr. Itkinson.

"I'm glad you've come, Doctor," she said. "This man must be stopped. Just because he hates me for rejecting him, it gives him no right—"

"Mariana, please—" Dr. Itkinson began.

"He killed my uncle," Mariana accused. "I know how much he hates us."

"You know that's not true, Mariana," said Itkinson.

"It certainly is not!" huffed Vlasenko. "Of all the—"

"Let me take care of this, Karl," Itkinson interrupted as he put an arm around Mariana. "I'm so sorry about your uncle, my dear. No one could have done anything for him. It is a miracle he survived as long as he did. It's no one's fault."

"No . . . no . . . it's his fault. . . ." Mariana pointed a finger at Vlasenko, but even as the force of her accusation weakened, so did her outstretched hand. Her arm dropped useless to her side. "*It's my fault.*" Her voice shuddered over the terrible realization.

"Neither is that true, dear. Come with me; we can talk in my office, have some tea perhaps."

The very mention of returning to the hospital wards filled her with utter revulsion. "I . . . I . . . can't . . . It's too . . ." Her tortured eyes met Dr. Itkinson's. "My uncle is dead."

Then she turned and ran down the stairs.

Mariana ran for three blocks before she realized she had no place to run. There were no quiet places of retreat in this war-ravaged city, no parks or public gardens where she could sit in safety and try to make sense of an existence that was crumbling like the mortar of the bombed-out buildings. Even if there were, it was dark outside, hardly the time to stroll through a garden.

Where else could she go?

210

Then she thought of Daniel, and how desperately she needed a friend. He had known great loss; he would understand. He would be there for her.

35

A cold mist from the sea enveloped the town. Mariana shivered in the night air. More haunting than the darkness was the silence—a quiet almost as unnerving as the constant shelling had been. The fighting forces must be regrouping after the most recent battle—the battle that had taken Ilya Burenin's life. Only the distant report of gunfire from a stray sniper filled the misty air.

Darkness and fog shrouded most of the squalor in the Chinese section of town where Daniel's inn was located. Being on the outskirts of town, it had escaped the heaviest effects of the bombing, but there were still bombed-out buildings lining the roads and gaping craters in the streets.

Mariana's frantic pace slowed, and her natural wariness took over. She didn't want to think of what might lurk in the shadows. But Daniel's inn was down a back street. She didn't know exactly where, for he had only told her about it; she had never been there.

The Imperial Palace it was called. She could hardly imagine anything equal to that lofty appellation in this run-down neighborhood.

She searched down two streets without success. There was not a soul around to ask directions, and she grew more apprehensive by the minute. A cat's shrill meow caused her to jump and gasp. The sound of a voice in the distance made her flatten herself against a wall for fear of being seen, in spite of the fact that a human was exactly what she needed in order to get some directions. She had brought no coat and was trembling with both cold and fear.

Then she turned a dark corner and collided with a dark figure.

They both cried out in shock, then the stranger scrambled to hurry away.

"Please, wait!" called Mariana as she regained some of her wits.

The person slowed. Perhaps he felt safe knowing the intruder was only a female.

Mariana gathered her courage and ran after him. "Please, can you give me directions?"

The man answered in Chinese. Mariana could not understand a word.

"Imperial Palace?" she said several times, hoping the message got across.

He answered with another stream of unintelligible Chinese, then pointed. But that gesture could mean anything, and Mariana shrugged her confusion. It took a moment, but he finally perceived that this Russian girl had no idea what he was talking about. He grabbed Mariana's hand and tugged at it, indicating for her to follow.

In less than five minutes, he brought her to a door in a row of squalid buildings. The Chinese characters over the door told her nothing, but the faded likeness of a pagoda-style palace under them was unmistakable.

Mariana wanted to hug the stranger. She gave him a ruble instead, and he obviously appreciated this far more.

Three Chinese locals, two men and one woman, sat inside. Mariana was hoping one spoke her language, when the woman said in broken but decipherable Russian, "You want help?"

"I'm looking for Daniel Trent, the American."

"He not here."

"What?" It was more an indication of frustration than a question.

"I say, he not—"

212

"Where is he?" Mariana's distress and disappointment infused her tone with impatience.

"How should I know? He no tell me."

Mariana spun around and left. What her hurry was, she did not know. She had no place else to go. Perhaps she just didn't want the people in the inn to see her in such a state. She had wanted to see Daniel—needed to see him. Where was he at this hour? Probably after some stupid news story. Why wasn't he here when she needed him? Didn't he care? Didn't—

She stumbled aimlessly down the street, and would have laughed at herself had she been able. How could she blame Daniel for not being home? He had his own life, and work to do—important work. She was expecting too much of him to be there for her every whim. But ever since that day during the bombing when Daniel had rescued her, Mariana had come to depend on him more and more.

But this wasn't a whim. She was in trouble, lost, confused. She had never experienced such heartache before; she didn't know what to do.

"Why couldn't he be there, Lord?"

She took a shuddering breath that caught on a tearless sob.

Sometimes he went to Saratov's. But that was on the other side of town. What if they missed each other? Could she chase all over town after him? Again, she realized she had no other options. She thought briefly of Philip, then dismissed the idea. Daniel was her best friend. He would understand her pain and confusion. Something told her that, though Philip meant well, he would never understand.

She began to retrace her steps through Chinatown, down the same dark, scary streets. Even the same cat uttered its night call. By now her mind was in such turmoil she was hardly paying attention to where she was going, trusting instinct to carry her toward Daniel. Instinct, and silent prayers she hardly perceived she was thinking.

"Mariana, is that you?"

He came toward her from a side street, shrouded in mist, his face shadowed by the darkness. Only the dear, familiar sound of his voice told her she could rest; she was safe. She ran into his arms, uttering his name over and over between choking sobs. As she felt the warmth and strength of his embrace, tears—real, cleansing tears—poured from her eyes.

"Daniel . . . Daniel. . . !"

"What is it?" he said softly, stroking her hair.

"I was afraid . . . I couldn't find you . . . Oh, Daniel, I need you!"

"I'm here now," Daniel murmured. His own mind was in a spin. *She* needed *him!* That was simply too incredible to absorb.

It thrilled him.

It scared him to death.

He never used to doubt his own prowess and abilities, and yet here he stood, quaking at the prospect of being needed by a woman like Mariana. This was completely new territory for Daniel; he had always been too footloose and unfettered to allow himself to be in such a position. More importantly, since his father's death, he had been more acutely aware of his own shortcomings than he often liked to admit.

What did he have to give someone like Mariana? Money, yes. But emotional support? Spiritual guidance? Comfort? Was she truly looking to him for these things? In his mind, she had always been the strong one in these areas. Now she was turning to him? He had a paltry store of wisdom for such an occasion.

Only one bit of logic came to him at the moment. "Let's go back to the inn where we can talk."

She nodded, then clung to him all the way back.

The same three people were in the inn's common room. Daniel and Mariana easily found a table in an isolated corner. The woman innkeeper brought them hot tea.

"You must be nearly frozen," Daniel said as he poured tea and placed a steaming cup in her shaking hands. "Just hold it a minute and let it warm you." He didn't have to tell her that, he knew, but he had never really had to care for someone before, and he was rather awkward at it. Surprisingly, as he began to warm up to it, he enjoyed the sensation. Or perhaps it was just that he enjoyed caring for Mariana. He knew she didn't need him—not really. But it felt good, for a short time, at least.

It took several minutes before the tea had warmed Mariana so that her trembling lips could form intelligible conversation. Then the events of that terrible day gushed out like a river breaking through the winter's ice.

Just the telling helped, and hearing Daniel's supportive responses, and seeing the look on his face that said, *I will help you carry this burden.* The questions that had plagued her were still there, but she no longer despaired that there were no answers.

"Daniel, why didn't I stay with my uncle? What am I going to tell my mama? Because of me he died alone. I could have—"

"No more of that, Mariana," he said sternly, like a benevolent father. "Believe me, I know what little good recriminations do."

"It hurts so much."

"But at the same time, you don't think it hurts enough," he said gently. "You feel like a failure, and you want to keep punishing yourself with blame. It won't work, Mariana. You're only going to make it worse."

She nodded. Her head was clearer now. Dear Uncle Ilya was gone; she couldn't do anything to change that awful fact. Daniel was right. And as she gazed at Daniel through tear-filled eyes, she realized how much he had grown since their time in Russia. He wasn't speaking mechanical words of comfort, but rather sharing from the depths of his soul, giving to her from the pain he had known.

"I knew you'd understand," she said.

He shook his head sadly. "I do, dear," Daniel said. "If I learned nothing else from my father's death, I did learn that I can't bring him back, and I can't change past mistakes."

Mariana sniffed and tried to blot her tears with her hand. Daniel handed her his handkerchief.

"Down deep, I guess I know that," she said after a moment. "But I'll still always wonder if I might have done something. Maybe if I had prayed more. Maybe God would have healed him."

"Mariana, if God wanted to heal your uncle He would have found some way to do it without your prayers."

"Then why even bother praying?"

215

A corner of Daniel's mouth twitched in a partial smile. "You're asking me? I'm a lot newer at this praying business than you."

"Papa and Mama could tell us the answer."

"Someday you and I can ask them. And I'll have countless more questions, while I'm at it."

"Oh, Daniel!" For the first time that dismal day, Mariana was reminded that joy did exist. "I can't wait! How I miss them and our happy, peaceful home; Mama's smiles, Papa's poetry, the tuneless song Grandmama hums, even my little brothers' shenanigans."

"I wish they could be here for you now, dear Mariana."

Mariana dried her eyes with the handkerchief. "But as much as I want my family," she said in a clearer, more assured tone, "I'm certain God sent the right person, Daniel. He knew just what I needed, and He brought you to me."

"Whatever would God be doing using a wishy-washy nincompoop like me, who has far more questions about God than answers?"

"It's like I said before—He sees your heart." She smiled. "And I, for one, am glad you don't have all the answers. How would you grow otherwise?"

They fell silent for a few minutes, sipping their tea and enjoying the surprising peace of the time. Mariana couldn't believe that two hours ago she had felt as if her world were crumbling. In a sense, nothing had changed—except for herself.

"When I came here tonight," she said, "I was ready to run away from Port Arthur. I never wanted to see that hospital again. I think I can go back now."

"I'd like to find a way to take you away from here." Daniel took her hands in his. "But you'd never be happy with yourself if you didn't return. You're too strong and brave for that." He brought her hands to his lips and kissed them tenderly. "I love you, Mariana."

I love you.

Those words floated between them for a long moment; they had surprised even Daniel. Yet he knew, even as he heard himself speak them, that he had never meant anything more fervently in his life.

216

Before Mariana had a chance to speak, he added, "Don't say anything now, Mariana. It was poor timing on my part, I know. You're not only grieving your uncle, but you've been under so much stress. There'll be time enough to respond when life is back to normal."

"I can tell you how I feel now, Daniel." She paused and held his eyes with her gaze. "I love you, too."

The intensity of her response sent a thrill through his body, but he found it difficult to accept the reality of their exchanged words of love.

"You don't think it's the impulse of the moment that's speaking?"

"Daniel, I think we've been destined to speak these words to each other for years."

"Nevertheless, it may take a while for it to sink in."

Daniel walked Mariana back to the hospital. He hated to leave her at the door. He knew Mariana was as true as gold in her declaration, but this was war, and life was unpredictable, changing from minute to minute. Even if a heart was true, so many outside events could happen to unravel the best intentions, the strongest love. As he turned away, back into the cold, dark street, he had a deep sense of how fresh and new their love was. Was it strong enough to withstand the fires of adversity that were sure to come?

VIII

UNRAVELING THE PAST

36

After five years Count Dmitri Remizov was still congratulating himself on the wisdom of returning to Russia. This was where he belonged, not traipsing all over foreign lands, allowing himself to be put on display by fawning, giddy women. In Russia he was more than a mere novelty.

With men he found the camaraderie of shared experiences—school, the Guards, war. With women . . . well, it was somewhat the same as during his travels. They were still fawning and at times giddy, but they were Russian women. More and more he was discovering in himself a much greater affinity for things *Russian*. He was almost as bad as the tsar in that respect. But his heritage, and leaving a mark on the future, was more important to him than it had been in the past. Why, he was even considering remarrying—a younger woman who could bear him a son to carry on his name.

He almost chuckled as he thought of that time of near despair in America when he thought he might die alone and in disgrace. He was still in the prime of life. And he need not worry about his daughter forgetting him. She was simply a gem in that respect. But even when she married and left him for good, he wouldn't have to spend his autumn years in solitude. There were droves of women interested in him.

He glanced at his reflection as he passed the French doors. Ah, yes, he did cut a fine figure for a man of forty-seven. What was he saying? He could hold his own with men half his age.

"Dmitri, Dmitri!"

Remizov turned to find Countess Alice Tolgskij. Dmitri had been engaged to her before he married Katrina, but Alice

221

didn't hold his fickle youth against him. She had ended up marrying well, and had been widowed a year ago. Since then she'd had her sights on Dmitri. She was still attractive, and her money was even more so. But she was at least forty-five years old, and no amount of makeup could hide the lines around her eyes. If Dmitri did take the matrimonial plunge, he was set on it being with a woman still of childbearing age.

That determination, however, did not prevent him from being friendly. "Alice, how good to see you." He paused to puff on his cigarette, as always in its six-inch holder. "Isn't this a delightful party?" They were at the home of Prince Velemir Cerni, celebrating his seventieth birthday. "And the 'season' hasn't even begun. We are in for a grand winter."

"If the war doesn't put a damper on things."

"But we must do something to maintain our spirits during this dreary time. My own daughter is over there, and I would go absolutely crazy if I didn't have something to distract my worry."

A servant passed with a tray of champagne. Dmitri plucked off two glasses, handing one to Alice.

"Let us toast our brave young people so gallantly defending Holy Russia!" They clicked glasses and sipped at the expensive drink.

Another woman joined them. "I heard your toast," she said. "If I had a fresh glass, I would lift it also. My brother is fighting in the war."

"Then let's get you a glass, by all means!" Dmitri hurried away, snatched another glass from the servant, and returned. With a flourish he gave it to the newcomer, appraising her carefully as he did so. He didn't recognize her as from the St. Petersburg social set. She was in her early twenties and pretty, in a plain, understated way. She had gentle brown eyes and looked as if she'd be far more comfortable in a church than at this party.

The three clicked glasses again and Dmitri noted with pleasure that Alice was giving the newcomer a rather critical scrutiny.

"I don't believe I've had the pleasure of your acquaintance," said Alice formally.

"I don't get to St. Petersburg often—you know how Muscovites are." She smiled, and her plainness was suddenly replaced by a glowing beauty. "I'm Yalena Barsukov."

Dmitri clicked his heels smartly and, bowing, took her slim, graceful hand in his and kissed it. "A pleasure indeed! I've heard the name, *Princess* Barsukov, isn't it?"

"Yes."

"An old Moscow family, to be sure. In banking, among other things. But it seems I've heard the name in relation to something else recently. Now what was it . . ." Dmitri stroked his goatee thoughtfully.

Alice wasn't about to be left out of this tete-a-tete. "I am Countess Alice Tolgskij."

"I'm glad to meet you," said the princess. "And you, Count Remizov, need no introduction. I inquired of our host about you—you see, I have heard of you recently also."

"Is that so? I am most intrigued."

"My brother and your daughter have made each other's acquaintance in Port Arthur."

"Ah, yes! Now I remember. The last letter I received from Mariana—in fact, the last since the Japanese tightened down on the siege. Your poor brother was wounded and was a patient of my daughter's. He is well, I hope?"

"He, too, managed to get a letter to our mother. He wanted to allay her fears in case word of his wound had reached her. He was quite well at that time. But there hasn't been mail from Port Arthur for months."

"It only adds to our anxiety."

"When I learned that you would be at Count Cerni's party, I wanted to meet you. From my brother's description of your daughter, I think I'd be safe in assuming that she did not see fit to tell you the whole story of my brother's hospitalization."

"The whole story?"

"Philip was about to have his leg amputated, but Mariana did not feel the severity of the wound warranted such a drastic measure. She stood up to Philip's doctor and insisted another surgeon be consulted. As a result, his leg was saved."

Dmitri beamed.

"You have every reason to be proud," said Yalena.

"Why, Dmitri," interrupted Alice, in another attempt to make her presence known, "your Mariana is a real heroine!"

"And it is so like her." Dmitri made no attempt to hide his affection. "A girl of real principles, and the strength to stand up for them. Not that she is bold or brassy, mind you," he added quickly. "A sweeter, more gentle girl you'll not find anywhere."

"You don't need to sing your Mariana's praises to me," smiled Yalena. "My brother has already done so in no uncertain terms. He is quite taken with her."

"Really? How kind of him."

"Thank you for allowing me to interrupt your conversation," said Yalena. "I shall leave you to yourselves."

"It was the most pleasant interruption of the evening!" Dmitri plied Yalena with his most charming grin.

"It was good meeting you." Alice infused a definite finality into her tone as she repositioned herself subtly to inch Yalena out.

But Dmitri stepped around her and caught Yalena's attention once more. "Princess Yalena, how long will you be here in St. Petersburg?"

"A week more. I am visiting my aunt and uncle."

"Perhaps our paths will cross once more. In the meantime, thank you for telling me about Mariana."

"It is the least I could do. I am more grateful to your daughter than words can express. I have added her to my daily prayers, and I light a candle for her safety each time I attend Mass."

Sometime later Countess Eugenia Remizov, in attendance at the same party, managed to get her son off alone.

"I saw you talking with Princess Barsukov earlier. What was it all about? You realize the Barsukovs are among the richest, most influential families in Moscow—probably in all of Russia. What did she want? It seemed a most pleasant exchange."

"Oh, my dear mama. It was! It was!"

"Well, tell me about it?"

"If you would read Mariana's letters," he said with just a hint of rebuke, "perhaps you'd know."

"My name may be on the envelopes, but it is obvious her letters are for you. I don't put my nose where it doesn't belong."

"I think it is sweet that she includes you. You never write to her."

"And would she care to hear from me?" Eugenia sniffed with derision. "Now, tell me about the Barsukovs."

"Well, it seems my Mariana saved their son's life. Princess Yalena is most grateful, as is her brother. Apparently he is quite taken with Mariana."

"Taken. . . ? Hmmm, this sounds promising. What a match that would be! I couldn't have come up with a better one had I worked night and day. Perhaps her crazy notion of being a war nurse wasn't so bad after all."

"Is that all you think of, Mariana's marriage?"

"Why not? Regardless of her feminist notions, the girl will have to marry one day; there's no reason why it can't be to a man of family and substance. I might remind you, my suddenly idealistic son, that a Barsukov dowry would set you up for life."

"There is more to life than money, Mama."

Eugenia laughed at that. "Maybe if you had to pay your own bills for a change, you'd think differently."

"Besides," Dmitri said, adroitly skirting the touchy subject of his financial accountability, "Mariana also mentioned in her letters that she has met that American fellow, Trent, in Manchuria. They were quite taken with each other four years ago, and I rather liked the man."

"That uncouth reporter? Bah!"

"Well, Mama, I must tell you unreservedly that I wish for Mariana to marry for love, not position."

Eugenia had begun to discover that her self-centered, rather foppish son, who in most cases could be easily manipulated, was almost impossible to argue with where Mariana was concerned. Eugenia had made an enormous mistake in backing down the first time he had stood up to her, over the issue of medical school. Now he seemed to think he had complete license where his impudent brat was concerned.

But Eugenia wasn't going to give up easily on this issue. They all stood to gain from a good marriage. "Do you mean to tell me you'd consent to her marrying a foreigner—an *American*?" She slurred over the last word as if it were the same as saying "leper."

"Well, I—"

"Ha! And you, who so extol the glory of Russia! How you spout off about your pride in being Russian. It all must be rhetoric in order to ingratiate yourself to the powers that be."

"I mean every word of it!"

"But you'd permit Mariana to marry a foreigner?"

"You know Mariana; it doesn't much matter what I *permit*. She does have a mind of her own."

"And it is about time you took her in a firm hand. If you don't have the heart for the job, then let someone who does do it. You must not let your insipid sentimentality spoil Mariana's future."

"I'll take what you've said under consideration," Dmitri said rather sulkily.

————

Dmitri was relieved when Eugenia excused herself, but he continued to reel from her harangue. It took a good ten minutes before he could get back into a proper mood for the remainder of the party. Still, his mother's intractability took the edge off his enjoyment; the only further bright spot was another brief conversation with Yalena Barsukov. She was a lovely woman—well, *young* woman. But so mature for her age, so poised and gracious. And he had found out, much to his satisfaction, that she was unattached. How such a lovely woman had made it to the ripe age of twenty-seven without getting snagged by some worthy Moscow aristocrat, Dmitri had no idea.

Dmitri made a point of learning her aunt and uncle's address so he could visit her before she left the capital. Perhaps he could make both his female relatives happy by obtaining a share of the Barsukov money without involving Mariana.

But, who knew? Perhaps Mariana was interested in Philip, after all. Wouldn't that be quaint? Father and daughter marrying sister and brother.

37

Three days later, on Vassily Island across the street from the humble residence of Anna and Sergei, a lone figure hid in a dark alley.

It was only about seven-thirty in the evening, but darkness came early in November. Basil Anickin had made the best use of the early winter shadows. He had been positioned in this alley for an hour, waiting, watching. He had made a habit of keeping this residence and that of Dmitri Remizov under surveillance—not every day, but often enough so that he had a very good idea of their routines. He and Jack had also made the acquaintance of a couple of the Remizov servants, frequenting a certain saloon where the two, a chauffeur and a grounds keeper, were regulars.

Patience and perseverance were Basil's closest allies these days. And, by the look of the situation in Manchuria, it appeared as if Basil would be rewarded by soon getting Katrina's daughter back in the nest. Only then could he strike at his blood enemies.

This night he was more weary of his quest than usual. It had snowed the night before, and his feet were numb and frozen. But his vigilance had reaped a small reward. He didn't know quite what to make of it, but if it had any significance at all, he'd find it.

Anna—her surname was Christinin now—had had a most

peculiar visitor earlier. He was, in fact, still in the house, probably partaking of the evening meal. It had been years since Basil had seen the man, but he would recognize the aloof and distinguished countenance of Prince Viktor Fedorcenko anywhere.

What was the mighty prince doing visiting a poor Vassily Island home?

True, Anna had once served his household, but according to Basil's sources, she never returned there after Katrina's death. She had secretly raised Katrina's daughter in the mean peasant village of Katyk. There she had married that Christinin fellow and had two sons of her own. So what would Fedorcenko be doing here? He had been there almost as long as Basil had been in the alley. Was it logical to assume that such a lengthy visit had to be something other than business?

Possibly it had to do with the granddaughter, Mariana. The old man might have a letter to share. Basil had assumed the same thing a few days ago when Count Remizov had visited Anna's home.

Mariana must be the link.

But Basil was not one to accept obvious answers. Life was not simple, and you missed too much if you just studied it on the surface. Because his own designs and desires were complex and convoluted, he expected the same from others. And this Fedorcenko clan had proved more inscrutable than most.

In ten more minutes Sergei and Viktor exited the house. They were chatting amiably as a fancy coach came around from the back of the apartment building. Both men climbed in and the carriage drove away.

Basil knew that Sergei had a regular tutoring session at the Assembly "clubhouse" tonight. There was also to be a board meeting of the Assembly leadership, to which Basil had contrived an invitation. The old man was probably just giving Sergei a lift to the meeting.

This connection might turn into nothing. But Basil had some time before the meeting and determined to take advantage of it.

He went to the best place he knew to glean information—a neighborhood saloon.

A glass of kvass in hand, he sat at the bar and exchanged friendly words with the three or four other men around him. Basil could be friendly when it suited his purposes—so much so that people almost forgot about the alarming intensity of his appearance.

After a few minutes, he asked casually, "Did anyone see that fine coach drive up around the corner? I thought for a minute it might be royalty."

"Isn't the first time that rig has been round," said one of the men.

"Is there a dispossessed grand duke living on Vassily Island?" chuckled Basil.

"Don't know who exactly the fellow is, but I live a couple of doors away, and I've seen him there before over the years. Real friendly with Sergei Ivanovich and his family."

Basil drained his drink and said no more. No sense being too inquisitive and raising suspicions. Besides, what more was there to know? Fedorcenko had been there more than once—not just recently either, but before the war had taken the granddaughter away. The only other question this raised was one these men could not answer.

What was the significance of Fedorcenko's visits *before* the war, especially in view of the fact that Mariana had been living with her father for the last five years? Her grandfather would have no reason to visit Anna for the sake of maintaining contact with Mariana.

It was food for thought, but it shouldn't affect Basil's plans at all.

He rose, left the saloon, and headed to the Assembly clubhouse.

38

Father Gapon's Assembly had a clubhouse, as they liked to call it, in the Vyborg district of St. Petersburg. The workers were quite proud of it, for they had remodeled the rented building themselves and brought in whatever odd pieces of furniture they could spare from their own homes. They built benches to accommodate large groups, and they even had a piano. Gapon saw to it that portraits of Russian tsars hung prominently on the walls, along with an icon-adorned "beautiful corner."

The clubhouse had become a comfortable place where workers could gather in the evenings during the week, and for most of the day on weekends. No alcohol was permitted, but a samovar of tea was always available and baked goods were often brought in by the women. Along with the opportunity for casual socializing, there were regular, organized meetings, such as study groups in which the members could discuss current events, newspaper articles and, occasionally, even some government-censored literature.

Sergei was glad to have helped make possible the enriching of the workers' minds by teaching them to read. Otherwise, many would have obtained nothing from the discussions. It made Sergei's sacrifice well worth it when he watched his pupils accomplish even a relatively mundane task such as reading a newspaper.

Sergei was thrilled at Gapon's progress with the Assembly, and he liked the tone of the group far better than that of the revolutionary groups he had seen. For one thing, Gapon was no revolutionary. Though quite intelligent and educated, he spoke and related to others, especially the workers, in a simple, unsophisticated way. He thought little of theoretical debates. And Sergei was quite certain Gapon had read next to nothing about politics, and knew even less about the revolutionary movement of the intelligentsia.

In fact, like the workers themselves, he was rather conservative and nursed some suspicion of such organizations as the Social Democrats and Social Revolutionaries.

Sergei glanced up from his work as Gapon entered the clubhouse. The priest tried to be in attendance at the meeting place whenever possible. That was getting more difficult, however, with nine branches of the Assembly now open in the city and two outside, and with nearly five thousand members.

"Ah, here comes the dictator," said the worker Sergei was tutoring. "We'd better look smart." The man spoke with affection, and Gapon liked the tongue-in-cheek appellation of dictator. He had even taken it one step further and given similar "titles" to others in the Assembly's leadership, such as "Viceroy" and "Minister of the Interior." He called Sergei his "Minister of Education."

Gapon approached the table where Sergei and his student sat. "Preparing another future leader, I see," Gapon said to Sergei. Then, patting the worker on the shoulder, he said, "When will you lead our next study group, Sandro?"

Sandro laughed. "I'm barely out of the first primer. Give me a year or two."

"That's much too long for a bright fellow like yourself. I wager it'll be in six months."

"If I had the money, I'd bet you," said Sandro.

"If I were a betting man." Gapon laughed heartily at his jest. He then added, "Our group will be meeting soon; we won't be interrupting your studying, will we?"

"We're almost done," said Sergei.

"Good. We'll need both of you."

Several others entered the building just then, among them Oleg Chavkin and the two strangers he had introduced to Sergei several weeks ago. They could hardly be called strangers anymore, for they had both been frequent visitors to the clubhouse, and at the next members induction, Oleg was going to sponsor both as full Assembly members. Sergei had never really warmed up to the two men, though he could not specifically say why. Probably just personality differences. You couldn't like everyone.

Jack Caine immediately busied himself taking photographs. He had one of those little hand-held cameras that took pictures called "snapshots." Sergei had heard of them but had never seen one. It was quite extraordinary. However, he became uncomfortable when Caine turned the camera toward him.

Sergei held up his hand. "Some other time, Jack." He tried to sound casual. "You'll distract my pupil."

"Just one photo," Caine said in inept Russian. Sergei had always kept quiet his knowledge of English and other languages. Caine turned to Basil and said in English, "Rolf, would you tell this good fellow that I'm doing an article for an American labor periodical, and a photograph of Russian workers hard at their studies would be perfect. Not to mention the positive public relations it would foster."

Basil passed this along to Sergei, who shrugged, still lacking enthusiasm. He allowed the photographs, but he made Sandro keep his nose in his primer, and Sergei himself remained bent over the book with his student.

Gapon was better disposed to the photographing, especially when Caine informed him that there were Americans with money acutely interested in supporting a labor movement in Russia.

In about fifteen minutes the meeting began. About thirty men were participating. One of the members with ties to the Social Democrats wanted to discuss a Marxist pamphlet he had recently read. Gapon allowed this to continue for about five minutes, then steered the group into a discussion of an editorial in the workers' newspaper, *Russkaia Gazeta*, which praised Interior Minister Svyatopolk-Mirsky's administration.

The subtle change of subject wasn't lost on Sergei. Gapon was having a difficult time keeping out radical ideas. More and more workers with ties to revolutionaries were joining the Assembly. It was bound to happen. In order for the Assembly to broaden its power base, it had to increase its membership.

Five thousand members sounded like a lot for the fledgling organization, but not when compared to St. Petersburg's *two hundred thousand* workers.

They spent some time discussing a disturbing rumor about factory owners in the city. The owners had never been wholeheartedly in favor of the labor union idea, police sanction or not, and now, nervous about the growth of the Assembly, it seemed they might be preparing to damage the organization.

"We must be constantly aware of our vulnerability," said Gapon. "Our mission is too important to allow trivial matters to undermine it." Then, to close on a lighter note, he added, "Now, we must begin to plan our Christmas activities. Oleg, would you tell us about the children's parties you are planning?"

It seemed appropriate to end in this way. The future of the Assembly and the workers' labor movement seemed much too bright to dwell for long on ominous notes.

39

Cyril Vlasenko had been careful in selecting the site of this particular rendezvous. He had needed a place where three men could meet in obscurity, while insuring that he could not be connected in any way to the meeting.

He chose a church—the St. Nicholas Cathedral, one of the oldest in the city, near the Kryukov Canal. No one would be looking for Cyril Vlasenko in a church, especially in the middle of the week! They timed their meeting to coincide with the end of a midday Mass. In addition, a funeral Mass was being conducted in another corner of the cathedral. Thus, there were enough people coming and going on that Wednesday afternoon—worshipers, mourners, and sightseers—so that the presence of three men having a discreet discussion inside would go unnoticed.

Cyril waited in the small park facing the cathedral. From his strategic bench he had a good view of the main doors of the church. He took no note of all of the stately elegance of the building with its three small cupolas and tall bell tower. Such things had no appeal to the practical-minded man.

Basil Anickin entered the church first. Then, in five minutes, Anickin was followed by Cerkover. Cyril let another few minutes elapse before he heaved his frame from the park bench and entered the church also.

Inside, about fifty people stood at the front altar listening to the priest chanting Mass. To the right, thirty or forty people gathered around a coffin draped in flowers while another priest murmured the funeral litany. Another dozen people strolled about the other open areas of the church, some lighting candles in the hanging braziers. Others were simply tourists having a look at the striking interior. Cyril found the place stifling with its cloying stench of incense, the insidious weeping of mourners, and the drone of the priests.

Cerkover had purchased a candle and was lighting it at one of the braziers. Whether this was part of his cover, or out of actual faith, Cyril didn't know. It looked good, anyway, and when Cerkover walked quietly to the rear of the vast building, it seemed completely natural for him to stand with head bowed and hands folded together in front of him. The fact that he had come specifically to meet the tall, rather intense-looking man standing next to him was not apparent.

Cyril thought about following the same procedure, but he felt rather silly lighting a candle. He quickly genuflected at the altar, then strolled casually around one of the large carved pillars, one of three or four that divided up the main floor. Cerkover and Anickin were standing behind a pillar that bore an icon of St. Nicholas. The icon was as old as the church itself, but its beauty, accented by the flickering candlelight, was barely acknowledged by the pragmatic and agnostic Vlasenko.

Cyril said in a muted voice, "So, at last we meet Nagurski."

He and Cerkover had decided not to reveal to Anickin just how much they knew about his identity. Hints, of course, had been made in order to keep him in line, but other than that it was best to keep the man guessing.

Basil responded with a quick nod of the head.

"What have you to report?" asked Cerkover.

"A new branch of the Assembly has opened," said Basil. "That makes ten—"

"I could learn that in the newspapers," broke in Cyril sharply. "That's not what you're getting paid to report to me."

Basil was unruffled by the rebuke, and Cyril saw that he was indeed dealing with a tough customer. He'd have to watch his step with this one.

"I am getting to that, Your Excellency." Basil spoke in a curt manner, as if he had a right to be impatient with Cyril.

"Go on."

"At the last meeting with an attendance of about thirty," Basil continued, "there were no fewer than six known Marxists—Social Democrats and the like. They are becoming more prominent. I've heard there are even a couple within the leadership."

"Good . . . very good!" said Cyril. "The tsar isn't going to like that. But I'll need substantial proof. Names of men we can definitely link with the S.D.'s. Have you got that?"

"Names mean nothing among the revolutionaries, as I'm sure you must know. They change their names as frequently as their underwear—and, from the smell of some of them, even more so."

Cerkover chuckled at this, but Cyril silenced the mirth with another sharp statement. "So far, in my opinion, you've done little to earn the money we are giving you. Perhaps I can find someone else who is more willing to earn twenty rubles a week—twice as much, I might add, as I pay even my coachman. Do you have anything of subsequence, or not?"

Basil's reaction was sphinxlike. In a tone devoid of all emotion, yet infused with a rather disturbing authority, Basil said, "For a price, Count Vlasenko, I have exactly what you wish."

"As I said, I'm already paying you a pretty kopeck," said Cyril.

"That is for the time I spend attending insipid meetings and socializing with those dull-witted, pathetic workers. Perhaps you would care to exchange places with me for an evening—oh, no, that wouldn't be a good idea, would it? Considering no love is lost between you and the poor and wretched of the city, you might not leave with your life."

"You are rather impudent for being one step up, if that, from the poor and wretched yourself." Cyril only vented a portion of his contempt—part of him was a bit intimidated by this man, though he cringed to admit it.

"Do you want what I have?" Basil persisted calmly.

"At what price?"

"Two hundred rubles—"

Cyril snorted derisively. "That's highway robbery."

"You don't know what I have, yet."

"For anything—"

"Photographs?"

Cyril hadn't expected this. As the old proverb stated, one picture was worth a thousand words. But two hundred rubles? Perhaps if these pictures would convince the tsar to remove his benevolence from the workers' union, it might be.

Cyril turned to his associate. "Cerkover, are we still within our budget?"

"Barely, sir."

He looked at Basil. "I'll give you a hundred rubles."

"Sorry. I have my partner to consider, and we went to considerable trouble to obtain and develop these photographs."

"Come now, Nagurski, this is Russia, not America—here everyone barters, if you recall."

"Not this time. I am firm in my price."

At that moment Cyril considered exposing his knowledge of Anickin's true identity, threatening him with prison if he wasn't more cooperative. But he quickly thought better of it. Something told Cyril that Anickin was a valuable asset, a secret weapon that would come in quite handy someday.

"Show me a sample of what you are selling first," said Cyril reasonably.

Basil reached into his inside coat pocket and drew out a photograph of three or four workers taken at the last Assembly meeting. In the group was one known revolutionary, a Social Revolutionary who had just returned from two years exile in Siberia.

It was enough to tantalize Vlasenko. Cyril made arrangements to pay the two hundred rubles the next day.

40

Back in his office the following day, Cyril studied each of the photographs for the tenth time.

They were well worth two hundred rubles. If he'd had it, he would have given two *thousand* for them. One wide angle shot of the entire group, though a bit blurry, included several familiar faces—radicals who had been under police surveillance. Several other shots of smaller groups confirmed the presence of these unsavory types infiltrating the supposedly police-sanctioned union. One shot was especially pleasing to Cyril—it showed that sanctimonious Father Gapon in friendly conversation with the radical publisher, Prokopovich. This would make a very good argument for the belief that Gapon was courting revolutionaries.

One photograph perplexed Cyril. At first, it seemed to mean nothing, and he was about to toss it aside as useless. Then a spark of familiarity accosted him. It was of two workers seated at a table, looking at a book. One of the men was a big, thick peasant with a broad Mongolian face. The other was more slender by comparison, but by no means small. It was this man that caught Cyril's eye.

He looked like a rather odd cross between a peasant and an old student or professor, and it was this peculiarity that first drew Cyril's attention. The man had on a worn, academic-style double-breasted jacket, a collarless shirt, loose-fitting peasant trousers, and lapti boots laced to the knees. The photo could not show if the man's light hair was gray or blond, but he looked old enough to have more gray than blond. His hair was collar length and he wore a beard, trimmed short and neat, the same shade as the hair.

Yes, there was something familiar about the fellow. Cyril knew it; he felt it. And he couldn't let go.

He lifted up his telephone receiver and called a friend of his in the police department. In half an hour, a police artist was in his office.

"Look at this photograph," said Cyril. "Then I want you to draw a picture of this man—" He pointed to the peasant-student. "Without the beard."

"But of course, Your Excellency! Give me a minute."

It took more than a minute, ten to be exact, before the artist handed his drawing to Cyril.

Cyril shook his head. "No, the man in the photo is much older. Can't you see?" Cyril tossed aside the sheet and demanded another drawing.

The second drawing was more to his liking. He gave the artist five rubles and sent him on his way.

Cyril sat in his big desk chair, the springs creaking with his weight as he leaned back. He rubbed the creases in his chin, deep in thought. He never forgot anything, but sometimes it took a little work to freshen the memory. Usually the work paid off, as in this case.

Seeing the man without the beard helped tremendously. The beard had been short enough, and light enough in color, to hint at the man's innate familiarity. But looking at the sketch of the beardless man sealed it.

Cyril thought back some four years when a madman had chased him from his newly acquired property at gunpoint. Viktor Fedorcenko had snapped completely and tried to stop Cyril from taking possession of the St. Petersburg estate. One person had had the power to "soothe the savage beast," as it were. Vlasenko had assumed that man was a faithful family servant. The fact that the same man turned up in a meeting of the Workers' Assembly, which Vlasenko opposed, was no reason to second-guess that assumption. His infallible recall usually paid off handsomely. This time it was a dead end.

Cyril was a little disappointed that his efforts hadn't produced something juicer. But at least his memory was still as sharp as ever.

He returned his attention to Basil's photographs. He must compose a letter to the tsar requesting an audience. He was about to call in his secretary, when he realized it was well after seven in the evening and the woman had gone home. Cyril took a pen and sheet of paper in order to compose the letter himself; she could type it up in the morning. He began with writing the usual salutations, then stopped.

"How shall I put this. . . ?" he murmured.

He glanced at the photographs as if for inspiration. His restless eyes swept over his desk, over the artist's drawings—both drawings.

Suddenly his head jerked back.

The drawing!

He had carelessly cast away that first sketch as too young. The man in the photo, the man who had helped Viktor, was much older. But now, as his gaze rested on that first drawing, he was confronted again with stark familiarity. It wasn't just that this younger man resembled the older sketch.

This younger man himself was known to Cyril.

It was too incredible for words.

But how could this be?

Cyril shook his head. The more important question was: How could Cyril best use this astounding revelation if it proved to be true?

Cyril lifted his phone receiver again, more thankful than ever for this wonderful invention that gave such instantaneous fulfillment to his cunning desires.

"Cerkover," he said after a moment, "I have another job for you. It must be done with the utmost discretion." He paused as his assistant spoke, then answered, "For the time being, this takes precedence over everything. But it shouldn't take long, and it may involve some waiting due to the distances involved." Cyril listened. "No traveling. A telegram ought to suffice—too bad there are no telephone lines in Siberia." He paused. "Yes, I said Siberia. Now listen closely."

41

Paul Burenin had few desires in life except to work for Russia's freedom. But the task was wearing him down, fraying his nerves, sapping his happiness.

A few days of euphoria had followed his compromise with Lenin. All he had wanted to do was labor for his people, and Lenin gave him that opportunity. But within a week of that day months ago, he was again butting heads with Lenin and the Bolsheviks. Sometimes he thought they cared more about their petty agendas than about elemental freedom. They seemed to be losing sight of what it was all about. And more importantly, many had forgotten completely about the masses, the Russian *people*.

Paul's mind was so distracted that Mathilde feared he might walk into a bus as Lenin had done a couple of weeks ago. Thankfully, Lenin had not been seriously injured—some bruises and cuts, and a badly lacerated eye which he had nearly lost.

Mathilde had recently gleaned the cause of Paul's turmoil, and she had decided to tell him what she saw. She didn't want to add to his misery, but she believed taking such a risk—making him see the truth—might be the only way to help her distraught husband. She could not bear any longer to see him struggle between highs and lows, especially since the lows seemed to be getting so much lower lately.

She thought of the last gathering at Lenin's. Paul had taken the floor for a few minutes and had spoken so eloquently about the Russian people, the noble peasantry. He was desperately attempting to refocus the Party's vision and emphasis. An argument had ensued.

"You sound like a Populist," Stephan Kaminsky accused.

"Isn't the revolution for the people?" Paul said. "We mustn't forget that."

"That sounds like Social Revolutionary gibberish. Are you sure you're in the right Party?"

"Kaminsky, you are of the peasantry like myself. I should think you'd understand."

"I only understand that the masses are asleep. If the revolution were left up to them, it would never happen."

Paul restrained a desire to glance at Lenin. Kaminsky wasn't exactly spouting Lenin doctrine, but his line was far more accepted than Paul's.

"I'm afraid I will never give up on the people," Paul said.

"No one expects you to," said Lenin. "They are the heart and soul of what we are doing."

"It doesn't sound like it." Paul suddenly looked as if he were ready to square off with the leader of the Bolsheviks. "Sometimes I get the impression from some of my worthy associates"—he cast a pointed glance at Kaminsky—"that if the people unanimously agreed they wanted no revolution, the Party would go on anyway."

"That's poppycock!" yelled another of the young men.

"And it's a completely moronic statement," said Kaminsky. "Such a thing will never happen."

The debate had continued for several more minutes until Paul finally wearied of defending his position and sat down.

That evening had sapped more out of Paul than anyone—except Mathilde—realized. For the first time, that night she had a clear glimpse of what was at the root of his difficulties. Now, she must tell him. So she chose a quiet evening as they finished their simple evening meal of bread and sausages. Paul had drawn glasses of tea from the samovar, and they relaxed in their chairs at the plain deal table where they'd had dinner.

"Nothing soothes better than a hot glass of tea," Paul said, but his taut features and lined brow belied his words. "I

241

should get myself a tea plantation and spend the rest of my life doing something really useful for mankind."

"Oh, Paul!" The bitterness in her husband's tone made Mathilde suffer as well, and strengthened her resolve. "I've been thinking . . ."

Paul leaned forward, instantly interested. "What is it, my wife?"

"It isn't easy to say, and certainly it won't be easy for you to hear."

"I'll brace myself, then. But do go on."

"It disturbs me to see you so distressed," she said. "Last summer you were depressed, then you spoke with Lenin and were cheerful—for a few days; then you sank down again. You were happy for a short time again when we went to London. Then—"

"Please don't remind me, Mathilde." Paul sighed. "You make me sound like a bouncing ball."

"I'm sorry, but I must speak plainly."

"I would not want it any other way. Forgive me for interrupting."

"Paul, you have been vacillating terribly, and I believe that is part of why you are so weary. But there is something more, too." She paused, swallowed. "For the last six years you have been playacting—and that can take a great deal out of a man. Since meeting Lenin, you have tried to fit into his mold. You have tried to be a Marxist, and it doesn't fit you. You have tried to be a Social Democrat, and it doesn't fit you. You have tried to be a Bolshevik, and it most definitely doesn't fit you. I've seen how you struggle over an article in order to fashion it within the Bolshevik parameters, while maintaining your personal integrity. That must eventually undermine a person's mental and physical strength. I wonder how you have maintained this long? But, my dear husband, you are being pulled in too many directions. It must stop. I can no longer watch you fall apart."

He didn't speak for a long time, and Mathilde wondered if she had said too much. Usually he appreciated it when she spoke her mind, but this might have struck a chord that was just too personal, and too impossible for him to change.

The silence lingered for two or three minutes. "I don't want to fall apart, Mathilde," he said plaintively. "But what can I do? You and I both know that if there is a revolution in Russia, Lenin will lead it."

"That sounds fatalistic to me."

"I wouldn't be involved here if that were my only motivation," Paul said defensively. "There is much of merit in Lenin; you know it. I respect him enormously as a man and a leader. If only . . ."

"And that is the crux of it all, Paul. If only he embraced democracy more than Marx; if only he wasn't so set on his central committee. But those are the basic elements of the entire Party. You would not even be content as a Menshevik. You have never been comfortable with the Marxist doctrine. Sometimes, Paul, the end does not justify the means." She peered closely at him, measuring her next words carefully. "When you were a boy and fell in with the terrorists, you believed that philosophy for a while until you saw a better way through your study in Siberia. I thought you had matured beyond such notions. But here you are immersed in it again. Sometimes the end isn't nearly as important as *how* you travel there."

"So, if I follow my personal agenda and it leads nowhere. . . ?"

"You will at least be content in knowing you stayed true to your heart."

He smiled, but the gesture was rather pathetic. "Like the hunter who goes after a buck with his favorite rifle, even though the weapon is old and decrepit. He catches nothing; his family starves, but at least he did what made him happy."

"I will not starve; the Russian people will not starve. I suppose the biggest consideration is your own motives, Paul. Do you, like Kaminsky and the others, look to the revolution for its own sake and for the power it will give you?"

"I hope you know the answer to that."

"Yes, I do. But I also know that power can have a great allure, and it could be easy to rationalize about all the good a man in power can do."

"Frankly, I have thought of that—often."

"Do you think Ilyich would tolerate anything but his own agenda?"

Paul stared at his wife. She had hardly changed from that first time he'd met her in Siberia. She did not mince a single word. "How have *you* survived these last six years, Mathilde? They can't have been easy for you in a Party to which you were opposed."

"I was with you, Pavushka." Smiling, she reached out and grasped his hand.

"So, what do I do, wife? Throw out six years of work? I have honestly hoped I could make a difference in the Party, smooth out some of the rough edges, moderate some of the mountains. Have I failed?"

"You have only failed if you give up."

"But you just said I should leave the Party, leave Lenin. Or did I not hear you right?"

"I believe you need to find where you belong. It seems to me the only way to do that is to leave Lenin."

Paul nodded. "I think I'm starting to feel a little better already. Spinning one's wheels in the mud is hard work."

Mathilde rose and went to the samovar to freshen their tea. When she returned, they sat quietly for a while; they had never been ones to muster trivial conversation. At times Mathilde wished they could be like couples they had observed—couples who indulged in playful banter. But they were a serious couple, intense—sometimes too intense. Mathilde often thought they ought to take a vacation from their doctrines and philosophy, and the all-consuming revolution for a while. But she was a little afraid to suggest it because it might be impossible.

After several minutes, Paul broke the silence. "Mathilde, I know where I belong, at least where I can best find where I belong. What do you think about going back to Russia?"

Mathilde's fine, serious mouth broke into an unreserved grin.

Paul returned the grin. "I see that you don't disagree."

"Indeed not! But can you promise me something if we return? I would like to spend some time in your Katyk with your mama. I want to learn how to make bread."

"Bread?"

"A secret desire of mine."

"There are other considerations, you know. But perhaps after so much time, we will not need to be so careful." He paused, and she smiled at his response. It was so like him to temper impulsiveness with reason. "Wife, I don't know if I can promise anything, but I will give it much serious thought."

42

The very presence of the tsar seemed to give courage to the departing soldiers. As he stood on the platform of the train station, garbed in his finest military regalia, Nicholas did indeed look the part of the caring, benevolent father. The troops paraded past him in precise, orderly ranks. He was proud of them, and he thought they sensed it.

He had passed out hundreds of small icons of St. Seraphim to the troops and asked for God's blessing on them as they left for war. He wondered if this would be among the last shipments of troops to the front. How much longer could the war last? Secretly, he hoped it ended soon; the entire war with Japan had resulted in deep humiliation for Russia, both at home and abroad. As tsar he could have put an immediate end to it by surrendering. But after so much had been invested, ending it was as difficult as continuing. A surrender would mean that all those lives had been lost in vain.

How could such a disaster have happened? They—he!—had underestimated the prowess of the Japanese. But who would have believed that, in less than a generation, Japan could have gone from an isolated feudal society to a nation that could challenge, and defeat, the Holy Russian Empire.

The Japanese army of six hundred thousand had faced off with Russia's three-million-strong army—and beaten them at almost every turn. At the beginning the Japanese had hit hard and strong with nearly all their might, while Russia had responded sluggishly by comparison. The millions and all their supplies had farther to travel, and by the time they reached the front in full force, the Japanese had already gained the upper hand. The Russians were never able to recover.

Nicholas tried not to consider the other reason for the failure of the army—the disorganization and ineptitude of the commanders. After all, as tsar, he had been instrumental in appointing most of them.

Nicholas was well trained in public decorum. The thousands of soldiers parading by saw nothing of his despair and depression. He waved and smiled as a proper leader should. The common soldier would never know the burdens that weighed upon Tsar Nicholas.

In addition to everything else, only days ago, Russia had nearly involved itself in a war with Britain. As it steamed out of the North Sea on its way to rescue Port Arthur, the Baltic Fleet had encountered a British fishing fleet and had actually fired upon them. One British boat sank, and two or three lives were lost. The British were understandably outraged. Nicholas had immediately wired "Uncle Bertie," Edward VII, King of England, to express his shock and regret.

Though it was no secret the British supported the Japanese—if not materially, at least in spirit—it appeared as if Great Britain would cool down and not attempt a standoff with Russia. Nevertheless, the last few days had been extremely tense.

It seemed odd that the British should be allied to Russia's enemy, since Bertie was Alexandra's blood uncle. But then, all the crown heads of Europe were intermarried; there probably wasn't a single one who wasn't related to the tsar. Such connections could make decisions rather sticky at times, but national interests usually had a way of taking precedence over family interests.

Nicholas took his private train back to St. Petersburg that day. He didn't like to be away from his family for so long. And he was exhausted with the role of inspiring leader. He almost wished he could hole up in his boudoir, in bed all day long, as Alix was doing lately.

The uncertainty about their son's physical condition was distressful, but life had to continue. Especially when you were the ruler of a mighty nation.

43

Misha had to admit that his duty back at Tsarskoe Selo, fifteen miles south of the capital, was most pleasant. The tsar made his residence here almost exclusively these days, except when he and his family went down to the Crimea. Misha had been back in his old post as Imperial Cossack Guard for the last two years.

He had recently returned from accompanying the tsar for over a week on his rounds of visiting the troops. It was a welcome relief to return to the serenity of Tsarskoe Selo. Perhaps as Misha grew older, he did not have as much need to be in the heat of the action. He had, of course, applied to join the troops at the front, but had been denied on the ground that the Imperial Cossack Guard could not suffer because of the war. He was not as disappointed as he might have been twenty years ago when he had practically *lived* for a good war.

On his way to his post that morning, Misha encountered the grand duchess Tatiana, the tsar's second oldest daughter. At seven, she was a tall, lanky child, graceful and self-assured, and there was no doubt that this one was a child of royalty. Very much in possession of herself, she was a born leader and even her older sister, Olga, deferred to Tatiana.

"Good morning, Misha," she said in a friendly, casual manner.

All the children were down-to-earth and friendly, especially with the servants and staff. They never lorded their position over the servants; in fact, they often were found working right along with them at their chores.

"Good morning, Your Highness—"

"Please, none of that. You know how we hate it."

"Forgive me—uh, Tatiana." Misha would never be quite comfortable with such familiarity; he was thankful the tsar didn't require it also.

"Tell me, I heard a rumor that Lieutenant Nogin is going to be a father. Is that true?"

"I heard a similar rumor." Nogin was one of the younger members of the Cossack Guard.

"My sisters and I want to make something for the baby. Could you let us know the due date so we know how long we have?"

"Of course I will. That's very kind of you."

"Babies are so wonderful. It was so exciting when Alexis was born. I simply adore him. I only wish—" She stopped suddenly then made a complete change in the direction of the conversation. "And what of you, Misha. Why haven't you found a wife yet?"

"I thought you knew. I am waiting for you to grow up, Tatiana."

She giggled. "But by then you'll be older than my father."

"I'm already older than him."

"Oh, really?" She gave this some thought. "Please don't tell him I thought differently."

"Believe me, I won't."

"Anyway, Misha, we need to find you a wife."

"Thank you for your concern, but I think I am too old for marriage. Besides, I'm fairly content as I am."

"But you have no family. Don't you get lonely?"

"Occasionally, I suppose. But my best friend's family is like my own. I am 'Uncle Misha' to his children."

"What are their names?"

"Yuri is fourteen, and Andrei is twelve. Then there's Talia,

248

who is eleven, I think. She isn't their sister, but she's such a close friend that she might as well be part of the family."

"They sound nice. I'm glad you have a family."

Misha thought about that insignificant conversation as he stood guard at his post later in the day. Had he missed something in never marrying? He was happy with his life, and he had a high purpose in his job. He had made a conscious choice not to marry, because he felt a soldier's life did not lend itself well to a family life. And even as a captain in the Cossack Guard, he would have found it difficult to support a family properly. He liked being 'uncle' to Sergei and Anna's children—it provided all the fun and none of the responsibility of parenthood. But occasionally he did envy Sergei.

Was that the only reason he envied his good friend? On some level, he knew that part of the reason for his bachelorhood was the special attachment he felt toward Anna. His feelings were in no way dishonorable, or disloyal to Sergei. But once or twice he had found himself looking at Anna and wishing things had been different.

Perhaps he should have married and tried to wipe away those thoughts by focusing on another woman. Over the years, there had been several other women he could have married. Even now he could easily find a wife among them. Misha was still a handsome, physically fit man. He did indeed look younger than the tsar, who was eleven years his junior.

Ah, well, he told himself, it was too late in life for regrets. And he would never want to do anything to spoil the special camaraderie he had with Sergei and Anna and their children. Those bonds were much too important to him, for they were indeed his family.

———

The very next day, Misha was to go ice-skating with Sergei and Anna and the children. The river was finally frozen solid enough for skating; they were going to bring a lunch and make a day of it. Misha arrived about ten in the morning. He climbed the steps to the front door of Anna and Sergei's building and was about to open the door, when he heard a sound and paused, turning to see if it was one of the children. He

249

then caught a brief glimpse of a figure in the alley across the street. His natural instincts prompted him not to let on that he had seen anything. But it was unusual for someone to be just standing there in the alley, especially on this cold winter day.

Misha entered the building, climbed the stairs to the second floor, and knocked on the apartment door. Raisa welcomed him in. In the flurry of departure, he gave no more thought to the man in the alley. Andrei was having trouble getting a knot out of his lace, Talia couldn't find one of her skates, and Anna was trying to convince Yuri that he could get another season's wear out of his skates.

Raisa chuckled. "The first skating party of the season is always the same. You'd think we'd learn to prepare the day before." Then she joined her daughter in the skate search.

Misha laid aside his own skates and offered Andrei his assistance with the knot. Sergei came down the steps wrapping his wool scarf around his neck.

"It doesn't look as if we'll get off on time," Sergei said.

Misha shrugged. "The ice isn't going anywhere."

In ten more minutes they were all trooping out the door, chattering and laughing. They planned to walk to the tram stop a couple of blocks away, then take the tram to the ice. Misha glanced toward the alley once more. The same man was still there, but this time their eyes met briefly. Misha looked away quickly as if the incident had made no impression upon him. Perhaps he had spent too many years as bodyguard to the tsar, but something about it just did not set well with him.

He casually sidled up to Sergei and subtly indicated for him to fall back from the group a few paces.

"Sergei, I noticed someone hanging out in the alley when I arrived. He's still there. Try to get an inconspicuous look, if you can."

Sergei stopped walking and bent down to tie his shoe, catching a glimpse of the alley as he did so.

"There's no one there," he said.

Misha looked. The alley was vacant. He shrugged and shook his head. "Rather peculiar, isn't it? That someone should loiter there for a good fifteen minutes, then the minute he is noticed, he runs away."

"Some street vagrant, probably."

"Yes, I suppose so. But you ought to take care, nevertheless. I've heard of burglars who spy out a neighborhood before striking."

"Well, he'd have to be a pretty desperate thief if he plans to rob this neighborhood. Most of the residents don't have two kopecks to rub together."

"I'm probably making something out of nothing."

"Let's catch up with the others."

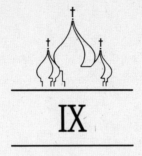

IX

PROPOSALS

44

Mariana had found the strength to return to the hospital. The initial euphoria of Daniel's expression of love helped carry her through the next two days of ceaseless labor.

Her uncle's funeral was a struggle, even though Daniel and Philip stood by her. Ilya was buried in a graveyard with hundreds of other fallen soldiers, thousands of miles from home. Mariana tried not to think of her family, especially her grandmama, who would never be able to visit her son's grave.

The work of the hospital continued in spite of her grief. The wounded and sick never seemed to stop coming. The deaths never got easier. They were completely out of anaesthetics, and the morphine supply was so low it could be used only on the most critical patients. In the past, Mariana had been disturbed by the plenteous amounts of vodka in the besieged city because many of the male hospital attendants were drunk all the time. Now she was thankful for it and had often sent those same attendants on black market "raids" to obtain it for hospital use.

The physical condition of the hospital staff was also deteriorating. Long shifts and poor diet had reduced most to utter exhaustion. Mariana herself, even days before her uncle's death, had noticed bleeding in her gums—a suspicious symptom of scurvy.

Mariana, indeed, had been bolstered by her recent encounter with Daniel, but life had not improved one hundred percent, or even fifty percent. She was simply able to continue to survive—and in the present conditions, that in itself was nothing short of a miracle.

The day she returned to work after Ilya's funeral, she met Dr. Itkinson in the corridor.

"Dr. Itkinson," she said, "I want to thank you for attending my uncle's funeral. It meant a great deal to me."

"It was the least I could do, Mariana. You are certain you are ready to work?"

"What else is there to do, Doctor? It occupies my mind, and sometimes I even forget to notice the bombing."

"I was on my way to find you," the doctor said after a short pause. "I have a bit of a proposition to offer you."

"Really?"

"The Japanese have offered us a small concession in return for the cease-fire we granted a few days ago."

"That's unusual, isn't it?"

"Not entirely. We are fighting an honorable enemy, I suppose."

"What is their concession?"

"They are going to allow a Red Cross boat safe passage from the harbor in order for us to evacuate some of our wounded. Stoessel has lined up a German freighter for the job. After some remodeling, it will accommodate about one hundred and fifty wounded. I know it seems a minuscule number, considering all the thousands we have, and, in my personal opinion, it is hardly worth the effort because of the accompanying personnel we will have to lose. But Stoessel is adamant that we accept the gesture. I'm in the process now of surveying all the hospitals to select the patients for the journey."

"They won't all be officers, will they, Dr. Itkinson?"

"Not if I have any say in the matter," Itkinson replied with conviction. "The largest percentage will be common soldiers. Whoever goes, however, must be seriously wounded, but with a high chance of recovery. It's not an easy selection to make. Even more difficult is staffing the boat. Choosing a physician was no problem—Vlasenko volunteered for the duty, and I saw no reason to deny him. He is the one person on the staff I can afford to do without. The nursing staff was another matter. You are all invaluable. And I know no one would volunteer to leave. But I have chosen you, Mariana, to go with the boat."

"Dr. Itkinson, I know my work has suffered lately—"

"Don't misunderstand me, Mariana," Itkinson quickly interjected. "I'm not sending you away because I am unhappy with your work. You are the best nurse I have."

"Then, why?"

"My dear, you have been through enough—and you have given enough. I am a doctor, remember? I can tell your health is suffering."

"I am not the only one."

"Nevertheless, I am sending you. But don't think for a minute you are being sent on vacation. The waters between here and Vladivostok, your destination, are rife with their own dangers. And once you have turned over your patients, you'll have orders to report by train to Mukden, where the next major battle of this war will most likely be fought. I would be reluctant to let you go, Mariana, if I didn't believe they will soon be needing you there more than we do here."

Mariana shrugged. "If those are my orders, what can I say?"

He gave her arm a paternal pat. "The military is wonderful in that way—making all our difficult decisions for us."

"When will we leave?"

"As soon as the ship is refitted. A few days at best, but we want to get off before the harbor closes up with ice."

————

Mariana couldn't get away from the hospital, but she sent a message to Daniel, asking if he could come see her that evening.

She was changing a patient's dressing when she had a visitor. It wasn't Daniel.

"Philip, what a surprise."

"I heard about your orders. I don't know whether to be thrilled or depressed."

"Let me finish here, then we can talk."

In five minutes she led him to two vacant chairs at the nurse's station where they sat facing each other.

"I have mixed feelings also," Mariana said, picking up on Philip's last comment. "A few days ago, I wanted nothing more

257

than to get away from this place. But now I feel like I'm letting everyone down."

"It's not your choice, Mariana. But my feelings spring from a different source. I am glad you are leaving the dangers and privations here. I could see, though you have tried to hide it, that you have been sick for days. It's good you are leaving before it gets worse. But—" He sighed heavily. "My selfish side wants you to stay. You have made this war bearable for me, and I don't know what I will do without your sweet smile and your soft, dear voice."

"Philip—"

"Please, let me finish. I love you, Mariana, and I want you to be my wife. I know wartime sometimes breeds fickle hearts, but I am certain you are the woman for me."

"Please, Philip, I can't let you go on."

"I know you don't love me in the same way," he continued in a rush. "But that doesn't bother me as long as I can be with you always, caring for you, protecting you. I can think of nothing else but spending the rest of my life with you."

"Philip, you are such a dear man, and the depth of your affection does me great honor—"

"As I would do for all of our days together."

"But, Philip, you deserve more. You deserve a woman who can love you with all the passion you yourself can give. You deserve to be unreservedly adored—and I know you will find her one day."

"But it is not you?"

"Not when I love another."

He shook his head, disappointed but not crushed. "Ah, I see. Daniel Trent."

She nodded in reply. And, to avoid hurting Philip too much, she tried to subdue her joy at simply hearing Daniel's name. But she knew her feelings were evident on her face.

"To be honest," Philip said, "I thought I saw it the first time I saw the two of you together. But, as neither of you indicated anything to me, I hoped it was my imagination, and I might still have a chance with you."

"We only just discovered it a few days ago ourselves—I

think it was brewing for a long time, though. I hope I didn't do anything to lead you on."

"Only by being your natural, angelic self."

"I'm sorry, Philip."

He chuckled warmly. "Thank you for saying so, anyway. I'll recover in time."

"When you return to Russia, a decorated war hero, there will be dozens of women ready to fall madly in love with you. And, if it hadn't been for Daniel, doubtless I would have been one of them."

At that moment, she glanced up to see Daniel approaching. Philip rose immediately and held out his hand, grinning at a somewhat bemused Daniel.

"You are a lucky man," Philip said, giving Daniel's hand a vigorous shake.

"What's this?" Daniel glanced back and forth between Philip and Mariana.

"Mariana has just turned down my marriage proposal in favor of a certain American correspondent."

"Daniel and I haven't discussed marriage yet," Mariana said quickly.

"What?" Philip turned toward Daniel with shock, partly feigned, partly genuine. "My dear fellow, what are you waiting for? Do you realize what you have in this girl? A priceless gem, an incalculable treasure! Don't risk letting her get away." He gave Mariana a wink. "She won't have far to go."

For one of the few times in his life, Daniel was nearly speechless. Mariana laughed. She felt bad for him, but it *was* a sight to behold. Nevertheless, she came to his rescue.

"Philip, you'll scare the poor man away," she said lightly. "You know how Americans are, fiercely independent. I thought we'd ease gently into the subject of marriage."

Philip and Mariana laughed, and even Daniel managed a chuckle or two.

At last he was able to speak. "You are taking this quite well, Philip."

"Above all, I want Mariana's happiness, and I know she would never be happy with me as long as she loved you."

Philip paused and became serious. "In that vein, Daniel, I would make a request of you."

"Say on."

"You must accompany Mariana to Vladivostok—"

"Where?"

"Daniel, that's why I asked you to come this evening," Mariana said. "I've been ordered to accompany a Red Cross ship to Vladivostok. The Japanese are going to allow this in return for the cease-fire we granted. I'll leave in a few days."

"And we cannot let her go without protection," Philip put in.

"Of course I'm going with her." Daniel spoke without a moment's hesitation.

Mariana nearly protested the idea that she needed protection. But the prospect of having Daniel along on the journey was too attractive to resist.

"Now, I must return to my duties," said Philip. Before departing, however, he asked Daniel, "May I give Mariana a parting farewell, in the Russian style? She did, after all, save my life and I shall be forever in her debt for that."

Daniel nodded his approval, and Philip gave Mariana an enthusiastic hug.

When Philip was gone, Daniel smiled. "Imagine him asking me for permission to hug you. He is a bit old fashioned, isn't he?"

"Just a little."

"Did he really propose to you?"

"Practically on bended knee."

"I may not be able to top that."

"You don't need to, Daniel. And I don't expect you to propose marriage to me this instant, either."

"But someday. . . ?"

"What do you think?"

"I definitely plan to, Mariana."

She smiled and nodded. "But first, let's just get used to this idea of being in love. It's quite a big enough step from being friends—for the time being."

He gazed at her with open love. He seemed ready to sweep her into his arms with far more than a Russian-style embrace.

Mariana felt the romantic tension and diverted their attention to another matter.

"I'm glad you're going with me, Daniel, even if I don't really need protection. On second thought, Karl Vlasenko will be along, so perhaps I might need protection after all."

"Now I'm more sure than ever!"

"Daniel, you won't mind leaving the action to accompany me?"

"You know me, Mariana, I can find news wherever I go. But I came here in the first place to be with you, so there's no reason for me to stay if you're gone. And, when I see you safely ashore, I can always return to the war."

"I'm to be assigned to Mukden afterward."

"Then we can go there together."

45

Despite Stoessel's war on the press, Nojine had some friends in Port Arthur's high command. When he heard of Stoessel's plan to use the hospital ship to get vital information out of Port Arthur, he immediately thought of Daniel, who had mentioned that he would accompany the boat.

He told his contact, Smirnoff's aide, about Daniel. What better decoy to use as a spy than a foreign correspondent who had no direct ties to Russia?

Nojine approached Daniel the day before the boat was to leave.

"Daniel, I have a great opportunity for you."

"I hope you're not going to try to get me to stay. My mind is made up."

"Not at all. How would you like to turn this voyage into a real coup for your newspaper?"

Daniel shrugged, amazed himself that he wasn't more interested.

Nojine continued, "Stoessel has some information he must get out—"

"Hold on! Are you suggesting I act as a spy for Stoessel, of all people?"

"I think this could be extremely beneficial to you."

"Why don't you do it?"

"They'd rather have a foreigner in order to distance themselves in case—well, just as added insurance. Besides, someone has to stay behind to report the fall of Port Arthur."

"How would this be beneficial to me?"

"You name it, Stoessel will give it to you in return for your services."

Daniel leaned forward, growing more interested by the minute. "Are you sure?"

"You can talk to them yourself. Smirnoff's aide will meet us in an hour at Saratov's."

An hour later, Daniel, Nojine, and Captain Zinkov sat at a table in deep discussion.

Zinkov explained what he wanted. "We captured a Japanese officer and under interrogation he revealed information about troop movements. The Japanese have recently landed eight thousand troops. We need to apprise Kuropatkin of this situation, for it will have a direct effect on his operations. Another contingency of troops will be landing before the end of the year."

"Don't you think that using the Red Cross boat in this way will place them at risk?"

"You, of course, would have to be willing to take all responsibility upon yourself. On the remote chance that the boat is scrutinized, the Japanese will no doubt accept your story that you acted completely on your own. We wouldn't do this if we thought there was any danger at all to the passengers. Even you should be perfectly safe disguised as one of the wounded. However, a disguise should be a last resort. We feel it would be best if no one else on the boat knows of the situation. Their ignorance will give you the best cover."

"Well, I'll play that one by ear," said Daniel.

"Does that mean you'll do it?"

"I'll expect certain compensation."

"Of course. What did you have in mind?"

"A guarantee of free movement at the front. I'll be going to Mukden after the boat excursion, and I want to cover Kuropatkin's spring campaign. And I want an exclusive interview with Kuropatkin himself."

"The assignment to the front, we can arrange. But it is difficult to speak for General Kuropatkin."

"Come now, Captain. I'll be taking a great risk here; surely you can arrange one tiny interview. Remember, the general should be quite grateful to receive the information I'll be carrying."

"All right, Mr. Trent, you have my word on it."

"Then it's a deal."

"The ship will be leaving tomorrow morning with the tide. Stop by my office before then for the documents."

The captain bade the two correspondents a good evening and left. Nojine folded his arms together with a self-satisfied grin on his face.

"Was I not right? A real coup, eh?" he said.

By now Daniel was completely caught up in the thrill of such an adventure, not to mention the prospect of great material for future articles. He had been toying with the idea of writing a book about his war experiences in Manchuria; now he was certain he'd have all the ingredients for a bestseller. Any initial reluctance he might have had was quickly fading into thoughts of glory.

"How can I thank you?" Daniel said, eyes glinting.

"Dedicate your book to me."

"You've got it, my friend." Daniel forgot for the moment that he'd already promised himself that if he did write a book he was going to dedicate it to Mariana.

46

Mariana breathed in the cold fresh sea air in a hungry gulp. She had never sailed on the water in her life, and she was enjoying the ocean in spite of her queasy stomach.

"You'll get your sea legs before you know it," said Daniel, coming up beside her.

"I hope so. We can't spare stomach medication for the nurse."

"Only about half the patients are seasick."

"The poor boys. Most are peasants, you know—farmers, not sailors."

"It's you I'm most concerned about."

"Oh, I'll be fine as long as I can breathe fresh air."

Mariana lifted her eyes to take in the surrounding sea. She had never seen anything like it. Dark blue water under a pale winter sky, gentle swells with occasional whitecaps. It seemed to go on forever. There was a constancy to the ocean, a strength that gave her an odd sense of security. She knew it could be fickle and dangerous, but it didn't frighten her the way war did. The ocean was entirely God's creation, and because of that she felt safe.

They were into the second day of their journey. Port Arthur and all the horrors and dangers of the siege were far away. The coast of Korea, though unseen at the moment, was miles off to their port side. The skipper said they were approaching the southern tip of Korea, and by tomorrow they would be entering the Tsushima Straits. There, they would come as close to Japan as ever on the journey. If they were to experience trouble, it was likely to be in the well-patrolled straits.

Mariana hardly had a chance later that morning to come up for air. A hundred and fifty patients with only one doctor, one nurse, and three attendants made for unending work. Mariana just didn't have time to think of her stomach. Even Karl Vlasenko was working like a trooper, despite his constant complaints of having to do woman's work, which was how he viewed nursing. Mariana ignored his whining—and the odor of liquor on his breath.

On the afternoon of their third day, they had crossed the Tsushima Straits and were heading up the Sea of Japan on the last leg of their journey, a day out of Vladivostok. Daniel had come below to lend a hand with the patients in hopes of a chance to visit with Mariana as she worked. They were now in the main hold of the ship, which had been converted into a large hospital ward with about fifty beds. The remainder of the patients were distributed among the other cargo holds and cabins; the crew and other passengers were crowded into two cabins. Mariana, as the only female, had her own cabin despite Karl's grumbling about unfair treatment. As ranking officer, he believed he should have his own quarters.

Daniel was helping to turn a rather brawny corporal as Mariana changed his soiled linens. They were nearly finished when an attendant poked his head into the ward.

He motioned Daniel and Mariana aside and said in a low voice, "Just spotted a Japanese cruiser about two miles away and closing fast. Better pray they're not trigger-happy."

The attendant scurried away after delivering his ominous news. Alarm coursed through Daniel. He tried to hide it from Mariana, but she obviously saw right through him.

"We're flying a Red Cross flag," Mariana said reassuringly. "What can they do but request to board and inspect us? They'll find we are exactly what we claim to be."

Daniel nodded but was unconvinced.

"Daniel," Mariana went on, "I should think you'd be thrilled—you know, an opportunity to interview the Japanese navy."

"Yeah, of course." He tried to shrug off the incident as trivial.

They returned to their task, but the moment Mariana turned her back to gather up the dirty linens, Daniel quickly took Stoessel's documents from inside his shirt, where he kept them at all times for security, and started to slip them under the patient's mattress.

Unfortunately, Mariana turned back too soon. She saw the pouch just before Daniel hid it.

"What's that?" she asked, brow furrowed.

Daniel couldn't lie to her. "Documents," he said simply.

"What are you doing with them?"

Before he answered, Daniel noticed that the corporal was taking a keen interest in the exchange. Placing the documents back in his shirt, he nudged Mariana to a far corner where they could talk privately.

"Mariana, please don't be upset with me, all right? But . . . well, you may as well know. Stoessel recruited me to get vital intelligence out of Port Arthur. I would have told you, but they thought that, for your own safety, no one else should know. However, they assured me no danger would come to anyone on the ship."

Mariana was silent for a long time as she absorbed Daniel's confession. Finally she said, "Now I see why Stoessel was so adamant about accepting the Japanese offer. The self-serving fool—"

"Mariana, I'm no fan of Stoessel's, but you must remember that the information I have will benefit the Russian army, perhaps save thousands of lives. If there was any risk at all to this ship, I wouldn't have agreed to do it."

"Then why are you hiding the documents?" Mariana asked incisively.

"Hiding what documents?" came a new voice from behind.

Karl Vlasenko had entered unobserved, hearing the last part of Daniel and Mariana's discussion.

Daniel groaned inwardly. This thing was getting out of hand. "Nothing," he said defensively. "It's really not a big deal, I tell you."

"I demand to know what is going on!" boomed Vlasenko.

By now all the patients were turning their heads toward the rising altercation.

"Let's discuss this outside," Mariana said. When the two men hesitated, she added with authority, "Now!"

They followed her out, and she closed the door behind them.

"Daniel is carrying secret intelligence out of Port Arthur," she told Vlasenko.

"Extremely important intelligence," Daniel added as if this validated his actions.

"You are using this ship for espionage?" exclaimed Vlasenko. "You could get us all shot!"

"Oh, simmer down—both of you." Daniel had had enough of their overreaction. "No one's going to get shot, for heaven's sake! There is absolutely no reason to panic." He forgot his own panic a few moments ago when he had impulsively tried to hide the documents. "*If*—and that is a huge if—my so-called espionage is discovered, I will simply say that no one here had any knowledge of my intentions. That will be the truth. In that case, I'm the only one who's gonna get shot."

"Oh, Daniel!"

"But at the very worst, they will probably just detain me for a while, then slap my hands and release me." Daniel sounded quite certain. In reality, he wasn't so sure at all. Maybe they *would* shoot him. He began to wonder if the promise of a juicy assignment at the front and an interview with Kuropatkin was worth the risk. It had seemed so at the time he had accepted, but now, with the Japanese breathing down their necks, he wondered. Why did he throw aside all good sense when it came to his job?

"I will not jeopardize my patients or my staff," declared Vlasenko, his voice shaky.

"I wouldn't ask you to," said Daniel.

"Just so you understand," Vlasenko continued. "I would just as soon feed you to the sharks than—"

"I get the point," broke in Daniel impatiently, perturbed at Vlasenko's sudden and uncharacteristic paternal interest in his patients.

"I'm going to go topside and see what's happening," Vlasenko said. "I would suggest that you, Mr. Trent, stay out of the way."

When Vlasenko was gone, Daniel said to Mariana, "I know you must think this terribly irresponsible of me, but I truly did believe it was an important duty."

"But why would you place yourself at such risk, Daniel? You're not even Russian. And as a correspondent, you are supposed to be neutral."

"How can I be neutral when the woman I love is Russian?" He paused, struggling over the real truth. Then he looked at Mariana and knew he had to tell her everything. "Stoessel offered me some compensation for my efforts, so what I'm doing isn't entirely altruistic—" He stopped and corrected himself. "It's not at all altruistic. I'm doing it for a prime assignment at the front with Kuropatkin himself, and an exclusive interview with the general."

Mariana smiled.

"What's that supposed to mean?" asked a baffled Daniel.

"The very things I love about you also make me so angry at times. I hardly understand it myself. But I guess at the root of it all is that I do love you, and I can't expect you to be perfect."

"I'd be forced to disappoint you far too often, if that were the case."

They paused as they felt a change in the ship's movement. The engines were slowing. No doubt the Japanese cruiser had signaled for them to stand ready to be inspected.

"What are you going to do now, Daniel?"

"I'll hide the documents."

"What if they are found?"

"I'll confess. In the meantime, perhaps if you gave me a stethoscope to wear around my neck, I'll look at least as much the part of a doctor as Vlasenko."

They started to reenter the ward, but Daniel laid a gentle restraining hand on Mariana's arm. "Thank you, Mariana, for not getting too angry at me. You are far better than I deserve."

She quickly brushed his cheek with her lips. "I think that's what true love is all about. I can't promise always to be so understanding and reasonable, but I'll try when I can."

47

Karl Vlasenko had no intention at all of going topside. He wanted to get as far from a possible encounter with the enemy as he could.

Immediately after leaving Mariana and Daniel, Vlasenko went to his cabin, the tiny cell he was forced to share with Daniel and the three attendants. He had to remind himself once more of what a magnanimous fellow he was. His father would not have been so generous as to share his quarters with peasants and a mere American.

His father—ha!

Cyril Vlasenko would not have allowed himself to have been placed in such a position in the first place. He would have demanded private quarters as a physician and as commander, by proxy, of this floating hospital. Karl had suggested such an arrangement to Dr. Itkinson, who had merely replied with an ironic chuckle and a patronizing explanation of how they must squeeze a hundred and fifty beds, staff, and crew on a ship barely large enough for a fraction of the passengers.

"We must make do, and rise to the occasion," Itkinson had crooned.

Karl had backed down, mostly because he was afraid that in balking too much, the chief of staff might find another doctor to accompany the boat. That was a possibility Karl was not willing to risk. He had been desperate to get out of Port Arthur. Why he had volunteered for the Army Medical Corps in the first place, Karl could not remember. He had more than likely been drunk at the time. The liquor had lulled him along with some insane visions of glory. The reality he found was not what he had expected. Another minute in that stinking town, with the maddening roar of bombs, and bleeding men with shattered arms and legs and faces, and Karl would have surely cracked. The hospital boat had provided him with the perfect and honorable escape.

Now that idiot, Trent, threatened to bring upon him as much danger—if not more—as he'd experienced in Port Arthur. Karl's hand shook as he opened the cabin latch. He slipped inside, then stopped. What was that? The engines were slowing. The Japanese were going to board the ship! They were all going to be arrested and tossed into some Japanese prison camp. Karl had heard all about those vermin-infested pits, unfit for decent humans!

Karl hurriedly stepped to his sea chest and rummaged about in it for a moment, finally drawing out a bottle of whiskey and a small shot glass.

He needed some steadying.

He tossed back two or three shots. Or was it four? He lost count after a while. But the tremor in his hand stopped, and the burning in his stomach seemed to take his mind off his panic. In a few more minutes, he capped the bottle and replaced it in the chest. But before he shut the lid, he paused as something else caught his eye.

A revolver.

The Smith and Wesson .38 caliber pistol that his father had given him before he entered the Army Medical Corps. He would never forget his father's words upon presenting the gift:

"Who knows, maybe besides your lily-livered doctoring, you'll actually get to kill a few Japs while you're at it."

Not the kind of words a son dreams of hearing from his father, but in Karl's case he was happy to get any words at all from his critical parent.

Karl turned the weapon over in his hand. His eyes were so blurry he didn't notice his hand had begun to tremble again. He had never used the pistol—and had prayed he never would! But suddenly Karl found himself tucking the gun inside his belt. His father would not allow Japs *or* arrogant Americans to push *him* around. Karl had always desperately wished he could be that kind of man, and maybe this was his opportunity. He wasn't sure what he could do, with a single handgun, against a Japanese cruiser, but the feel of the revolver pressing against his side under his coat convinced him he was brave enough to face whatever came his way.

Not that he had any intention of leaving the safety of his cabin. It was important that he protect himself—for the benefit of the patients, of course. He was, after all, the only doctor.

He was startled by a pounding on his door. His stomach lurched and the blood drained from his face. He hesitated before moving. But the pounding persisted. Finally he lumbered to the door and opened it.

———

The German skipper, his first mate, and about half a dozen Japanese sailors, including two officers, greeted Vlasenko.

"Who's this?" demanded the Japanese commander through his interpreter.

"Our physician," said the skipper. "He's the officer in charge, so I thought you ought to speak to him." Then he explained to Karl, "This is Commander Otami of the Japanese cruiser *Niitaka*. They don't believe we're a Red Cross ship; said the Russians are not known to use hospital ships. I told him of the special circumstance, even showed him our papers signed by General Nogi himself."

"They could be forged," put in the commander.

"This is an outrage!" Karl blustered. "We were promised safe passage."

"If you are what you claim to be, you will not be harmed," assured Commander Otami. "Now, we will continue our search. Show us the way." He gave Karl a pointed look.

Karl glanced at the skipper in hopes of being relieved of the leadership suddenly thrust upon him. But for the last five days, Karl had been telling the German skipper that, as chief physician on the vessel, he was the ranking officer. Vlasenko didn't think a mere skipper ought to have the final say. But now his plan had backfired, and the skipper merely grinned at him, then shrugged, feining helplessness, and stepped aside.

Karl, swaying a bit on his feet, led the way to the main hold. If that place with wall-to-wall beds didn't convince these idiots of the ship's noble mission, then nothing would. The hard metal bulge pressing into his skin was comforting as he opened the hatch.

48

"Nurse, what's happening?" a patient called to Mariana in alarm. "The engines are stopping."

"It's nothing to worry about, Private Karskij," Mariana replied. She turned to the other patients. "Just stay calm. We may be boarded by the Japanese for a routine inspection. Our papers are in order, and there should be no problem."

"They better leave us alone," warned Karskij. "They got my arm and my leg. I'm not going to let them dirty Japs do no more harm to me or my comrades."

"Please calm down, private. No one's going to be harmed—"

At that moment the door swung open, and a pale, slightly wild-eyed Vlasenko entered, followed by his entourage of German and Japanese sailors.

The Japanese pushed past Vlasenko and began fanning out purposefully through the makeshift hospital ward.

"Be careful there!" huffed Vlasenko. "These are sick men. It's obviously a hospital."

Ignoring him, the Japanese commander turned on Daniel and Mariana. Since Mariana's identity was apparent from her uniform, he asked Daniel, "Who are you?"

"I'm Dr. Trent, an American observer from the U.S. Surgeon General's Office."

The commander took in Daniel's hastily donned white laboratory coat and the stethoscope hanging around his neck, and was about to turn away, convinced, when Karl blundered forward.

"He's the man you want!" Karl cried. He stuck his hand under his coat and pulled out his hidden pistol, thrusting it in Daniel's face. "I was just about to place him under house arrest when you came," he told the commander.

"Doctor Vlasenko!" cried Mariana.

"The man's gone crazy," Daniel said, hoping to maintain his cover somehow. His accusation was believable, too, considering Vlasenko's strung-out appearance and the definite odor of alcohol that seemed to permeate him.

"None of us knew a thing," Vlasenko raved on. "He had documents—probably some defamatory clap-trap for the American press. He's a correspondent."

"Is this true?" asked the commander.

"First, would you make him put that gun down?" asked Daniel. "He might actually attempt to use it."

One of the Japanese sailors had instinctively drawn his weapon and aimed it at Vlasenko the moment the Smith and Wesson had appeared. Commander Otami was about to order Vlasenko to turn over his gun when a new burst of activity made everyone forget all about Vlasenko.

———

Private Karskij had been growing more and more agitated as he listened to the proceedings. The Japanese had made him a cripple for life. Since his wounding and the double amputation that had followed, he had thought of only one thing— to get home, kiss his wife and hug his children one more time, and then end what was left of his life. But now it seemed as if the Japanese were about to rob him of that, too.

He wasn't going to let that happen, not without taking a few Japs with him.

One of the enemy sailors had positioned himself near Karskij's bed and was momentarily distracted at the surprising altercation with Vlasenko, and the revelation of the presence of a spy. Karskij had one good arm and it was strong. With it, he snatched away the sailor's holstered side arm and cocked it before the hapless enemy sailor could respond. When, in the next instant, the sailor did make a move, the weapon in Karskij's hand fired and the sailor toppled to the deck.

"All right!" Karskij screamed, quickly raising the side arm and taking aim at a new target. "Who wants to be the next Jap to die?"

———

Everything happened in a flash. Those standing were barely recovering from their stunned shock at this turn of events before Karskij swung around his weapon, this time with Commander Otami in his sights. Even the sailor who had drawn his gun on Vlasenko did not act fast enough.

Karskij's agitation and distress impelled him to move faster than his mind could reason. He obviously didn't care about the Japanese sailor's weapon, or even Vlasenko's weapon; all that mattered was that he took a few of the enemy with him into welcomed death.

But the time it took him to yell his threat was a moment too long. Mariana, who was closest, took advantage of that instant and lurched toward Karskij with the intention of disrupting his aim. She flung herself bodily against him, sending his arm upward. When the gun discharged, the bullet creased the bulkhead near the ceiling.

At first, no one understood where the second shot, coming in close succession to the misfire from Karskij's weapon, had originated. Nor did Mariana immediately grasp the cause of the stunning blow to her body. She thought someone had pushed her, but with such force it made her head reel. She stood there a moment with a perplexed frown on her face.

Then she crumpled.

———

Daniel's eyes had first been on Vlasenko's Smith and Wesson, then his attention had shifted to Karskij. He hadn't even noticed when the Japanese sailor had drawn his weapon. When Karskij hesitated, the sailor took aim and fired at nearly the same moment Mariana made her move. When the report of the second shot echoed in his ear, Daniel had first thought

Vlasenko had tried to shoot him.

Daniel looked at Vlasenko, whose eyes had suddenly gone wide and glassy. The stark panic on the doctor's face was proof enough he'd never have the nerve to fire a gun. When Mariana fell to the deck, Daniel ignored Vlasenko and his toothless threat. He rushed to Mariana.

"I . . . I think . . . I've been shot." Mariana seemed surprised, as if there might be a possibility she could be wrong.

Daniel stripped off the laboratory coat he had stupidly thought would protect everyone from harm. He rolled it up and placed it lovingly under her head. As he bent over her, he saw the widening splotch of red in her left side. Then her eyes closed and her body went limp.

"No!" Daniel cried. "Mariana!"

The commander quickly shook away his own shock. Less than a minute had elapsed since Vlasenko had first drawn his weapon, causing the tragic chain reaction. The commander ordered one of his men to take Private Karskij in hand. Private Karskij's weapon was confiscated and a rifle was pointed at his head, but the distraught private no longer seemed much of a threat. After realizing the tragic result of his mad revenge, he had fallen back in his bed, a glazed, haunted look on his face.

Then Otami turned on Vlasenko and snatched the gun from his hand. "If you are truly a physician, help these wounded—now!"

In the meantime, all the other Japanese had drawn their weapons, training them warily around the room.

Daniel was oblivious to it all. He didn't care any longer about ships, documents, interviews! How petty and insignificant it all was. Nothing was important if Mariana was lost to him—

Then he felt a flutter of movement in the hand he had gripped in his own. Her eyes blinked.

"I . . . must have fainted." Her words were barely audible.

"Thank God!" Tears spilled from Daniel's eyes as they had not even done when his father had died.

Commander Otami, not entirely unmoved by the sight of the wounded nurse, and the overwrought doctor—or what-

275

ever he was!—kneeling at her side, took charge of the situation.

"I will take this entire ship into custody," the commander ordered. "You are all under arrest. I will escort this ship to the nearest Japanese harbor—"

"No!" Vlasenko jumped up from where he was tending the wounded Japanese sailor, who had received only a flesh wound. "You can't do this to me—us. You have to honor the Red Cross flag. We have papers. It's inhumane. It's illegal. It's—" He apparently couldn't think of any other arguments, finally ending in a desperate, "You can't!"

"I have a wounded man." The commander was not about to let anyone forget the fact that he had nearly lost a man in the unfortunate melee. "I have every reason to suspect this ship is engaged in espionage. You cannot expect me to let you simply sail away."

"But we'll be in Vladivostok tomorrow!" whined Vlasenko. Somehow he thought this should matter to the commander.

The last thing Daniel wanted to do just then was support Vlasenko. But with Mariana hurt, there was more reason than ever for getting to their destination. The wounded might receive care in Japan, but there would be too much uncertainty, too much delay. Shimonoseki was the nearest Japanese harbor, but it was at least a day farther away than Vladivostok. Even if Mariana did survive such a trip, would she then have to spend the duration of the war in a prison camp? Daniel could not accept that possibility.

He rose and faced the commander.

"Look here, Commander, you don't need to go to those extremes." Realizing he still had the stethoscope around his neck, he pulled it off and laid it aside, as if to give further credence to his next words. "Dr. Vlasenko is right. I am a spy. I'm carrying intelligence to Kuropatkin. No one on this ship had any knowledge of my activities until I was discovered shortly before you boarded. These people were carrying out a humane operation and should not be made to suffer for my stupidity. If you must arrest someone, then I should be the only one. Even Private Karskij there can't be blamed for his behavior. Look at him. He's lost an arm and a leg—can you hold it against him for going a little crazy when he saw you, his enemy?"

"How can I verify your words?"

The commander couldn't really want the inconvenience of escorting the German vessel. And maybe Mariana's attempt to save his life had touched him. Since the documents Daniel carried in no way revealed any Russian strategy, but rather information on the Japanese positions, Daniel saw no reason not to hand them over to the commander. He knew as he did so that he was also giving up all the concessions Stoessel had promised him, but after one glance at Mariana's fallen form, he had no hesitation at all.

The commander read the papers with the help of his interpreter, then he shook his head. "This is it? This would not have turned the tide of the war, maybe only affected a few battles." The Japanese officer stared at Daniel as his assistant interpreted his words. "But that is the nature of war, is it not? Risking so much for so little."

The commander's words burned like fire in Daniel's gut. He had indeed risked much—too much—perhaps even Mariana's life. And for what? A story. Words on paper that would ultimately line America's trash cans. If Mariana lived—oh, God, please let her live!—how could she ever forgive him? How could he ever forgive himself?

"There has been enough grief over this incident," Commander Otami said finally. "The ship is free to go to its destination. You—Trent, is it?—will come with me."

Daniel nodded. He had expected no different. "May I have a moment with the nurse?"

The commander nodded when the request had been interpreted to him.

By now Vlasenko, who had thought it expedient to treat the wounded enemy first in order to cull the commander's favor, was examining Mariana. Daniel knelt by her side opposite Vlasenko. He tried not to look at the pathetic doctor.

"Daniel," she said weakly. He had to bend very close to hear her. "Please be careful . . . I'm sorry."

"You have nothing to be sorry about, my love. You were

277

wonderful, brave. I'm so proud of you. If only I could be as brave."

"God be with you . . . and I love you so!" She reached for his hand and tried to grasp it, but she had no strength at all.

Daniel gave Vlasenko a beseeching look, wanting desperately to hear that Mariana's wounds were not as serious as they appeared. The doctor could only shake his head hopelessly in response. Daniel, suddenly filled with fury toward the doctor, wrapped his fingers around Karl's shirt front, pulled the doctor close, and said in a low but menacing tone, "She had better be alive the next time I see her, Vlasenko—or I'll see to it you go up on charges of murder!"

"M-m-me?" stammered Vlasenko. "What did I do?"

"There wouldn't have been any shooting, Vlasenko, if you hadn't drawn that stupid gun." This was probably not strictly the case, but Daniel wasn't ready to exonerate Vlasenko for his part in it all. "And I swear, you won't get off easily if anything happens to Mariana."

Daniel bent down and kissed Mariana tenderly on the lips. "I will meet you again soon in the Summer Gardens, Mariana, and I shall bring the picnic lunch."

"We will watch the lovely swans . . ."

"For hours and hours!"

Commander Otami was anxious to get on his way. "Come along, Mr. Trent."

Daniel kissed Mariana one last time, started to rise, then paused and cast Vlasenko one last warning glance. Mariana must live. Daniel could not bear another grievous loss.

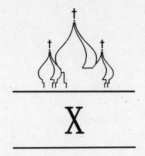

X

THE PAST CATCHES UP

49

Cerkover padded up the steps that led to Cyril Vlasenko's spacious office in the Ministry of the Interior building. He was in the habit of using the back way to the count's office rather than the front elevator. Though Cerkover was Vlasenko's official aide, it always paid to be cautious. The cunning and devious Count Vlasenko, who was continually spinning numberless plots and intrigues, would want it that way, at any rate.

Cerkover puffed heavily. At forty, he was no longer a young man and the years had not been kind to him. He reached the count's door and paused, not only to catch his breath, but to admire his surroundings—the wide corridor, carpeted with a Persian runner, the massive door with its brass hardware, and the gold-embossed plaque that announced "Count Cyril Vlasenko, Under Secretary of the Interior." The count's henchman envied all this and aspired to possess it one day. That he was this close was a small miracle in itself, for less than ten years ago he had been nothing but a minor constable in a dirty Ukrainian village. He had made himself known to Vlasenko, then governor-general of the province, by being an informant and all-around bootlicker. He had been instrumental in turning the blame for some civil unrest upon the Jewish populous. This coup had brought Vlasenko to the attention of the Imperial government, and when Cyril had been promoted, he didn't forget the constable who had helped make it all possible. For this, Cerkover was ever indebted to the count and would do anything for the man. He hoped Vlasenko's gratitude would be evident in promotions closer and closer to the seat of power. So far, he hadn't been disappointed.

Cerkover knew his mentor well enough to realize what he now carried to the man was one of the best coups of his career. He knew everything about Vlasenko's bitter vendetta against the Fedorcenko family. He didn't quite understand it—that is, he didn't understand why it continued, considering the fact that the count had squeezed nearly all possible life from the family. But, for whatever reason, Vlasenko seemed to glory in any misfortune that fell upon that hapless family, and all the better if the count himself was the cause of the calamity.

That being the case, what Cerkover now possessed ought to make Count Vlasenko ecstatic, and, as a result, give Cerkover quite a boost in the esteem of his mentor.

He entered the outer office. Vlasenko's secretary was busy shuffling through an open file drawer. She glanced up, gave him a pinched smile, and continued with her work.

"Is he in?" asked Cerkover.

"Approach at your own risk," she said dourly.

"Something wrong?"

"He just came from a meeting with the Interior Minister; that never makes him happy."

"Let him know I'm here."

"You brave man." The woman left her cabinet, returned to her desk, punched a button on the intercom, and informed the count he had a visitor.

In another minute, Cerkover was standing before Vlasenko in his plush office. The count was sipping a glass of brandy and puffing on an expensive cigar. He offered neither to Cerkover.

"This had better be good," growled Vlasenko. "After an hour with that blathering idiot Svyatopolk-Mirsky, I can't take more bad news."

"This should brighten your day considerably."

"Well, get on with it." Vlasenko finished his brandy in one swallow and then poured a second glass.

"You recall the task you sent me on several days ago?" Cerkover breathed the pleasant odor of cigar smoke, vowing to buy himself one downstairs when he finished with Vlasenko. He deserved to celebrate.

"Of course I remember. What do you take me for? Now quit

twaddling and tell me—what happened?"

"My first telegram to the Kara Prison was not promising," Cerkover said, trying to moderate his usually colorful and self-serving manner of reporting in order to placate his boss's present impatience. "They claimed that the prisoner Sergei Fedorcenko had been on the official rolls from 1881 to 1896, whereupon he died in a flu epidemic."

"You, of course, didn't accept that answer?" The brandy was warming Vlasenko, and the anticipation of some positive news seemed to be improving his disposition.

"You yourself, my dear count, taught me never to accept surface evidence. I got to thinking that for anyone to survive fifteen years in the Kara mines was a small miracle in and of itself. I also know it's common practice for those wardens to carry dead or escaped prisoners on their rolls for many years in order to extort extra money from the government, by pocketing the allowances for absent prisoners. I suppose that extra income is the only thing that makes their jobs bearable. Well, I have a friend who is an official in the region, and who also happens to owe his job to me—you may recall the fellow who helped us in another matter—"

"Enough!" exploded Vlasenko; even the brandy could not still his impatience. "Tell me, was it him, or not?"

"My friend was able to go in person to the mines and have a look at the books. That's why this has taken a few extra days." Cerkover knew he was pushing it, but he had to impress his boss with his investigative talents. "In 1896, a new warden took over the mines. Before the old warden retired, he purged his books—in essence, 'killing off' many already-departed prisoners he had been carrying for years. Fedorcenko was one of about a dozen who succumbed to the supposed flu outbreak."

"But what proof have you that he didn't die then, or at some other time during that fifteen-year period?"

"There was no flu epidemic. My friend confirmed this by questioning a couple guards who had been there in '96."

"Yes, but he could have died at any time before then."

"The only way to confirm that was to locate the retired warden."

"Yes. . . ?" Vlasenko took several anxious puffs off his cigar, not even bothering to inhale.

"He's very old now, still residing in Siberia, in the Lake Baikal region, living very nicely off his extortion. He was quite willing to talk when he realized he'd been found out—"

"Your friend traveled there to interview him?"

"Impossible this time of year because of the weather. But my Kara contact got in touch with a friend of his—you know how it works."

"Yes, and I suppose this is going to cost me a pretty kopeck."

"Knowing your financial limitations, Your Excellency, I promised promotions instead of cash. Believe me, they were quite happy for a promise of anything that would deliver them from the Far East."

"Very good. I've got government posts in abundance that ought to make them happy. Now, what did this retired warden say?" Vlasenko drained off the last of his brandy.

"His memory is not the sharpest—he's at least seventy years old. But he remembered well certain events in the summer of 1881. After all, it's not every day one has a prince and ex-Imperial Guard for a prisoner—not to mention a prisoner who made a rather flamboyant escape—"

"An escape! I knew it!" Vlasenko's flabby jowls shook as he pounded his fist triumphantly on his desk. "But that means he's been at large for twenty-three years."

"That is not all. I made inquiries about the fellow in the photograph. He is known among the workers as Sergei Ivanovich Christinin. He is married to Anna Burenin—"

"No!"

"You know the name, I gather. Peasants near your estate in Katyk. Christinin—or, rather Fedorcenko—and the girl were married in 1882."

"All those years!" exclaimed Vlasenko. "Right under my nose!" Cyril leaned back heavily in his chair.

"The man has cheek, I must say." Cerkover was pleased by his employer's shocked reaction.

"It all makes sense, though. The Burenin girl was a Fedorcenko servant for years—the young prince must have been carrying on with her all along. And, once he was a fugitive, he probably felt he couldn't do much better than the peasant girl, so he married her. Still, it took nerve, I'll give him that. And then to risk it all by helping his father four years ago."

"So, Count Vlasenko, what now?"

"What do you think, Cerkover? How can I, with a clear conscience, allow a fugitive from justice, a murderer no less, to remain free?"

50

Was there a finer sight on earth than that of women chatting amiably with flour up to their elbows, kneading bread? Paul Burenin could not help philosophizing on the profound implications of the scene, the simplicity of life at this level, the symbolism represented by bread, the staff of life. This was Russia at its best; and this was the reason for all his labors over the years.

Mathilde had been right. She had known what a return to Katyk would mean to Paul.

He watched with joy his mama, Anna, and Mathilde at their labor—their labor of love. Odd, how different the three women were—Mama Sophia's open simplicity; Anna's quiet strength; Mathilde's bold intelligence. Yet they worked together with such an easy camaraderie. Mama could not possibly understand half of what Mathilde said, yet she had taken her immediately to her heart as a true daughter. And Mathilde! Who would have known she was a child of the intelligentsia, who had grown up with servants and knew far more about books than the workings of a kitchen. Even in Siberia she had managed to have enough money to buy bread from the local peasants rather than make it herself. Paul never complained about this extravagance, because her own attempts had been practically inedible.

How proud she had been a few days ago over her first successful loaf of black bread!

Yes, the decision to come to Katyk had been pure inspiration. And the timing of their visit must truly have been the hand of God—Paul was becoming more and more of a believer. His appearance had been a balm to the family's time of grief over the death of dear Ilya. Mama said over and over how God did not take without giving something in return.

It still had not been easy to hear of Ilya's death—such a waste! That good-hearted bear of a man who so resembled Papa Yevno. All so the tsar could strut and bully in an attempt to prove to the world that the autocracy was a healthy force in Russia. It made Paul seethe and remember anew what lay at the root of his revolutionary zeal. The only good to arise out of the whole war was that it was showing the Russian Crown to be exactly what it was—a massive entity covered with gilt, balancing on feet of clay. Paul could not be more pleased that the war was turning out disastrously for Russia. This was surely going to wake up the masses. And for that reason, perhaps Ilya's death had not entirely been in vain.

The women were finishing their work. Three loaves were being placed in the oven.

"Now, we can take a little rest," said Sophia, wiping the flour from her hands.

Paul realized his mama was a very old matushka now. Her broad, plump face was liberally mapped with creases. The boundless energy he had always associated with her was taxed after making a loaf of bread. She wheezed slightly, and her old legs trembled as she lowered herself, with Anna's help, onto one of the table benches. She wouldn't be with them much longer. That she had lived this long was a miracle, considering that most peasants in Russia were lucky to see fifty or sixty. Sophia was well beyond that. Marfa had always done most of the housework. She and Ilya, with their three children, had lived in the old Burenin place since Yevno's death. When Anna had arrived to care for her grieving mother, Marfa went to her own mama's house for comfort in her time of grief. What they would do now that there was no longer a man in the home was still a difficult, unanswered question.

"Let me pour you some tea, Mama," said Anna. "You, too, Mathilde—sit and warm yourself with tea."

"Kneading bread is warming work enough," Mathilde answered, "but I wouldn't mind a glass of tea anyway."

"I know you women are exhausted," Paul said, "but I was just wondering if I could inspire a companion to join me on a walk."

"In this weather, Pavushka?" Sophia was aghast. What peasant went outside in winter when they didn't have to?

"The cold clears the cobwebs from my brain, and I need exercise no matter how cold it is."

"That's what comes of reading books and writing words—" Sophia grinned in spite of her comment. "But I couldn't be more proud of you, my Pavushka. Your papa would be beside himself if he could see all the wonderful things you have written."

After everyone had finished their tea, Anna said, "Paul, I will join you on your walk, if you don't mind. City life has made me more hungry for fresh air."

"Mathilde, are you up for some exercise?" asked Paul.

"I don't think I can face the ice right now. Why don't you and Anna go."

Paul smiled at his wife, knowing she was making excuses so he could spend some time alone with his sister.

They bundled up in their heavy coats and boots. Anna tied a wool babushka around her head, and Paul put on his fur cap, pulling the earflaps down snugly.

Anna and Paul started to walk down by the river, remembering how they liked that path as children, but after slipping and sliding on the icy path a few times, they decided they ought to take the road over the little bridge that led into the village proper.

Paul chuckled at the spectacle they had presented. "It is humbling, isn't it? I feel young on the inside, but, oh, how the years tell on the outside."

"Too true, Pavushka. But being here now with you is as good, perhaps even better, than being young," Anna replied. "Perhaps you forget how confused we were sometimes and how hard it was struggling between the new ways we wanted and the desire to honor the old ways of our parents."

"I remember all too well my confusion—but it's often no less difficult now." Paul paused, kicking idly at a fallen twig. "Anna, will I always be struggling with life?"

"Mathilde told me about some of the things that happened in Europe. You are a deep, thoughtful, man, Paul. Perhaps such struggles come with your nature. Sergei is the same way. In many ways, we more simple-minded folk are better off than those of you who are the great thinkers of the world. But, Paul, I thought you had worked some things out in coming here."

"Only to the point that I could not follow the Social Democratic way. I still don't know where I will go from here."

They walked a bit farther, across the footbridge and as far as their sister Vera's house. All Vera's family was snug inside on a day like this. Paul and Anna were silent for some time, each absorbed in their own thoughts and memories. Paul thought of his papa and missed his hearty chuckle and big heart. He wondered what counsel Papa Yevno would give him now. Yevno had believed firmly in placing his future in God's care. Yet Yevno was also a great proponent of not sitting back like a rich moujik, allowing life to sweep you along in its great flood. He probably would have suggested that Paul set a course and follow it for a while; if it didn't work out, at least he would have learned something from the attempt.

By coming to Katyk, Paul had done that very thing. He was moving, though he wasn't entirely certain in what direction. It felt right so far, and perhaps that was as much as he ought to expect. He could almost hear his papa say:

"Ah, Pavushka! Don't fret so over tomorrow. Isn't it in God's hands?"

Paul turned to Anna. "Mama has no one now to take care of the farm," he said.

"Vera's eldest, young Yevno, is almost nineteen and will marry soon," Anna replied. "They have talked of him taking over the farm. Vera will care for Mama."

"Yes, that makes perfect sense, doesn't it? In the meantime, Ivan and the boys can plant the spring crop and take care of things."

"It seems the best solution."

"Anna, what would you think if I told you I had, for a crazy instant, thought of becoming a farmer again?"

"I wouldn't be too terribly surprised. It seems a logical place for your path of self-discovery to lead."

"Really?"

"What better place for a retreat from the battles of life? I've come here myself for the same reasons."

"Perhaps it wouldn't be a mere retreat, but rather a permanent move."

"You, Paul? I don't think you could do it. Not that you wouldn't be capable of working the farm, but that you couldn't give up your life's work—not before it came to fruition."

"If it ever comes to fruition."

Anna said nothing, and as daylight was slipping quickly away, they turned around on their path and headed for home.

After a few moments they heard footsteps beating at the icy road behind them.

"Anna, is that you?"

Together Anna and Paul turned to see Vera's husband, Ivan, jogging up toward them.

Anna waved, and she and Paul stopped and waited. When Ivan halted before them, he was red-faced, and out of breath. It took a moment before he could speak.

"Is something wrong, Ivan?" asked Paul, doubting that the man would so extend himself for something trivial.

"I'm afraid so." Ivan looked at Anna with pity.

Anna's heart lurched. In an instant, she thought of all the tragedies that might have occurred to induce such a look from her stoic brother-in-law. Had something happened to her children or Sergei, who were still in St. Petersburg? Or to Mariana, at the front? She cast searching eyes on Ivan, but she couldn't bring herself to ask him any questions.

"I was in the tavern," he said, "and a fellow brought in this message. I couldn't read it myself, but the fellow said it wasn't

289

good news. It's from Prince Viktor Fedorcenko. You had better read it for yourself, Anna."

Anna forced herself to reach out and take the paper he held. With trembling fingers she opened it and scanned the few terrible lines, hastily handwritten by Viktor.

"It's Sergei," she said in a voice of shock and disbelief. "He's been arrested."

51

"It's got to be near here somewhere," said Anna, the strain of the last few days clearly evident in her frayed tone.

"Probably some little street without a sign," Paul said.

Paul looked again at the slip of paper in his hand, then glanced at Anna with a perplexed shrug. Neither of them was familiar with this part of St. Petersburg. They had taken the horse-drawn tram from Vassily Island and down Nevsky Prospekt about two kilometers and now were on foot. The address they were looking for was supposed to be about three blocks north of the Prospekt, but so far they'd had no success finding it.

They had left Katyk immediately upon receiving Viktor's message; there had been no question that Paul and Mathilde would join Anna. Paul had no idea what he could do for his sister, but he could not consider a leisurely farming life while she was in trouble. Upon their arrival back in the capital, Anna had been permitted to see Sergei only once. She was able to assure Paul—who, of course, could go nowhere near the Peter and Paul Fortress where Sergei was being held—that her husband was in reasonably good spirits.

Paul recalled, many years ago, when he had seen a despondent Sergei on their fateful trek to Siberia. There could be no doubt that Sergei was a different man now, full of hope and faith. Still, he was presently in a precarious position, and even he could not deny that his future did not look promising. He was a captured fugitive, tried and convicted of a terrible crime. There was no reason why the courts should not return him to Siberia to finish out his sentence—a life sentence to hard labor.

But those who loved Sergei were not about to allow that to happen without a fight. Viktor, who had heaped blame upon himself for Sergei's first arrest because he had not interceded for him back then, was not about to repeat that mistake. Although his influence in the government had declined greatly in the last twenty-three years, he still had some connections, and intended on using them to their fullest. He was at this moment scheduled to see the Minister of the Interior.

Paul would have liked someone such as Viktor, who was far more sophisticated in the ways of the law, along at this moment. He and Anna had an appointment to see a lawyer, and Paul had precious little knowledge of the law and felt intimidated in this realm. Besides that, he had little trust in lawyers, and he knew nothing about the man they were about to see except that the organization he worked for was active in providing free legal counsel to the poor working classes. Some members of the Assembly had given Anna the man's name.

Alexander Kerensky was a young man, fresh out of law school. Viktor had approached a couple of experienced society lawyers but they weren't cheap, and Sergei had insisted on trying the man recommended by the Assembly.

"I am now a workingman," Sergei told them, "and I feel more comfortable in that company."

"We'll see how this man is," Viktor replied with some skepticism. "If he's good, fine—if not, we will get one who is. We'll worry about expense later."

Viktor was fully prepared to sell the Crimean estate if he had to. He said he'd been thinking of moving back to the city, anyway. But Paul wasn't as concerned about this or the financial situation as he was about Anna. This shocking turn of events had been especially hard on her. Her life had settled into a comfortable place. She was entering the autumn of her life with a sense of security, and she had believed it would go on forever. Now it suddenly appeared as if it all would be painfully ripped away from her. And, as if all that wasn't bad enough, she was rebuking herself over the very fact that she was having such a hard time accepting Sergei's plight.

"I ought to be able to trust God," she told Paul, weeping. "But I'm so afraid!"

Paul had no answers for her. He was not Yevno, with all his papa's simple wisdom and boundless faith. He only hoped this Kerensky fellow could help them.

Paul stopped a passerby, but he could not give them directions. He asked a clerk in a store, but the man was new to the area and had not heard of the street. Finally, he stopped an old batiushka, carrying a basket of groceries on one arm and hobbling along with a cane gripped in her other hand, seemingly oblivious to the freezing winter day. She looked as if she'd lived in this neighborhood all her life. The old woman nodded and pointed with her cane. Yes, the street sign had fallen off the wall years ago and had never been replaced. She not only gave directions, but took Paul and Anna to the very place they sought.

The street was old and rather decayed, as were the buildings lining each side. Most had shops on the ground level with apartments on top. The office was in an old grocery store that had closed but still held the odors of sausages and stale bread. The display cases were gone, replaced with shelves of legal books, file cabinets, and a couple of old desks. No carpets covered the floor, no drapes hung on the large window which still bore the lettering announcing "Davydov's Market."

The whole ambiance of the place was that of a literal "shoestring" operation, and Paul was a bit worried. He hadn't expected a plush South Side office, but he had hoped for something more established than this to bolster his confidence.

A telephone on one of the desks was the one luxury in the room, and at that moment a female, apparently a secretary, was speaking into it. Seated in front of that desk was a coarsely dressed man, probably a factory worker. At the other

desk, a couple, also dressed like working people, were standing with a young man shaking hands.

"Don't worry about a thing," said the young man. "I'll speak
to your landlord about the matter."

"Are you sure he won't evict us?" asked the woman.

"I have a feeling that once he sees you have legal assistance, he will forget all about those threats. I'll contact you day
after tomorrow."

He escorted the couple to the door, then turned to Paul and
Anna. "Good morning to you," he said in a welcoming,
friendly tone.

"We have an appointment," said Paul.

"You would be Mrs. Christinin," he said to Anna.

"Yes . . ." Since Sergei's arrest, Anna hardly knew what
name she should use.

"I'm Alexander Kerensky. Please come and sit down."

The lawyer took his seat behind the desk, while Anna and
Paul settled themselves in two chairs facing Kerensky's desk.
Paul took a moment to appraise this fellow in whom they were
about to place their trust. He couldn't have been more than
twenty-four, though the boyish glint in his eyes gave the impression that he could be even younger. In most respects he
was a rather ordinary-looking man, with short-cropped brown
hair and a neat, almost fastidious appearance. He wore a blue
serge suit that was by no means expensive, but stylish nonetheless. His brown eyes had a slight squint, and though he was
generally warm and friendly, there was a hint of detachment
in those eyes. Paul liked him immediately and sensed he was
genuine, if nothing else.

"Before I hear the specifics of your problem," Kerensky
said in a distinctive baritone, "I would like to tell you a little
about myself so you know exactly where I stand. First, I have
only finished law school a few months ago and I haven't been
accepted to the Bar. It seems that a couple of the names I sub-
mitted as references were not acceptable to the powers that be
because of certain political differences. I tell you this only so
that you understand that the absence of Bar membership isn't
because of incompetence. When it is time to reapply, I will use
different references, and, hopefully, will be accepted. As I'm

sure you know, everything in this country is so political these days." He paused, glancing between Paul and Anna to insure they understood. "As a result of all this, I can only give you advice in an informal way; I cannot act as legal counsel in a court of law. But often all that is necessary is informing clients of their rights."

"Do you mean to tell me," said Paul, "that the common man in this country does have some rights?"

"Well, Mr.—ah, I don't believe I got your name, sir?"

"Pavlikov."

"Well, Mr. Pavlikov, there *are* laws in this country, and at times even the government can be made to recognize them." He gave Paul an incisive glance, then smiled. "We must at least attempt to honor those laws, or we'd be no better than revolutionaries, now would we?"

"We certainly could not have that," Paul replied drolly.

"May I ask your interest in this case, Mr. Pavlikov? You are a relative, perhaps?"

"Yes."

"From the little I know of the case, I can understand your skepticism, but you wouldn't be here if you didn't hope to find some justice for your relative within the confines of the law."

"My sister here and her husband hope for that," said Paul flatly.

"I see." Kerensky paused, then addressed his next comment to Anna. "Would you like to tell me the particulars of your husband's problem?"

Anna told the young lawyer everything, keeping nothing back. In the first few moments of the meeting with Kerensky, she, like her brother, had been favorably impressed. She wasn't certain if such a young man, green and inexperienced, could help, but she felt he was worthy of the opportunity.

Her account outlined Sergei's former place in society, his service in the Imperial Guards, the ill-fated book, the assignment in the East, and the altercation with his commanding officer that eventually led to his life sentence to Siberia, and finally his escape from there and his subsequent new life. Kerensky was obviously speechless when she finished. There was a long silence before he spoke.

"The name of Fedorcenko is not unknown to me," Kerensky said finally. "Of course, I was a mere toddler in Simbirsk at the time these events occurred." He paused, seemed to do some mental calculations, then corrected himself with a wry grin. "Actually, now that I think of it, I wasn't even born yet."

"Your home, then, is in Simbirsk?" asked Paul. Lenin had also been born in Simbirsk, and it was possible Kerensky might know of him. The Ulyanov family had caused quite a stir in that town when, in 1887, Lenin's elder brother had been executed for attempting to assassinate the tsar.

"Was—" Kerensky replied, "—until I was eight, when my father was transferred to a government post in Turkestan. Even at that, such an important name as Fedorcenko couldn't be completely forgotten."

"I'm afraid," said Anna, "that now the name is only important from the standpoint of historical significance."

"Why else would you now be consulting a mere fledgling like myself, whose most important client is a line supervisor at the Putilov Steel Works? I must admit that I am not certain I am equal to the task. When I made an appointment with you, I had no idea of the magnitude of the trouble. My best advice to you would be to find the best criminal lawyer in the country."

"But, Mr. Kerensky, twenty-three years ago my husband had the best lawyer, and he ended up in Siberia."

Anna regretted voicing that fact, for it left them momentarily silenced as the hopelessness of the situation confronted them once again. Even if Viktor could get the money to hire Russia's finest legal minds, would that be enough?

"Mrs. Christinin," Kerensky said at length, "if you will allow me a day or two, I will research this case and see what I can come up with. If I have nothing satisfactory by then, my recommendation would be for you to seek help elsewhere. That's all I can do."

"We appreciate your forthrightness, Mr. Kerensky."

Sensing the end of the interview, they all rose simultaneously. They shook hands, and Kerensky ushered them to the door.

"I will do my best," he said before they departed.

"Of course," said Anna with a brave smile.

Outside, Anna looked at Paul as they walked away. "I sense he's a well-meaning young man," she said. "I do think he will do all he can." There was, however, a question in her tone and her eyes sought assurance from her brother.

"Oh, yes, I agree." What Paul did not express was his fear that Sergei needed more than good intentions to deliver him from this crisis. Paul's entire life's work had been built upon the belief that there was no justice to be found in the Imperial government. Although he tried to be encouraging to Anna, he was hard-pressed to give her the kind of deeply felt affirmation she needed.

52

Anna chose to accept Paul's well-meaning affirmation. Down deep she feared Sergei's plight was next to hopeless, but for now she wasn't ready to confront that truth head-on. Sergei was always telling her how strong she was. And before her papa died, he had told her she had great strength: *"In your weaknesses, Anna, you have been made strong because you have, more than all my children, allowed God to dwell in His fullness within you."*

She didn't feel any of that strength now. She knew Paul was merely placating her, but she couldn't bear to hear anything else. And she resented the inner voice that kept telling her she must be strong. Didn't she have a right to feel despair and fear? Her beloved Sergei was sitting in the Fortress in a cold prison cell, and the possibility of his being sent back to Siberia was all too real.

But what about those who were depending upon her? The children would be coming home from school tomorrow and would have questions and fears of their own. Sergei had insisted that their schooling not be disrupted, and so they had not yet been told of his arrest. They would have the weekend to deal with it, then Sergei wanted them to return to school on Monday as usual. How could she face them? How could she comfort them?

And what of Viktor? His son's arrest was forcing painful memories from his past to the surface. He had confronted and reconciled with much of it four years ago, but Anna could see it was weighing heavily upon him. More than once in the last few days, she had seen a vacant stare in his eyes, as if he were thinking of retreating back into that safe fantasy world of his where there was no pain or suffering.

She would like to run away as well to a place where troubles did not exist, and where Sergei was at her side where he belonged! But for the moment, events did not seem to be designed with her emotional rest in mind.

When she and Paul had returned home, Raisa had greeted her with a letter from the war department informing her that Mariana had been wounded. She was now in a hospital in Vladivostok, and as soon as she was well enough to travel, she would be returning home. The letter gave no indication of the nature of her wound or how serious it was. Anna's relief at the prospect of Mariana's homecoming was overshadowed by the fear that her daughter might yet succumb to her wounds, or that she might be permanently disabled.

When Yuri and Andrei came home from school the next day, Anna was not in a frame of mind to be a support for them. But the presence of Paul and Viktor helped. Viktor had picked the boys up from school in his hired carriage and they all were now seated in Anna's parlor.

Both Yuri and Andrei expressed a sense of the unfairness of this happening to their family. After an initial outburst, however, Yuri grew quiet and thoughtful. Andrei, on the other hand, immediately began to think of actions to get his father back.

"Uncle Paul, I'll bet you know people who have escaped

from the Fortress. It can be done. Maybe when they bring Papa to appear in court, he can get away. Then we can go to Geneva or even London and live there. You did it, so it shouldn't be too hard—"

"No, Andrei," said Viktor, "your father has lived as a fugitive. He wants to be free, and he wants you to be free."

"Do you really think that will happen? They're going to send him back to Siberia, and we'll never see him again. That's true, isn't it, Uncle Paul? The tsar isn't interested in our family. Mariana's been wounded in his war, and he still doesn't care—"

"He probably doesn't even know about Mariana," said Viktor.

"Are you defending the tsar, Grandfather?" Andrei's tone, though respectful, was full of challenge. "All Papa did was write a book and a tsar destroyed his life because of it. I'll never believe in the tsar again."

"He may be our only hope."

"Then we'd better say goodbye to Papa."

Anna said in a detached tone, "I'll go to Siberia with him this time."

"Mama! What'll happen to our family, then?" Andrei's voice broke as tears rose in his eyes.

Paul interceded calmly, "No one is going anywhere. We haven't used all our options yet. What you've said about Mariana is a solution we haven't even considered. It is possible an appeal can be made to the emperor in view of Mariana's sacrifice for her country."

"That seems so cold," Anna said, "when we don't even know how Mariana is."

"Do you think she would mind, if it would save her papa?"

"Do you really think that will help?" asked Andrei.

"We must do everything we can, no matter how remote the chances of success are," Paul answered evasively.

Viktor grasped at the faint glimmer of hope. "I will write a petition to the tsar, mentioning Mariana. It may just work."

Then Yuri spoke for the first time. He had been following the conversation, but he had an entirely different concern. "I want to see Papa, before they take him away, before anything else happens."

"But, Yuri," said Paul, "they won't let children into the Fortress."

"I just turned fifteen." Yuri's voice was so serious, his expression so somber, that for a fleeting instant he did look far more a young man than the boy his family was accustomed to.

Anna leaned forward and looked at him intently. Despite Yuri's dark hair and eyes, he had always resembled Sergei, as much because of their similar personalities as because of any similar physical characteristics. Now he looked so much like a young Sergei that it made Anna want to weep. Yuri could almost be that nineteen-year-old young prince who had taken the time to teach a servant girl how to ice-skate. Sensitive and introspective, sometimes moody but also warm and caring, Yuri, like his father, had never looked for the easy path to follow. And Anna feared that whatever direction Yuri's life took, it, too, would never be completely free from troubles. A few days ago, Anna had told Paul that struggles were inherent to men such as himself and Sergei, and so it was with Yuri.

As a mother, Anna was tempted to intercede for him, to use what power she had to protect him from the pain that life and his own character were sure to inflict upon him. Then she thought about what had happened when Viktor had tried with Sergei—it had destroyed their relationship.

Anna studied her son as she fought her own inner conflict between motherly protectiveness and wisdom. Yuri turned and faced his mother. He didn't have to say anything; she knew he was bound to confront life in his own way, and her interference would not be welcome. Visiting his father in prison seemed a small thing. If it could be arranged, why not allow him? Sergei would probably be thrilled to see Yuri. Yet Anna knew that cruel place, with walls that echoed years of pain and suffering, would scar Yuri's sensitive heart, especially seeing his own father in such a place.

She so wanted to say no, but instead, she turned to Viktor. "Do you think such a thing can be arranged, Prince Viktor?"

"My connections have been next to worthless thus far, but

perhaps they can at least do that."

"Thank you, Grandfather," Yuri said, then turned to his mother. "Thank you, Mama."

Anna tried to smile but it was a feeble attempt. She had let go of Mariana at a terrible price. What would be the cost of Yuri's freedom?

Oh, God, she inwardly cried, *give me the strength to leave my children in your hands.* Why it was such a hard thing to do, she couldn't quite fathom. God was certainly worthy of such trust. Papa Yevno had often talked about letting the little birds fly from the nest. Had he ever said it would be easy? Anna didn't think so. But it was one of those things that had to be done. Parents had little choice in the matter.

She glanced once more at Yuri. No, she had no choice at all.

53

Yuri did not want to be impressed by his father's prison. But as he and his grandfather crossed the St. John Bridge, passed through the outer gate and approached the main gate of the Peter and Paul Fortress, he was profoundly aware of a sense of awe. The black double-headed eagle perched over the arched entrance seemed to beckon him into a world so rich in history that he nearly forgot the grave purpose that had brought him to this place. A quick scan of some of that history, however, immediately cleared his mind.

Despite its beautiful cathedral, with ceilings painted with likenesses of cherubs and angels, this fortress represented vi-olence far more than spiritual fulfillment. Almost since its beginning, the prison across the courtyard from the cathedral had housed political prisoners—most notably the Decembrists of 1825. A steady stream of so-called "enemies of the tsar" had filed through these gates. Some had been executed and tortured, some had gone insane from solitary confinement, and others had died because of the cold and dampness. Those who survived were often sent to Siberia. A few of the lucky ones returned to their revolutionary activities.

Now Yuri's father would be numbered among the thousands who over the last two hundred years could claim residence in this austere place. The part of Yuri that loved history was moved almost to pride by the fact that his father was now among the elite. He rebuked himself immediately, for such thoughts were in direct conflict with his fear that his father might never come out of this prison.

Yuri's ankle nearly twisted as he tried to match his grandfather's long strides on the uneven cobbles of the courtyard. Viktor had been quiet since he came for Yuri that morning, briefly answering a few questions and making only one or two comments, but now as they neared the guardhouse, he paused in his determined steps and turned to his grandson.

"Yuri, I know you believe you are old enough to come to a place like this, and if I didn't agree I wouldn't have gotten permission for this visit. But I must warn you, it may not be as easy as you think."

"I understand, Grandfather."

"Do you, lad?" Viktor did not expect a verbal response, but his gaze probed the boy as if the answer to his question lay behind his grandson's dark, brooding eyes. "You must be strong for your father."

Yuri nodded silently. What would he find, then, behind that prison wall? Was his father's condition so terrible that Viktor felt his words of warning necessary? Well, no matter what, Yuri would be strong; he would show his father and his grandfather that he was a man and worthy of their respect.

A guard admitted them into the dingy yellow building. Inside, there was little difference in temperature from the winter day outside. Yuri shivered as the guard led them down a gray, dank corridor which curved around in a U-shape with a branch bisecting the U. They walked for some distance, their heels clanging hollowly on the stone floor. They paused at a desk, whose lamp shed the only light in the corridor. This area was a little warmer because of a stove burning near the guard's desk, but it was apparently the only source of heat for most of the length of the corridor. Vents allowed some of this heat to enter each cell.

The guard accompanying Viktor and Yuri spoke to another guard seated at the desk. "Visitors for Fedorcenko," he said gruffly. The seated guard nodded and rose and the first guard turned and went back down the corridor the way he had come.

"Gotta search you," the remaining guard said with a hint of apology in his tone. Showing as much deference as possible toward Viktor's obvious nobility, the guard proceeded to give both Yuri and Viktor a thorough frisking. "What's this?" he said, taking a package Yuri was carrying under his arm.

"A book and some writing supplies for my father," Yuri replied with a concerted attempt at keeping his voice even and mature. But under the force of the man's scowl and rough demeanor, Yuri found it difficult to keep from trembling.

"Got no orders to allow such things in."

Viktor said, "I'll take full responsibility."

"Well, Your Excellency, that's all well and good, but rules are rules, you see and—"

"I have a letter of introduction signed by the Minister of the Interior himself." Viktor hitched back his shoulders and looked every bit the prince of Russia that he was. "Do you question my authority?"

The guard chewed this over for a minute, then shrugged. "I guess that's good enough for me, but I'll have to inspect it first—if you don't mind?" When Viktor nodded, the guard opened the package, found it to be exactly what Yuri had claimed, and handed it back. "All right, then, follow me."

During all this, Yuri stole a glance at his grandfather and realized for the first time that he was indeed an aristocrat. Yuri had known this for some time, even before his father told him of his family heritage, but now it struck him with full impact. Prince Viktor Fedorcenko may have fallen onto hard times, but the noble qualities that had been bred into him all his life would never be crushed completely.

They passed half a dozen cells before the guard paused, opened a small hole in a heavy iron door, and announced the visitors. "You got fifteen minutes," the guard told Viktor.

He opened the door with an ancient-looking key on a thick iron ring. A cold draft met them through the open door. The guard stood back to allow the visitors to enter the cell, then firmly locked the door behind them.

Sergei had been seated on his cot, the only furniture in the eight foot by eight foot cell except for a small table. He jumped up when he saw Yuri and gave him an exuberant bear hug.

"What a surprise!" he exclaimed. "How did you manage this?"

"Grandfather arranged it," Yuri said.

Sergei kissed his son's cheek before letting him go, then turned to Viktor and shook his hand. "Thank you, Father."

"Yuri requested it." Then Viktor added with a slight smile, "Actually, he insisted on it."

"I wanted to see you, Papa," Yuri explained. "I just—" He paused, not able to admit his real reason, not able to tell his father that he had been afraid he'd never see him again. If he made an admission like that, he'd probably end up crying, and he was determined to be strong as Viktor had requested. He changed the subject instead. "Andrei wanted to come, too, but he is too young. Mama gave up her time so I could come. I hope you don't mind."

"No, of course not."

"I brought something for you." Yuri gave him the package.

"You don't know what a godsend these things are," said Sergei after opening the package. "I was just thinking that a good book would make this place halfway tolerable. And to be able to write! I can't thank you enough." He placed the package on the table, then motioned for his guests to sit. "I think this old cot will hold all of us. Sorry it's all I have to offer."

Despite the upbeat tone of his voice, Yuri noted that his father did not look well. Perhaps it was the ragged look of his beard, which he had always kept so neatly trimmed; or maybe it was the old gray prison suit and the poorly lighted cell that made his skin look pasty. His father's voice was thick and gravelly, which he said was due to a slight cold he had caught a few days ago. But worse than all this was the fact that he never stopped shivering during the visit. At one point they all rose so he could pull up the single blanket on the cot and wrap it around his shoulders. He had to pause frequently during his conversation to cough.

He tried to shrug it off with a laugh. "I guess it wouldn't be prison if it had all the comforts of home."

"We're going to have you out of here soon," said Viktor, but Yuri thought his grandfather was just saying what was expected. His voice seemed to lack the force of real confidence.

Yuri said, "Papa, Andrei tried to make up an escape plan."

Sergei chuckled. "That sounds like him. But I'm too old for such antics. It was a foolish thing to do even as a young man, and it was sheer luck that I made it—on second thought, it had to have been the hand of God, for that's the only way I could have succeeded."

"You don't think God wants you to escape this time?"

"I can't say for certain, but I'm content to take a more conventional route this time. I was pretty desperate in Siberia. Besides, Yuri, I'm tired of living as a fugitive. I'm ready to—" He paused, running a hand thoughtfully over his graying beard. "To be a Fedorcenko again. After I told you and Andrei about our family, I felt uncomfortable with the secret life I was living. Oh, I realize it was necessary, but all that has changed now. I hate being in prison, but at least some good is coming out of it."

"Papa, does that mean we should tell people who we are now?"

"That's up to you, son. I know this must be hard on you, and confusing."

"I don't mind, Papa. But I want to do what's right."

"This isn't a case of right and wrong."

"That's what makes it so confusing."

"What do you want to do, Yuri?"

"Andrei wants nothing to do with the nobility; he says the working classes and the peasants are Russia and that's what he wants to identify with."

"And what do *you* think?"

Yuri looked over at his grandfather, then back at Sergei. He hadn't wanted to say these things or admit his ambivalence, but now that the conversation had unexpectedly taken this turn he felt he couldn't very well lie to his father.

He said, "We are what we are, Papa. We *are* aristocrats, aren't we? Nothing terrible happened when Mariana claimed her position; she still stayed the same good person at heart. I don't think it should matter either way, except that by taking our proper place in society, we might be able to do some good, make some positive changes in the system." He hadn't said everything he was feeling, but enough so that he didn't feel deceptive. However, he looked down as he spoke, not quite able to meet his father's eyes.

It was Viktor who responded. "Your attitude is quite noble, Yuri, and I don't like to discourage it. But I have always been an aristocrat and have done little good for this country even though I have spent the better part of my life trying—" Sergei started to protest, but Viktor held up his hand and continued, "Perhaps I'm somewhat cynical, but it's best that Yuri see reality so he doesn't end up disillusioned. And the reality is, son, that I was once a man of great financial power and influence. I had the ear of the tsar himself, but little good came of it. Should you take up your position in society, you will have only a name and a title, nothing else. Perhaps that will be enough to do some good, perhaps not. But it would be dangerous for philanthropy to be your sole reason for assuming your title."

"He's right, Yuri," said Sergei. "Whatever you do, it must be for *you*. I know that sounds a bit selfish, but in this case I think it is the best thing you can do."

The guard pounded on the door and yelled, "Five minutes!"

Yuri was relieved for the interruption. He hadn't been comfortable with the direction of the conversation. He quickly changed the subject. "Papa, can I come see you tomorrow?"

"I've been keeping track of the days, Yuri, though it hasn't been easy. But tomorrow is Monday and you must return to school. Besides, Sunday is the only day for visitors, and your mama should come next Sunday."

"I hope you're out by then."

"So do I, Yuri."

305

Viktor said, "We have a lawyer working on it. The one recommended by the Workers' Assembly. He seems like a good man."

"Good." Sergei turned to his son. "Yuri, I want you to concentrate on your studies, and tell Andrei the same. I want to be honest with you—I think you are old enough to hear these things. I haven't lost hope, but the possibility that I may never leave here definitely exists. If I am no longer around, you will be tempted to quit school in order to help with the finances. But that must only be a last resort. More than anything, my desire for you and Andrei is to finish school so that you will have good choices in life. In the end, that will be far more important than the name you choose, or if you have a title or not. It may be a struggle but—" His rising emotions momentarily choked him, causing a bout of coughing.

Yuri threw his arms around his father. "Oh, Papa! Don't say such things. Everything is going to be all right. It will!" And in spite of all his resolve, tears spilled from Yuri's eyes.

The sound of jingling keys penetrated the heavy door, and in a moment the door swung open. Their visit was over. One last embrace for father and son, then Viktor and Yuri were ushered out.

Yuri was silent all the way home. All he could think of were the changes that were certain to come to his life. But the worse thing of all was having to face these changes without his father. How could he do it? How could he make the right decisions? His father *had* to come home again. Yuri wasn't ready to let go right now. He tried to act grown up, to make people think that at fifteen he was a man, but it wasn't true. In many ways, he was just a confused and fearful child, a child who still needed his father.

54

It was obvious to Cyril that this business with Father Gapon was getting out of hand. And it was partly his fault for letting himself get sidetracked with his vendetta against the Fedorcenkos. Yes, seeing Viktor's son hauled off to prison was satisfying to Cyril, but was a few moments of satisfaction worth the cost of his work falling to pieces?

He had, therefore, eagerly accepted the opportunity to meet once again with Basil Anickin. This time the meeting was arranged to take place at a large bookstore on Nevsky Prospekt. Anickin had requested the rendezvous, and Cyril expected Anickin to ask for more money. What he did not expect was Anickin's tempting proposition.

They were appearing to browse among the shelves of books. Anickin, nearby, had pulled down a copy of *A Tale of Two Cities*. How appropriate. The book should have been banned, in Cyril's opinion, but the tsar didn't want to appear the dullard he truly was by scourging Russia's bookshelves of so-called classics.

Cyril lifted a book from a shelf, giving it a cursory glance to insure he hadn't inadvertently taken something equally incriminating. Dostoyevsky. Well, at least he was Russian. He opened it and thumbed through the pages, taking a moment to make sure Cerkover was within view. There was something disconcerting about this Anickin character, as if he'd have no qualms at all about running a knife through Cyril's heart. Cyril refused to meet with him alone.

"So, what do you want? Be quick; I am a busy man." Cyril took the offensive, knowing it always paid to stay a step ahead of a man like Anickin.

"The Okhrana hasn't been very successful in stopping Gapon," Basil said matter-of-factly. "He's opened another branch of his Assembly in the city, and several more are flourishing outside the city."

"I hope you didn't call this meeting to bore me with old news."

"My time is valuable too, Count Vlasenko, and I don't like wasting it on insignificant spying."

"If you're too good for the work, I can easily find someone else willing to earn the kind of money I've been paying you."

"I'm a man of action."

"Then you called this meeting to dissolve our relationship?"

"I take it, then, that you don't want action."

Cyril suddenly realized Anickin was building up to something, and as much as he hated giving the man latitude, he was curious enough to allow him to continue. "What kind of action would you be talking about?"

"There is only one thing that can be done to stop Gapon."

"Ha! Again, you state the obvious, Nagurski. As if we haven't tried eliminating Gapon. But if you had truly been doing your job, you would have noticed that he is constantly surrounded by his bodyguards—his doting workers."

"Let me have a chance at it."

"And what could you do that trained police operatives couldn't do?"

Anickin's features contorted into a twisted half-smile that sent a chill down Cyril's spine. It was a stupid question. This Basil Anickin, alias Rolf Nagurski, had probably made an art form of killing. According to Cerkover, that had been Anickin's primary activity in the United States.

"All right," Cyril said, not bothering to wait for an answer. "What do you plan on doing, and how much will it cost me?"

"You don't need to know my plan. Success hinges on secrecy. As for cost—twenty thousand rubles, up front."

"Up front?"

"That's an American expression meaning—"

"I know what it means!" blustered Cyril, the rise in his tone causing nearby shoppers to glance in his direction. He choked

308

down his ire, then, when curious eyes were turned away, he continued in a calmer voice. "If you think I will pay you a kopeck before the job is done, you are crazy."

"I have been told that." Basil's tone was chilling, like black ice in winter—difficult to see, but lethal.

Cyril swallowed. The man was positively unnerving! "Half *up front*, and half when the job is done."

Basil nodded. "In addition, I will want passport and identity papers under an assumed name for departing the country."

"What name would you like? How does Basil Anickin sound?" Cyril couldn't help himself. He hated the way Anickin always managed to get the upper hand.

Basil's lips bent again into a semblance of a smile. "A fine name, but I'd prefer something more generic, like Ivan Something-or-other."

"Anything else, Your Highness," sneered Cyril.

"I'll need some supplies, items that may raise questions should I attempt to procure them myself. TNT, detonators, fuses—here's a list."

Cyril stared at the paper in Basil's hand as if it were a poisonous snake. "I want nothing in writing."

"Some of these things are too technical for you to remember."

"All right, put it in that book; my man will pick it up."

Basil shrugged and did as he was told. "When do I get my ten thousand rubles?"

"Meet my man in a week, around noon at the Gostinny Dvor Market. At that time he'll give you the money and instructions on the delivery of the supplies."

"It's a pleasure doing business with you, Count." Basil tucked his list between the pages of Dickens' classic, snapped it shut, replaced it on the shelf, then ambled out of the bookstore.

Cyril watched Anickin leave, his only consolation the fact that whatever else Anickin was, he was indeed the best man for the job. Gapon did not stand a chance with such a lunatic stalking him. Cyril tried to smile at that prospect, but he was still quaking too much from the disconcerting meeting to find much humor within himself.

He was more certain than ever that the moment Gapon was gone, Cyril would need to take steps to eliminate Anickin. It was simply in everyone's best interests that such a dangerously insane person be removed from society.

55

Despite all Viktor had been through over the years, he was still not one to feel entirely comfortable asking others for help. Prince Svyatopolk-Mirsky, the Minister of the Interior, had been sympathetic enough on their first meeting almost two weeks ago, but not encouraging. But, after watching Sergei's health decline since his imprisonment sixteen days ago, Viktor determined to make another attempt. The minister was again sympathetic, but still not hopeful.

"The tsar is weighed down with such difficulties at the moment," he told Viktor. "And, to be perfectly frank, this is not exactly the best time to be requesting favors of him. Perhaps if the war takes a turn for the better..."

But that final statement was made with little enthusiasm. Though the spring campaign was still ahead, no one had any confidence it would go any better than in the past.

"He is still hearing petitions, is he not?" Viktor asked with one final flicker of hope.

"The barest minimum. Since the birth of the heir, the family has been in all but seclusion at Tsarskoe Selo. Although your son's plight is a grave matter, I do not feel at liberty to approach the tsar about it. Besides, your son's initial offense was against the tsar's grandfather, in whom he placed great store. Thus, I doubt he will look favorably upon a reprieve. Your best hope is to apply for another trial—"

"We are looking into that, of course," said Viktor a bit impatiently. In spite of everything, he hadn't been prepared for such a negative response. "But that process could take months, perhaps years, and my son's health is not good. Every day spent in the Fortress depletes him more and more."

"I can't promise anything, Prince Fedorcenko, but I will keep this matter under consideration. If there is an opportunity to assist, I will do what I can."

"I suppose that is all I can ask."

"I can supply you with arrest reports and other documents pertaining to the past case. Your lawyer will want such papers, I am sure." The Minister jotted a note on a sheet of paper and handed it to Viktor. "Take this to Count Cyril Vlasenko's office; his secretary will make you a copy of the report. I will have my secretary get the other papers—however that may take longer, since they are by now buried in the archives."

"What is Vlasenko's part in this matter?" This was the first he'd heard Cyril's name in connection to the arrest.

"I only know he asked to see the report several days ago, and to my knowledge, he still has it. He did mention to me he was related to your son in some way."

"A distant cousin."

"That must be it, then."

Viktor nodded and rolled his eyes. "His concern is touching."

As he left Svyatopolk-Mirsky's office, Viktor wondered about Cyril's association with all this. Four years ago Viktor had suspected Vlasenko of involvement in the sudden financial collapse that had led to the confiscation of the St. Petersburg estate, but he'd had no proof—and he no longer had the means to investigate. Now Cyril's name was associated with another Fedorcenko calamity.

Viktor did not believe it was coincidence.

He was tempted to go that moment to Cyril's office; it was just down the hall. But what good would it do to vent his suspicions and anger? Cyril was now such a powerful man that confronting him might only cause more of his wrath to fall upon Sergei. Why the man was so vindictive and hateful, Viktor could not grasp. This was carrying a family vendetta too far; but then, Cyril was that kind of man, with insatiable desires, unlimited greed. Such things drove him—in fact, Viktor would not be surprised to learn that Cyril Vlasenko actually received a good deal of pleasure from the demise of others.

Someday perhaps Vlasenko would pay for his evil deeds, but Viktor wasn't going to live for such a day—that would make him no better than Cyril. He had more important matters that required his energy.

Viktor turned a corner and looked up to see Sergei Witte coming toward him.

"Ah, Viktor Fedorcenko!" he boomed as he reached out to shake Viktor's hand.

"Mr. Witte, how good to see you."

"Don't tell me you have taken my advice and returned to government service?"

This brought an ironic smile to Viktor's lips. "Hardly. I'm afraid I'm here on a rather unpleasant errand." He briefly explained what had happened to Sergei.

"That is a shame. You have my deepest sympathy. Can I help in any way?"

"Only if you could get me an audience with the tsar."

"I'm afraid I haven't seen him in some time myself. He was not too pleased with my censure of the war. Since things have been going so poorly, however, I'm looking less and less the fool. Count Plehve's 'small victorious war' is turning into a nightmare. Rumor has it, though, that the tsar—how shall I say?—has more of an ear toward the voice of reason. My name has been suggested to lead the peace delegation."

"Then it is close to an end?"

"We can only hope." They had been walking together and now Witte paused. "Why don't you join me in my little office for a brandy?"

Viktor agreed. He wasn't in the mood for socializing but understood the importance of nourishing a friendship with such a man as Witte. The office was in the opposite wing, and as they entered Witte apologized.

"His Majesty doesn't want to cut me off completely, so he keeps me in a corner to call up at need. And, of course, I won't refuse his call. I could save this country if he'd let me, but—" He paused and shook his head. "Enough about me. Let's talk about your son. But some brandy first."

He poured out two glasses and they sat in leather chairs. Witte asked questions and Viktor filled in some of the details of the past. Viktor tried not to let his hope rise at Witte's interest—after all, if the Minister of the Interior couldn't help, what could Witte do? He might have known great political power in the past, but at the moment, he was almost as ineffectual as Viktor. Still, Witte was a smart man, extremely savvy in the ways of the government. Perhaps he might suggest some loophole.

"Well," Witte said at length, "if those revolutionaries could hear your story, they would see it is not only the masses who suffer injustice at the hands of the government."

"And I suppose the real irony is that I am even now *not* a revolutionary. I gave the better part of my life in service to the tsar, and though I saw great Imperial fallibility, I would not want to destroy it all. Too much of what Russia is is wrapped up in her monarchy. It's a proud heritage and a rich history we have. We don't need to burn down the whole building in order to get rid of a little dry rot."

"It's more than a little dry rot, I'm afraid. Your own situation points that out only too dramatically. If a man of your standing could be so fouled by the government, then there is truly something amiss."

"I can't argue there. Still, I've always believed we could have the best of two worlds in a constitutional monarchy."

"But our august leader may end up losing everything if he continues to refuse to give a little. I suppose that's why I don't wash my hands of the whole mess—I want to see our world salvaged somehow, and I believe if Nicholas will only listen to me, we will be saved."

"You have my support, for what it's worth these days."

They fell silent for a moment, Witte thoughtfully stroking his graying goatee. He drained off the last of his brandy, then said, "I wish I could do something for you, Viktor. Both for

313

your son, and in restoring you to your former place in government. I know by rights you deserve your retirement. But for a man of—sixty-five?"

"Sixty-nine, to be exact—almost seventy."

"Well, you appear remarkably fit for your age. When I come back into power, I'm going to see to it you receive a post."

Viktor noted how Witte used the word *when*, not *if*, he returned to power. No one could accuse Witte of modesty or lack of self-confidence. He was perhaps the most brilliant man in government, and he well knew it.

"Now," Witte continued, "I have a suggestion regarding your son. As I'm sure you understand, the tsar, even if he were favorably disposed toward your case, is in a difficult political position. This war has lowered his esteem even among the masses. If he should make a point of exonerating the son of a nobleman, it would not make him look good. He must do everything he can right now to improve his image, and that would never help him. But you mentioned that your son has, during his years as a fugitive, lived as a peasant and among peasants. I take it he was well esteemed by them?"

"Very much so."

"And he has for some time now been tutoring men of the working class?"

"Yes, and I've spoken to some of these men. They think the world of Sergei and are distressed at his plight."

"He was involved in this Workers' Assembly?"

"To some extent. More on the periphery, I believe."

"Then here's what I suggest. An appeal to the tsar should not come from you, my dear prince, but rather from these workers. You see the beauty of it, I'm sure."

Viktor grinned. For the first time since Sergei's arrest, he felt some hope.

56

Lack of hope had been Daniel's biggest difficulty during those first weeks of his imprisonment. Long after he passed the point where he feared being executed as a spy, he continued to be dogged by despair and misery. What did it matter if he lived, if Mariana was lost to him?

At last he truly understood how two lives could be so intertwined that one was almost useless without the other. It wasn't easy for him to admit to such a mawkish sentiment, he who had always prided himself on his hardheaded, cut-to-the-chase, eminently practical qualities. But in the weeks since his capture, he'd had the time to thoroughly dissect his values, to scrutinize the man he'd always thought he was. At first, he had been so despondent that the result of his introspection hadn't been very pretty.

Daniel Trent was nothing but a selfish, self-serving reprobate who deserved to rot in a Japanese prison camp. He could see no reason why Mariana could have possibly loved him. Even at the end—

"Oh, God, please, don't let that moment on the ship be the end!"

She had never condemned him, or held his foolishness against him. He thought of her final words:

"God be with you . . . and I love you so!"

He didn't deserve such love; he didn't deserve her.

For the first two weeks of his confinement in a dingy POW camp in the south of Japan, he had thought of little else but how miserable his life was, and how deserving he was of just such a life. Even if Mariana was still alive, he was determined to do her a huge favor and never see her again.

In addition, he was burdened with the fact that he was once more in deep trouble and in need of God. But he stubbornly refused to pray or even think of God. He'd thought he had gotten over that kind of pride, but he still detested being such a *"foul*-weather" Christian. He had hoped he would have a chance to test out his new spiritual insights in normal, untroubled waters; but that apparently was not to be. Many times, in spite of himself, his thoughts would stray to things he had read in the Bible, or something Mariana had said. But he tried to shut those thoughts down immediately.

Mariana had said, "What better time to turn to God than when you are in trouble?"

Still he could not shake the sense that this was wrong, at least that it was hypocritical. But the harder he tried to turn his mind from spiritual paths, the more it would wander in those directions. It was uncanny. Crazy.

He soon became nearly obsessed with this battle. One afternoon he collapsed on his bunk, exhausted, when he hadn't done a bit of physical work all day. He fell asleep and began dreaming—weird, nonsensical dreams, bits and pieces of his whole life, but in a surrealistic milieu. He awoke a few hours later in a cold sweat.

He could remember only one part of the dream collage—the strangest part of all. He was in the desert, surrounded by tents, and seated with a particularly thick, heavy piece of canvas, which he was trying to sew. The "needle" he was using was a huge, unwieldy thing that looked like some animal bone. He tried to push it through the canvas, but it wouldn't go in because the tip was so blunt. He kept at it, grunting and groaning, sweating with the labor, but his attempts always proved unsuccessful. Then suddenly Mariana appeared, dressed as an Arabian princess, dancing around him, singing in a sweet cheerful tone, oblivious to his struggles. Her words were almost taunting in their singsong sweetness:

"It's not easy to kick against the pricks, Daniel. It's not easy . . ."

She repeated the words over and over again. He finally started to scream at her, but the dream abruptly ended and he jerked awake, trembling and sweating. He thought he might have screamed in reality, too.

Mariana's words in the dream kept coming back to him. They sounded familiar, though he was almost certain he had never actually heard her say them. Why were they so familiar, then? And why did he keep thinking about it? Why couldn't that part of the dream just go away like all other dreams?

While exercising in the prison yard the next day, he struck up a conversation with some of the other POWs. They all agreed that they hadn't slept well since coming to the camp and had experienced many bad dreams.

One fellow said, "It's that stinking Jap food. I think the fish they give us is raw."

"As if Russian food is any better," Daniel countered.

"Bah! What do you Americans know about food? Everything you have is from other countries, anyway."

One man spoke with more sincerity. "My father believes dreams are from God. He's a village priest, so he should know."

"All dreams?" asked Daniel.

"Hmmm, I dreamed about my sweetheart the other night," said another.

"Well, maybe not all," said the priest's son.

"What do you think of this one?" Daniel proceeded to describe his dream.

"Oh, yes, yours definitely is of a spiritual nature, because it has Scripture in it."

"Scripture?"

"A man sewing tents and the verse: 'It's not easy to kick against the pricks.' The apostle Paul was a tentmaker, you know, and when he was converted to Christianity—"

"Oh, yes!" exclaimed Daniel. "Now I remember where I heard it. The story about the road to Damascus." Daniel shook his head, incredulous. "You don't think . . ." But he couldn't verbalize the rest of his thought.

Other men began telling about strange dreams they'd had, urging the priest's son to try to interpret them. He quipped that he felt like Joseph in the Egyptian prison, but he made a sincere attempt to expound on each dream.

Wrapped up in his own musings, Daniel wandered back to

his barracks; it was too cold to be hanging about outside for long, anyway. He lay on his bunk and tried to digest what the priest's son had said. A dream from God? It was unbelievable! But he couldn't deny that his dream was uncannily related to Scripture he had once read. And even stranger was the fact that it so obviously related to his present struggles.

Once he decided to accept the dream as it was, he had to deal with the message. What was God trying to tell him? He didn't have to search far for the answer to that question. It was almost as clear as that blinding light the apostle Paul had seen on his way to Damascus. The more he fought God, the more miserable he was. Daniel realized that the most contented he had been in his life was during that time right after his father's death when he had been seeking and not fighting. Mariana was right when she told him that God wasn't going to hold his human weaknesses against him.

The most incredible aspect of this entire dream incident was that God had never given up on him, pursuing him even in his sleep! Such a God could not possibly mind his failures as much as He appreciated Daniel's successes. He didn't expect Daniel to be perfect, or, at least, He knew it wasn't going to happen this side of eternity.

Daniel stopped fighting that day.

Sometimes he berated himself for forgetting to pray and think about God. But many times he remembered. Sometimes he struggled; sometimes he didn't. But he accepted his humanity as God had, and he discovered peace.

Taking advantage of the next days of inner calm, Daniel interviewed several of his fellow prisoners—no sense letting this POW experience go to waste. He believed there was a story angle in every aspect of life. Perhaps one day he'd even write for the religion editor of the paper, but he didn't feel nearly competent for such an undertaking yet.

Three days later, he was transferred to Tokyo. No one told him the reason, and he sat in a Tokyo jail for three more days before anyone finally communicated with him. At last a guard unlocked his cell and escorted him out of the prison, into a waiting wagon and to a building about a mile away—a military office, from the look of the many men there dressed in uniforms. They ascended a flight of stairs to a rather nicely appointed office, where a small man in his early forties, dressed in the uniform of a colonel, greeted Daniel in crisp English.

"Have a seat, Mr. Trent, please. I am Colonel Shiamura."

"Thank you, Colonel." Daniel sat in a straight-backed chair facing Shiamura's desk.

The colonel smiled, and Daniel thought he detected an ingratiating aspect in the man's expression. "You must be wondering what your disposition is with the Japanese government."

"Curiosity is one of my biggest faults, I'm afraid," Daniel said noncommittally. What *was* going on?

"We have been amiss in not keeping you informed, but . . . ah . . ." Shiamura cleared his throat. "Your presence in our prisoner of war camp was not made known to the proper authorities until only a few days ago. And since then we have . . . ah . . . been at something of a loss as to what exactly to do with you."

"I don't believe I understand."

"According to Commander Otami's report, you were caught—shall we say?—in the act of espionage."

"I've already admitted that. I agreed to transport some information in order to get a story for my newspaper. In retrospect, a foolish thing to do. I suppose I deserve to be shot as a spy."

"Under normal circumstances, we would be within our rights . . ."

"But. . . ?" Daniel prompted.

"Your capture, Mr. Trent, has placed us in a diplomatically untenable position."

"Really?"

"You have no idea the stir you have caused. Otami thought he was arresting a mere American correspondent—imagine his chagrin when he discovered he had imprisoned the owner of one of the largest steel companies in America. In fact, the Japanese navy owes a great part of its strength to Union Steel. Well, you can see the position that places the Japanese government in."

Daniel restrained a grin. He could see their dilemma, although this was the first time it had occurred to him. The Japanese couldn't very well execute the person responsible for keeping their war effort afloat. Daniel was a bit chagrined to discover that his company was doing business with Mariana's enemy. He, of course, was supposed to be neutral, but as he had told Mariana, that was not easy considering his deep ties with Russia. Nevertheless, he thought it unwise to mention these things to Shiamura.

Daniel responded as simply as possible. "Yes, I do."

"At the request of your President Roosevelt, the American ambassador has spoken to our Prime Minister."

Daniel cocked an eyebrow. He had spent so much of his life spurning the family position that he had forgotten—or never really realized—just how much power the Trent name held. In an instant, all sorts of practical uses of this power spun through his mind, but he shook them away as one would an annoying cobweb. Let his brother have all that. Daniel was content to be on his own, calling upon company profits only for his basic needs.

But President Roosevelt? The Japanese Prime Minister? Hmmm . . .

Not now, fellow, he told himself firmly.

He was not too proud to use the family name to get out of this present jam, however—especially when the alternatives were either a firing squad or rotting away in a Japanese POW camp.

"So, now what?" Daniel said.

"I am instructed to give you a severe reprimand, then release you into the custody of the ambassador's assistant. I have been told that I do not need to apologize for my government."

"I don't expect you to. What I did was wrong."

"You are an honorable man, Mr. Trent."

"I'm simply sorry for what I did. I lost sight of my proper place in this mixed-up war."

"I understand that the young Russian woman who was wounded on the ship was rather close to you."

"Very close."

"Love does tend to cloud political issues." Shiamura gave Daniel an understanding smile. Then he continued more formally, "I believe this brings to a conclusion our interview. Consider yourself reprimanded, Mr. Trent. Now a guard will see you downstairs, where you will be met by an escort from the embassy."

Daniel rose. He shook hands with the colonel, then bowed Oriental-style. "Thank you very much."

The colonel walked him to the door, and Daniel paused. "I don't suppose it would be possible to *see* the Prime Minister?" He simply couldn't help himself; the newspaperman in him *had* to be appeased.

And he was shocked when Shiamura said, "I believe that can be arranged."

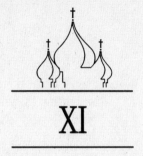

XI

COMMITMENTS

57

Nicholas looked again at Svyatopolk-Mirsky's proposal. Matters of state must progress despite a disastrous war and a sick child. Life goes on.

He wished now he had never given his blessing to the Minister of the Interior for the Zemstrov Congress held last month. He had been under the impression that its agenda would involve nothing more than the usual inconsequential matters. Instead, they had come up with a proposal that included an appeal for a representative body in the government. At first Nicholas had agreed—perhaps in a moment of weakness, out of despondency over the war.

Then he'd had second thoughts. He called his Uncle Sergei up from Moscow for advice, and even consulted with Witte. Both were opposed to the proposal. Of course, Sergei's reactionary tendencies were well known, but who could guess Witte's reasoning when he had always been hounding the tsar about a constitution? Probably the arrogant Witte simply couldn't abide any reform that he wasn't author of. Nevertheless, with checks by these men whom the tsar respected, Nicholas reconsidered his stance.

Stabbing a pen in an ink well, Nicholas scratched some notes in the margin of the proposal, then, on a clean sheet, wrote a brief letter informing Svyatopolk-Mirsky of his final decision. This done, he called in Prince Orlov, chief of the tsar's Private Secretariat.

"Could you see that the Minister of the Interior gets this?" He handed him the pages. "Tomorrow is soon enough."

"Of course, Your Majesty." Orlov waddled forward and

took the papers. Prince Orlov was so fat he could not see the tips of his shoes past his belly. It was hard to believe that one of Orlov's ancestors had been Catherine the Great's lover.

"Now, I must prepare myself for the reception tonight," said Nicholas, pushing back his chair. The French president, Loubet, was visiting St. Petersburg, and as much as he and Alix were shying away from social gatherings these days, it did not pay to offend the French. The alliance with that nation was still a very important part of Nicholas's foreign policy.

"As you wish, Your Majesty. This other matter can wait."

"What other matter?"

"Nothing important, I assure you. A petition from a group of workers."

"Well, all things considered, I should probably take time to at least look at the workers' petition."

Orlov handed over the petition and Nicholas read it with interest. It contained nearly two hundred signatures—in some cases only marks or illegible scrawls—and requested the tsar to review the case of Sergei Viktorovich Fedorcenko, and then to grant a pardon to the man. The tsar, of course, was familiar with the Fedorcenko name, though for the last twenty years it had not frequently been mentioned in society. The petition left no doubt that the Sergei Viktorovich mentioned therein was a scion of that famous family. It outlined the man's offenses, then went on to sing his praises.

This man risked his own anonymity by stepping out of his private existence to meet a vital need among this community's deprived citizens. He gave of himself without the prospect of financial gain, spending countless hours tutoring working men. He could have melted into the city's thousands, a safe existence for himself and his family, and then gone to the end of his days undiscovered by the authorities. Perhaps we cannot condone his flaunting of the law, yet we all bear witness to the fact that Sergei Viktorovich has always been a good and upright man. We believe that a reevaluation of his case will show that twenty-three years ago he was little more than a victim of circumstance. Even the crime of which he was convicted was an act inspired by the best of motives. And

*it shows he was an aristocrat who cared for others, plac-
ing their welfare above his own.*

*We, the undersigned, ask of our most august Imperial
Highness only that you review his case, confident that
upon doing so Your Majesty will conclude with us that
Sergei Viktorovich Fedorcenko has paid sufficiently for
the indiscretions of his youth.*

Orlov smiled sardonically as Nicholas looked up from
reading the document. "Next, they will want the man canon-
ized," he said.

"They did go a bit overboard, didn't they?" Nicholas fingered his moustache thoughtfully. He had never met Prince
Sergei Viktorovich, who was more than ten years older than
the tsar. Though they had moved in the same social circle
twenty-three years ago, their ages had distanced them. But
Nicholas knew that Viktor Fedorcenko had once been a favorite of his grandfather's. Nicholas had been at the impressionable age of thirteen when Alexander II had been murdered, and he still vividly recalled that horrible time. Only a
few years ago, he had built an ornate cathedral on the spot
where Alexander had been killed. He remembered Viktor Fedorcenko's genuine grief at the funeral. Not long after Alexander's death, the elder prince had gone into seclusion.

He wondered why Viktor himself had not appealed to the
tsar. There had been rumors that Fedorcenko's tragic circumstances at the time, including the death of his wife and daughter, had unhinged the man. So, now were there only peasants
and the like to speak up for Viktor's son?

"Do you know anything of all this, Orlov?"

"I took the liberty of procuring the file on Prince Fedorcenko and perused it briefly."

"It's curious, isn't it, that the young Fedorcenko returned
to Russia after his escape from Siberia when he could have
struck out for foreign parts? Well, I'd like to read the file myself. It should prove a fascinating diversion if nothing else."

"There are many more pressing matters—"

"I always liked Viktor Fedorcenko."

"Showing aristocratic favoritism at this time might be in-
advisable, Your Highness."

"Then you propose I ignore these workers? It appears to be a sizable representation."

"It does put you in a sticky position."

"This Prince Sergei has some cagey proponents." Nicholas fingered the petition thoughtfully. "Tell me what you think, Orlov."

"The Fedorcenkos were never close friends of mine, Your Highness."

Nicholas managed a thin smile. This was probably a sublime understatement. The Fedorcenkos, especially Viktor, had always been political moderates; the Orlovs represented the more reactionary end of the spectrum.

"Do you think they are revolutionaries?"

"There is no evidence that would lead me to draw that conclusion. I have never agreed politically with Fedorcenko, but he was always a staunch monarchist. I made a few inquiries; Viktor Fedorcenko has returned to St. Petersburg and seems quite recovered from the . . . ah . . . mental affliction that forced him into seclusion. I spoke with Witte this very morning, and he also believes Fedorcenko is loyal to the Crown. In fact, Witte wanted to give the man a government post."

"But what of the son?" Nicholas wasn't surprised that Orlov had looked into this matter so thoroughly. It was his job to be well informed and to keep the tsar informed also.

"For most of the time after his escape, he lived a simple life of a farmer in a peasant village. No political affiliations whatsoever. He moved to St. Petersburg to be near his niece, whom he had raised in the village, but who at that time left to live with her real father."

"And what of his association with the Workers' Assembly?"

"It appears to be exactly what the letter indicates—philanthropic, as it were. I'm sure he has liberal views or he wouldn't have written the book in the first place that got him in trouble with your grandfather. But a revolutionary? I doubt it. For one thing, Gapon, who heads this Assembly, is most careful not to associate with rebels. I've been told that Gapon himself is a loyal monarchist. I doubt he would give such lavish support to a revolutionary. You may not have noticed, but his signature was also affixed to the petition."

"I'm going to give this matter careful consideration, Orlov."

"Yes, Your Majesty."

"But tomorrow. Now I must face the French. Alix is waiting for me."

58

Alexandra Fedorovna wore a pasted smile across her face as she received the hundredth fawning subject. She knew none of them liked her, and their flattery was as phoney as her smile. But she had her duty, as she supposed they did also. At least the French didn't hate her as much as the Russians, and there were a couple dozen of them to divert her.

However, she was glad when dinner was finally over and the group retired to the ballroom for dancing. There she could sit on her dais overseeing the festivities, while isolated from them as well. The music was lovely, and Nicky was at her side. Everyone else was occupied with dancing and didn't bother her much. She was somewhat miffed, then, when Princess Barsukov approached the royal couple. Still, she smiled. Yalena Barsukov was one of the more genuine of the nobility.

"Your Majesties!" Yalena bowed deeply. "Might I impose upon you for a moment to have a word with you?"

"Of course, Princess." Nicholas signaled for one of the footmen to bring a chair near them.

"Do sit down," said Alexandra.

"You are most kind." Yalena sat in the red velvet chair. Even for a woman like herself, who moved in the best circles, it was an honor to sit in the presence of the emperor and empress.

"What is on your mind, Princess?"

"I have a story I would like to share with you, Your Majesties. I would hesitate in bothering you at all except that I believe in time of war such stories as this are as vital to the war effort as guns and ammunition."

"Do go on," Alexandra encouraged.

"I wish to tell you about a young woman who deserves recognition, a woman who has selflessly sacrificed almost all for her beloved country. She was first brought to my attention when I learned how she saved the life of my brother, who had been wounded at the front."

"We know of your brother also," said Nicholas. "A courageous man. I was proud to award him with the Order of St. Andrew. But what of this young woman?"

"My brother, Philip, has informed me of some of the deeds of the young nurse, Your Majesty. She has worked within range of enemy fire, tending the wounded, and she served in a hospital in Port Arthur, suffering the privations and bombings of the siege. Sometimes she worked eighteen and twenty hours without rest. I realize many others are sacrificing too, but this woman did not have to go to war. She could have remained in her comfortable home, attending parties, and doing all the other things young noblewomen are apt to do.

"Then, not long ago," Yalena continued, "she was seriously wounded while undertaking the dangerous mission of transporting wounded through the enemy-infested sea. This young woman expects no laurels for her deeds—in fact, I have been told she would be discomfited by such attention. However, I believe in this difficult time you, Your Majesties, would want to know of the heroic deeds of your countrymen and women. I hope, too, that hearing might encourage you and brighten a dark hour."

"Indeed it does." Alexandra's smile, this time, was genuine. "Who is this girl?"

"Her name is Countess Mariana Dmitrievna Remizov."

"I don't know the name," said the empress. "I'm sure it would be uplifting, as you say, to meet such a young woman."

"You said she was wounded?" asked Nicholas.

"Yes, Your Majesty. But she is home now, in St. Petersburg."

"Nicky," said Alexandra, "I would like to bring her to the palace."

———

As soon as Yalena left the emperor and empress, another woman appeared. She was the grand duchess Militsa, one of the Montenegrin princesses who was also married to one of Nicholas's cousins. She, along with her sister Anastasia, were among the few people whom Alexandra could truly call friends.

"Your Highness," Militsa said, "I have brought with me tonight a guest I thought you might like to meet."

"Really?" Alexandra was curious; after all, Militsa had introduced her to the French doctor Philippe, and other itinerant monks and healers and miracle-workers. Even Alexandra had to admit that some of these had been charlatans, but she was so enthralled by the mystical that she continued to hope one day a true holy personage would find his way to the palace.

"He is a *starets*, a holy man, from Siberia. His religious mentor is none other than Father John Kronstadt." That was a high recommendation indeed, for Kronstadt had been Alexander III's private confessor. "Shall I get him for you?"

"By all means, Millie, especially since he's come this far."

The grand duchess scurried away, and in a moment she returned with a rather striking man at her side.

He was a tall, lean, large-boned man in his early thirties. Dressed as a peasant, he would no doubt have come quickly to the attention of the royal couple in that aristocratic gathering even if Militsa had not introduced him. But it was more than the man's attire that was notable.

"Your Majesties," said Militsa, her tone containing an air of anticipation as if she were privy to a fantastic secret, "I would like to present Father Grigory Rasputin."

The priest bowed low. "Your Majesties, this is a singular honor."

"Father Rasputin," said Alexandra. For a brief instant, their eyes met, and she forgot what she had been about to say—in fact, she was momentarily speechless. Rasputin's eyes were black like obsidian, like a moonless night, like the depths of a cave of many secrets. Alexandra nearly lost herself in those depths.

Nicky, beside her, stirred and spoke. "Father Rasputin, we are honored likewise to meet a man of God. What brings you to St. Petersburg from Siberia?"

"Ah, Your Highness, the answer to that question is so long and involved it would no doubt bore you. Suffice it to say, I am a wanderer, ever seeking spiritual enrichment."

"As are we," said Alexandra, finding her voice at last, though it was breathless with wonder at what was happening inside her.

"That doesn't surprise me, Your Highness."

"I should like to speak further with you."

"I am at your service."

The remainder of the evening passed far more pleasantly for Alexandra. She spoke for several minutes with the priest and felt as if she had discovered a truly remarkable individual. After the priest left for the evening, she continued to think about him and wonder what such a man could do for her and her husband. He was a simple priest, not a politician, but deep down Alexandra thought the government would be better off with fewer politicians in charge. She didn't entertain great hopes of this Rasputin having such importance, of course, yet Nicky could do a lot worse. But there surely was a better calling for such a *starets* as this Rasputin. Little Alexis flickered through the empress's mind. But the child had been doing better lately. It was possible she had worried for nothing. The malady had probably played itself out. Thanks be to God, he would have no need of healers and miracle-workers.

59

Snow had been falling all morning. A lovely sight. Peaceful, clean, like a promise of good things to come.

Mariana needed such a promise now. The trip back from the war had been long, and the whole ordeal had left her exhausted. She had arrived home a week ago, excited that she would be home for Christmas. But she had landed in the middle of a family crisis, and a dreary holiday had passed with Papa Sergei in prison. The family gathering had been a glum one to say the least. Mama Anna had tried to minimize Sergei's plight to her recuperating niece, but the strain, evidenced in new creases around Anna's brow, was obvious. She tried to be cheerful, but her voice was thin, as if tears were not far away.

When Mariana had imagined her homecoming while lying in the hospital in Vladivostok, she had envisioned Anna's tender arms holding her, comforting her, assuring her that all would be well, that Daniel would return to her, and that she could maintain hope for her future—for their future together. Instead, Mariana had been called upon to offer words of comfort and assurance to Anna, and hope for *her* future. She didn't begrudge this unexpected turnabout, but . . . oh, why couldn't life be smooth for a change?

Watching the quiet snowfall from her bedroom window was like a balm to Mariana. A brief respite. It changed nothing, but even a little reminder that peace did exist was something to cherish.

The respite didn't last long. Her door suddenly burst open, letting in a cold draft—along with Eugenia Remizov.

Mariana had wanted to stay at Mama Anna's to recuperate.

But her père, Dmitri, had been so overwrought with joy at her homecoming, she could not hurt him by revealing her true desire. Besides, Anna had enough to deal with without having to nurse Mariana. She was recovering steadily. She could walk to the water closet by herself, and had even ventured for short treks in the corridor outside her room, but each excursion had left her quite exhausted. The doctor had told her she had lost so much blood that it would take much time before she regained her strength back. There was even a hint that she might never return to her previous vigor. Anna didn't need a patient on her hands.

But it meant Mariana had to put up with her overbearing grandmother. Why didn't the woman fulfill her constant threats and move back to Moscow?

"Mariana!" Eugenia exclaimed with a rare look of pleasure on her long, angular face. "Today is surely the best day of your life!" She waved a letter in Mariana's face.

All that Mariana could think of was that she had received word that Daniel was on his way back to her.

"What is it, Grandmother?" Mariana had finally conceded in addressing Eugenia as grandmother, but the title would never come easy. Often she had wished she could have known Princess Natalia—who, she had been told, had been a sweet, gentle lady.

"A letter for you, my dear."

"I assume you read it?" Mariana indicated she was irked at this invasion of her privacy.

"In your own best interests," defended Eugenia. "I would not want to expose you to any undue shock in your delicate state of health, Mariana. It's my duty."

"Well, let me see the letter—or, isn't that permitted?"

"I will not let your insolence spoil this great day." Eugenia was spilling over with goodwill, and she was determined to be the imparter of the good news rather than let Mariana read it for herself. "You, my dear, have received an invitation from His Majesty the tsar!" Triumphantly she dropped the letter on Mariana's covers.

"Oh," was all Mariana could say. She should have known

that Eugenia wouldn't have been excited over a letter from Daniel.

"Is that all you can say? Why, you ungrateful child! This is the turning point of your life. Our family fortunes have finally improved. I'll be able to get you the best match in Russia—"

"That won't be necessary, Grandmother! I already have the best man . . . in the world!"

"That American? Bah! We can only hope he never gets out of that Japanese prison camp."

"Countess Eugenia! How can you say such a thing? How can—?"

"Oh, simmer down, child. I suppose it *was* an unkind remark." Even Eugenia knew when she had gone too far. "But it distresses me so to see you ruin your life. I still can't believe you turned down Prince Philip Barsukov. The richest family in Moscow, and the elder prince is easily one of the most influential men in all of Russia. What were you thinking? Just count your blessings that you've been given this new opportunity. An audience with the emperor and empress will enhance your social fortunes to no end."

Mariana sighed, then laid a hand across her forehead. "Grandmother, I think I feel faint." She closed her eyes, and lolled her head to the side.

"Mariana?"

In a weak whisper, Mariana said, "Perhaps a cup of tea might revive me . . ."

Eugenia clucked her tongue and gave a frustrated shake of her head. "You better work on building your strength." It was an order, not a concerned request. "You can't miss the appointment at the palace."

Eugenia strode from the room. Mariana carefully opened an eye to make sure her grandmother was gone, then the other eye popped open and she breathed another sigh. She'd had her fill of Eugenia's railings—another minute of it, and she really would have fainted!

Absently she picked up the letter. Looking at the fine linen paper and the gold Imperial seal, she had to admit that it was rather incredible. She slipped the letter from the envelope. A personal note from the tsar. Well, a closer inspection showed that it had probably been written by one of his secretaries—but handwritten, not typed.

> "To Countess Mariana Dmitrievna Remizov, From Their Majesties, Emperor and Empress of all the Russias, Nicholas II and Alexandra Fedorovna: Be it known that you are hereby requested to attend an audience with Their Royal Majesties. Their Majesties wish to meet a true hero of the war in which our beloved country is now engaged. In consideration of your current illness Their Highnesses will await your suggestion as to the date and time. Please reply at your earliest convenience."

Mariana smiled. The tsar was bowing to *her* "earliest convenience"? Incredible. And "true hero"? Who had he been talking to? It must have been Philip, or perhaps the sister he spoke of so often. The Barsukovs were the only people she knew who had any knowledge of her time in Manchuria, and who were also close to the tsar. Mariana's father had also mentioned his blossoming friendship with Philip's sister.

But what had the tsar been told? She felt a little silly to think that he had been given misinformation. She was no hero. And what would he think if he knew she had taken a bullet in order to save a Japanese commander? Perhaps that part had been omitted. It might be best for her to decline the royal invitation.

Eugenia would have a seizure!

In spite of the fact that disappointing Eugenia would give her just a touch of pleasure, Mariana did think she'd rather take advantage of the invitation. It wasn't every day someone was given the opportunity to meet the tsar. It would be a memorable experience. She would tell Daniel all about it and he would probably write—

The thought of Daniel deflated all her rising excitement. *Would* she see him again? Where was he? How was he? He had to be all right! And, if he was, would he then be worried about her survival? How would he ever know from a prison that she had survived?

Then she remembered to pray. Crossing herself, she uttered simply, "Dear Lord, wherever Daniel is, protect him and help him to know that you are near. And, please, bring him back to me!"

60

Eugenia saw to it that a pot of hot tea was sent up to Mariana. Though it seemed to her that her granddaughter's fainting spell had been terribly convenient, she did think it expedient that she do what she could to stay on the girl's good side. That wasn't easy, to be sure, what with her phoney self-effacing manner, and her stubborn flaunting of her peasant simplicity.

But this was no time for Eugenia to lose her patience. She had put up with the girl for this long, and now, with an audience with the tsar in her near future, she would have to continue her forbearance.

But what would she do if that flighty child insisted on marrying that idiotic American? Eugenia had thought she had put an end to that relationship a few years ago, when she had destroyed the American rogue's letters before Mariana had a chance to see them. Apparently he was a persistent lout.

For that day and the next the question hovered over her like a cloud. No wonder she was getting a headache. On the afternoon of the second day, she retired to her boudoir for the remainder of the day. But, lying on her daybed, with a cool cloth over her forehead, she could not escape the dread that she might not be able to control her granddaughter. And it didn't help that Eugenia's milksop of a son was determined to give the girl anything she wanted.

If only she could think of something that even Dmitri would have to concede to, a line he would not step over even for his daughter. Something so socially repugnant—

Eugenia smiled as the perfect solution came to her devious mind. It was really very simple. In fact, Mariana herself might have to accept it as an insurmountable stumbling block to her marriage to that loathsome American.

An hour later, Dmitri came by to inquire of his mother's health. She hadn't seen him since the royal letter had come. She assumed he had been on one of his all-night gambling sprees, but instead of rebuking him Eugenia welcomed him into her boudoir.

"Dmitri, have you heard the good news?"

"The audience with the tsar? It's unbelievable, isn't it? I never thought Yalena would actually speak to the tsar."

"What do you mean?"

"Well, I must admit that I planted the idea in her pretty head. We were talking about the discouraging progress of the war and how distressed the tsar was. I mentioned that if only he knew about some of the heroes of the war, he'd probably feel much better. I said it lifted my heart every day when I thought of my Mariana's courage and how she was wounded for her country. It didn't take Yalena long to come up with the notion of telling it to the tsar."

"Why, Dmitri, I'm impressed. I didn't think you had such cunning in you."

"I never dreamed it would actually work! It had been merely a stab in the dark."

"Well, it did work, and now your daughter will soon be presented to the royal family."

"I wonder if the tsar expects me to present her?"

"You're her father, aren't you?"

"My name wasn't mentioned."

"That's the least of your worries, my dear son."

"Worries? In my mind, I thought this would end most of my worries. Fifteen minutes ago, I called up Alexsie Kozen— you know, the banker. He's been tighter with money than a poor muszhik's lapti. I tried for a loan a few weeks ago and he refused; he said the house was mortgaged to the hilt and I simply had no more collateral. Today, I casually mentioned my daughter's good fortune, just to see what might happen. Well, of course, he's heard—the St. Petersburg gossips haven't failed me yet! And guess what? He is going to extend me a five-thousand ruble line of credit. That ought to keep me—that is, us—in business for a while."

Eugenia was not impressed. She had more important matters to consider. "Money isn't everything, Dmitri. Someday Kozen—and who knows who else—is going to expect you to pay back all those loans of yours. Then what? I'm more concerned with future security. What if Princess Yalena decides not to marry you? You're old enough to be her father, you know. In fact, come to think of it, I do believe her father is a year or two younger than you. Do you really think you can snag such a girl?"

"I have snagged her, my dear Mama!" Dmitri grinned like a love-struck schoolboy.

"What!"

"Lovely Yalena has all but agreed to my ardent marriage proposal."

" 'All but'?"

"She wants to wait for an official engagement until her brother returns from war. They are quite close—"

"Her father approves?"

"Two years ago Yalena's heart was broken when her fiance was killed in a yachting accident. They were deeply in love, and she mourned him intensely. She almost joined a convent. Her father is so happy she has had a change of heart that he'd be the last to stand in our way."

"So, it doesn't bother him that you don't love her, and are just after her money."

"Mother! I am appalled! I love her as I have not loved a woman since Katrina."

"Is that so?"

"Well . . . almost as much. Men my age are not expected to fall in love in that way any longer. But I care for her deeply, I truly do. I would do anything for her."

"In return for which, she shall finance your luxurious lifestyle."

"I didn't think you could be so crass, Mother."

"I'm not complaining, mind you. It'll be a nice change to have another woman pay your way. But I don't much like what the gossipmongers are saying."

"Forget them! They'll bite their wagging tongues now that we have the ear of the tsar."

Eugenia smiled. The conversation had come full circle, back to where she wanted it. Let her son do with his life what he wished; it was too late to help him. Mariana was another matter.

"Mariana is not even sure she wants to see the tsar," said Eugenia.

"Nerves. She'll get over it."

"As I hope she will get over her silly infatuation with that American."

"Don't start on that again, Mother."

"You don't care if she ruins her life?"

"I've said it before, and I'll say it again—I like the fellow. And I still can't see how marriage to him would ruin her life. Besides the fact that they love each other, Mariana will never have a financial worry again. The Trents are quite wealthy, Mama."

"Money, money, money! Is that all you think of?"

"What else is there?"

"Have you ever thought about your daughter's eternal soul? Have you considered the fact that this American is not Orthodox? Will you have your daughter marry outside the Church?"

Dmitri's bright enthusiasm faded. In fact, he had never considered this. Spiritual matters were the furthest thing from his mind. He lately had tried to patronize Yalena, to whom such things were important, but basically he was far too pragmatic to be mystical. Yet the *Church* was a different matter altogether. He never attended, except at Christmas and Easter, but neither would he dare ignore the external forms of religion. When he married Yalena, it would be in the Church; if they had children, they would be properly baptized into the Church; when he died, he would expect Last Rites, and a proper Orthodox funeral. To do otherwise simply never dawned on him. The thought that his daughter's marriage might not be recognized by the Church, implying that she'd be living in sin—well, it was distressing at best, staggering at worst.

Eugenia knew from his speechlessness that she had him. She repressed a triumphant grin.

"What do you plan on doing about it, Dmitri?"

"Must we do anything right now?" asked Dmitri, lamely, hopefully. "I mean, the last Mariana heard from young Trent, he had been captured as a spy. You know what they do to spies, Mama. I hate to say it, but our young man may already be out of the picture."

"And if not?"

"Oh, let's not worry about it now. I don't want to ruin this wonderful time. Who knows? After this audience with the tsar, many eligible men will be introduced to Mariana. She may change her mind on her own."

Eugenia shrugged. She couldn't count on Dmitri for anything sensible. He forgot that many handsome men had already been paying court to Mariana, and she had snubbed them all. But Eugenia said no more. She had planted the proper seeds for now. She would keep pressing the issue of religion, and when—or if—the time came she would be in a very strong position to thwart a marriage not befitting a family of their station in Russian nobility.

But Dmitri was right about one thing—perhaps that awful American would never return. Then all their problems would be over, indeed.

61

Mariana finally decided to accept the tsar's invitation only when Viktor suggested that the audience might greatly help her papa Sergei's situation. She reluctantly allowed herself to get caught up in her father's enthusiasm; it would not have been proper to appear before the royal family glum and depressed, worried over the uncertainty of her dear Daniel's disposition. It helped a little when Dmitri, who had knowledge of such things, assured her that it was unlikely the Japanese would execute an American citizen.

"And he is a Trent, you know," her father assured her. "If anything happened to him, it might cause an international incident. The Japanese are in no position to risk war with America."

Mariana had never thought much about the importance of Daniel's family. He hardly ever mentioned it. She wondered if her father might be exaggerating a little. But it was something to hang on to, and a reason for hope.

The preparations for the big day helped take her mind from her worries. She let the beautiful new dress cheer her. Again, Eugenia outdid herself, proving her taste impeccable, and Mariana showed her good sense in letting her grandmother have her way. Eugenia knew that white was in fashion, especially for afternoon wear, and she chose a filmy white gauze with soft gathers in the skirt, three rows of horizontal tucks above the hem, elbow-length sleeves with the bodice and long basque of *broderie anglaise*. A blue sash at the waist was clasped with silk roses. Mariana's hair was pinned up, and she wore a wide-brimmed hat decorated with ostrich feathers and chiffon.

After so many months in her nurse's uniform, which was usually stained and wrinkled—or, more lately, in bedclothes—it did feel good to dress up. But it felt somewhat odd, too. She thought of her friends at the front, and all the soldiers who were still suffering danger and deprivation.

At two-thirty in the afternoon the hired troika came for Mariana and her father, who, much to his ecstasy, was to accompany her. He, too, had dressed for the occasion in a new, and expensive, gray pinstripe cashmere suit, gray Homburg, and black cashmere overcoat with a fur collar. He looked almost as exquisite as his daughter. But this was a big moment for Dmitri, for he had never been presented to any tsar. And, though he was only along as chaperone, he knew this was as much his great social opportunity as it was Mariana's.

Their appointment was for three-thirty, and it would take most of the preceding hour to travel to Tsarskoe Selo, where they were expected at the Alexander Palace. Mariana bundled up in a rabbit fur coat, and Dmitri insisted that his daughter be tucked warmly into the sleigh with several thick furs and blankets.

Before the sleigh reached the palace gates, they drove through the town clustered around the tsar's residence. All around were many mansions of the aristocracy, whose occupants' entire existence was dominated by the royal family and the life of the court. Dmitri chuckled with satisfaction as they passed through.

"I'll warrant we're the talk of the town today, Mariana," he said.

"But why, Père?"

"The Court gossips miss nothing out of the ordinary, my dear. So when a couple of nobodies like ourselves are presented to the emperor and empress, you can be sure there is talk. I expect our mail delivery will be full of invitations—everyone dying of curiosity about what transpired. Our social prospects are about to soar!"

"I thought that happened a few years ago when you and Grandmother had that big party for me."

"That was but a pale shadow of the future. After today we will have stepped into an even more elite circle."

Mariana said nothing. Why spoil her father's excitement? But she had no desire to reenter society, especially one that was more elite. Her time in Manchuria might have had its difficulties and stresses, but she had never felt more alive with purpose. She understood why Daniel had such a passion for his work—it fulfilled him, gave his life meaning. She had no heart to return to the world of aristocratic idleness. She wasn't sure what exactly she would do, but she did know that what she had experienced on the front line in the war had forever altered her direction in life.

In a few minutes the troika pulled up in front of the palace gates. Within the eight hundred acre compound of the Imperial park there were two palaces. The Catherine Palace was the larger and more ornate of the two, built by Peter the Great's daughter, Elizabeth. Its blue facade with elegant white columns and gilded trim matched Versailles in grandeur. With two hundred rooms, it was a study in opulence, literally dripping with gilded carvings on the ceilings, the wainscoting, and the window and mirror frames. The walls were resplendent with works of art, and the floors were inlaid wood of the most intricate designs.

Nearby was the Alexander Palace, built by Catherine the Great for her beloved grandson who was to become Alexander I. It was simpler than the Catherine Palace, with only one hundred rooms, but in no way lacking in Imperial richness and decor. Here, in one of the wings, Nicholas and Alexandra made their home. Alexandra had redecorated to give it the air of an English country estate.

Mariana and Dmitri were taken by a servant into one of the formal drawing rooms of the Alexander Palace to await the arrival of the royal couple. The furnishings were of cherry, and the sofas and chairs were upholstered in bright chintz of mauve, Alexandra's favorite color, yellow and blue. The gold brocade draperies were closed, since it was almost dark outside. A tall stove covered with intricately decorated tiles kept the room at a comfortable warmth. Several vases of fresh flowers shipped in from the Crimea were placed around the room.

Mariana and Dmitri waited in silence, both struck with jitters. In ten minutes the door opened suddenly and in came a rather striking black man dressed in a gold-embroidered jacket, red trousers, white turban on his head, and shoes with curved toes like that of an Arabian prince. His entry signaled the imminent arrival of Their Majesties.

Father and daughter, schooled in Court protocol by a lady-in-waiting for days before the audience, immediately rose and faced the door. Mariana stole a quick, nervous glance at her father. He was a shade paler than normal, and she thought she detected a tremor of his lip beneath his moustache. She was definitely shaky herself and wondered if she remembered the proper curtsy. It eased her nerves a little when she recalled Anna's oft-told story of her encounter with the tsar, Nicholas's grandfather, Alexander II, and how he had nearly run right in to her in a corridor of the Winter Palace. Except for Uncle Misha's gentle prodding, Anna would have forgotten to bow. But Alexander had smiled warmly at the frightened servant girl that day. Mariana hoped Nicholas II would be as benevolent today.

Then they came.

Nicholas stepped aside to allow his wife to enter first. She was tall, slim, and attractive, as elegant as fine porcelain. Her features, which tended to be slightly angular, were softened by reddish gold hair and dark blue eyes. She wore a simple gown of ecru lace, belted at the waist with matching satin. Several strands of pearls hung around her long neck, and her hair was piled up into a bun near the top of her head. She wore no other adornments; it was as if this audience was just a part of her daily routine. Mariana felt better and began to relax at bit. She curtsied, and Dmitri offered a low bow.

Nicholas, dressed in a plain military tunic with dark trousers tucked into knee-high leather boots, doted on his wife with obvious affection. He saw to it that she was seated comfortably, even though a footman was there for that purpose, and motioned for Mariana and Dmitri to sit. Mariana perched near the edge of her chair, her back straight, uncomfortable about being seated in the presence of the royal couple.

"It is an honor to meet such a courageous young woman," Alexandra said. "When my husband and I heard about you, I felt you should come to our home so we might in some small way repay you for your services. I know there are so many others over there who are deserving of recognition, but in extending our hospitality to you, it gives us a sense that we are touching them also."

"Your Highness, your words make it so much easier for me to accept being singled out. Whatever I have done was so little compared to what others have suffered and are at this moment suffering."

"Tell me, Countess Remizov," asked the tsar, "what is the prevailing mood of the men over there?"

"I'm probably not the best judge, since I only see the soldiers after they have been wounded. To be honest, I must say some of these are bitter and resentful, but most of their hostility is focused at the Japanese. Many, even among the wounded, are proud to have served Russia. They love their country, Your Highness."

"And what of their tsar?" He quickly added with an apologetic smile, "I'm sorry—I won't make you answer that."

Alexandra interceded. "Did you enjoy your work as a nurse, Mariana Dmitrievna?"

"Oh, yes, Your Highness, very much so. I felt so useful. However, I did nearly quit when my uncle died."

"Your uncle was an officer with which regiment?" asked Nicholas.

"He was a private in the Ninth Infantry, sir."

"A private?" Nicholas cocked a curious eyebrow.

Out of the corner of her eye, Mariana noticed her father shift nervously. She supposed her peasant ties were a skeleton he would have preferred to have remained in the closet. But Mariana was proud of that part of her life.

Alexandra said, "This is most interesting. Do tell us all about it. But first, I believe tea has arrived."

During tea, prodded by the tsar and tsaritsa's questions, Mariana related a concise sketch of her unusual family. She kept vague Dmitri's role in the tale, but implied that he had been forced by circumstances to leave the country. Nicholas was more interested in Sergei and Anna, anyway.

"This Sergei Viktorovich would have sacrificed his position for the woman he loved. A true man of honor," said Nicholas.

"Oh, yes, he is, Your Highness."

"And, I recall the same to be true of your grandfather. How is he now?"

"He is well, sir. But distressed, as we all are, about my uncle Sergei's recent difficulties."

"I was sorry to hear about that."

"It's not your fault, Your Highness."

"Thank you for saying so, but I am involved because the original offense was against my grandfather. And also because I am in a position to affect the situation."

"Your Highness, I am appreciative of your concern, especially since you have so many other things on your mind, with the war and all."

"I would like to help your uncle. I would like to pardon him and restore him to his full place in society."

"You . . . you would?"

"You deserve no less. You and your family have served the Crown well, even if perhaps you haven't always agreed with it. I believe you have all paid enough for past indiscretions."

Sudden tears spilled from Mariana's eyes, and the empress actually rose and laid a comforting hand on her shoulder. "My dear, I should like to visit with you again sometime."

"Thank you, Your Majesty," said Mariana through her tears, then, in a sudden impulse she kissed Alexandra's hand tenderly.

On the ride home, Dmitri was positively bursting with pleasure. Though he had been practically ignored during the interview, he was obviously proud at how his daughter had deported herself. Mariana realized with amusement that as Dmitri recounted the experience over and over her father's role in the event seemed to be growing as they moved farther from the palace, but she didn't mind his exuberance. Realizing that Dmitri's monologue would continue, with or without her participation, she returned to the privacy of her own thoughts.

She had met the emperor and empress of Russia—and had not made a fool of herself! In fact, they had actually seemed to like her and wanted to see her again. That alone was almost too much for her to fathom. But on top of it all, Papa Sergei would be freed from prison! And he could be Prince Sergei

Fedorcenko once more. Mariana knew that since Viktor's recovery and reconciliation with his son, Sergei had regretted more than ever that he couldn't claim his real name.

She was so happy for them. Would her mama now claim her proper title? Princess Anna Fedorcenko. It would fit her very well, for Anna was the most noble person Mariana had ever known.

Only Mariana's uncertainty about Daniel marred her complete happiness—not only because of her worry for him, but also because he was her best friend and she couldn't share this extraordinary day with him. He had been in her thoughts, as always, first thing that morning, and was still on her mind and in her heart as the troika pulled up before Anna's building on Vassily Island. Mariana had asked Dmitri to stop there before going home so she could tell Anna the good news. She wished now she would have asked the tsar more specifically about when he thought Sergei would be released, but it was wise, when one received a boon from an emperor, not to push too far.

Anna answered the door, and Mariana was surprised to see her mama smiling; Anna had been so dismayed about Sergei that she had fallen into a persistently glum mood. Why was she smiling now? Had she already heard the news?

"Mariana, you must have heard," said Anna.

"About Papa, you mean?"

"No . . . I thought you came here because you had been home and heard about—" Anna stopped abruptly, all color draining from her face. "What about Papa?" Her voice was filled with alarm.

"It's okay, Mama! Don't worry—I have good news." Mariana threw her arms around Anna. "The tsar is going to pardon Papa!"

"Oh, my—!" Sudden tears cut off anything else Anna might have said.

Dmitri came up and patted Anna on the shoulder. "I am so happy for you, Anna," he said with deep sincerity.

"And so am I," came a familiar male voice from the parlor doorway.

Mariana's head jerked up.

"Daniel!"

She left her mama and ran into his open arms, weeping and laughing. For all his lack of brawn, Daniel easily swept her up and swung her around joyfully.

62

As they had promised each other so many weeks ago before their parting, Mariana and Daniel took a walk in the Summer Gardens the next day. It was winter now, and there was no fragrance of lilacs; the pond was all frozen and the swans had been taken to warmer quarters. All the statues had snow collecting on their heads and shoulders, but the two lovers did not care.

They held hands and walked along the icy paths as if it were spring. Pausing by the canal that separated the park from the busy street, they talked about their experiences since that awful day on the ship when they thought they might have lost each other for good.

Daniel was truly awed that Mariana had met Nicholas and Alexandra. He laughed, his merriment mingled with just a little surprise, when she hinted that the experience might make a worthwhile story.

"Mariana, I didn't think such things interested you."

"I guess at times I was so busy being critical of a few things that I forgot to give proper credit for the real importance of what you do. I want to be more supportive."

"That means a lot to me. But, Mariana, it is a bit ironic, because everything that has happened to me has helped change my perspective on many things—the importance of my job included."

"Would you like to tell me about it?"

"I have been wanting to since I first saw you yesterday, but there was so much going on then. Besides, the timing is much better now. Are you warm enough? It may take a while."

She slipped her arm around his and snuggled close. "Now I am. Do go on."

He told her all about his time in the Japanese prison, about his discouragement, and finally about his dream and how persistent God had been with him.

"Like a certain reporter I know," chuckled Mariana.

"Which reminds me of another struggle I've had. For a while I thought that being a reporter might not fit in with serving God. Sometimes I have to be pretty aggressive and hardnosed to get at the truth; and there have been times when reporting the news has made people, sometimes even innocent people, uncomfortable. But I've realized that God is more interested in the truth than anyone. My job only conflicts with God's will in terms of my perspective, approach, and priorities. I don't suppose I'm going to change overnight, but I'm going to trust God that He will continue to be persistent with me and not let me go off the deep end."

"From the moment I saw you yesterday, I sensed there was something different about you, Daniel. You are confident now—not just cocky, but . . . it's hard to explain. Before, you were depending so much on yourself that it made you nervous. And the more nervous you were the more cocky you became."

"Now I'm off the hook!" Daniel said cheerily. "I don't have to protect myself so much anymore. It feels good to be able to lean on God. But—and this is really the spooky part—I actually feel stronger than I did before."

"My papa says that with God, things are often the opposite of what we expect them to be. He's fond of the Scripture, 'In your weaknesses are you made strong.' "

"I like it. I'll have to memorize it. By the way, I can hardly wait to talk with your papa Sergei. I have a million questions."

"The tsar assures us that he will be home soon."

350

"You'd think they could release him the minute the tsar gives the word."

"Russian bureaucracy, you know. We better not push it; something could go wrong."

"I suppose I can wait until then," Daniel said with a chuckle. "There's something else I want to see him about—and perhaps I should see Dmitri also."

"Oh . . . what's that?"

"Will you forgive me if I don't kneel in the snow—oh, never mind. You are worth it—" He dropped to the ground on one knee in the cold, wet snow and took Mariana's hand in his. "Mariana, if you'll have—what is it Countess Eugenia so fondly calls me, among other things?—an obnoxious American, I would like you to be my wife. Mariana, will you marry me?"

"My grandmother doesn't know a thing, Daniel. She refuses to use your proper name, and she won't accept that you are the most wonderful, exciting, dear man I have ever known. I have been waiting for years for this proposal."

"You have?"

"Most of the time I didn't even know it myself. But if you will have a barbaric Russian, I would be honored to have an obnoxious American. My answer is yes! Yes!"

Jumping up, he took her in his arms and kissed her.

In a few moments when their exuberance had calmed a bit, Daniel said, "You know, Mariana, I don't think Russians and Americans are really that different. Oh, there are the obvious things, but deep down there are a lot of similarities, too. I wouldn't be surprised if one day our two countries will be standing shoulder to shoulder as world powers."

"Or nose to nose," quipped Mariana.

"But you and I will never be nose to nose."

Mariana smiled. "Oh, I wouldn't be surprised if it happened occasionally. Our differences make things interesting."

"All I know is that I love you, Mariana!"

And they were in each other's arms again.

After a few moments, they started walking again. Before long they had left the Summer Gardens and were walking along the river. They were quiet most of the way, speaking of only a few trivial things in passing. For the most part they just quietly enjoyed each other's presence.

At last the physical exertion of the walk began to wear Mariana down. Shortly before they reached the Winter Palace, she was too exhausted to continue. Daniel hailed a droshky to take them the rest of the way. After a few moments of rest in the carriage, with several blankets pulled up over them for warmth, Mariana was able to resume a more intense conversation.

"Daniel, I'm so happy now, I can hardly describe it. But there are two things troubling me."

"Only two?" He winked and chuckled. "The path of true love never runs smoothly, you know."

"These are serious, I think."

"I'm sorry for making light of it. Please tell me."

"Well, I feel foolish for the first problem—I just need to have this out in the open and hear your reassurance." She shifted nervously and looked down for a moment. "It's just this, Daniel: Have you thought about how marriage might interfere with your work?"

Relieved, Daniel grinned. He had no trouble with the answer to that. "I've thought about it a lot. At first it scared me to death. I thought I'd have to give up everything for marriage. I wanted you, but I couldn't give up my work. But I meant what I said before. My priorities are different now."

"I don't want you to give up your work for me. I don't think I'd like you to travel as much after we're married, but then, I can go with you sometimes."

"Of course! That would be great. But while we're on the subject, what about *your* work? I'm not one of these men who would require you to subjugate yourself entirely to me, you know."

"I enjoy nursing, but it's not my lifeblood. I only know I want to continue to do something meaningful with my life. It doesn't have to be nursing." She glanced up coyly at him. "It might be very meaningful to raise our children, Daniel."

He paled perceptibly. "*Our* children?"

"You like the notion?"

"It's exciting, yet a little frightening. But I'll definitely get used to it. That raises another question. Where will we raise these children—America or Russia?"

"I think our children will be citizens of the world, Daniel, and they should be familiar with *both* their homelands."

"We certainly should be able to afford to keep two homes. You realize that, don't you, Mariana?" He paused, and spoke as if offering an apology. "The Trent name comes with a bit of money."

"It's an awesome notion, but I'll try to get used to it." She gave a mocking, long-suffering sigh.

They laughed together, then Mariana turned serious once more. "Daniel, I need to say one more thing. There is something you should be prepared for when you speak to my parents. Countess Eugenia has hinted at it already, and I think Dmitri will probably feel the same as his mother. I'm not sure how Papa Sergei will feel. It's about our different faiths."

"We are both Christians."

"But in the Orthodox Church, that isn't enough. The Church has strong taboos about marrying outside the faith."

"Yes, I suppose I knew that; I just didn't want to consider it."

"I'd like to know how you feel about it, but let me tell you what I think. The Orthodox Church in Russia, as I'm sure you know, is a major part of just about everything and everyone. My parents have known *nothing* else. And part of the subtle teaching of the Church is that other so-called sects, even Christian ones like Protestantism, are almost as close to evil as you can get. Other Christian 'sects' have even been persecuted in the past. I know Anna and Sergei don't believe all that. They taught me that all Christians are brothers and sisters— the church they attend isn't as important as their faith in Christ. But I doubt even Mama and Papa have ever thought about going to any other church. *I* don't care what church we belong to, Daniel. I know our spirits are one in Christ. But they may expect you to convert. That's a serious step, and I don't want to ask—"

"Mariana, say no more. If that's what I must do, then I'll do it. But I'd like to think about it all first, before I—or we— make any rash decisions. I've never really considered any of

353

this before, and I want to make the right move. But I feel certain this won't keep us apart."

"It worries me a bit." Mariana's brow creased and some of the joy of the day faltered. "You don't know my grandmother Eugenia. She can't even accept the fact that you are an American, much less a Protestant."

"Thank God, then, that I won't have to approach her!"

Mariana grinned. "I didn't think about that. For once male dominance shall be welcomed."

"Oh, my liberated woman!" chuckled Daniel. "What have I gotten myself into?"

"You didn't think marriage would be simple, did you, Daniel?"

"No. That's why I've avoided it for so long. But a complicated life with you, my love, will be far better than the lonely simplicity of the past."

They rode in silence for a while until the droshky neared the street where Raisa's flat was located. "Daniel," Mariana asked, "when will you speak with my father and my uncle?"

"As soon as Sergei gets out of prison. That should give me plenty of time to give some thought to this matter of the Church."

"My mama has already said we will have a big family gathering to celebrate Papa's homecoming."

"That will also give me time to get up my nerve. Most suitors only have one father to face—I'll have two!"

Daniel walked Mariana to the door, and when Anna answered it, she insisted they both stay for dinner. They accepted immediately; they didn't want such a special day to end—the most wonderful day of their lives. Soon enough they must confront practical realities, but for now they wanted to bask in the joy of their hearts finally united in committed love.

63

Even Yuri and Andrei, who were home for the weekend, could feel the charged excitement around the dinner table that night. Yuri watched Daniel and Mariana with interest, but Andrei was more stoic—to him, romance was more an embarrassment than a blessing.

Soon after Daniel and Mariana departed, the rest of the family retired for the night. The lamps were out, and the house was dark, but Andrei's stomach was growling—it was three whole hours past dinner, after all! He couldn't get the sweet rolls Daniel had brought from a bakery out of his mind. There had been several left over, and when Daniel left for the evening he said with a wink at Andrei, "I'll bet they won't go to waste if I leave them."

Andrei crept from his bed and tried to open the door quietly, but he forgot about the creak in the hinges. His brother stirred.

"Where're you going?" Yuri asked sleepily.

"I'm hungry."

"Don't be so noisy." Yuri rolled over again.

But a few minutes later, when Andrei was in the kitchen slicing some cheese to have with a roll, Yuri appeared.

"Couldn't go back to sleep," he said. "Then my stomach started talking. What've you got?"

"Just a roll. Want one?"

"Sure."

Andrei tossed his brother a roll and Yuri reacted quick enough to catch it before it landed on the floor.

"That cheese looks good, too, but don't throw it at me, okay?"

Andrei plopped a few slices of cheese on the table. He was cutting more cheese when the kitchen door opened again. It was Talia.

"I thought I heard a noise in the hall," she said.

"You're brave," said Yuri. "What if we had been burglars?"

"What would burglars be wanting to steal here? Mama says that's the blessing of being poor—the robbers don't bother us." She glanced at Andrei. "Some tea would be good with that—and some plates."

"Too much trouble," said Andrei.

"Well, at least some tea. The samovar's still hot. Just a minute."

In five minutes the three were seated around the table in the light of a single oil lamp with sweet rolls, cheese, and tea sitting before them.

"It's been a long time since we've talked like this," said Talia. "Seems when you come home from school you always have assignments to do."

"The work is hard," said Yuri. "You'll find out when you go."

"I don't think I'm going to go," she said.

"What?" Yuri was surprised and just a little affronted. "Has my mama been spending all this time teaching you so you could quit your education before it even gets started? Only to marry and have babies? I thought you wanted more out of life."

"There's nothing wrong with being a wife and mother, Yuri. I mean, someday." Talia was a romantic, perhaps too much so. She had been completely enthralled watching the two young lovers earlier that evening.

"Yeah, Yuri," put in Andrei, "that's what girls do best."

Yuri groaned. "Where do you get these archaic ideas, Andrei? Not at home, that's for sure. This is the twentieth century, and enlightened people know women have more to offer than that."

"That's true," said Talia, who wanted to be enlightened especially if Yuri thought it was important. "But I think marriage is wonderful, too. Look at how happy Mariana and Daniel are."

356

"They're not married," said Andrei.

"But they're going to get married."

"How do you know that?"

"Couldn't you tell? They are so much in love. It's wonderful."

"Wonderful?" sneered Andrei. "I'd die if someone gave me all those cow-eyed looks they were giving each other." Andrei shook his head with disgust. "I remember Daniel from before, and he used to be a sensible fellow. I liked him. But since he's been back, he kind of reminds me of gooey sweet candy—always staring at Mariana with a silly look on his face. He hardly notices anyone else. 'Oh, Mariana, can I help you?' 'Mariana, you say the cleverest things.' 'Did you make the cake, Mariana? Oh, it's heavenly.' "

Yuri and Talia laughed as Andrei perfectly mimicked a love-struck Daniel.

"I still think it's wonderful," Talia said. "Don't you want to fall in love like that someday?"

"Ugh!" Andrei said emphatically.

Yuri thought for a minute before he responded. "I guess we all will someday. But do you know what that'll mean?"

Andrei nodded. He knew very well what it meant, and he didn't like the whole idea.

Talia shook her head. "What, Yuri?"

"We'll all probably have to go our separate ways. Of course, Andrei and I will always be brothers. But, Talia, your husband might mind your best friends being boys—and our wives might mind the same about you."

"That's ridiculous!" Talia said with more passion in her tone than usual. "We'll always be friends. I wouldn't marry anyone who'd be that narrow-minded."

"I guess you never know who you might fall in love with," said Yuri.

"No you don't," said Talia dreamily.

"Talia, you're starting to sound like Daniel and Mariana," said Andrei. "And if there's any more of this silly talk, I'm going to lose my appetite."

"Ha! That'll be the day," taunted Yuri.

"Yuri," said Talia, "do you remember last summer, when

you found out about your father's noble background, and we decided then that we'd always be friends?"

"Yes." Yuri would never forget that day. And he'd never forget the secret he'd made Talia swear never to reveal.

"That still goes—no matter what," Talia said with simple confidence.

Andrei turned serious and practical. "We ought to do something that seals our friendship. I've read where friends will become blood brothers by cutting themselves and mixing their blood."

"I don't like that," said Yuri.

"Are you squeamish? And I thought you wanted to be a doctor."

"It's not that . . . It's just that, well, it wouldn't be right to cut Talia."

"Why not?" Talia asked.

"You're more delicate. I—"

"I can do it," she said, trying to be convincing, and her determination was evident in her soft voice. "But first I have something to tell you both. I've told you a little about my papa, how he came from a good family—not anything like yours, but his father had some money from a partnership in a textile factory, and a country estate. But he disowned my father when he married my mother—she was the daughter of a peasant near the estate. If you remember, a year or so ago my grandfather died. He left everything to my father's brother, so I haven't suddenly become an heiress. I hardly know my father's relatives because my grandfather forbid any of them to associate with my father after his marriage. Well, I've told you also about the relative who is wardrober to the grand duchess Zenia. I met her recently—not the grand duchess, of course, but the wardrober, and she's a very nice lady. She never liked what my grandfather did, but out of respect for him she heeded his wish. Now that he's gone, she wants to make up for that injustice. I guess she wants to take me under her wing, sort of improve my lot in life—" Talia paused and giggled lightly. "She couldn't understand that I'm pretty happy with my life. But I do like what she wants to do—Mama said it was my choice. She wants to sponsor me at the ballet school! She thinks I'd be good at it, though girls usually start a couple years earlier than this. I want to give it a try, anyway. What do you think?"

"I think we better hurry and be blood brothers and sister," said Andrei, "before you become a prima donna and forget all about us."

"I think it's great, Talia," added Yuri. "You'd be perfect for it; you look just the part."

Talia blushed. "Okay, how do we do this blood thing?"

Andrei jumped up, found a sharp kitchen knife and a dishcloth, then returned to the table. Without a moment's hesitation he sliced his finger with the knife.

"Who's next?" he said, biting his lip in order to hide the pain.

Yuri took the knife and did the same, hesitating only slightly as he passed it to Talia. She tried to be as bold as Andrei but her first cut didn't draw blood. Her face went pale.

"We don't have to do this," Yuri said.

"Hurry, our blood is drying," Andrei said.

Talia pressed the knife harder, wincing as it dug deep. Tears welled up in her eyes, but there was a lopsided smile on her face as a drop of blood appeared in the cut.

"Now!" said Andrei.

They held their fingers together for a long moment, struck silent by the profound solemnity of the childish rite. They had been friends for years, but now they had a single moment in time to remember, no matter where life took them, when they knew the bonds between them were real and strong.

"We should say something," suggested Talia.

There was a moment of silence as they tried to think of something that matched their reverent mood.

Finally, Yuri said, " 'A threefold cord is not quickly broken.' "

They all solemnly repeated it together. It was like a hope and a desire and a prayer all in one.

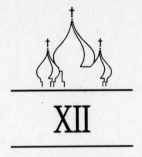

XII

GATHERINGS

64

Epiphany was a high holy day. Some believed it to be even more important than Christmas, because it celebrated the manifestation of Christ's divine power through three important biblical events: the appearance of the Wise Men at His birth, His baptism, and the miracle of turning water into wine at Cana. In Russia few such days passed without proper recognition.

Besides the usual services, this day was traditionally set aside for the blessing of waters. In St. Petersburg, the Neva would be blessed and the tsar and his family would be present.

The crowd that gathered on the bank of the river near the Winter Palace was not unusually large, and it was kept in very strict order by the cordons of Cossacks. The additional presence of several military regiments also gave the occasion an appearance of security. Misha, nonetheless, kept a sharp lookout.

The tsar and tsaritsa and their four daughters stood at the forefront, bundled to their royal chins so that it was hard even to recognize them. The tsar appeared particularly at ease, seemingly untroubled by the rising turmoil in the city. But isolated as he was at Tsarskoe Selo, it was impossible that he truly could be oblivious to the problems in St. Petersburg.

The trouble had begun at the end of December with the fall of Port Arthur. Rumor had it that Stoessel had simply handed over the fort to the Japanese against the wishes of his officers who desired to continue the fight; they had argued that there was still enough food and ammunition in the fortress to carry them for quite a while.

More than likely, the strike at the St. Petersburg Putilov Works which followed had nothing directly to do with the national humiliation over the fall of the fort. Its direct cause was the unfair treatment of several Assembly members. But the Putilov Steel Works was the largest industrial operation in St. Petersburg, and the walkout of twelve thousand workers was no small matter. Within days thousands of other workers in the city went on strike to support the Putilov workers. In less than a week eighty-two thousand St. Petersburg workers were on strike, all but paralyzing the city.

In view of the strike, the relative quiet of today's ceremony was eerie. Rumors hinted that the workers were gearing up for a rally, or perhaps they were simply biding their time to confront the tsar. But Misha was less concerned about workers' rallies than he was about a lone assassin who could sneak into such a gathering armed with a bomb.

That possibility seemed remote, however, as the high Metropolitan of the Church delivered his Mass, then, sprinkling holy water over the river, blessed the Neva. The final raising of an impressive cross carved of ice drew applause from the royal family. The ceremony concluded with an artillery salute from the Peter and Paul Fortress.

Then suddenly the ceremonial cannon fire turned deadly. A round of live ammunition ripped over the heads of the crowd, shattering windows in the Winter Palace. Screams and pandemonium broke out. The sensible people flattened to the ground, but others panicked and ran in all directions. Misha and several other Cossacks threw themselves toward the royal family, who had already ducked to the ground.

Daniel had no lack of news opportunities since his return to St. Petersburg. In fact, the war was almost old news compared to the charged atmosphere in the city. No one, least of all Mariana, expected the recent developments in their relationship to quell his zeal for his work, especially when events began to escalate into a national crisis. George Cranston at the *Register* office practically begged him to stay on top of things and deliver some dispatches.

He and Mariana had been present at the Epiphany ceremony. Thank God, it had not turned tragic—only one policeman had been wounded, and that had been by flying glass. A few windows in the palace would have to be replaced, but the royal family had not been harmed. Nevertheless, all of St. Petersburg was in an uproar over the incident. The Okhrana immediately went to work, asserting that it had been an accident, that live ammunition had mistakenly been mixed in with the blanks. Daniel hoped it was true, but he seriously doubted it.

He took Mariana home immediately, then went directly to his office to file his dispatch about the incident. He had only worked about half an hour when the door opened and Sergei entered.

He was looking better today than when he was released from prison two days ago, but he still had a worn, drawn appearance about him. He had hardly allowed himself enough time to recuperate before resuming his duties, especially tutoring the workers. They and Father Gapon had been instrumental in his release, and he was determined not to let them down.

Daniel had not seen Sergei since one brief encounter the day of Sergei's release. Daniel had hoped not to see him again until the family dinner planned for tomorrow night; it was going to be difficult to keep from mentioning his and Mariana's plans. The only thing that kept him quiet was that he knew Dmitri must be present when he brought up the subject of marriage.

"Good afternoon, Prince—"

"Please, please!" Sergei broke in. "Never mind that 'prince' business." Sergei did not intend to change a thing about his life because of his pardon. But then, he was hardly in a financial position to change much. Princess Gudosnikov had invited him and Anna to dinner as her way of welcoming him back to the fold. But Sergei no longer fit into that social circle, and he didn't wish to. And despite Mariana's recent meeting with the tsar, many others among his former noble acquaintances would have nothing to do with him even if he had wanted it.

Sergei continued, "You must call me Sergei. You may think

me too old for such familiarity, but Mr. Fedorcenko sounds so formal between friends—and Mariana speaks so highly of you, Daniel, that I would like us to be friends."

"I'd like that, too," said Daniel, "and for the same reason. Mariana has said so many wonderful things about you; I would be honored to consider you a friend."

"Excellent! You know how to make an old man feel good." Sergei slapped Daniel on the back. "Now, I know how you are always looking for news, and I think I have something for you."

Daniel raised his eyebrows. "Go on."

"Father Gapon is planning a march on the Winter Palace on Sunday. He has a petition he wants to present personally to the tsar."

Daniel had been wondering about Gapon, and this might be his best chance to find out. "Do you think Gapon organized the strikes? I can't get anyone to confirm this."

"I don't believe he did. I think it was more of a spontaneous reaction of the workers. But I have no doubt that Gapon intends to use it to his best advantage. The strike will certainly give teeth to his petition on Sunday."

"What kind of march will it be?"

"Peaceful," Sergei said with emphasis. "All Gapon wants to do is present the workers' petition to the tsar."

"And he really believes the tsar will meet him?"

"He has the utmost confidence in the emperor, Daniel. There's going to be a planning meeting of the Assembly tonight; why don't you come and see for yourself? Perhaps you can even talk personally with Father Gapon."

———

Later that night, Daniel accompanied Sergei to the Assembly. Over two hundred men were crammed into the hall that had once been the Old Tashkent Cafe. It was freezing outside, but the crowded building was hot and stuffy. Still, no one complained; an air of excitement and anticipation filled the place.

Daniel had never seen Gapon, and he was surprised when a young man in his early thirties mounted the platform to address the group. His dark eyes were intense, as if focused on sights too awesome for the common man. Yet he spoke with a vibrant warmth and in ordinary language, seemingly very much in tune with his beloved workers.

"Sunday we will see the dawn of new life—a resurrection! Our dear Little Father will come to us, take our hand, and lead us at last to prosperity, to the security all men deserve. The great day is at hand when we will rise from our tomb, when the workers, the lifeblood of the country, will come into their own."

When Gapon paused, the crowd chanted back, "Into our own . . . into our own!"

"And if the tsar does not meet us, then there is no tsar!" Gapon cried. "But we will always stand together, and, if need be, we will die together."

"Then there is no tsar!" shouted the crowd.

"We will die together!"

When the speech was over the crowd surged around Gapon shaking his hand, or having him bless their children. It took five minutes for Daniel and Sergei to inch their way to the front.

"Ah, Sergei," Gapon said with exuberance. "It is good to see you. You look none the worse for your terrible experience."

"It's good to be free," said Sergei, "and I understand I have you to thank."

"Many were involved, but on their behalf, I accept. Bless you."

Sergei introduced Daniel.

"Another American reporter. All this must greatly interest your people."

"They want to know what's happening in the world," said Daniel. "Can I ask you a few questions?"

"Only a few; there is so much to do before the big day."

The crowd continued to press around and chatter excitedly. Daniel practically had to shout to make himself heard.

"Father Gapon, what are the workers going to ask the tsar?"

"Only that he help his children, lift their suffering. That they be treated as human beings, not cattle."

Daniel scribbled furiously in his notebook. "Any specific demands?"

"What all men deserve. Decent working conditions, an eight-hour day, fair pay, safety. Freedom of speech and assembly."

"What if the tsar doesn't meet you? Do you have anything more forceful in mind?"

"Absolutely not! This will be a peaceful gathering. We only wish to be heard. We will be willing to send a smaller delegation to the tsar if he requests it, but it must consist of men I have personally selected. I have sent a letter to the tsar giving my word that he need fear nothing from us. We love him and believe in him. He can face us without misgivings."

Daniel couldn't ask the final question lingering in his mind: What if, even then, the tsar ignored the workers? It was a possibility no one wanted to consider.

65

Basil surveyed the table crowded with supplies—wires, fuses, tins, clocks. Cyril Vlasenko had been faithful thus far in fulfilling his part of the bargain. He had delivered a portion of the supplies and half the money. But Basil did not plan to be as faithful. He cared no more about Father Gapon than he did about an ant in the road. The days when Basil lived for revolution, anarchy, assassination, were over. He had no intention of killing Gapon—not because the man's cause meant anything to Basil, but rather because Anickin had far more important uses for his supplies.

And the time was at last ripe for his dream to be realized.

Grinning, Basil picked up one of the precious fuses. His sources had informed him that little Mariana Remizov was home from the war, wounded. Ah, how thankful Basil was that the Japanese had not spoiled his joy by killing the girl. That pleasure was to be left only for him. And as soon as he received the remainder of his supplies and completed his bombs, he'd be ready. Then all that would remain was to wait for the best moment to attack. He had missed the small family Christmas gathering because he hadn't received his supplies, but the occasion gave him the idea of striking the entire family at once. The beauty of such a prospect was even more alluring than the thought of watching Dmitri in mourning. Why waste a good bomb on just one person?

Gently he set the fuse back on the table. He had an appointment. He grabbed his tattered coat and left his hovel in a tenement on Grafsky Lane. Taking a tram partway and then walking, it took him half an hour to reach the rendezvous. His limbs were nearly frozen, but a fire burned in his eyes. Everything on that table back in his room would mean nothing if this meeting failed. Basil was about to receive his most vital delivery.

Cerkover was waiting for him, just as they had planned, at the foot of the Nicholas Bridge on the south side of the river. The traffic was heavy at that hour in the late afternoon, both with vehicles and pedestrians. It was almost dark, for the winter sun set early in those northern latitudes. No one gave a second look at the two men who paused to talk; to all appearances, the better-dressed of the two was asking directions of the other. Cerkover set down the battered suitcase he was carrying and took a pencil and pad from his pocket in order to jot down the directions. Basil pointed and gestured as if to accompany his verbal explanation.

As Cerkover pretended to write, he said, "That's a lot of dynamite you've asked for."

"It's all there?" Basil did not hide his concern. Everything hinged on the explosives.

"Yes, but I didn't much enjoy carting this all over town."

"It's much more stable than you'd think."

"And you need this much for one bomb?"

369

"You don't think I'm going to count on one bomb, do you? There can be any number of complications. I need to have a couple of backups."

"This wasn't easy to get. There better not be any 'complications.'"

"Don't worry. I'll be successful. No one will escape."

"We hope it won't be too messy, Nagurski. Of course, there are bound to be innocent bystanders involved, but we want this as clean as possible. Try to get him alone."

"I always try."

"When can we expect completion?" asked Cerkover.

"It could have been much sooner had you been quicker in this delivery."

"As I said, it wasn't easy to procure this much material without rousing suspicions. We've heard Gapon is planning some big public rally. We'd like it to be before then."

"I can't say for certain. There are too many variables. But you don't need to know the exact time, anyway."

"Don't you trust us?" Cerkover was affronted.

"I don't trust the legions who work for you."

"Why do you think we have taken such pains to keep our meetings so secret?" Cerkover said. "No one knows of this operation but Vlasenko, you, and myself."

"And not the secret police you've had following me?"

"No one has been following you—at least none of our people. I tell you, Vlasenko and I are the only ones who know of you or your job."

"That's all I wanted to know." Anickin was relieved. "I don't want half the Okhrana after me when this is done."

"Neither do we want them after you—or us. You will have no problems getting away, so long as you get the job done and we don't have a bunch of innocent deaths on our hands."

"Only those who deserve it will die," assured Basil.

Cerkover tried to hide his involuntary shudder at Basil's words, but Basil saw and was pleased with the effect he'd had on Vlasenko's henchman.

Cerkover couldn't get away fast enough. Since there was nothing more to say, he pocketed his pencil and pad, gave a perfunctory "thank you" to the "direction-giver," and hurried away.

No one noticed that the man had left his suitcase behind. As Basil bent down to pick it up, it seemed quite natural, especially since it was as worn and frayed as the man who now carried it. For all anyone knew, he was a poor traveler just arrived in the city from the provinces.

Basil paused a moment to watch Cerkover disappear into the crowd. *Ah, yes*, he thought, *all who deserve death will die!* Including mealy-mouth government lackeys and their pompous bosses.

Cerkover said he wanted a clean job, and that was Basil's desire, as well. But for Basil it had a slightly different meaning. When he was finished, there would be no one left who could link him to the dastardly deed. Two bombs would be for Mariana Remizov and her father, in case he couldn't get them together. The third bomb would be for Count Cyril Vlasenko. He had different plans for the elimination of Cerkover. Too many bombs would simply be redundant.

Basil had just verified what he'd suspected all along, that Vlasenko had kept Basil's involvement quiet. It was logical that the count would not want anyone, even his Okhrana buddies, knowing that he was dealing with someone like Anickin. And Basil had no delusions as to the fact that Vlasenko and Cerkover knew his real identity. With them gone, no one could link him to the bombings, or, by the time anyone did, he'd be long gone. He would never receive his final payment or the promised travel documents, but Basil's personal satisfaction would be payment enough.

Hefting the weighty suitcase in his hand he leered slightly as he walked back across the bridge. He wondered what these passersby would think if they knew he carried enough power in his hand to both fulfill and shatter many dreams.

66

The flat was filled with all the good fragrances indicative of a holiday. They had spent a dreary Christmas because of the uncertainty over Sergei; now they could really celebrate. Anna and Raisa, with Mariana's and Talia's help, made all the traditional Christmas treats. Daniel had made a gift of a huge ham, in addition to a big box of sweets and an excellent imported coffee.

There would be sixteen people crammed into the small flat—Anna, Sergei, Raisa and the three young people, of course; but also Viktor, Sarah, Mariana, Daniel, Paul and Mathilde, Dmitri, George Cranston from the *Register* office, and Misha. Even Eugenia had decided to grace the group with her presence—it was, after all, in her best interests to appease Mariana now that her social prospects had so improved.

Half an hour before the guests were due to arrive, Sergei wandered into the kitchen.

"Just thought I'd see if I could help with anything," he said, suddenly aware of being in the way.

"We wouldn't hear of it!" said Raisa. "You're the guest of honor, after all. Now, shoo with you!" She wagged her hands at him. "Go, sit and rest."

"I've been resting all day," Sergei complained. "I'm the most rested man in Russia—and the most bored."

"There's nothing wrong with a little boredom once in a while," Anna said.

Sergei just shrugged, not convinced.

"Can you spare me a moment?" Anna asked Raisa. "I think I'll try to entertain my husband for a few minutes."

372

Sergei grinned instantly, took Anna's hand and led her away. "That's all I really wanted," he said. "Some time alone with you."

"We'll have a lifetime to be alone together, Sergei."

Sergei's merriment faded and he didn't answer for a moment. "If there is one thing I realized while in prison, Anna," he said at last, "it's that life isn't predictable. We must savor every bit of it, not take for granted a single second."

He led Anna into their tiny bedroom.

"Sergei?" Anna said coyly.

He smiled again. "It's the only place where we can be alone."

"And why do you want to be alone?"

"I am a greedy man, my dear wife. After weeks away from you, I don't think I will soon get my fill. And, as I said, life is too short to pass up opportunities when they arise."

He took her in his arms and kissed her passionately.

"My, my!" Anna said, breathless. "You make me feel like a girl again."

"And I feel like a young man. Perhaps I've been around Mariana and Daniel too much, eh? All that young love rubs off."

"Young love . . ." Anna sighed contentedly. "It doesn't seem that long ago when we were like them."

"'Were'? Oh, Anna . . ." He gently ran a finger along her cheek. "I feel exactly the same. I remember the exact moment I knew I loved you, as clearly as I remember ten minutes ago. I had kidnapped you from the ball at the Winter Palace—"

"I was hardly *at* the ball," corrected Anna.

"No, you were too fine for that. You were the most beautiful girl there. We walked together in the Palace Square."

"Talking about poetry."

"All I wanted to do was tell you I loved you and take you in my arms."

"I would have fainted with shock and fear."

He smiled. "Yes, I'm afraid you would have. That's the only reason I waited."

"Oh, Sergei . . . here we are old people now, waiting for our daughter to announce *her* engagement. It doesn't seem possible."

"So, do you think the big announcement will happen soon?"

"Mariana confided in me that Daniel is only waiting to talk to you and Dmitri. Don't be surprised if he gets you two alone this evening."

"Good! It's about time those two got together. He's a good man. I've had a bit of a chance to talk to him. I never knew anyone to ask so many questions."

"Was he interviewing you for his paper?"

"Well, some of his questions might have had that intent, but, believe it or not, most of them were about spiritual things. I haven't seen anyone so hungry since . . ." He paused, smiling at the pleasant memory. "Since another young man met a Scottish missionary in China. Anyway, I don't think our Mariana could have made a better selection for a husband. I'm glad she waited and didn't capitulate to Eugenia's pressures."

"Mariana has a mind of her own."

"Like her mother."

"I am happy for them, Sergei," Anna went on. "But with Daniel's home being in America—it's hard to accept that Mariana may go so far away from us."

"Perhaps they won't be. Daniel seems very attached to Russia."

"I guess we must accept the time when our children will grow up and start lives of their own. I don't want to be the kind of mother who holds on too tightly."

"Just remember, Anna, you will never lose your children. Don't forget our favorite old proverb: Let your children choose their own path, and it will always lead back to you. You have done this, and you *will* reap the fruits."

"*We* have done it, Sergei. And *we* will reap the fruits."

"Yes, of course . . ." Sergei's voice trailed away, and for a moment his focus turned inward. "Anna, if I am not always around—"

"Sergei, what are you saying?" scolded Anna. "I won't hear of such a thing. I just got you back—to keep for a *very* long time."

"I suppose my time in prison made me think of the future— it made me realize I am not immortal. God does not always give us what we think we want or need. I just feel it is best to be prepared for . . . well, whatever God ordains for us, that's all."

"How would you feel, Sergei, if I said such a thing to you?" Anna said, slightly miffed. "If I said I wouldn't be with you forever?"

"I'd feel you were being practical."

"Ha! You'd be devastated."

A sheepish expression slipped across Sergei's face. "You know me too well, Anna."

"Does all this just have to do with your time in prison, Sergei, or are you not telling me something?"

He shrugged, trying too hard to appear casual for it to work. "I suppose, like everyone else in this city, I'm a bit on edge."

"Is it Father Gapon's march?"

"We have no guarantees all will go as planned."

"Then don't go, Sergei!" Anna said emphatically.

"You know I can't do that. It's going to be an important day in our country's history. I have to be there."

Anna nodded and tried to shake the momentary pall over the conversation with a quick grin. "All right. But I'll have no more such talk about uncertain futures, especially on *this* grand day. We are celebrating your homecoming, my dear husband. And that's all I want to think of—how happy I am to have you back."

Anna put her arms around her husband and pulled him to her in a fervent embrace, and she held on for such a long time Sergei wondered if she would let him go in time to greet their guests.

67

Daniel decided to approach his two prospective fathers-in-law before dinner. He would never be able to enjoy the meal otherwise. His main problem was how to get them alone in the crowded house. A large table of boards had been set up in the parlor to accommodate all the people, and at the moment, Sarah, Mariana, and Talia were there setting out dishes. The kitchen, of course, was out of the question, which left only the bedrooms available for privacy.

He chose his moment while Viktor and George were deep in conversation, and Misha had gone out with Yuri and Andrei to carry in firewood. Dmitri cocked a curious brow when Daniel asked if he could speak to them in private. Sergei had a slight smirk on his lips and a twinkle in his eyes.

They went to Sergei and Anna's tiny room, for they were less likely to be disturbed there. When Sergei closed the door, a sudden attack of "nerves" struck Daniel. He walked to the little window by the writing desk, hoping the minor physical activity would ease his anxiety. He wished he could have stood forever gazing out the window at the falling snow, but then he thought of the life that lay ahead for him and Mariana, and that gave him courage to begin. He cleared his throat and turned back toward the men. Dmitri was seated in the desk chair, and Sergei on the edge of the bed.

"Thank you for leaving the festivities for a few moments," he said. "I . . . have . . . something I wish to ask of both of you."

Neither Dmitri nor Sergei looked especially surprised. They had both known this was coming.

"I thought it best to speak to both of you because you are

both such an important part of Mariana's life. I hope there is no offense taken in that," Daniel said.

It was appropriate that Dmitri spoke first, for he was the one most apt to be offended by Daniel's method of approach. "These are rather odd circumstances, and I am the first to admit that Sergei, here, has as much right as anyone to be involved in my daughter's affairs. Do go on, Daniel."

"Well, Count Remizov—Prince Fedorcenko," he began in a formal tone, "I would like to ask Mariana's hand in marriage!"

Both men grinned, and Dmitri turned to Sergei. "What do you say, Sergei? I value your opinion."

"This is by no means a surprise," said Sergei. "And, if it were entirely up to me, I would give my wholehearted blessing. I have one concern: Where will you make your home? We are close to Mariana and hate to think of her leaving us for such a faraway place as America, but we understand that is your home, Daniel."

"Mariana and I have discussed this, and we feel we can keep a home here and a home in America, dividing our time equally between the two places. I am pretty much indispensable to my newspaper on Russian affairs, so I'll be called upon to spend much time here."

"That relieves my greatest worry—and Anna's, too," said Sergei.

"You have my blessing also, young man," Dmitri began. "But—"

Daniel's hopes rose, then immediately fell at the word *but*. "Yes, Count Remizov?" said Daniel in a foreboding tone.

"We must consider the matter of your different faiths, Daniel."

"Mariana and I have discussed that, and I have given this a great deal of thought." Why, then, did he now have a knot in the pit of his stomach? He'd had it all worked out in his mind and was confident that he had a solution that would make everyone happy. But his confidence suddenly fled.

"May we hear what you have been thinking?" asked Sergei.

"In the past I was never a very religious person." Daniel tried to put in his voice the assurance he lacked in his heart. "My father was Presbyterian, and though he didn't attend

377

church regularly, he was far more faithful than myself. I darkened a church doorway twice a year if I was lucky—you know, Christmas and Easter. When my father died four years ago, I experienced a—how shall I call it?—spiritual awakening. There have been ups and downs during that time, and I am far from mature in the spiritual or religious sense. But my faith in God has become very important to me. Because I have traveled so much, even in the last four years, I have never affiliated myself with a particular church. When I was home, I attended the Presbyterian church where my father was a member. I found it to be a nice church where God seemed real and alive. I've also attended churches of other denominations—some good, some bad. I've gone to some Presbyterian churches that I didn't like. What it boils down to in my mind is that the kind of church you attend isn't as important as whether God can be found there or not."

Daniel paused, glancing back and forth between the two men as if trying to gauge what their reaction might be to his next statement. "I've attended some Orthodox churches here in Russia as well," he went on, "and I have to admit I never felt comfortable in those services. Even when my Russian became fluent, I received very little in the way of spiritual food from them. Perhaps the emphasis on form and recited liturgy was just too alien to me. However, I must say I have only attended two or three services in all my time in Russia. It may be I have just not found the right Orthodox church—"

Sergei held up his hand. "Before you go on, Daniel, let me say that our church is indeed based largely on form. How a man *performs* is their major consideration—more so, I think, than what is in his heart. You will find many who dwell on the external acts hoping to insure their salvation in this way, hardly giving a thought to Christ."

"The same kind of people exist in the Protestant church."

"I will confide something to you," said Sergei. "I have attended a Protestant church here in St. Petersburg a couple times and I enjoyed it very much. You Protestants are given much more liberty to approach our Lord directly, and I like that. But I have been an Orthodox all my life, and at my age change is not easy."

"You mean you have considered changing?" asked Daniel, incredulous. There was also an audible gasp from Dmitri.

"Like you, Daniel, I want more than anything else to grow close to my God. I want to be open to how God may want to accomplish that deed. I can grow in the Orthodox Church because my heart is seeking. Others may attend and not change a bit because they want only to fulfill the law, as it were."

"Well, sir," said Daniel, feeling a bit more relaxed, "that is just how I see it. At first I thought it might be hypocritical to convert in order to marry Mariana. But now I see it as getting the best of two worlds. There are some beautiful things about your church; there are some good things about mine. With the proper inner attitude, I think they can both be beneficial."

"There's more involved in converting," said Sergei, "than only attendance."

"Do they forbid you from attending other churches?"

"It is frowned upon. Other churches are not considered to be the true faith."

"I was thinking we could divide our time between the two."

"Would the Presbyterian Church permit that?" Dmitri asked.

"I probably couldn't be a *member* of both denominations, but I could attend both."

"Not so in our church," said Sergei. "If you did what you're proposing, you'd have to be somewhat secretive about it. Of course, if you were far away in America, I suppose it would be easier to practice such a—"

"Deception?" put in Daniel. He suddenly saw the faulty logic of his simplistic resolution, and an uneasy feeling crept over him.

"Sort of sounds a bit like that, doesn't it?" said Sergei.

"I feel rather naive," sighed Daniel. "I thought I had the perfect solution." He looked once more out the window. The snow had stopped. He had never imagined this interview would go quite like this. He'd thought he had worked it out so well. Dmitri and Sergei would give their blessing, and he and Mariana could marry in peace.

Suddenly it was falling apart.

"Will you convert?" asked Dmitri.

379

Daniel sighed again. While he had been deliberating these things earlier, he had tried to ignore the fact that the Orthodox Church was unbending toward other Christian faiths. He had hoped it wouldn't be an issue. But it was—a very big issue. And he knew instinctively where he stood on this matter.

With hesitancy in his voice, but with conviction in his heart he could not deny, he said, "I . . . don't think I could be part of a church that won't accept other Christians simply because they belong to a different church. I don't pretend to be an expert, but it sounds similar to what the apostle Paul was battling against when the Jewish Christians wouldn't accept the Gentiles on equal terms. I just don't think Christ would judge Christians of different levels like that."

Daniel didn't notice the approving glint in Sergei's eyes because Dmitri spoke up immediately. "This must be hard for you, Daniel," he said. "But I respect you all the more for the fact that your principles mean so much to you that you will give up Mariana—"

"What?" gasped Daniel. "I haven't given up Mariana."

"But she cannot marry outside the Church."

Daniel only gaped silently at this flat, seemingly unmovable statement.

"Dmitri," said Sergei, calmly, reasonably, "don't be so rash."

"You would allow such a thing?" exclaimed Dmitri. "Thank God, I am her legal parent and the final decision rests with me."

"Dmitri, Mariana is of age," said Sergei.

"She would not defy me!"

"Don't place her in such a position," implored Sergei. "You will alienate her. She loves Daniel and, I believe, has for a long time. We all saw this brewing. Why didn't you oppose it from the very start?"

"Because I . . . I—"

"You wanted Mariana's happiness," prompted Sergei.

"I hadn't given thought to this other detail."

"It's not such a big thing, Dmitri. Mariana will not burn in hell by marrying outside the Church, contrary to what they'd have us believe. Only socially—"

"*Only socially?* Sergei, what else is there?"

"I remember a time when you didn't give a fig about what society thought. You used to laugh at the pompous gentlemen and the pampered ladies and all their meaningless rules. Don't you remember, Dmitri?"

"It's different when you're older. I have to think of what people will say."

"Our families have had to live with a lot worse irregularities and have survived. What matters most is that this will not tear us apart as a family. Mariana has chosen a man of faith, a man of honor, and a man of principles."

Dmitri uttered his worst fear. "What about my mother?"

"Surely you can handle Countess Eugenia." Sergei said it with such conviction that Dmitri gave him a double take.

"I can? Ah . . . well . . . of course I can! I am the head of the family."

"That's right."

Daniel had listened silently, amazed at how adroitly Sergei was handling Dmitri. Dmitri seemed to be breaking.

––––––––––

Dmitri glanced at Daniel and could not help but be touched by the young man's earnest countenance. Although Dmitri hadn't followed most of Sergei's and Daniel's religious talk, he still felt more inclined to give his blessing than not. After all, he did like Daniel. Hadn't he been the one to discover Daniel in America and bring him to Mariana's attention? He had seen promise in the lad from the beginning. And the Trents were worth millions. Who cared what church they went to next to *that*? Besides, they'd be in America most of the time, so who would notice?

But tradition kept hounding him. A marriage outside the Church? How would that affect their current status with the tsar? Nicholas and Alexandra were extremely religious people. But Dmitri had thought Sergei would oppose it, and he hadn't at all. Were the emperor and empress as peculiar in the matter of religion as that?

"It's just so irregular . . ." Dmitri mumbled, hardly realizing he was speaking aloud.

At that moment, Mariana threw open the door.

"Père, you can't withhold your blessing!" She knelt at his feet and took his hands in hers. "Please, don't stand in the way of our happiness!"

"Mariana," said Dmitri, also in a pleading tone, "there are so many things to consider."

"But, Père, have you thought of the most important thing?" Mariana jumped up and strode to Daniel's side. "What of the fact that we love each other?"

Dmitri looked at his daughter, then at Daniel—his future son-in-law?—who was returning Mariana's devoted gaze.

Look at them, Dmitri thought. *How often is it that such depth of love comes to two people? They are truly meant for each other. What I wouldn't give to have someone love me in the way she loves him. And what father would not give everything to know his only daughter will be loved as Daniel so clearly loves my Mariana? This is a match made in heaven. It's impossible that heaven could, or would, destroy it.*

Dmitri stood and walked to Mariana and Daniel, laying his hands over their joined hands. "Ah, love," he said in a thoughtful tone. "In one's autumn years, it's easy to forget such things. My dear children, you have my blessing also!"

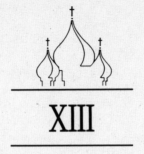

XIII

BLOODY SUNDAY

68

Cyril's patience was growing thin. Things were simply not going well.

The release and pardon of Sergei Fedorcenko was enough to sour Cyril for life. Those rascals always managed to get the better of him! How did they do it? Did they have some kind of guardian angel looking over them?

In addition, he had to face the disheartening realization that Basil Anickin might not get to Gapon before the big march on Sunday—tomorrow!

Drat that Anickin! But Cyril Vlasenko knew it was hardly fair to blame Anickin entirely for the fact that Gapon was still alive. The priest had been a slippery devil these last several days. Gapon was keeping an extremely low profile lately, and even when he did appear in public, he was better protected than the tsar himself, constantly surrounded by his body-guards.

Gapon knew he was a marked man.

Warrants had been issued for his arrest, but they had been denied on the ground that the priest's arrest would only worsen the situation. Besides, no one could get close enough to the man even to arrest him.

But Anickin had better do something soon. If the workers' march wasn't stopped, Cyril had no doubt that he, himself, would be the prime scapegoat for whatever the march brought.

What was taking Anickin so long? True, he had only recently received his explosives, but he had known the importance of getting the job done quickly. Cyril was beginning to wonder if the fellow could be trusted. He had known Anickin was deranged all along, but he felt it had been worth the risk, considering that the lunatic was probably his best hope for eliminating Gapon. If Cyril was wrong . . . well then, he had just given a crazy man enough explosives to blow up half the Winter Palace.

Cyril just couldn't think of that now. But something had better happen soon or he was going to pull Anickin in. Vlasenko's nerves couldn't take much more of this.

Cyril might have to resign himself to the fact that neither he nor anyone else would be able to stop Gapon's planned march on the Palace. Fullon, the mayor of Petersburg, had telephoned Gapon in an attempt to talk him out of it, but the priest wouldn't even speak to him. The best Cyril could hope for now was that the march came and went without incident, forcing Gapon's demise by his own ineptitude.

Failing to halt the march, the ministers met that afternoon in an emergency meeting to prepare a plan for dealing with the situation. Cyril attended the meeting. All were present except Witte. Cyril wondered if Witte had been purposely ignored because the others feared he would side with the workers. More than likely, though, the pompous idiot was staying away in order to distance himself should something go wrong. The conniver!

The ministers discussed the deploying of troops in the city and the importance of keeping the marchers away from the Winter Palace. Thousands of troops from as far away as Pskov had already been called in. The tsar, of course, would be nowhere near the Palace; he had returned to Tsarskoe Selo immediately after the Epiphany service.

Any benevolence the ministers might have felt toward the workers dissipated when the Minister of the Interior showed the group a letter he had intercepted—from Gapon, intended for the tsar.

Don't be deceived by your ministers, it had declared. *They are lying to you about the true state of affairs in Russia. They don't want to see the people rise out of the depths of poverty. But the people know that Your Majesty would help us if you knew the truth. We have faith in you! So, we have decided to come to*

*you tomorrow at the Winter Palace at two in the afternoon. Fear
not to stand before your people and hear our petition. You will
not come to harm.*

The man had gall. Gapon had indeed gotten much too big
for his cassock. Thank God the tsar would never see the letter.

The final topic on the ministers' agenda was the question
of when they would inform the workers that the tsar was not
in the city. No decision was made. It was probably too late,
anyway.

During the night, gusts of frigid wind blew in from the Baltic. Snow swirled in the streets of the city. It was no night to
be outside, but a soldier had no choice in these matters. Misha
had been transferred from his duty at Tsarskoe Selo to assist
in the bolstered patrol of the city. A few days ago three thousand troops had been present in St. Petersburg; now that number had more than tripled. Over ten thousand troops, including Cossacks, along with thousands of police—all to keep
order for a *peaceful* workers' march.

Warming his hands over a drum fire, Misha turned down
the vodka that was passing freely among the troops. They were
cold and bored, and even they did not expect tomorrow's
events to require more of them than their stoic presence. The
soldiers got drunk; they danced and sang. But Misha could not
indulge in the night's revelry. He didn't like the look of what
was about to happen. It reminded him too much of something
in the past.

Khodynka Field.

It had started as a peaceful gathering of common folk—
and ended in disaster. Why couldn't the leaders learn from
such things? Misha hadn't yet figured out just what could be
learned, but there had to be something. Sergei would know.
There was probably no relation at all between the two events,
but Misha could not get Khodynka out of his mind. And a knot
formed in the pit of his stomach that would not go away.

Misha did not pretend to know or understand Father Gapon's designs, but Sergei had faith in the man. No matter what
he intended for Sunday's march, and regardless of how peace-

ful he wanted it to transpire, it seemed that with such a forceful military presence there could only be trouble.

———

Gapon smoked several cigarettes and drank a glass of tea, but he could not eat. His throat was raw from all the speeches. Even away from the crowds, in the flat of one of his workers, he could not relax. There had been another meeting that night; he hadn't gotten away from it until quite late, and he was exhausted. But there were last minute preparations to attend to.

The leaders of tomorrow's various contingents wanted a final blessing from the priest. Six columns of marchers would be originating in various parts of the city. They would begin at different times, depending on their distance from the city center, with the farthest having about ten miles to traverse. The times were synchronized so that all the columns would converge on the Palace Square at the same time. Gapon had given detailed descriptions of the routes to the police. He was determined to keep this within the law. The marchers didn't expect trouble, but they were nervous anyway. The increased military presence hadn't gone unnoticed.

At the last minute, Gapon told the leaders to discourage women and young children from joining the march. As much as Gapon wanted to believe that tomorrow's event would be peaceful, a gnawing fear persisted in him.

Finally, long after midnight, Gapon went to bed, and at last fell into a restless sleep.

———

Sergei returned home around eleven. Daniel had gone with him to the meeting with Gapon, and afterward he rode with Daniel back to his boardinghouse, then took the same droshky back to his own home. The flat was quiet and dark when he arrived. Everyone had gone to bed.

Sergei was quietly tiptoeing down the hall when a footstep behind him caused him to stop.

"Papa," said a soft voice.

Sergei turned to find Andrei, and even in the dim light, Sergei could see his son had a solemn expression on his young face.

"You're up late, Andrei."

"I didn't want to miss you."

"You wanted to talk?" When Andrei nodded, Sergei said, "Let's go sit in the kitchen so we don't disturb anyone."

They sat at the table and Andrei hurried into his concern without further preamble. "I want to go on the march tomorrow, Papa," the boy said earnestly.

"I don't think it will be appropriate for children to be present, Andrei."

"Papa, will I always be thought of as a child just because I am the youngest?"

"Son, this is serious business, not a lark." Somehow Sergei sensed he didn't have to say that to Andrei, but he was anxious to think of some deterrent to his son. Everyone firmly believed this would be a peaceful event, but the presence of the troops was disturbing nevertheless.

"I know that, Papa. Haven't you noticed that I truly believe in freedom? I've listened to students at the university, and I've read things, too. Sometimes everyone jokes about the political things I say, but I think I am a revolutionary, Papa, like Uncle Paul. And I'm even more so now since the injustice done to you."

"Son, I'm sorry if I have made light of the things you feel. I suppose I never realized how deeply you felt them. I will try to be more respectful in the future. But, Andrei, one thing troubles me about what you've said, and I may as well mention it now. I don't want you to follow the path of a rebel out of revenge for me. Injustice was done, of course, but remember, too, that it was the tsar who pardoned me."

"I'll try to. But a tsar sent you away, and a tsar pardoned you—so it seems to me that only evens the score."

"Still, he is our ruler, and that is what tomorrow's march is all about. Father Gapon is loyal to the tsar above all else."

"I don't hate the tsar, Papa. You taught me not to. That's why I'm asking to be part of this. When I grow up, I want to be able to say that I marched with the men who brought freedom to Russia. Please, Papa! Let me walk beside you."

"All right, Andrei, you can come. But you must stay with me the entire time."

A huge grin replaced Andrei's solemnity, and a knot formed in Sergei's stomach. This was his baby, Anna's baby. Yes, he was almost as tall as Yuri, and certainly huskier, but it still was not easy to let him grow up. Perhaps inevitable, but never easy.

69

The blustery weather of the night abated by Sunday morning. When the sun rose at eight-thirty that winter day, it brought with it a crisp, clear sky. The temperature rose to twenty-five degrees. As if God himself had ordained it, they couldn't have had a better day.

Sergei rose at dawn, dressed in his best clothes, and breakfasted with the family. The women opted to remain at home. Anna hated crowds. For a while Yuri was undecided about what to do. Since Andrei had received permission to go, he would also be allowed to attend. But he didn't demonstrate Andrei's enthusiasm. Sergei suspected that the boy didn't want to risk disappointing his father by staying behind on such an important day. In the end, he left with his father and brother at half past nine.

The Vassily Island contingent of marchers was already gathering for the procession. Oleg Chavkin and some of the workers Sergei had been tutoring had asked Sergei to join Gapon's group, which would depart from Nevsky Prospekt.

It was a forty-five minute walk to Gapon's gathering place, and Sergei used the time with his sons to explain what was about to happen. They had a good discussion. Sergei was surprised by how much Andrei knew about the revolutionary movement, and—for a boy who hated schoolwork—how much he had read about political philosophy.

On the way, they met a friendly gendarme who, upon learning their destination, wished them Godspeed and assured them there would be no trouble. The clusters of Cossacks and soldiers, however, seemed to belie the man's words. Sergei wondered if Misha was in town. He thought he recognized a couple members of Misha's regiment.

Some fifty thousand had already gathered on Nevsky Prospekt. They got underway at about eleven, Gapon at the front surrounded by his guard. A huge portrait of the tsar was carried in the vanguard, and many smaller pictures of the emperor and empress were also held aloft. Many people also carried icons and crosses, and several men hoisted a huge banner that said: *Soldiers! Don't fire on the people.*

The marchers moved unimpeded down the wide avenue. They were a solemn group and radiated more of the atmosphere of religious ceremony than that of a parade. Many had experienced misgivings the night before when they saw the troops and had written farewell letters to their families. A confrontation seemed inevitable; many declared that they were prepared to die. But as the actual march began, they seemed to have put aside these fears. Instead, there was a sense of holy purpose, a sincere belief that this march would end, not in tragedy, but in a beautiful coming together of the "Little Father" and his people. Police even helped clear the way for them. And when the workers began singing hymns, many of the police even doffed their caps out of respect.

"Save us, O Lord, Thy people!" rang tens of thousand of voices in united melody.

In such a huge mob, it was no small miracle that Sergei saw Daniel shouldering his way through toward him.

"I knew I'd find you if I kept toward the front," Daniel said. "Do you realize that by the time all the groups meet at the palace, there could be as many as two hundred thousand people marching? This is absolutely incredible. I doubt my readers will believe it when they read it." He held up his little Kodak camera. "I've got some good photos, though."

Sergei chuckled. "It makes me believe we might really get results this time."

"I hope so." Daniel lowered his voice. "I've heard a rumor that the tsar is not even in town."

"I pray to God that's not true, Daniel." Sergei glanced around at the mob of people. How easily this procession could turn into a riot!

"Anyway, I'm glad Mariana and Anna didn't come."

Sergei restrained a glance at his sons. Had it been wise to let them accompany him? He had a strong suspicion that Andrei would have found his own way here had Sergei forbidden him. History was being made today, no matter what happened. It seemed right that his sons, whose Fedorcenko name already made them very much a part of Russian history, should be here this day.

The throng passed the Kazan Cathedral and neared the Alexander Gardens not far from the Palace. Ahead, Sergei saw the great monolith of Alexander I dominating the Palace Square. Was the tsar Nicholas in residence at the Winter Palace? Was he now peering out a window at the procession, preparing to step out on a balcony to receive his people? It seemed like so little to ask of a ruler. These were simple folk who really did not want much—only peaceful lives, free from sickness and starvation, and the freedom to make of their lives what they could.

With a single word, the tsar could grant his subjects' deepest desire. It would cost him so little, and in return he would gain their undying devotion.

Are you there, Nicholas? Are you waiting?

Cyril Vlasenko wiped a bead of perspiration from his forehead as he stared out his office window.

By the saints! What a mob of people!

His failure had allowed it to happen, although he'd never admit that to anyone but himself. But even he had never dreamed—it would have been more of a nightmare!—that the inconsequential priest could have organized such an event.

He tried to think if there was any way he could directly be

held accountable for whatever happened out there—especially if Anickin decided to strike during the march, though at this point that was highly unlikely. Nevertheless, all the funds paid to Anickin had been completely laundered. Only Cerkover knew of his involvement. Anickin and his American cohort—what was his name?—were the only other links. Anickin couldn't have involved anyone else, for Cerkover had reported that the fellow didn't even want to divulge his plans to Vlasenko.

One thing Vlasenko hadn't considered: What if the march were successful? What if the tsar did manage to receive the workers? But that was impossible. The tsar was twenty miles away in Tsarskoe Selo.

There would be a massacre today. How could it be avoided?

———

The troops had strict orders not to allow the marchers near the Palace Square.

The only reason Misha could imagine for such a directive was that the tsar had no intention of receiving the workers. Did the officials think the mob would just disperse the minute the troops barred their way?

Look at them—they were on a holy mission!

Could a mere word from a soldier stop that? Misha prayed fervently it could. But he knew otherwise. And he had already decided his personal response. He would not use force, and he would order his unit to do the same. But his unit was only a fraction of the thousands of soldiers present. Did he really think it would make any difference? Was this just another way to assuage his conscience?

The mounted Grenadiers were the first to move into position, forming a barrier across the avenue. Behind them were troops of infantry, their weapons held tensely. Did these men think they would use those weapons? Surely none of them *wanted* to.

A bugle sounded and the crowd paused momentarily. Then, when no one made any real attempt to stop them, they began marching again. The police seemed actually to be encouraging them. Perhaps nothing would happen after all.

Misha called to his unit, "Hold your fire."

Some of the Grenadiers fired into the air when the people started moving again.

Some of the mob shouted, "We are going to see the tsar!"

Then it happened.

The Grenadiers charged the crowd. But the people grasped one another's hands, still singing, and tried to hold firm. The Grenadiers broke ranks, but in an orderly fashion. At first Misha thought they were going to give way, after all. Then he saw with a sickening lurch in his gut that they were merely making way for the infantry. They were going to let the infantry do their dirty work.

The foot soldiers broke through the opening the Grenadiers had made and started firing—not in the air this time, but directly at the crowd!

The first to fall was an old man carrying a cross; he was trampled by the panicked marchers.

"What are you doing?" a worker yelled.

"Protecting the tsar," shouted a soldier.

"But we love the tsar. We wouldn't hurt him."

No one was listening anymore.

70

Daniel watched, horrified, as the infantry drove into the procession, rifles blazing. This simply could not be happening.

But it was!

A man crumpled to the ground right in front of him and he would have stumbled over the body had Sergei not grabbed his arm, jarring him back to his senses, and nudged him around.

Another regiment was rushing toward them from the Admiralty, while other troops were attacking from behind. Daniel was no novice to danger or battles; he had been in military encounters before. But this was different—the victims were unarmed. They were singing hymns, for heaven's sake!

"Sergei?" Daniel implored. He could think of nothing else to add, he simply had to reach out to someone; he had to touch some element of sanity.

Sergei just shook his head. His face was white, and he clutched Andrei and Yuri to him as if he would shield their young eyes from this horror. But he was not successful. The boys watched as men and women fell, bloodied and screaming. Pale and terrified, they clung to their father.

Still the crowd would not give way. They had come to see their "Little Father." He would save them if only he knew such things were happening.

A woman stumbled, and Daniel stopped to help her. She looked up at him with plaintive eyes. "Where is the tsar?" she asked, tears streaming down her face.

No words came to Daniel's lips. All he could do was stare silently at her. She turned to another, a simply clad worker, and tugged at his sleeve, repeating the same question.

The man's broad, friendly features were knotted with confusion. Then Daniel heard the man utter the most incredible words he would ever hear from a common Russian man:

"There is no tsar!"

"Oh, God in heaven! Help us!" wailed the woman, stumbling on.

An instant of panic gripped Daniel as he realized he had lost sight of Sergei. He didn't want to be alone in this. He had heard Anna tell about Khodynka Field, and now he knew exactly how she had felt. He would be all right if only he stayed with Sergei. Wildly, Daniel looked around, a mumbled prayer on his lips.

He pushed against the surging mob. Shots were still firing. Then just as he caught a glimpse of Sergei, he heard another shout.

"The priest has been shot!"

That had to be Gapon. Daniel was almost to Sergei. The boys were still hanging on to their father, but Sergei, hearing the shout about Gapon, now started forward. Daniel knew that Gapon meant something to Sergei, but was Sergei going to the very front of the throng, exposing himself and his boys to such danger?

As if Sergei had read Daniel's thoughts, he stopped and turned back. Then he saw Daniel.

"We've got to get out of here," Sergei said, pushing his way to Daniel.

"There's no place to go."

They had to try. Sergei attempted to steer them toward the edge of the street. Because they were so near the Square, there was little cover from buildings, but they could at least get out of the middle of the crazed melee.

In the noise and confusion, Andrei's scream could hardly be heard. Daniel didn't even notice anything until he saw Andrei let loose of his father and fall to his knees, grasping a bloody shoulder.

When Andrei fell, Sergei spun around and threw himself on both his sons in a frenzied attempt to protect them. Fear, fury, panic marked his expression.

Daniel saw a soldier with his rifle still aimed in the direction of Sergei and his sons. Instinctively he charged the soldier, but the man was too far away. And Daniel was suddenly blocked in his hapless effort as a dozen workers unwittingly knocked him to the ground.

The soldier fired another round before Daniel could do anything.

By the time Daniel got to his feet, it was too late. Although screams were rising all over the place, one scream now seemed to echo over them all. It was no louder than the others; only its sickening familiarity made it stand out.

When Daniel spun toward the sound, he saw Sergei still crouched over Andrei. But now Sergei was sprawled over his son, a huge, ugly splotch of dark red staining the back of his best Sunday jacket.

Daniel's legs felt wooden as he forced himself toward his companions.

Yuri was crying. "Papa! Papa!" he sobbed.

There were no tears in Andrei's eyes though he bit his lip, obviously in physical pain from his shattered shoulder. He just sat there, staring at his father's fallen form draped over his own legs.

Daniel knelt by them and tried to lift Sergei, but he was heavy—dead weight. Daniel couldn't accept that. Sergei must only be unconscious. Perhaps he could bring him around.

"Sergei, can you hear me?" Daniel laid a hand on Sergei's shoulder and gave it a little shake. But there was no response.

"Is he. . . ?" Andrei began, but he couldn't finish the awful thought. And Daniel couldn't have found the courage to answer, anyway.

All Daniel knew was they could not stay where they were, still very much in harm's way. Panicked, confused crowds surged around them, and the soldiers were still attacking. He had to get Sergei and Andrei to safety, to help. But he also knew he couldn't carry Sergei. He uttered a silent prayer for help, then looked wildly around as if God's answer would come from the crowd itself.

And it did.

A huge worker by the name of Ivan, whom Sergei had tutored, stumbled toward them. "Sergei Ivanovich?"

"Yes," Daniel said. "He's wounded. We have to get him away from here."

The big man bent down and lifted Sergei into his muscular arms.

Ivan looked at Daniel. "I think he's . . . gone."

"No!" said Yuri almost pleading. "He's wounded. He needs a doctor."

"Come on," said the worker. No sense arguing now with the poor child.

Daniel tried to help Andrei up, but the boy had barely started to stand on his feet when he crumpled to the ground in a faint. Daniel gathered him into his arms, and urging Yuri forward, they headed after Ivan.

The events of that day did not end until long after midnight. Even after the majority of the workers had dispersed and gone to their homes, others roamed the streets, looting and vandalizing. On Vassily Island, the workers threw up a barricade and tried to fight back with guns burglarized from a local gun shop. But in the end, a deadly quiet fell over the city. The workers' noble quest had failed. What they had most feared, and what the revolutionaries had often tried to tell them, was true after all.

The Little Father did not care. There was no tsar.

———

Anna and Raisa and Talia had stayed indoors all day. They had heard many shouts and much commotion outside. And the gunfire. It had been frightening, not knowing what was happening.

When Anna heard a noise outside the front door of the flat, she prayed it was Sergei and the boys returning. She would not rest until they were safe at home. She rushed to the door, flung it open and was greeted by Daniel's drawn and haggard face, his arms laden with Andrei's semiconscious form.

"Anna, I'm sorry—" Daniel began.

For a moment, her stupefied gaze fixed only on Andrei. When the boy moved, she realized he was alive. But she had no time to feel relief, for Yuri threw his arms around his mother, new sobs wracking the grief-stricken boy.

"Mama! It's Papa . . . he's . . ."

Before Yuri could finish, Anna's eyes shifted, focusing over Daniel's shoulder to a big, coarse-looking worker.

And Sergei in his arms.

71

Heroic deaths and poignant death-bed farewells are more often elements of fiction than fact, Daniel wrote, pounding at the keys of his typewriter as if somehow that would relieve his grief. *On Sunday morning, January 9, when Sergei Fedorcenko left his St. Petersburg flat, kissing his wife goodbye, he had no reason to think he would not return to her that night. She did not know it would be the last time she'd see him alive.*

Sudden death came to Fedorcenko, as it also came to over two hundred workers that day. A bullet through the heart brought instantaneous oblivion to Fedorcenko. No chance for last wishes, or even last rites. No chance to tell his wife how he loved her. Nor to embrace his sons and offer a final word they could carry with them in their hearts. Lingering death-bed scenes make for good stories, but sometimes they just don't happen in real life.

Daniel pulled the page from the typewriter, read it, then crumbled it up and threw it into the trash. Somehow he had to write a news story about the day's events, but his frayed emotions kept getting in the way. Although he tried, he just could not erase from his mind the scene in Raisa's parlor earlier that evening—the shocked faces, the empty, dazed stares. It was simply impossible to come to terms with the fact that Sergei was dead. When Mariana arrived, the disbelief had dissolved once more into tears. When the tears abated, the shock set in again.

Mariana had given what medical attention she could to Andrei, and, except for the lack of proper supplies, probably did as much for him as a doctor could. He would recover—from his physical wounds, at least.

For the next two hours they sat together waiting for the undertaker to come for Sergei's . . . body. Anna kept looking toward the door, but it wasn't the undertaker she was looking for. She kept expecting Sergei to enter at any moment. He was the only one missing from that family gathering—his warm voice, gentle humor, unaffected wisdom. His absence had to be only temporary; it couldn't be forever.

Daniel's experience with his father should have helped him, given him some basis on which to offer comfort. But it didn't. He knew more than anyone that nothing can soften the shock of sudden bereavement. They just had to be numb for a while. And they had to weep every few minutes when they realized anew that Sergei would never be with them again.

Raisa prepared a meal out of habit, mostly to have something to do; no one touched the food. After dinner, Misha came to the house.

It was some time before Misha recovered from his own shock at the news of his friend's death. When he did, his original reason for coming seemed unimportant. He had thought Sergei would want a report of the aftermath of the day's tragedy. But mostly he had needed to talk to his friend, to hear his valued wisdom and try to make some sense out of what had occurred.

Daniel saw that the Cossack was having trouble controlling his emotions. Several times Misha had stood staring out a window, his face turned away from the others; occasionally his hand would brush his eyes. Daniel had done the same thing himself, and several times he had been caught in the act and his tears seen by all. No one thought any less of him for it. Nor did he or the others think less of the burly Cossack.

Daniel tried to engage Misha in conversation. Anything was better than this stark, empty gnawing they were feeling.

"How bad was it?" Daniel asked.

"Several thousand wounded," said Misha. "The . . . death toll keeps changing. Last I heard it was up to two hundred."

"What happened? Why did they fire?"

"It was the only way the troops knew how to follow their orders."

"Which were?" Daniel's tone was suddenly intense, hard.

400

He forgot for a minute he wasn't grilling a source. "I'm sorry," he apologized. "I forgot myself, and I forgot who you are."

"As usual, I am the enemy," Misha replied in a choked tone. He bit down on his trembling lip, but continued. *"That's* who I am! My job is to protect the devil. I do it well . . . I'm very good at it. There is none more loyal than I. The fact that I never fired a gun today doesn't exonerate me. I stood with the villains. I—"

For the first time that day, Anna stirred to life. She jumped from where she was seated and ran to Misha.

"Stop! I won't hear any more of this." Anna laid a hand on his shoulder. "You are our friend, Misha. You were Sergei's best friend. He loved you as a brother."

"Then, Anna, why am I forever opposed to him? I wanted to fight *with* him, like we did in the Balkans. Why must I now be numbered with his murderers?" Suddenly the dam of his grief broke and unabashed tears flowed.

Anna placed her arms around him and let him cry like a child on her shoulder. And somehow, comforting Misha seemed to give Anna strength. She was always best in the role of giver and servant.

"He's gone!" wept Misha.

"I know . . ." Anna said as if this were the first time she truly realized it herself. And Anna wept freely as well.

———

Daniel returned his thoughts to his work. He had come to the office immediately after leaving Anna. Mariana would stay with her; Daniel had felt too helpless to remain any longer. He wanted to lose himself in his work. Maybe he could even be of some use that way. He would publish the truth, expose the government for the heartless animals they were. Then maybe he'd discover some sense in Sergei's death, in all the deaths that day.

His hands flew once again over the keyboard. He wrote only the cold, hard facts this time. *They* were incriminating enough.

It was after ten and Daniel was putting the finishing touches on his article when a knock sounded at his office door.

Through the glass he saw a familiar, shadowed face.

He opened the door immediately.

"Paul Yevnovich, come in please."

Daniel shook Paul's hand, then Paul introduced his companion. "This is Alexander Kerensky."

Daniel shook the man's hand. "Why do I feel as if I have met you before?"

"I feel the same way, but I am also at a loss," said Kerensky.

"Well, come in and have a seat."

Daniel led the men into the office and dragged two chairs from the other desks over to his.

"I just saw my sister," Paul said.

"Then you know?"

Paul nodded. "So tragic, so senseless."

"I'm glad to see you, Paul, but I am curious why you've come here."

"Alexander and I were at the march, mostly as spectators. I suppose our reason for seeking you out is that we needed to tell our experiences to someone, preferably someone who might put it to good use. At Anna's, your name was mentioned and it just seemed you were the right man. I understand the power of the press, Mr. Trent, and I believe the revolutionary cause in this country could be well served—"

"Hold on," said Daniel, respectfully but firmly. "The press is powerful only if it remains objective."

"You take me wrong. It's not my intention to manipulate the press—just to impart the facts, from my perspective. Include the government viewpoint also, if you must—that should make for excellent reading."

Kerensky added, "I'm here to offer an entirely different perspective."

"May I inquire what your perspective is, Mr. Kerensky?" asked Daniel. "Mariana has told me a little about yours, Mr. Burenin, and I would like to hear more directly from you. But for now, go on, Mr. Kerensky."

"I am a strong supporter of the Populist movement," said Kerensky. "I wasn't a follower of Father Gapon's, but I do have a strong affinity for the common man, and for democracy—"

"Now, I remember!" said Daniel. "Forgive me for interrupting, but I've figured out where I know you from. About four years ago you and I were in jail together."

"Ah, yes, I shouldn't have forgotten that, either. It's not every day a Russian gets to share a cell with an American."

"Now that that's cleared up, please go on. But first, is there any word about Gapon? I heard he had been shot."

"I heard that, too, but later a worker assured me the priest was uninjured and had escaped. Presumably he will be leaving Russia secretly at the first opportunity."

"I'm sure Lenin would love to get hold of him," said Paul.

The three conversed for over an hour—an American, a Russian liberal, and an ex-Marxist. Oddly, they developed an immediate camaraderie, as if they'd been close friends for years. And somehow the talk, recapping the events of the day and pouring out opinions and feelings, helped ease some of the pain and grief they were feeling.

When the two visitors departed, Daniel returned to his typewriter. He worked all night, and by morning he had before him a tall stack of pages. It was not a news story—that, too, would be sent to the *Register*. This was more of a tribute to all those who had sacrificed so much that day, and especially a tribute to Sergei. It could never be published in Russia; Daniel would be risking a great deal just in attempting to smuggle it out of the country.

He slipped a final sheet into the typewriter and pecked out the words: "To Sergei Fedorcenko, whose sacrifice sprang out of love."

Daniel thought of the man who, but for the unfairness of a lead bullet, would have been his father-in-law. He thought of all the questions he had wanted to ask that wise man of God, a man he had come to love and admire. A surge of anger rose in Daniel at that thought, at the realization of how he had been so robbed, how they all had been robbed of such a remarkable man.

He and all those who loved Sergei had already cried out to God: *Why did you take him from us? We still needed him, God. He had so much more to give.*

But Daniel knew Sergei would not want his death to separate anyone from the God he had so loved and served. Such a response would make a mockery of the man's life. Somehow they must use Sergei's death, instead, to draw closer to God. That's what Sergei would have wanted.

XIV

HEROES

72

Basil had to move fast now. Because he had not been able to strike at Mariana Remizov before the workers' march, he had to complete his plan quickly, before Vlasenko had a chance to catch his breath from all the excitement in the city.

Basil looked at his worktable. Everything was coming together nicely. With his needle-nosed pliers he twisted a wire in place around the appropriate gear of the clock he was using as a timing device. Then he snipped the wire with wire cutters. All that was left to do was attach the dynamite, which he would do just before he made use of the bombs. No sense risking blowing up his own home, wretched hovel that it was.

There would be no more waiting, no more missed opportunities. He had already missed the family dinner to celebrate Sergei Fedorcenko's homecoming since he had received his explosives too late. Too bad, too. He would have greatly enjoyed raining death and tragedy upon such a joyous family gathering.

Now he'd have to settle for a funeral.

How thoughtful of Sergei Fedorcenko to die and thus give Basil another prime opportunity to complete his evil designs. And this time Basil would be ready. His bombs were set to go, and he knew the exact time and place. There would be another family gathering, of course, following Fedorcenko's funeral. Everyone who mattered to him would be there.

Tomorrow.

He could hardly wait. He had not felt this much eager anticipation since—well, perhaps never. So, it was about time. He was due some satisfaction in this good-for-nothing world.

But first he had another small job to do. He left his apartment. It was quite late and pitch dark—perfect for what he had in mind. He met Jack Caine in a tavern.

"You delivered the message as I asked?"

"Yes," said Caine. "He's going to meet you in front of the Marinsky Theater."

"Good. He'll never make it, of course."

"We'll see to that."

"Let's get on with it, then."

———

Would the pain ever stop?

Anna believed she would go to her own grave with that inner ache still seizing her, the feeling that when she looked up or heard a noise, Sergei would be there. Mariana had told Anna once about the "phantom pains" amputees experienced, and she thought what she was feeling now was very much like that. An important part of her had been traumatically cut off, yet often she felt as if Sergei were still here. She could still smell his presence in the flat, in the pillows on their bed, in his hairbrush still sitting on their dresser. The book he had been reading still lay by his bedside, a bookmark at the page he had last read. He would never finish it.

All at once tears choked Anna. The suddenness of her emotional eruptions no longer surprised her. She was on the verge of tears constantly, and any small thing was apt to cause her to break down again.

Mariana had been trying to distract herself in a book. She was staying at the flat now, present for moments just such as this. She glanced up, laid aside her book, and went to Anna.

"Mama?" She put an arm around her.

Anna tried to sniff back the flood. "I'm sorry, Mariana, I just can't stop thinking . . . or longing for him . . ."

"It's all right, Mama. Cry all you want." Mariana's words opened up her own floodgate, and her tears poured out, too.

"I don't know if I can face tomorrow."

"We'll do it somehow. I've been praying."

"Your papa would be so . . ." But Anna couldn't finish. It took several minutes for her to regain at least some of her composure. "I'm so glad I have you, dear child, and Raisa, too. I wouldn't be able to make it without the two of you."

"Yes you would, Mama. You're—"

"Don't say it, Mariana. Don't tell me how strong I am. Half my strength, I think, was from Sergei. Without him I am . . . just a poor, scared servant girl. I can't bear it, Mariana."

"Mama, I love you so. I'll try to help you."

Anna tried to smile but it didn't work. Her lips just would not stop trembling. Mariana moved close to Anna, keeping her arms around her mama and laying her head comfortingly on Anna's shoulder. She really wasn't certain who was comforting whom.

After a while Anna said, "Your papa told me just before he died that his time in prison had taught him to savor life, not to take any of it for granted. I wish I had taken more of what he said to heart. I wish I had—" She bit back a fresh rush of tears. "I don't know why I do this to myself. If I could only stop talking about him, stop *thinking* about him. But I have this horrible need to do that very thing!"

She was silent for a few minutes, then she went on, more musing out loud to herself rather than speaking to Mariana. "Maybe he was trying to tell me something that day when he was talking about the prison. Maybe, without his even realizing it, he was trying to prepare me—maybe God was trying to prepare me—for this very day." She intoned a short, bitter laugh. "Wasn't that good of God?" Her tone was hollow, empty. Mariana had never heard her mama speak so of God.

"Mama, you mustn't—"

"No, I *must* say what I'm feeling. I have a right, Mariana. I have served God all my life. I don't deserve for Him to be so cruel to me. Is this how God treats those who love Him?"

"You've told me many times, Mama, that life isn't supposed to go smoothly all the time, that we couldn't grow if it did."

"I've grown enough!" Anna's voice grated harshly.

Mariana stared, aghast.

That look of frightened panic on her daughter's face was like a steadying slap in Anna's face.

"Forgive me, Mariana. I didn't mean all those things. I haven't given up on God. I'll get over this. It'll just take some time."

Anna wondered as she spoke if her daughter could tell she was just saying what was expected of her.

"Mama, no one would think any less of you if you didn't go tomorrow."

"What? Not go to my own husband's funeral?" She shook her head. "No, I need to go—for myself if no one else. Maybe it will make it all more real to me."

"Then we can cancel the gathering afterward. Everyone will understand."

"Raisa's been preparing all day for this. I think it's her way of dealing with . . . everything. And it will be better for us to be together afterward—we will need each other. I'm not the only one who is grieving."

As she spoke, she thought of her sons. Andrei, especially, had not been himself. Of course he was still recovering from his wound, which was serious enough. Yesterday he had been in surgery to have the bullet removed. That trauma, along with the blood loss, had kept him in bed and in pain. He insisted that he would attend the funeral, and Anna could not refuse him. Misha had volunteered to carry the boy, but instead that job had been assigned to one of the workers. Misha, Daniel, Oleg, Dmitri, and two other workers would be casket-bearers. Viktor, of course, was too old to be expected to carry either a casket or a strapping twelve-year-old boy.

But Anna was more worried about Andrei's uncharacteristic silence. He hadn't spoken more than a handful of words since Bloody Sunday, two days ago.

Yuri was grieving deeply also, crying a lot, though he tried to hide it. He was spending a great deal of time alone. In fact he was behaving much like his younger brother, but it was far more in character for him than for Andrei.

But then, neither of Anna's sons had ever experienced any real loss in their young lives. And this was probably the deepest loss, next to a spouse or child, that they would ever feel. Sergei had never been like many fathers, distant and authoritarian. They had lost the most important man of their lives.

Anna hoped, as with herself, that the funeral would help them come to terms with the fact that their father was gone. She wished she could be there more for them, but she was barely holding herself together.

She was glad that God was there for them, and He was bearing the burden of their grief. She knew the truth of God's presence, but she had been unable to pray since Sergei's death. Words of prayer seemed to catch in her throat.

She didn't hate God for what had happened. God was also too much a part of her—it would be like hating herself. Yet part of her did blame God a little—and yes, maybe that meant she also blamed herself.

It was totally illogical. She could have done nothing to save Sergei. As far as God went . . . well, she had to accept the fact that He had some great purpose in what had happened. She kept telling herself that, at least. Over and over and over and . . .

When will I *believe* it? she silently asked herself. *When?*

Well, in the meantime, life would continue its never-ending flow. They would do the things they must do. They would survive. But Anna felt as if survival was more a punishment than a blessing.

73

Basil awoke early in the morning. Although it was still dark outside and he'd had a busy night, he was completely alert the minute his eyes opened. He had slept soundly. The previous night's work had not bothered him in the least; it had been more exhilarating than disturbing. The elimination of that government lackey, Cerkover, was but the first step in the realization of Basil's long-desired dream. And just as Cerkover himself had wanted, it had been a clean job—no one would be able to trace the apparent street mugging to Basil.

Now Basil had to complete the second step in his plan. It was trickier, because Cyril Vlasenko was a much more "high-profile" man than his lackey. But Cyril was also a prime target of the revolutionaries—it was a miracle the man had survived this long! No one would suspect this morning's bombing as anything but another act of political terrorism. No doubt some Social Revolutionaries would be eager to accept the blame, even if they hadn't been responsible for it.

Basil looked at his worktable where his projects were waiting. He had to admit he'd done a fine job. They might not look like much, with their rag-tag assortment of wires and fuses, some of which he'd had to scavenge for himself. But he was experienced in this field and knew he had produced two fine implements of destruction. The larger one was laced with enough TNT to blow a house and all its occupants into the sky. Basil picked it up, caressed it lovingly, and placed it in a large handbasket. He covered it with a linen cloth he had procured in a secondhand shop; he didn't want it to look too new or expensive.

The second bomb was smaller; it only had to destroy a carriage. Basil carefully placed this bomb, intended for Vlasenko, in a suitcase—the very one Cerkover had used to deliver the explosives. Basil could not keep from delighting in the fact that Vlasenko would be killed with his own explosives.

He ate an unhurried breakfast, then slipped on his overcoat, hat and gloves, took the suitcase, and left his room by seven. He had until eight-thirty to complete his work. Vlasenko was in the habit of leaving for his office every day at eight-thirty sharp—he never varied from this routine.

It was still dark when Basil reached the South Side palace, ironically the old Fedorcenko estate. Basil stealthily made his way to the carriage house, and—there it was! The troika Vlasenko rode each day to work. It was already in place for the horses to be hitched up, but the stable hands had gone off to do other chores until the time of Vlasenko's departure.

Basil glanced all around before approaching the troika. He could hear faint voices in other parts of the building. He would have to be quick.

412

His mind wandered momentarily as he thought of the many times years ago he had covertly entered these grounds to spy on the beautiful Princess Katrina. At first he had come as an adoring suitor, dreaming of the day they would be married. The dream had been so close to realization—

The faithless hussy!

She thought she could spurn him and get away with it. Well, she had paid dearly for that misjudgment. But not dearly enough!

Basil's breath suddenly was coming in quick pants, sending white puffs into the freezing air. His hands trembled as he opened the suitcase.

"Calm down," he reminded himself. How quickly the thought of that broken heart years ago could upset him.

But he found himself suddenly in a hurry. This business with Vlasenko was a nuisance. Of course it had to be done if Basil intended on surviving after his deed was completed. But he was anxious to get on to the main part of his three-pronged plan—the grand finale. Quickly then, he slid under the troika with the bomb in hand. A couple of screws in the attached brackets, and the bomb was in place under the right rear runner.

He stopped dead still as he heard footsteps. Were they ready to hitch the horses?

Then a voice shouted: "You young dolt! You took the wrong harness. We have a new one."

The footsteps quickly retreated. Basil let out his breath, then wasted no more time. He set the timer for 8:35. The moment he was sure it was working properly, he slid away from the troika, grabbed the suitcase, and jogged away.

He was sorry he wouldn't be able to stay around to watch the results of his handiwork. But he had other more important matters to attend to.

———

Vlasenko had distanced himself from Sunday's events so that when Gapon was assassinated, no one would ever suspect his hand in it. Although the assassination idea had failed, Cyril's actions had a way of turning out for the good anyway.

413

Immediately after Bloody Sunday, the tsar had fired Svyatopolk-Mirsky from his position as Minister of the Interior, and Cyril was again in line for the job. This time, however, he was practically a shoo-in. Nicholas had spoken to him and all but assured him that, except for a few formalities, he could expect to be in his new office by the end of the week.

Naturally, Cyril was ecstatic.

But he couldn't bask too long in this one good fortune. Too many other things were going wrong. For one thing, he had heard nothing from Basil Anickin. Because Gapon had already slipped out of the country, there was no need for the lunatic Basil, but Cyril didn't like the thought of the man roaming around Russia with those explosives. Cyril hated to think what kind of mayhem a man like Anickin could cause in this town with all that TNT.

With the Minister of the Interior position glowing in his future, Cyril didn't want Anickin out there without supervision. He could only hope that Cerkover was keeping on top of things.

Cyril's worry over Anickin, however, didn't dull his appetite. He ate two big helpings of eggs and ten sausages to go with it. His wife was obviously bursting to scold him for his gluttony, but he pretended he didn't see. He belched loudly, then took out his pocket watch.

It was time to go.

He almost dreaded going to the office today. What new national calamity would greet him? But he refused to capitulate to his fears. It did make him almost wish he had decided to attend Sergei Fedorcenko's funeral today. But Cyril thought he might gloat too much at the grieving family, and even he had enough decency to know where to draw the line.

"Remember, Cyril," said Posnia as her husband donned his greatcoat, "we have seats at the ballet tonight."

"How could I forget?" He hated the ballet, but because it was the national passion he pretended to enjoy it.

He went outside. It was cloudy, and a cold wind hinted of an impending storm. The troika was waiting right in front as usual. The driver had just extended a hand to help Vlasenko into the carriage, when a footman hurried toward them from the house.

"Your Excellency, there is a telephone call for you."

"I must get to the office. Have them call me there," said Cyril.

"It is the police. They said it was urgent."

With a perturbed sigh, Cyril returned to the house and took the phone receiver.

"Yes?"

"I thought you would like to know, Count Vlasenko," said the person on the other end, "of a terrible tragedy."

"Now what?"

"Your aide, Cerkover, was discovered about an hour ago—dead."

"What? Are you sure?"

"Yes, he's been positively identified."

"How. . . ?"

"A street killing, Your Excellency. Stabbed and robbed. I'm very sorry to have to tell you."

Cyril was stunned and felt an emotion akin to grief. He had liked Cerkover, and loyal assistants were hard to come by.

The police inspector filled Cyril in on a few more details, then Cyril said, "I'd like to have a look at the body myself, and see your reports. I'll come by in an hour."

"We will be expecting you, sir."

Cyril was in a daze as he left his house once again. He simply could not believe such a thing could happen. What was Cerkover doing in a place where he could get held up at knife point, anyway? Cyril rubbed his chin in disbelief, shaking his head as he neared the troika.

He took out his watch again. He had a meeting with the ex-Minister of the Interior at nine, but that should give him plenty—

The sudden blast threw Vlasenko ten feet. He landed on the cobbled driveway, the weight of his body smashing his pocket watch to bits with the force of its fall.

74

Two hundred mourners had attended the funeral services at St. Andrew's. Most were workers, but many students were there also. There were very few from the noble classes.

Oleg said more workers would have come except they feared the authorities' reaction to a large gathering—and with good reason, too, after Sunday's senseless tragedy. There had already been several funerals, including two mass funerals of about fifty caskets each, and so far no incidents. Nevertheless, a couple squadrons of police were in strategic positions around the church.

Nothing happened.

It had been a beautiful and moving service. One of the workers Sergei had tutored read an essay he had written for the occasion. In it he called Sergei the "Worker Prince," an epithet that would undoubtedly accompany Sergei's name for many years into the future. To the workers, Sergei had become a hero because of how tirelessly he had served them.

Anna had hoped the funeral would help her say goodbye to her beloved husband. But she could not even bear to look at his casket. She needed to accept his death; still, she could not bring herself to look at his empty, dead shell.

Andrei filed by quietly, and he did look at his father, for a very long time. Tears spilled from his eyes, but they were the only indication of his anguished heart.

Yuri wept, even sobbing and sniffing at times. Maybe he was better off than his mother and brother for his ability to express his grief in that way. He laid his favorite book in the casket next to his father, then impulsively kissed his father's cheek.

Then all the family and close friends, that same group that had gathered a week ago to welcome Sergei home from prison, left the church and went to Raisa's flat.

———

Basil watched as each mourner arrived. They were all there now—at least all that mattered. It took him a few minutes to complete the next phase of his plan. The streets were practically deserted; sensible people were indoors at this hour. Though it was only four in the afternoon, it was already dark out.

But Basil needed someone—

There! The perfect lackey. A boy, fourteen or fifteen years old, was hurrying down the street. There was no telling what he was doing out, but he'd probably not turn down a chance to earn a ruble.

Basil stepped out of the alley and called, "Hey, boy!" When the youth's footsteps hastened rather than slowed, Basil called again, "Listen, I mean you no harm! I have a little job for you." The boy slowed but didn't turn. "You wouldn't mind earning a ruble, would you?" The boy turned. Basil grinned.

He gave the boy the handbasket, instructing him carefully about what he was to do and say. He also gave him the money.

The youngster skipped away toward the building. He was to go to the second floor, to the Sorokin flat. As it turned out, he lived on the third floor and knew the two families, having played occasionally with Yuri and Andrei. He was pleased to be a part of the surprise. He knew of the family's mourning— several people in the building had already sent baked goods and other food to show they cared and to help ease the burden of grief. He said he was happy to deliver this man's gift; it made him feel as if he'd had a part in helping the poor family who had lost their father.

———

The flat looked almost as it had for the party days ago. The same board table was set up in the dining room. It was laden with food—mostly gifts from neighbors, although Raisa had been busy cooking also. As Anna had guessed, it had been her way of dealing with the loss of a dear friend.

Everyone was milling about, chatting quietly. Even though the table was the same and the people were the same, the mood was far different. How jubilant the group had been that other day, especially after Sergei had joyously announced Mariana and Daniel's engagement. Raisa had hardly been able to quiet them down so they could say the blessing and eat. Now, little more than a whisper would have gotten their attention.

Raisa was carrying out a heavy platter laden with chicken when a knock came at the front door.

Hands full, she glanced helplessly at the door. Then she continued on to the parlor and snagged the nearest person to help; it happened to be Misha.

"Would you get the door, Misha?"

Misha didn't recognize the boy with the basket, but he wasn't around often enough to know all the neighbors.

"I am to deliver this to Anna Fedorcenko," said the boy.

"And what might it be?"

"A gift."

"Who from?"

The boy shrugged. "I was just told to deliver it. The fellow wanted to offer his condolences, but he didn't want to intrude on a family gathering."

"That was thoughtful of him. Perhaps there's a note inside."

"Are you the master of the house?"

"No, but I'll see that Anna Fedorcenko gets it."

"I suppose that'll do."

Misha smiled. "I assure you I am fully trustworthy."

"All right. Good-night, then."

Misha carried the heavy basket to the parlor. At first he thought the peculiar sound he heard was his imagination.

Anna came up to him as he set the basket on the table with the other food. "So many people care. I didn't think we knew this many folks in the neighborhood."

"I suppose we shouldn't let all this good food go to waste."

"You're right." Anna turned to the group. "Please, everyone, let's enjoy this fine food our friends have provided."

Anna reached toward the basket to lift the linen cloth.

Tick . . . tick . . .

"Anna!" Misha called sharply. "Stop!"

"What?"

"Stand back! Everyone stand back!"

Everyone obeyed the command of the Cossack—he was, after all, captain of the Imperial Guard.

Slowly, Misha lifted the cloth cover.

———

Basil could have disappeared the moment the bomb was delivered. It was foolhardy to stick around. Yet what did he have to fear? When the explosion went off, he would simply blend in with others who would gather at the scene. It was worth the risk, anyway. He had waited twenty-three years for this moment. Nothing in earth or heaven could prevent him from seeing its wonderful, terrible climax. His limbs were frozen with cold as he stood transfixed, his gaze fastened on the building across the street.

No, he couldn't miss this. *At last, Katrina, you will pay for the way you so heartlessly spurned me. Everyone will pay for all the suffering they caused me.*

———

Amazingly, general panic did not set in when they learned the awful truth. They all seemed to instinctively know that panic was the surest way to get them killed. Some of the women had tears in their eyes, and some of the men had weak knees, but they kept their heads regardless. And the best thing they did was look to Misha who was by far the most experienced in these matters.

"What'll we do?" asked Anna.

"This is a timed device. No way of telling for certain when it's set to blow. But we must assume it will be soon."

"Throw it outside," said Dmitri.

"That might endanger innocent passersby." Misha looked at the bomb. "I want you all to hurry and evacuate this building. Try to clear all the other residents out, especially those in close proximity to this flat. I'm going to try to disarm it."

"Misha—"

"Hurry!" Not even his most experienced recruits would have argued with the tone of Misha's voice.

Within seconds the flat was cleared out. Misha told Anna to see that the women got outside, while the men raced through the building pounding on doors and rousing the residents. There were only three floors to the building, with about a hundred residents. Thankfully, it was still early in the evening and most people had not yet gone to bed.

———

Dmitri pounded on only a few doors. He tried to look surprised when he reached the main entryway of the building within a few moments, in fact only seconds before Anna and the women. At this point, he told himself, it was best to try to save what they could. Who knew if that Cossack really had any idea what he was doing?

But Dmitri did have some pride, and seeing only the women about to exit made him feel truly the fool. A coward.

Before his death, when they were talking to Daniel, Sergei had reminded Dmitri of the past, of when he had been a daring young man who had defied society and made an art of taking daredevil risks. What had happened to him? Had he fallen so low that he would succumb to his fear and number himself with women and children? He was still a man, wasn't he? He was not so old that he had lost that, had he? He was about to marry a beautiful young woman. Could he face her knowing just what kind of poltroon he was?

Somehow his inner debate forced some of his courage to return. He would go back inside—he had to if he were ever to live with himself again.

Anna had thrown open the door, and before Dmitri turned back, he took one wistful look over the heads of the women to the outside and safety. He saw a man standing in the alley across from the building. In itself, this was hardly unusual—but this man's gaze was focused directly on the Sorokin flat.

It was no coincidence.

No one could know what was happening in there. Only a man who had planted a bomb would skulk in an alley taking such interest in his potential target.

Dmitri hurried in front of the women, blocking their way to the outside.

"Anna," Dmitri said urgently, "stay inside a few moments longer."

"Why?"

"I think the man who left the bomb is in the alley. Let me try to get to him before he suspects we've discovered anything. Don't let anyone out of the building for thirty seconds."

He prayed they had that long.

"All right. Be careful, Dmitri."

———

Basil looked at his pocket watch. It should be nearly time. That was always the tricky part of this kind of operation. You had to set the timer, allowing for enough time for the bomb to get to the right place at the right time, but you didn't want too much of a leeway for fear of discovery. In case of discovery, Basil had taken some precautions. He had built the bomb in such a way that it would be almost impossible to disarm. Perhaps an expert might have a chance, though even that was doubtful. And there were no experts in that flat tonight.

Nervously he glanced at his watch once more. There should only be a few minutes left, but he couldn't tell exactly. The cold seemed to be making his watch run slowly. He hoped it hadn't affected the clock on the detonator!

Three more minutes—

Suddenly he saw people exiting the building. Just residents who happened to be going out for the evening? No! There were too many.

He had been discovered.

But that wouldn't matter. They could not do anything about it. If anyone tried, the bomb would just blow up—and take half the building with it.

He tried to calm himself. He ought to make his escape, but he could not leave without knowing if he had been successful.

———

Perspiration beaded on Misha's forehead. He prayed he

could figure this thing out. After the Palace bombing twenty-four years ago, and the assassination of Alexander II, Misha had made it a point to learn all he could about bombs and explosives. He might not be an expert, but he knew enough to build a bomb—and, he hoped, to take one apart. With his pocketknife he had unscrewed and gently lifted the outer casing to reveal the inner workings of the device.

A drop of sweat trickled into his eye. He tried to blink it away, but it only burned and blurred his vision. Wiping a sleeve across his brow, he focused once more on the bomb. With each tick of the timer, he felt his own time slipping away.

He had to lift the casing to get at the timer. His hands were uncommonly steady. Thank God!

There was the clock! Whoever had built this thing knew what he was doing—and meant business. The clock had been shielded so that it could not be seen without the risk of moving the device—a delicate procedure without knowing how sensitive the explosives were. So far, God was with him. But the clock revealed that if he didn't disarm this thing in one minute, it would indeed take a heavenly miracle to prevent scores of lives from being lost.

The wires were so twisted, and in a jumble—a very calculated jumble! Misha studied the thing for a moment. It was hard to focus, knowing that his minute was quickly dwindling to seconds. But rash judgment would only get him blown to bits. He took a steadying breath.

Following the many wires with a trained eye, Misha discovered what had to be the two main leads. Experience told him that pulling the wrong one would be disastrous, prematurely triggering the detonating device.

Wiping his brow once more, he took a deep breath and pulled one of the wires.

75

Basil slapped his watch against his hand. Cursed thing!

More people were pouring out of the building now. There were fifty in the street, and more coming.

He ground his teeth in anger. It was all over. There she was! Katrina's daughter. Safe, as were the rest of her miserable family.

Basil knew he had to get away. He had to be free so he could strike again. He wouldn't give up. He had invested too much of his hatred to abandon the quest now. He had to move.

But his cold legs did not respond as quickly as his frantic mind was urging them. He did not turn fast enough.

Dmitri crossed the street and crept along the side of a building until he was within inches of the man in the alley. He flew at the killer with all the force his two hundred pounds of muscle and flesh could muster. He was hardly as fit as he had been as a twenty-four-year-old Imperial Guard, but for the moment surprise gave Dmitri the upper hand.

And he knew to take full advantage of the moment. On the offensive, he launched another attack at his fallen adversary just as the man was attempting to gain his feet. Dmitri aimed blow after blow at the bomber's face and torso.

But dealing cards and wooing ladies had left Dmitri's hands soft. After half a dozen blows, they were raw and bleeding. Dmitri's arms couldn't keep up the momentum.

The instant he let up out of sheer exhaustion, the man leaped to his feet. He sent a fist into Dmitri's face, clipping him on the chin and sending him back against the wall. His eyes widened when he saw who his attacker was.

"Dmitri Remizov!" he exclaimed.

Dmitri still hadn't had a good look at the man in the alley, but he wasted no time in trying to figure how this man knew him and what it could mean. He leaped forward, aimed a hard blow at his stomach, and while the man was doubled over, Dmitri kicked him in the face.

The culprit stumbled into the street.

Dmitri's adrenaline was rushing now. He felt almost twenty again, and able to take on a horde of villains. He lunged again, ready, and fully believing, he was about to deliver the finishing blow.

The bomber twisted to the side, but Dmitri was quick and delivered a relentless barrage of facial blows. The man fell back against the foot of a streetlight. Suddenly, as Dmitri paused to catch his breath, he saw—through the blood and the imprint of the years—that he had faced off with an old adversary. Basil Anickin had come back from the dead! The bomb was his doing. He was still bent upon his old vendetta.

Dmitri struck again, but his shock at seeing Basil after all these years took some of the edge off his momentum. Basil got in a fierce right upper-cut that rattled Dmitri's jaw and clouded his vision. As Basil rained blows down on him, Dmitri retreated, his arms shielding his face. He didn't see the fist smash into his stomach. Doubled over, Dmitri only heard the sound of retreating footsteps.

For a moment all Dmitri felt was relief. He tried to tell himself he'd done his best. He had tried and failed—again. But he was an old man. What could he do?

He watched the culprit run. That battle years ago with Basil still haunted his mind. He knew it had been the turning point of his life—the moment in time when he had abdicated his manhood. He had tried to hide it, even from himself, in his frivolous, superficial lifestyle. But it had never been far from the surface, and now, as he faced an almost identical repeat of that day, the horrible realization of his failure assailed him again.

What could he do?

He knew now, if he had not realized it before, that Basil Anickin's thirst for vengeance would never be quenched. He had come back after twenty-three years, and he would keep coming back until they were all dead—everyone related to Katrina, everyone she had loved and would have loved.

Dmitri had only two choices: Let that happen, or die trying to prevent it. He thought of Sergei's heroic death. They had been best friends, equal in prowess if not in character. The thought of his friend infused him with courage. Dmitri had once been a man; it was not too late to become one again.

With the greatest effort of will he had ever expended, Dmitri forced his legs into motion. Basil was halfway down the street, and Dmitri's lungs were not in much better condition than his soft, weak hands. But he poured every bit of strength he had into his legs. Basil must have thought he was safe, for his steps slowed, and Dmitri closed the distance between them.

Anickin obviously heard the footsteps pounding behind him. He turned.

"Give it up, Remizov!" Basil taunted. "I need little excuse to kill you tonight. But I'd rather get you all together."

"I won't let you do that, Anickin." Dmitri's voice came in gasps. Blast! How he hated being old!

He lunged toward Basil, who had started to move again. Dmitri caught hold of Anickin's greatcoat; just a handful of the heavy wool, which he wouldn't be able to keep for long. He yanked hard before the fabric was wrenched from his hand by Basil's resistance. But it was enough to slow him down.

Dmitri threw his hands around Basil's neck and pulled him down. For a minute or two they tussled on the frozen street until Basil managed to get his knee up. The forceful thrust dislodged Dmitri.

As Dmitri poised himself for another attack, a knife appeared in Basil's hand. It happened so quickly, Dmitri hadn't even seen movement. The knife slashed violently at him, slicing at his jacket—the expensive new one he'd bought to see the tsar in! As Basil pulled back for another strike, Dmitri reached forward, trying to grab the hand that held the knife.

Dmitri missed.

Basil thrust with the knife again. This time it found flesh and blood. Dmitri's left arm was sliced below the elbow. In pain, Dmitri fell back, grasping his bloody arm.

Basil took off again. Dmitri shook off the pain that coursed through his wounded arm and sprinted in pursuit. For several minutes they ran through the streets, Dmitri just barely managing to keep Basil in sight. They were nearing the river. Ahead, Dmitri saw the expanse of the Nicholas Bridge. How would he ever catch Anickin? And why hadn't a policeman interceded in their mad chase? Where were they when you *wanted* them? His age was definitely telling now. His chest ached, and the muscles in his legs screamed. How did Basil keep going? They were the same age, for heaven's sake!

Just as Dmitri thought he could not continue, Basil slipped on the ice. Dmitri watched in disbelief as Anickin went down, sprawling on his face in the snow. Then he saw a metallic flash as Basil's knife fell from his hand, landing a couple of feet away from his fallen body.

Dmitri leaped for the knife, palming it and turning toward Basil in one swift motion.

The fall had knocked the wind out of Basil, but he was too full of hate to allow himself to be defeated so easily. As Dmitri grasped the knife, Basil rolled over and had nearly gained his feet when Dmitri, knife in hand, swung toward him.

Basil stopped, eyeing his assailant. He had been stalking Dmitri for months now and had a good idea of what the man had become over the years. Basil did not fear him.

"Go ahead, Remizov. Use that knife, if you can."

"It's the only way to stop you."

"Then use it!" Basil sneered with derision at Dmitri.

Dmitri hesitated. He knew the only way to be truly free of Anickin was to kill him. But he had lost the killer instinct, the soldier's instinct of his youth. His shoulders sank with the awful realization, and the hand holding the knife relaxed slightly.

Basil laughed.

"I knew it, you sniveling coward! You couldn't save your wife, and you won't be able to save your daughter. She is dead, Remizov! Do you hear me? Dead!"

Basil's words seemed to clear Dmitri's head. Mariana's life

depended on him. Her life, her future, depended on the hollow shell of a man he had become—the whining, primping dolt he knew he was.

But there was no time for self-recrimination. Anickin was already turning; soon he'd be running again and Dmitri knew he had little stamina left for another chase.

Like a madman himself, Dmitri charged, and the knife in his hand met flesh and bone—he heard it grind at Basil's body. It was an instant before Dmitri realized he had only impaled Anickin's shoulder. But it drew a scream from Anickin, and he turned savagely on Dmitri.

Dmitri lost hold of the knife and it fell to the ground, but he had no time to worry about that. All he could do was fend off Basil's blows.

He neither saw nor heard the wagon approach. Police were clamoring toward them before Dmitri realized that help had finally arrived.

"What's going on here?" yelled a policeman.

Twenty-three years ago it had been Dmitri, not Basil, who had landed in jail. That couldn't happen again.

"This man is responsible for a bombing," said Dmitri.

"At the Vlasenko place?"

"What?" said Dmitri confused. "No, a bombing a few blocks from here."

"There has been no—"

Taking advantage of the momentary distraction, Basil dashed away.

"He's getting away again!" Dmitri shouted. And to his own surprise, he ignored the police and shot off after Basil.

Basil had reached the bridge, but it was slow going, for the bridge was thick with ice. They both skidded and slipped several times.

Dmitri was the first to see the droshky approach. Basil was glancing over his shoulder to assess Dmitri's proximity. When he turned back, it was too late.

The driver gave a sharp jerk on his reins. Basil tried to stop, but he slipped again on the ice. He went down inches from the oncoming horses. The animals, frightened by both the painful lurch of the reins and the sudden commotion before their eyes, reared wildly.

Dmitri watched the scene in both horror and wonder. And he heard Basil let out a single, terrified scream before the deadly weight of the animal's hooves crashed down on him.

76

Everyone cheered as Misha exited the apartment building, hands raised over his head in victory, a grin plastered on his face that could mean only one thing.

The ordeal was over.

They crowded around Misha, slapping him on the back, shaking his hand, giving him a hero's reception. Misha forgot how his legs had felt like rubber, and his hands had shaken seconds after yanking the wire that diffused the bomb. He forgot how his life had paraded before his sweaty eyes—sins, mistakes, everything. He forgot his last thought—that he'd never see Anna's sweet face again—for which he had rebuked himself instantly.

Now it was over. By a true miracle of God, the lives of those he loved had been saved. But he hardly felt deserving of all the praise. He had only done his job. It could never make up for Bloody Sunday, for what had happened to Sergei.

"Thank God for you, Misha!" said several voices at once.

"Please, that's enough. Any of you would have done the same if you had known how." Misha turned to the gathered residents. "Go back to your homes," he said in a tone that was almost an order. "It's safe now." He turned to Daniel, who was standing nearby. "Did anyone call the police?"

"Yes," said an older man in the crowd. "Did I do right?"

Daniel and Misha looked grimly at each other and nodded. They would have liked to continue to bask in their relief at being spared, but they knew the ordeal was not entirely over. Someone had left that bomb, and the sooner they discovered who, the better.

Anna approached. "Misha, Daniel, you ought to know that Dmitri left a few minutes ago. He said he had spotted someone across the street in the alley who looked like a suspect. I saw them fighting, then I got distracted. When I looked back again they were gone."

"Dmitri? Are you sure?" said Misha.

"Yes. And if that was the culprit—"

But she was interrupted by Mariana's voice.

"Père!"

Mariana broke away from the group and ran to her father, who had just stepped out of a police wagon. Mariana had never seen her father look like this before. His clothes were disheveled and torn, and under the dull light of a streetlamp, she could see his bruised and bloodied face. Then she noticed his bleeding arm.

It took only a few moments of convincing from the gathered residents to exonerate Dmitri before the police. There would be no time in jail for him this day. Misha took the police into the building to show them the bomb. And the attention, much to Misha's relief, shifted to Dmitri.

Pursuing Basil had been the first really heroic thing Dmitri had done in years. No one blamed him for milking the story dry as Mariana tended to his wounds. When they returned to Raisa's, they let Dmitri tell the story several more times, and no one protested that he embellished the facts more with each telling.

Unlike Misha, Dmitri reveled in the attention. He couldn't wait until Yelena heard the story—preferably not from him but from someone else, so he could act the part of true modesty. But the real moment of glory for Dmitri came as he was about to leave that evening.

"What you did tonight, Count Remizov, took true courage," Anna told him. "Had you not stopped Basil, there's no doubt he would have tried again. You saved us; you saved Mariana. Katrina would have been proud of you."

"I'm just thankful it's ended."

"We are all in your debt."

"Heavens!" Dmitri chuckled wryly. "Don't say that, Anna. You know how bad I am with debts."

Anna laughed with tears standing in her eyes—this time tears of affection, not grief. She embraced Dmitri for the first time, as her friend, not as her superior. And that meant more to Dmitri than all the heaps of praise he had received that evening.

77

When all the excitement was over, the guests gone, and Raisa, Mariana, and the children were in bed, Anna found herself alone in the parlor. It was still hard to go to her and Sergei's room. His presence was still too painfully evident there, and she had not yet had the heart to remove his things. Maybe she never would. Viktor's wife, Princess Sarah, who had lost her first husband many years ago, suggested that it was all right and normal to hang on for a little while. She had known people, and so had Anna, who had cleared out all their deceased spouse's possessions in an attempt to erase the ache. It usually didn't work, anyway. And the memories and things of a loved one, besides causing some pain, were a great source of comfort also.

Sarah said Anna would know when she was ready to put away Sergei's things and keep her best memories of him in her heart.

A few days ago Anna would never have believed Sarah. She had been in a dark tunnel with no end in sight. She had felt, as never before in her life, a longing to die also. That she should have to live, to continue an empty, hopeless existence without her dear Sergei, seemed the cruelest fate imaginable.

But something had happened to Anna within the past few hours. A glimmer of light had appeared at the far end of her tunnel, a small hint that her despair was not destined to be endless. Oddly, that perception had been prompted by the bomb scare. The moment she had set eyes upon Basil Anickin's bomb she had been beset by fear—gripping fear, the kind that only springs from someone who is afraid to die. Someone who *desires* to live.

When Misha had exited the building grinning his success, Anna had cheered as loudly as anyone.

It had shocked her at first. Then she had felt just a little guilty about it. How could she want to live when the most important part of her life had been snuffed out?

Yet she did; she really did.

She had no idea at the moment just how she would go on, how she would survive day by day. Most of the time it seemed impossible. But she would.

Perhaps it was the strength everyone, even Sergei, was so fond of extolling in her. Sometimes it was such a burden to be strong. But as usual, she would no doubt come to the place where she could thank God for it.

———

"Mama?"

"Mariana, come in."

"If you want to be alone. . . ?"

"No. Come and sit by me."

"I woke up and you weren't there." Mariana was sharing Anna's bed, partly because there was no other room in the small flat, but also so her mama would not be so lonely.

"Don't worry so about me, Mariana," Anna said gently as her adopted daughter sat on the worn couch by her side.

"I can't help it."

"I'll be all right."

Mariana peered at her mama through the dim light of the oil lamp. How worn Anna looked. The strain of her grief etched in new creases in her delicate features. But for the first time in days the dull void seemed gone from her eyes. The smile that touched her lips reached up into her eyes, instilling a hint of life into her face.

"Will you?"

Anna nodded. "Yes. There's too much to live for. Now I'm beginning to understand what Sergei meant by savoring life. I know that's what I must do—for him, for myself, and for those I love. I want to be part of your future, Mariana—yours and Daniel's. I want to see my sons grow to be men. If I'm lucky, I'll get to see my grandchildren."

"It's what Papa would have wanted for you, Mama."

Anna nodded. "But Mariana, it's also what I want, and that makes all the difference."